WALLOWING:

The Joys and Pains of a Common Joe

WALLOWING:

The Joys and Pains of a Common Joe

Michael Stull

Northwest Publishing, Inc.
Salt Lake City, Utah

Wallowing: The Joys and Pains of a Common Joe

For information address: Northwest Publishing,
6906 South 300 West, Salt Lake City, Utah 84047
JC 08 30 94
Edited by Davis Team

PRINTING HISTORY
First Printing 1994

ISBN: 1-56901-194-X

NPI books are published by Northwest Publishing Incorporated,
6906 South 300 West, Salt Lake City, Utah 84047.
The name "NPI" and the "NPI" logo are trademarks belonging to
Northwest Publishing Incorporated.

PRINTED IN THE UNITED STATES OF AMERICA.
10 9 8 7 6 5 4 3 2 1

Table of Contents

1. Making Choices 1
2. Slow Down 5
3. The Shadows on My Wall 12
4. Penny for Your Ketchup 18
5. Metal and Flesh 23
6. "No Way, It Couldn't Be." 30
7. Enjoyable 35
8. Sure 39
9. Give Me A Beat 41
10. The Horse Without A Rider 48
11. Marx 57
12. The Heavy Hand 66
13. Stroke the Fury Conscience and Ego 76
14. Harvest 83
15. A Terrible Ode 87
16. "Come On, Give Me A Break!" 98
17. Morissey and the Shiverless 108
18. Lighten Down 118
19. Sitting Next to Expectations 131

20.   Long Walk in A Black Gown 135
21.   Lord, Buy Me Something Nice 144
22.   Slippery Straw 152
23.   Needle, Sunset, Junk 158
24.   Sipping Red Through A Funnel 167
25.   Sliding in Galoshes 174
26.   LM and IS Curves 179
27.   Bad IV 181
28.   Toothpicks Dipped In… 194
29.   Pretending 200
30.   Pickin' Apples 213
31.   Licky, Licky Lie, Somethin' in the Sky 225
32.   Nobody Really Knows 233
33.   Song to Speak 238
34.   The Man Touching His Nose in Elusiveness 249
35.   Rubber Sheets 254
36.   "Come On, I Can't." 257
37.   J.G. Is Gratefully Dead 262

Author's Notes

I am sitting at my desk attempting to make the day go by painlessly. Lately, avoiding the pain of a monotonous boredom has become harder. Why? Well, my unchallenging and unrewarding job with a large, money center bank can explain my lowly situation. My given job description, within this bureaucratic nightmare, has provided me with the freedom to choose my work load and to choose my work ambitions. Unfortunately for the company, I have chosen to avoid all responsibilities. On average, this job coupled with my work avoidance has given me 117.25 hours to kill during a month, or about five hours a day. The yearly figure adds up to be 1,305 hours. Slightly exaggerated? Sure, but I do have a lot of time to kill that a bathroom and the *New York Times* can't save.

Secondly, the boredom has become less bearable due to the rigors and routines of everyday, adult life. Every week I do my laundry; I shop; I go to the dry cleaners; I go to the same bookstore; etc., etc. These processes go on every week, every day, and every every. My schedule is the following: during the weekday, I go to work; I have bologna sandwiches for lunch with my girlfriend; I suck up to my boss; I finally go home; I go to the gym to impress; I cook chicken for dinner; and I go to bed. On weekends, I get drunk too early and too quickly on Friday winding up in bed too early; I go to the same diner for breakfast, which is a bargain for New York at $1.65; I read the paper; I go to the gym to impress; I do nothing; I go out again, winding up home too drunk and too early. Sunday is a repeat of Saturday, but the going out stuff is replaced by watching the same meaningless T.V. and wondering why I can't drink so much anymore.

Don't get me wrong, I'm not one of those so called "Slackers," nor do I want to be. The problem is a lost thirst for life. Tomorrow comes to me like an alarm clock with an easy snooze button to hit.

Today is the day, though. Like the smoker deciding today is the first day of their new life, the revelation has hit me. Like the movies or other books, this day has come only during the lowest of lows. However, my resolution is clear, my mind is set, and a fire continues to enlighten my head. Now, I begin to fulfill the dream. "Enough is enough," I whisper in my office to all who wouldn't listen and couldn't hear.

Also, I would like to thank this corporation for providing this grant of time that they unknowingly gave me.

The Prologue

Life is simply a big story and if you are not living a story to tell or telling a story you've lived, then one is not truly living. Currently, I am not truly living and have entered a zombie dimension, wearing a cheap suit and a knit tie to compliment. To make a change in my life, I am starting slowing and opting for the easier side, which is to tell the best story that I can imagine which I have lived.

So instead of waking up every morning to a buzz, shaking my head while making odd attention obtaining moans, and saying, "Another day, another one hundred after tax dollars," I am going to have a new motto, "Another day, another one hundred after tax dollars, another story to tell," which officially makes me a professional story teller.

Vonnegut told me once (through reading one of his books, and not in person) that he believed a book should start out with etc., because there is never a true beginning or ending in any story. (I'm not actually sure if it was Vonnegut or Vonnegut quoting another author, so no credit will be officially given to either.) Of course, conventional religion agrees with this notion, but I must state my disagreement of the powers that seem to be and Vonnegut; life and death are the beginning and the ending. Since a birth is not beginning the book, I will follow his advice.

To Lisa

ONE
Making Choices

The Commencement

Etc…to begin again. The night and sea engulfed the over-booked plane, leaving me nothing to look at but my blistered hands. With the progression of the last couple of months, the blue, bulging veins represented an unworthy, yet healthy, reflection of my soul. My true, inner reality existed in self-deprivation and self-denial which swirled, hidden in my neat attire, in colors that were approaching a heavy black.

This growing black had left me alone on the plane with only the dreams of Kristie and how it was supposed to be. Mom had always painted such a beautiful picture of love, but it had not included the likes of Kristie or myself. Thus, this commencement, that the uncomfortable plane represented, left me ecstatic at the upcoming possibilities of something more.

However, the sudden consciousness of excitement hesitated like the joyful pain of meeting a blind date for the first time. Fortunately for me, I still had hope which could turn the unseen date into a lingerie model that cavorted on the sticky pages of a Victoria Secret's catalog. I scanned the plane for that very prospect, but the reluctance of leaving remained and took root. Deserting everything with nothing in front of me just wasn't my style. Still, I sat in the stuffed plane readying for takeoff.

Losing myself in the feel of the plane's wheels elevating above the rushing ground, I slumped back into the earth tone stripes that wrapped around the steel framed seat. The long trip ahead with only a Walkman and the unstoppable departure of all sane life, as I knew it, drifted me back to the memories of why I was so glum and desperate to try something different.

"The famous tale of the naive, Midwestern kid fits you pretty well," I had to talk to someone. "Things started for you, like most, under the shadow of the griping will of parental regrets. Suddenly, college began for you and your new, but secondary, life blossomed. Too bad your parents had already done the damage. I know, you tried, you really tried. But here you are, two and half years later and same as you ever been."

"So why so glum? You have it a lot better than most." The plane leveled. "Sure you know what it is. Age is coming upon you and you are acting the part, a part you aren't yet comfortable with. And how can you be grown up without a woman to share it with? But why did you have to choose Kristie? Anybody would have succeeded in fulfilling your need to be accepted by a member of the opposite sex. I can't believe you told her that you loved her. How silly you are." The angry words formed, but stopped short of embarrassing sounds.

"The way you two met would sum it up, or at least should have given you a clue. You and your friends decided to play that flippant and degrading game to determine who could get the most sex from the most amount of women in the least amount of time. Everyone else on campus was doing it, but you included some rules, gave it a name, and bet a case of beer that would never be anted up. Formalizing the mating period and making it into a competition seemed like a justified and novel approach to college night life, but didn't you consider yourself above that shit?"

"Back to the story, would you?"

"Needless to say you were not the victor. Your roommate, Jack, won, as he always does with his tall, dark, and blue-eyed approach. However, you did not end up the big loser, either. You met a few women, but none of them would bring home the case, or should I say that you couldn't bring home the case with any of them. Anyway, one of the women was a pretty freshman, named Kristie, from Southern California who seemed relatively intriguing. She would only let you kiss her, but offered up several pleasurable games of enticement and denial. Those moments still sizzle your desire for her, but have not returned, have they?"

"No," I turned to the woman next to me who was wearing a

Walkman. Her head rocked up and down in rhythm with her left knee, obviously missing my escaping grunt.

"So you jumped on the chance and decided on a phone call. Next was one of your less than famous dates, but it was successful. I will give you that. Your novel and cheap approach of wine, talk, and music set the tone for the upcoming months and took all pressure off of any future impressing gestures. Don't say it. I agree with you, good, drunken quality time is always the best way to get to know someone, plus you're a stingy bastard."

"Things went well. Kristie and you were going at each other like cats in heat almost immediately. She fulfilled all of your whims, but there were only so many whims and times to fulfill them. Things began to fizzle."

"Yeah, I know."

"Your lifestyles quickly became perfectly meaningless. You would study all night during the week and she would watch TV and get high. After you finished studying, she would come over and you would act like those crazed, love cats and then go to sleep. You would wake up, do the cat thing, and go to classes, leaving her alone in bed only to come home to find her already gone. Then, the process would begin again. On weekends, the same story held true, except your classes were replaced by bars and friends, while her T.V. was replaced with parties and friends. Don't you see the meaningless efforts in your relationship? It's just sex."

"Yeah sure, but sexual convenience has its pluses."

The conversation finally ended in my head, as I plunged into the present reflections of how much I missed her and how stupid I was for leaving the country. Even though I couldn't admit it, my conscience was more than accurate. It could ignore my aching heart that throbbed anew without her, but I couldn't. Not long after we started, I held us together with my emotional cowardice and self-inflicting lack of confidence, both of which were now sitting next to me on the crowded plane laughing at the promises I had just made her. The thoughts embarrassingly stung. Still, I sadly clung to the necessity of a relationship. "What an easy escape from a worsening situation. Why do I want to blow it?" the conversation started again in my head.

Trying to grab some sense, my fist came down hard upon my thigh, bringing me back to my future of an upcoming semester abroad in Brussels. Kristie left in remembrance of the coup of my parents. I had offered them the dream of studying International

Economics in Europe and the selling point of the associated low cost and the fact my sister had gone to Europe in high school as part of a bell ringer church group. Reluctantly, they agreed and supplied.

I touched my side, underneath the arm pit, to feel the money holster that contained everything they had dutifully given me; a passport, fifteen hundred dollars, and a Eurorail pass. The bulging purse brought relief. Once again, I allowed myself to look at the familiar faces of my soon to be fellow class mates. The sight of us snuck into my cringing face. We were one hundred white, fortunate kids who had hopped on a plane expecting to cross the ocean in order to play around as tourists, to act like assholes, and to earn transferable grades with little effort in studying and lots of effort in traveling. The situation was a can't miss.

The continuing flight had a pleasant, party atmosphere which hid the uncomfortableness of Iceland Air. Iceland Air, our school's preferred airline, offered by far the cheapest flight to Brussels and the only one our school would book for us, so everyone was on board. Unfortunately, I could not share their feelings, because the aircraft, which was either designed for short Europeans or for extra seats, did not allow my six foot two inch frame to fit into its allotted space.

Making the best of my knees smashing into the head rest in front of me, I tediously perused the flight for at least one friendly face. Finding none, I looked at the women, their faces and their bodies, none of which really struck any immediate fancies. Turning inward, I had nothing left to do, but to watch the flight pass and to allow the thoughts of Kristie, which were convincing me to live by our empty promises in vain, to remain.

TWO

Slow Down

The flight never passed the point of horrible with the only highlight coming in Reykjavik when I received Iceland currency after paying in American dollars. The large coins floated among my fingers, as if made of foil.

"Hey, now I'm getting somewhere," but the lady didn't even bother to look up at me from her work. Regardless, I smiled at her blue paper crown.

Traveling was awing and completely foreign. I knew not how to be cool doing it, but I was trying. The blame lay in a childhood that had only brought a barely memorable trip to Myrtle Beach and to New York. My parents had believed in the basics, a canoe and a tent or making progress on finishing the necessities around the house.

Even through my travel naiveté, the students who bought Reykjavik Hard Rock Cafe sweatshirts at the airport were rightfully deemed uncool. So many of them reboarded with their chest proudly thrust outward displaying the yellow circle of the Hard Rock Cafe. I noted each smiling face with the appropriate label, "geek."

"But who, the fuck, am I?" I thought. "I definitely don't reek of James Dean, but these clowns, they hover above the boundary of ridiculous."

As they continued past without a word, these fellow students, that were already subjected to my stereotypical mocking, reminded me of my own social ineptness that was created during a distressing childhood of a typical sheltered life of prefab friends in a prefab environment. Its own victim, my mind blanked as I continued to wallow alone, sitting stoically.

So I began the search for my only known friend who was also going to Belgium. His name was John. Actually, John wasn't a true friend, but a friend of a friend. However, he was someone whom I knew well enough to say hi to. My lone hopes in him were high, because according to the friend, "he's the funniest guy I know." So I looked for the familiar blonde, wavy hair and pink, German nose.

Locating him, we talked briefly, but I discovered that neither of us had too much to say. Our confused minds were simultaneously transporting back to the never livable past. So I was left to settle for the quickest remedy of them all, sleep.

When Brussels' soil arrived in my lightened T.V. set window, my mind freaked out my entire body with the deliberations over the actual time as compared to the real time that my body knew it to be. My watch was of no hope, because I couldn't remember if I had been anal and set my watch forward to European time, kept it at Eastern Standard for sentimental value, or had been cool in Reykjavik and set it for some crazy time zone in the middle of the Atlantic Ocean. The face said four forty-three. I had no idea.

"Hey, what time is it?" I said to the woman next to me who still had her Walkman going at full speed. I repeated the question after she turned the yellow knob on the side of an expensive product of Sony. Her face crinkled, then paused, uncrinkled, then paused, then recrinkled. My exact realizations occurred in her olive skin forehead.

She went through some sort of logical thought process with the face of her watch and an index finger. "Okay, if there is a six hour difference…" she mumbled away. I looked for someone more knowledgeable, but surprisingly came up empty.

She announced, "Okay, it's twelve forty-five. We left at ten o'clock and it's an eight hour flight plus the six hour time difference and we are a half hour away." She picked her head up with the gratifying pride of happening upon the solution to a Calculus equation. Besides this huge smile, her face divulged a large nose that rode outward just below thick, black, poodle curls and that was wrapped by a Middle Eastern stain.

Not able to take her beam, I took her same logic and my own index finger to the face of my watch. However, the pointing finger couldn't remotely explain how the hands read four forty-five, but the second hand was, at least, still moving.

"Thanks, I'm Don." As I looked down in slow motion, our hands awkwardly met and began to shake in unison. Besides her face, she was absolutely tiny. Her hand placed in mine made me laugh in the absurdity, like the Tom Petty video when he does a spin off of Alice in Wonderland; a huge chair, plate, utensils, and a regular Tom Petty. (I think it was "Don't Come Around Here No More.") For her, it was the inanity of her little body in this huge chair and a huge smile, nose, and hair.

She eased up on my hand and said, "I'm Erin."

I unequivocally hate shaking hands, especially in informal situations. She noticed my reluctant response and pulled hers away quickly. Feeling bad, I couldn't help wondering about the ritual of shaking hands, who had started shaking it, and why it represented selling out and sucking up to me. A bent formula of money, power, success, and handshakes flashed above her mop.

The plane began its final descent and I tightened up my seat belt until my knuckles whitened. This panic into a strict adherence of the seat belt rules was a result of the mechanics of flight and the simultaneously hitting of the wheels to the ground without tipping, all of which mesmerized my mind.

With stuff in hand, the plane and its passengers unboarded. I slid in line right in front of John, "Don, this reminds me of *The Mouse That Roared*. I keep looking for Peter Sellers to walk up behind me and to say high." His head poked over my padded shoulder.

Uncertain, I agreed with a confirming nod figuring that *The Mouse That Roared* was a movie about Europe, but I kept quiet concealing my ignorance.

The moment was too good to be true. One by one, we climbed down a portable set of stairs and walked across the runway about a half a mile to a hanger and through an inefficient customs department. Even the weather was just like the picture of Europe, that I had sold to my mind, rainy with heavy clouds, but not too cold. Behind me in the customs line, John kept mumbling with jerks of his body about *The Mouse That Roared*.

After customs, we were marched off to a bus by some of the administrators of our new school. One guy, who looked our age but balding, was running around and giving everyone advice about our upcoming meeting with our "house parents." Telling me that he was "the representative for the students on the administration side, you know, the student coordinator," he invaded my space.

He continued, "Moyen, I'm Andy, that is hello in Belgium's native tongue. Hey, sweet backpack. All of those pockets will really come in handy on the train." I gave him that blank look to make him go away and inform him that his Sesame Street tone should go along with him.

John and I sat together in the very back row of the upper deck of a sight seeing bus. "John, I remember you rushing our fraternity. Then you dogged us." The plastic smell of the bus company's disinfectant unclogged my passages.

He pulled back and let his mouth rip apart and downward, "Man I don't know. I was really torn, but my dad couldn't understand why I needed to join and I really couldn't come up with a reason to join. So I didn't."

Taking his lead, I turned to look out the window and shut up. The flowing countryside solaced the failure of my first attempt to make conversation with my only friend. I remained quiet and uncertain of him, besides the fact that he was the funniest guy in the world and that he didn't want to be in my fraternity.

On our way to the school, we took a brief tour of town. The man giving the tour was the school's Dean, Dr. Lorkis, a once very esteemed professor who had come to Belgium to end out his teaching days gracelessly.

We passed the King's palace as he spoke into a microphone somewhere hidden on the first level of the bus, "when the king is home, the flag is at the top of the mast. When the king is out of the country, the flag is at the bottom of the mast." The words almost soared in their monotone and slow consistency.

I turned back to John, "and when the king is not home, but in the country, the flag is at half mast," mimicking his sliding paraphrase. It sounded dumb, but it was much better of an ice breaker than questioning his rejection of my fraternity.

The city contained many old fortifications. Sensing our curiosity, the bus paused, letting us walk through an elderly valley that split the city in two. The common theme of Belgium and its swirling green forests, that were encased by a hard coating of cement and ancient grey, was exemplified in these heightened, natural walls and plush floor of the valley. "Wow, this is it. This is Europe. Look at that green grass. Now Don, that is fuckin' green. Green as my National Geographic. Green," he ranted onward until the descriptions blurred into a moan.

Personally, I got stuck on the grey. Every building was made of cement and the sky was heavy and threatening. Belgium was just as grey as green.

"Belgium is a country of a couple million people in about the area smaller, but of similar shape as South Carolina. The country is basically tri-lingual with French, German, and a Belgium dialect being spoken. The dialect is used in the streets and understood, but not in the classroom. The country with its rolling, green hills has a fair amount of woodland area. The major industries are wine, beer, the European Community, and offshore banking. Part of the Alsace valley, Belgium has some very best white wines, besides several breweries." I stopped listening to the pamphlet-like presentation of our Dean to look around myself.

My eyes swung back and forth, pausing to blink. The only thing that I knew about Belgium was that the city of Brussels, besides being the capital, was a European Community Capital. It has something like the European Court and perhaps a European Congress, but I couldn't remember. I had learned little and retained nothing about the country from our one day seminar, except that everyone was a banker, who laundered a lot of drug and oil money, and that the make up of the people were partially natives, but a strong minority of Italians and Spanish which added a nice flavor.

The tour ended with our arrival at school. "Our families would be the last fuckers to show up." John and myself stood outside waiting to be picked up and taken to our new homes.

"Yeah, mine are suppose to live like five minutes from here. Hey, let's try to hook up tomorrow. Let's meet up here 'round one," John's nerves did the talking.

"Sounds good man. My walk is s'pose to be about twenty to twenty-five minutes to get here, but we should meet here since it's the only place we know?" I searched the area wondering which way home would be.

The rain slowed as almost everybody had finished the awkward moments of meeting their new families and had left. I looked back at the school, "John, this is small. I thought it would be like a couple of buildings and a courtyard with grass, benches, and the such."

"One building? It looks like a house." He joined my search, "Great, we are right by a synagogue and what is that…the Bulgarian Embassy. I'm sure we won't get fucked with too much having those two as neighbors. Hey, where is the main part of town anyway?" his voiced raised to an angry level.

Off a couple of hundreds yards, a park laid while the beginnings of what seemed residential ran the opposite way. The same grey buildings were everywhere, no matter where you looked.

Finally, a grey haired guy jumped out of a little, red, Renault sports car. "I bet this is my guy." Since only a few were left and I knew that I lived with an elderly gentleman, I was certain, so I carefully studied his movements. Like a local politician, he jovially approached the school's dignitaries and then flirted with the ladies making jokes and sexual innuendoes.

"Don, Don?" I motioned him towards my location. In less than a flash, he whirled around, grabbed my bags while offering a greeting, then started up the car. Luckily, I was able to stop his momentum just long enough to get his phone number and to relay it to John. The ease of his English was a tremendous relief.

"Thirty-nine, eighty-two, forty-two."

"All right, Larry Csonka, John Stallworth, and D.J. Dozier. Got it," the words trailed away as we took off, leaving John to fend for himself.

Sitting captivated, I was held in check by his mouth which motored away at the same illegal speed as his little, red car. The only thing that was attainable from his raving was that his name was Albert. Still, without me, he continued onward with his tales.

Shaking off the long trip and lightening up, I desperately tried to follow him and to make my own conversation, but my body wouldn't respond in its despondent needs for sleep. The efforts were honest, but failed in the drowning dreams of what kind of bed I would soon be in.

The bed and its cool sheets danced blissfully in the windshield, even though I was pissed at not immediately connecting with Albert. A long time ago, I had made the resolution that my mood would be sociable and friendly to my new house dad, regardless of my fears. However, his speed and intensity coupled with my desires to sleep made me a fly on the wall.

"Do you have any brothers and sisters?"

"I have a sister."

"I got your letter. Your French seems very good," he smiled forward not wanting to leave the road.

"Well, actually it is rusty. I haven't used it in quite awhile," the guilt of having my French teacher from high school proof the letter snuck into my empty stomach.

"Where are you from?"

"Pittsburgh, Pennsylvania."

The conversations continued in threads the entire trip home and through the early afternoon dinner that he greeted me with. Happily and voluntarily, he went into the tales of his many students that he had housed before and his trip to visit them in America.

Succumbing to exhaustion, I forgot the pressure of conversations and allowed myself to enjoy the stories and the meal which was steak, French fries, and lots of wine. Everything filled my body and mind making my new bed look like deserved heaven. As soon as the food was gone and his anecdotes ran out, I went straight to my dreams.

THREE

The Shadows on My Wall

Waking up at two-thirty in the morning while your body was certain that it was eight-thirty the night before was a horrible experience. I was frustrated, tired, bored, and awake plus I had no idea what I should do with the time. "What to do?" echoed against the grey walls in my little song.

I studied the room. It was an odd shape, kind of like a square, but with one corner hacked off, thus making it smaller and adding a fifth corner.

The bed, that was built to match my short European forefathers, left about six feet of my six foot two inch frame hanging over the edge. Luckily, I slept in the fetal position. The bed sat in one of the corners and faced towards the single, large window on the opposite wall. On top, only one, thick, white blanket with faded yellow stripes was provided, but it was filled with a heavy foam that was actually quite comfortable. This lone blanket had one serious flaw; it couldn't handle extremes. If the night became too cold or remained too hot, I ended up struggling through the night with sleep and the blanket's limited temperature control.

After the bed, the configuration presented a night stand which nestled into one of the corners created by the hacked-off edge of the otherwise perfect square. Next, the doorway was on the wall that was slashed. With the original square starting again, the closet emerged with triumph of its largeness, especially for my one suitcase worth of clothes. Eventually, its emptiness would gnaw at my confidence. Also, a dresser nicely fit next to the closet for handy storage of such things as underwear.

The next wall housed a desk which sat below the window. It looked like an old kitchen table that still had the plastic tablecloth to prove it. The window stared out into the front of the house and into, most unfortunately, the orange buzz of a street lamp. When I read at night in the melancholic dark or watched the rain cry through its artificial glow, the street lamp was nice. But most of the time, I was paranoid at its bug killing aura.

The walls were a sterile hospital white with a matching floor which was made of brown and green tiles along with a little rug thrown over top. Without this crucial rug, the room had the ambiance of the old folks home that my grandmother spent her last years dying.

Directly across the hallway of my bedroom, the second floor contained a bathroom that was really the only other frequented room. The bathroom contained the basics; a sink, a toilet, a bathtub, and a mirror. Two oddities existed. First, the hot water heater, a little bugger that was stuck on the wall, had to be lit every morning. Every morning, I had to first light the pilot, then take a shit while watching the blue flame warm my bath water. Secondly, the bathtub, on first glance, looked nice and big, but upon using, it lacked the dire necesssitics, a curtain and a shower head. Without either, I was very uncertain in how to properly clean myself. In four months, I could not master the bath and the involved washing process.

With my curiosity contained, I sat down at my desk to contemplate how I would shower and to figure out that I could officially wake up around seven. Then, I opened up my nice little leather bound travel diary that my mom had so thoughtfully placed in my stocking at Christmas. I began to write my first song to REM's quirky melody of "I Believe."

I believe in death,

I believe in pro-choice,

I believe in highly socialistic societies,

I believe in health and happiness through leisure,

I believe in meaningless pursuits,

I believe in being alone,

I believe in death,

I believe in living,

I believe in barter,

I believe in Santa Claus,
I believe in the power of ignorance,
I believe in the shame of knowledge,
I believe.

I continued on with a story, "A bum asked me for money and I smiled at him, so he followed. He began to tell me his plight, but I cut him short. Tell me something good and something funny and my pocket of change is yours."

He paused and I waited patiently as he considered if I was being condescending or if I was a genuine saint. He looked up from his feet and curiously looked at my wire framed glasses. "I can't tell you anythin' good or anythin' funny, but I will tell you what I believe."

"Fair enough."

"I believe in the work ethic, but nothing seems to be working for me. So what the hell do you expect me to believe in?"

I smiled at him stopping his growing rage and handed him my change, "Most profound statement I've heard in years. Thank you."

He counted the money. "Thank you."

I felt weary from my first and last Journal entry. I fell back to sleep.

When seven A.M. finally came, I awoke to the sounds of my new roomie, Albert, fussing around in the kitchen downstairs. Ignoring him, I prepared for a shower and to face the new day. After letting the pilot light kick in, I turned on the water and plugged up the drain. Slowly, the cold tile and the hot water wrapped comfortably around me. The experience of sinking into my new European bath tub left me thrilled and excited.

I lathered up and tried to rinse. I, scrubbing and soaking in my own dirt, realized why showers were developed. In a tub, one can only lather, but never really rinse. Then I figured out the hand held aspect of the tub. Just like a removable showerhead, the tub had a removable spickethead. So I emptied the water to rinse and instantly the floor became soaked. A wet floor on my first attempt threw me into a panic. Trying to dry it as much as possible, I even opened the window to let a drying, winter breeze chill the tiles. Today was not a good start.

By the time I was ready and went down stairs, he was on his way to church. He put out the breads, jams, and spreads of the typical continental breakfast. 'No wonder these guys are so small. Don't they know that a good breakfast is the key to a good day? It felt like days since I had talked to anybody.

"Don, or is it Donald?" I shook my head indifferently. "Don? I must show you the alarm. It is very important. I was robbed once. No, no, not a lot of money, but they robbed me. It is not like it, uh, how do you say, like it once was. Now, Don, this is very important. Do not forget. If you want to go anywhere, you must turn on and remember to turn it off as soon as you get home," his dialect rolled and hooked in his tongue's confusion of applying French and German to English.

"Like this. Turn key, like so. Take the key and hide it above the windowsill. Please do not hide anywhere else. I must know at all times where it is, so I don't call the police on myself," he laughed.

"Okay, Okay, you try it. Now, this is how to turn it off. Remember twenty seconds you have until it goes off. Watch. You must not go too fast or it goes off and you mustn't turn too slow. Like so. You try."

I turned too slow. That bell-less box blared into my lungs. I knew that it was going to go off, but it had still scared the shit out of me. I tried two more times until finally succeeding.

"Here are your keys. I go to church and then maybe to my son's in the country. I do not know." Then, he was off like a prom dress.

Nothing to do and nowhere to go, I investigated. First, that damn alarm thing was located in the bathroom to the left of the front door. It was just one of those toilet and sink only bathrooms. I walked down the length of the hallway and decided between the living room on the right, the basement door on the left, and the kitchen straight ahead.

The living room was wide open, seemingly formal and also part-timed as the dining room. The chairs looked old and uncomfortable. Generally, the room had no character, but a couple of books, a map of America with pins marking visits, and pictures. The picture on the coffee table between the two chairs was of his deceased wife, who was a little manly, but still managed to maintain an edge of femininity that helped her attractiveness. The other pictures were of former students like me, except women. Staring at the smiling faces, I wondered how they had showered and if he had really housed women.

The room was fronted with a series of huge windows which were held back with heavy drapes that matched the dark green of the felt covering of his chairs and couch. The curtains kept the room dark and formal.

The complimentary color of the walls was tan and the floors

were wooden with an oriental rug to give the scene some spice. He was obviously neat and organized.

The living room continued, changing into a family type room which was much more livable. A T.V., a paper, a book case, a telephone, and a worn couch gave the room a little needed lift. This room was mostly covered in browns except the burgundy couch. Finishing the right side of this room, another row of windows, without curtains, showed a barn off to the right and a rambling green field with a soccer goal off to the left. Its picture was charming.

I began leafing through the channels on the television set. German, Italian, French, and even English was spoken. A couple of soccer games, a German talk show, and music videos couldn't hold my attention. So I continued along the back of the house until I came to the kitchen. It was humongous with lots off empty spaces and few modern appliances. I sat down to my food.

"La Vache Qui Rit light. Hey, I can even watch my fat intake with the laughing cow," I said to bolster my confidence in comprehending French. I ate bread until boredom came quickly after conservatively finishing a small glass of orange juice.

Playing with some crumbs, I checked out the kitchen and watched the fog out of the back window. He seemed to have a very small back yard with a chair, bird feeders, and a ten foot by ten foot garden being its only possessions. Shortly, it turned into a field that looked like it belonged to the barn, but I couldn't be sure.

The kitchen itself was very bright with a light yellow paint job, white cabinets, and the back wall entirely filled with windows. It was definitely the most lively room in the house. "Where are the appliances?" I speculated while trying to put my breakfast away properly.

The dorm style refrigerator, that sat on the floor and came up to my knee caps, was in the back corner away from his family type room and next to the windows. Opening it, I placed the spreads, butters, jams, and juices in their hopefully proper places. It was easy because nothing else was in there to worry about disturbing.

The rest of that wall was countertop and cabinets. I placed my dishes into the two tub sink. Again, there was the miniature hot water heater hooked up to the faucet. I went through each cabinet and drawing, finding the silverware, the glasses, the dishes, the utilities, the tools, and the such. The only other appliances were a tiny stove and a tiny deep fryer where he made my french fries the day before. Nothing excited me at all, except his backyard window.

The lacking refrigerator, except for continental breakfast supplies and an endive, worried me. "There's got to be another refrigerator and or a freezer. The basement."

I climbed down the stairs to find a landing with two doors. I unlocked the door straight in front of me and discovered the empty garage. Trying the other door, I opened it and found a storage area that every cellar has. "Voilá, the freezer," my first attempt at French.

The freezer was the kind that sat on the floor and had a sliding door on the top, just like an ice cream parlor. I peered in only to see some meat and bread. The rest of the cellar was lined with shelves that contained various canned foods, tools, and alcohol; all boring.

Well, I had been up probably a good eight hours since my journal entry. So I climbed up to my bedroom and took a nap at eleven A.M.

FOUR
Penny for Your Ketchup

"Fuck," I was already late to meet John. It was now four o'clock and we were suppose to me at one.

I frantically got ready, but then presented myself calmly to Albert. "Albert, Hi. How was your day?"

"Oh, Don. It was fine."

"I must go meet a friend."

"Oh, I was going to take you to Pasha tonight. Will you be back?"

I paused trying to gain some semblance of Pasha and what it meant to me. Having no idea, I went with it, "Yeah, we are going to walk around for awhile and then get something to eat. Then I will be back."

"About what time? Oh, what do I say? You do not know. Bring your friend back with you. We will all go together," his breathing quickened with odd excitement over the friend idea.

"Oh yeah, how do I get to the school?" Slowing down, I continued, "I mean, school, that is where I am meeting him."

"Go outside, walk up the street and turn left onto the Rue de Dix Septembre. It is on that rode about thirty minutes away. Or you could take the bus. Here take a bus schedule," he kept explaining about the complexities of traveling to town and about the bus system in his broken English, as I continued out the door. Without a choice, he gave up and I was off.

I followed Avenue de Dix Septembre which was really called

Avenue Monterey, but the signs eventually renamed it Dix Septembre. "What is Dix Septembre? The tenth of September, um?" Its four, well traveled lanes gave it the appearance of the city's major artery to and from the west side of town.

The road bent here and there, presenting pretty much the same picture with each change. Brussels contained an endless supply of residential homes that looked like square brownstones made out of the ever present grey concrete, one of the sad results of World War II. Hitler's lasting impression was converting Central Europe into these prefabricated skeletons that ran right up to one another. These houses, at least, had their own little lawn that began as soon as the abundant sidewalks stopped. However, the houses started only a few feet from the end of the sidewalks. The beautiful green was being pushed aside by the stiff grey. Occasionally, a house would not really be a house, but some sort of little grocery store or butcher shop.

A few old, ugly, and pale people, whose sights never left their feet, crept past or slipped behind me. Conceding that making lots of European friends was an improbability, I was more than content with their disregard.

Up ahead I saw the bobbing yellow head which belonged to John. "Hey, man. Sorry about…" I had already begun my apology when he did the same. But I cut him short, "amazing, I can't believe we both overslept to about the same time and still had the fortune of running into each other randomly on the street. Hey how's your family?" Our luck and destiny caught me slightly surprised and very eager.

"Oh you have gotta see 'em. It's amazing," his eyebrow rose to the bottom of his bangs. "They all come up together in this 1960 hunk of a car. This little guy with huge arms and legs jumps out and takes my bags without a word. He is my housedad. You know this guy is probably out there all day waxing and tinkering with his piece of glorified shit and it still runs bad, but runs. I hopped in and two minutes later we are there. It is five minutes from school." Each uniquely exaggerated syllable enticed me further into his tale.

"Well, anyway, you have got to see this place. You know that valley we were in yesterday, that cuts through the city? Well it goes right behind the school and it's my back yard, my fucking backyard. It's amazing. I feel like it's part of a Disney movie set with the grass, the trees, the little river, and the little people walking around with nice costumes.

"So they fed me this huge meal and I was dead asleep. I woke up and walked around with Marco. Oh Marco, you've gotta see this guy. Marco, he's their son that lives at home and works for some bank. He must be some fucking dork or something. I don't really know. He looks fourteen in the face with a little dirt lip, has a body of my grandfather, and he is actually thirty-five. But there is something about his innocence that you think he is one of those guys that talks little kids into doing sexual deviances for him and turns them into gay rapists for the rest of their lives.

"The parents, at least the mother, are the nicest people. I ate just tons. Actually, the guy never said anything. He just stared. I don't know what his deal is." He captured some air in his mouth after his non-stop oration. After a few hearty seconds, the air filtered slowly out of his nose.

"How's your room?"

"Nice, it's up in the attic with a desk and a huge and amazingly comfortable bed. Oh, it had this huge green pillow on it. I didn't know if I slept under or over it. How 'bout you?"

"It's all right. I do have my own bathroom, but you know there is no shower in there. I already got it fucking soaked. It had this hand held sprayer that I could rinse myself off with, but there is no curtain, no nothing. He also got me drunk yesterday before I fell asleep. I have this funny feeling about him."

"Well, where should we go? Marco says the town is that way. There is even a McDonald's." We both turned to the East facing the same park as we had noticed yesterday.

"Let's see how we have Americanized this place."

I followed John's pointed finger. After our school and a couple of other buildings, most notably a synagogue, the park engulfed the skyline hiding the bustling metropolis. The quaint park was a small square typical of a city park with a few benches and a playground, but managed to completely engulf its area.

"I live right on the other side of that park. Right down the hill," his head wiggled in disbelief.

Quickly, the street became densely populated with people, cars, and stores. We had no idea what we were doing, but it was definitely an urban setting. Eventually our sidewalk turned into a huge, deserted square that couldn't decide if nobody liked it or if it was just too big for itself.

"Hey, there she is, McDonald's." Seeing a fast food restaurant and relying on it so quickly let me down from my expected adventures.

McD's was exactly like every other one that I have been in, but everything was in French.

"Seven Francs for ketchup. Look, there is even biere, here." We did some quick calculations in our heads and in our pockets and left. Basically, Belgium francs sucked and took about thirty-eight of them to equal a dollar, or they equaled between two and three cents. Somewhere between two and three cents did not exist in our minds, thus the Francs sucked. Also, they sucked because of a lack recognition, since they have the same name as French currency.

"Someday before we go, we've got to get a biere here. Which do you think came first beer or here? Was here decided on after beer was? You know, beer here is so catchy, but biere ici, that's bad."

"What?! That's one of the stupidest thing I've ever heard. In fact, that is the stupidest thing I've ever heard." He laughed, but not at me. "That's why we are going to have so much fun here."

I ignored him, "John? Albert, you know, the guy I live with? Well, he wants to take us out to some place. I don't know if it's a bar or restaurant, but I have a feeling that we might get fed."

"Sounds fine by me. Let's go," he led me out from under the golden arches empty handed to the evening. In its newly produced darkness, the night took us back along the only road I knew to home.

"Ah, Don, you are home I hear," hurrying away from a blinking T.V. "This is your friend, I see. Hello."

"Hi, I am John," came out in an overly loud, overly slow, and unique, German accent. I would quickly grow accustomed to this manner of speaking with or being spoken to by foreigners.

Albert wasted no time and steered us into his car while speaking of Pasha. "Pasha, you like Pasha, pretty women and Americans. You like." His smile was sinister and alluring.

I had no idea, but I pictured topless waitresses at this so called Pasha. That excited look in his eyes told a tale of sorrowful old man lust that was associated with topless waitresses. Plus that name, Pasha, sounded so exotic.

Upon entering, we were disappointed to unearth only a bar. According to Albert, all of the American students, which was us, went to this bar every single night, but we saw none. However, the English bartender and waitresses made us comfortable. We sat down at the quiet and dark bar to drink beers. Albert only had one before buying us another and quickly leaving us to our own lacking devices.

Not really eating since this morning's bread, the beer whirled around inside of me. After a couple beers, I was queasy, hungry, and sleepy.

Unable to continue, I abruptly announced, "John, I'm taking off. I'll see ya tomorrow. We have orientation, don't we?" A long, drawn puff ran through my numb lips, "I hope I can find my way home."

"Me too," his face swung towards the bar and whirled up to the entrance. He disappointedly pointed to the door.

At home, Albert was still awake, but in his pajamas and ready for bed. After rubbing his eyes below his glasses, he began speaking softly, "Don, to stay healthy you must have drink every night before bed. Hold on, I will get it." He ran downstairs with resolution in his steps. His voice approached and echoed up the stairs, "I received this bottle from a father of one of the students that stayed here. Real Kentucky whiskey." He smiled familiarly at the bottle, almost impressed by himself. "Now, do not drink like a child. Enjoy, sip it, catch the flavor. It is the key to health."

Finishing, I went upstairs and threw up. I slept like a baby until my body decided three A.M. was, once again, the preferred hour to rise. I couldn't wait for the jet lag to wear off.

FIVE
Metal and Flesh

School sucked, no matter what country, even the infamous semester abroad in Europe. University life has become the discipline of memorizing and the skill of regurgitating it. All learning stemmed from who did what when or what happens if, "the objective test," or what does my teacher believe in and what style of writing is pleasurable to them, "the subjective questions." Systematically, college drilled in the feelings of the status quo and brain washed the next generation of leaders into keeping the order intact.

Also, the extreme costs, the unaffordable commitment, and the slighted acceptance process of post secondary education was not forgotten. Through these steadfast rigors of obtaining a permission slip to continue onwards, the chosen were allowed to carry the torch, generation after generation. To sum higher education was a bullshit way to provide the means for the upper class to remain on top and unchallenged. With these thoughts and Led Zeppelin's "Going to California," roaming through the hallways of my brain, I walked into class.

I was less than excited for my first day of school, but I didn't even hesitate to continue on with my chance at being powerful and rich. "Liberal Arts, my ass! Preparation for my life's work, my ass!" My eyes circled the radius of the area nearest, hoping nobody had noticed my words.

My only excitement for school was the first day and checking out all of the faces in class. To make a good initial impression, I had a distinct plan of attack. Showing up a couple of minutes early insured a seat in the last row. This last row seat was key for looking at everyone's entrance. Looking at the faces, clothes, and amount of prepared supplies, I would guess where everyone would sit and predetermine their grades for the semester. Books and notebook in hand, meant the front of the class. Nice chinos or a skirt with the proper supplies meant the first row, the true go-getters. However, nobody impressed me more than the kids in the Wrangler jeans, the too small sweaters, the Zip tennis shoes, the glasses and the mussed hair. Oblivious to their supplies or to their sitting arrangement, they simply slid into class, unnoticed and unnoticing. Nobody would ever get to know them or see them study, but they would always have the high score. Whenever the teacher would announce the high score achiever only a few, who would use a little logical deduction, could figure out that it was the kid in the Wranglers. My enjoyment of their successes culminated with the dismay and disgust of the cotton and polyester first row crew.

Following my planned regimen of the day, I attended my semester's schedule; International Economics, Comparative Economics, French, and Twentieth Century European History (1929-1950).

International Economics was taught by Hitler's twin, or at least a good impersonator. Honest to god, the classes' jaws had to be lifted up after Dr. Stullir walked into the room with his greasy, black hair parted to one side, his burnt black, cigar mustache, his pasty skin, his short, stocky body, and his overly exaggerated method of speaking with a German accent. Actually, Dr. Stullir would later tell of his escape from the Communists in East Germany when he was a small boy right before the Berlin Wall was constructed. I knew better, he was Hitler, reincarnated into a wonderful professor who was beginning the process of making up for all of his historical travesties.

Comparative Economics was taught by the director of our university, the frail minded Dr. Lorkis. The self-proclaimed doctor's loss of mind and monotone presentation provided me time to catch up on sleep, to work on an imitation of him, and to practice my drawings of tired old men. His saving grace was his ability to find really good speakers and his insufferable tolerance of the student's sophomoric gestures.

French was a piece cake because it was first year French and I had previously tested into third year. Also, the teacher was a woman who had a hidden flirting and personality category on each test for all of the men. It was another sleeper.

Twentieth Century European History was just as it sounds, hard and intimidating. The teacher was in the same mold as Leonardo da Vinci. I don't know why or how, but he was filled with an intense amount of knowledge on every event and person in history. He knew and did it all and didn't know or care that he actually could do it all. Eventually developing some courage, I asked the burning question, "Did Hitler die a virgin?" Scared, I qualified the statement, "I remember when I was little and I read the *Book of Lists* which provided a list of the most famous virgins and Hitler was number one."

He scrunched up his face, gave me a stern but proud glare, "We can speculate all we want, but not in this classroom. Now that is for talk in a bar over a couple of beers. Maybe, one of these days I will be invited in one of your outings and I will tell you all that I know on the subject." He laughed knowing he would never be invited.

He also gave an original copy of *Mein Kompf* for the person with the highest score in his class. A great idea, but most everyone just wanted to finish the class.

After the first day, every day in school was the same. Most of my time was spent wondering why we learned so many unapplicable facts about things that have nothing to do with anything and why we learned about so many things that I would never face in my life. However, I studied, knowing that was essential, if I wanted to work and make a lot of money. If I wasn't questioning, the rest of the time was spent drawing or watching others draw. Fortunately, my seat in Economics was next to a guy named Tim who could draw the most amazing pictures of airplanes. He had talent.

The first day of classes wound up and we all slowly drifted back into our formative years when everything was fresh and everyone was confused about their clothes, bodies, and hair. The socializing and stratifying process began along with the status and image games of youthful colleagues. Joining in, I proved my lack of wisdom, something that would never find its way to me.

I had already picked John as my friend and one was enough, but he was much more social so I followed along without any other alternative. As he began telling the group that would be the popular ones, about his home life, I enlisted in their circle.

"When I wake up in the morning, birds fly into my window and grab my clothes for me. I go downstairs and breakfast is waiting along with two sandwiches for lunch. " Each word of John's was loitering with attention maintaining delight. "The dolphins come up next to my house and I hop on and they take me to school. It is fuckin' Disney, I tell you. I went outside last night and tried to eat a little bit of my house to see if it was gingerbread. I'm telling you, Disney created my backyard." Each movement and pause kept the whole crowd intrigued and eventually made us decide to check out "John's Valley" and drink some wine in it.

About an hour later, we were following John down a winding cobblestone path that brought us to the base of the valley and to a small stream. We entered upon a small, stone footbridge. He pointed up to his new home on the hillside. "Perfect," we all romantically chanted in unison.

A club immediately took form in the honor of John and his Valley. I fell in behind his leadership and began the initiation, "Take these corks and offer it to the gods of John's river. Demonstrate your love of life with this offering to John's dolphins." The last wine bottle was opened.

Counting to three, we threw the corks off of the bridge and into the cement filled bottom of the stream. "Drink now from the bottle of knowledge and life. Drink deep and thirstily and you can begin to capture the perfectly beautiful essence of John's valley. To our king, John."

We drank ourselves into a wild John frenzy, yelling his name and calling out for his creatures. The idea became the god and the inspiration of the day. It cradled our new found fear and sense of adventure and banded us together into a gang of emotional protection of the unknown of tomorrow in an unknown land. I was inspired, but cynical to the auspicious start to my life.

The seven of us picked our new roles, the King, the Minister of Defense, the Grand-pere, the Sacrificer of Virgin, the Court Jester, the High Priest, and the Chief Justice. Society had taught us well and we were unable to continue on with a club, if we didn't have assigned roles of power and a purpose for living. They reflected ourselves and what we wanted out of life in a sad, but accurate account of society and its formations. True Communism and Anarchy don't have a shot at success.

Another shameful commentary was the men's decision to give lesser roles to the women who had accompanied us. They were the Demoiselles of John. It was a perfectly disgusting act of sexism and injustice performed by men which indicted us and our Western culture.

Upon finishing our bottles, we wound into the night and through the valley for our first taste of night life in Belgium. Although fun was had by all, our adventure would become the quintessential picture of our first nights together trying to bust out in Europe. John threw up in the bathroom and disappeared without anyone knowing how, where, or when. Two, politically stupid goons got into a fight, yelling at each other until finally being thrown out. And the rest of us tried to pick up women. The end results foreshadowed the quintessential view of our upcoming lives; John woke up in the bushes a couple hours later, the rest of us had empty pockets and masturbated ourselves to sleep, and all Americans were banned from the bar.

The specifics of my night were blurry, as I sat quietly, watching the happenings around me. I was a mellow drunk who, if given the chance, shamefully wallows in their pity. Eventually, I became drunk and horny enough to begin the mating process and forget any of my heavy problems. I looked across the table from me and noticed a woman, who was a fellow student with a nice ass, smiling at me. Even though the smiles showed a set of braces on a twenty-year-old woman, her tight long ass was seducing, so I joined in her and her friend's conversations about the origins of the great tastes of Belgium waffles.

After a couple of exchanges of smiles I got up to piss, to find John, and to decide which road to take. John was nowhere in sight, so I helplessly went back to the metal head with my decision already made for me.

"This has been fun tonight," her voice was surprisingly a tenor.

"I'm sorry, but I don't think I know your name."

"Leslie."

"Yep." We sat staring at each other wondering what to do next. Luckily conversation didn't impress her.

I decided to continue attempting to have her, "Let's go somewhere else."

"Well, I really should be getting home."

"Where do you live?"

"It's only about fifteen minutes from here. Do you want to come and check it out?"

"Why not?"

Briefly, Kristie, who was probably doing the same thing that I was, penetrated my intentions. She was much prettier than Leslie, but I got up and walked her home. I even ignored the reality of my road that was leading me nowhere to another night of masturbation.

We walked a few minutes and I made my move, going for a kiss. She obliged giving me my first experience of kissing someone with braces, let alone a twenty-year-old woman with braces. It was all right. She rubbed up against my tight jeans and I caressed her breasts and ass, occasionally running my hand through her reddish blonde, frizzy hair. The blood left my brain to fill my drunken crotch.

"Fifteen minute walk, my ass," the words mumbled inside of my mouth. For forty-five minutes, I walked and listened to promises of seeing her bedroom.

We finally arrived. "Good night, you better not come up. I don't know what the rules are in the house and I don't want to piss anyone off." She didn't bother to give me the hopes of more.

I was pissed, drunk, horny, and hungry. "Do you have any idea how I can get home?" I lashed out against my failure. She looked back and pointed in the direction we had come, then disappeared inside after a kiss with which I tried to convince her of letting me stay one last time.

In moments I was cold, but the wind and rain became my only saviors by staying away that night. I started walking back and glanced at the little hand of my watch pointing towards three. It was time for my body to wake-up so I eagerly started the long, lost walk home.

I jogged to the other side of the valley and realized I had no idea where I was or where I lived. I crossed a six-lane highway and snaked through the deserted streets. The cold was extreme against my unprotected structure.

Some sirens passed by and stopped in the front of a house. Tired, I stopped to rest and to check out what was happening. Right in front of me, an old lady was being wheeled out of her home on a stretcher. She was shrunken from years of not moving with only the bones for her skin to wrap around. Upon passing her black sunkenness, my beady eyes connected with her own, grotesquely beautiful eyes that were peering our of her balding silver head. She gummed away at her teeth while the world around her moved slow and unconcerned. Nobody bothered to handle her with care, which she didn't. In her mind she was already dead, but her body was no longer connected to it. She looked at me blankly then closed her eyes deliberately, as if she wanted to pretend to not have seen my escaping youth. She disappeared behind the closing doors, while her daughter locked the front door to her childhood and to the eventual devastation of age. I could see the daughter's nightly drinks and daily crossword puzzles that deadened her to the slow painfulness of the inevitableness of her mother's life and of her own.

The sudden rush of mortality struck. No remorse could be found for this dying old hunk of organism. I had never realized that I could die before so I tried to visualize my death. Old? Violent? Sad? Would I be missed? Would anyone cry at my funeral? I hoped that anyone who truly cared would dance upon my grave.

I searched inside for the answers and the feelings, coming up empty. "Shit," I still felt immortal in the ignorance of youth and I hoped it would all end that way. With tomorrow still on my mind, I knew mortality would strike when that same tomorrow came in the form of dread. The breath of today was gone, but the old lady and her daughter were scared and tried to hold it in. Their long uphill to death had begun.

I continued home.

SIX

"No Way, It Couldn't Be."

"I woke up, got out of bed, dragged the comb across my head. Doo doo do doo do doo. On the way downstairs I had a smoke, someone spoke and I went into a dream. Ah, Ahahah, Ahahhhah ah ah."

Where else would be our first European trip, but Amsterdam? The drugs and the whores were the circus attraction for all young Americans. Feeling the obligation, one hundred of us got onto the same train to see if the rumors were true and to huddle in the safety of numbers.

The whole gang was at the train station for the 12:38 to Amsterdam. It was on time and we fought for seats. I originally sat with a couple of guys from John's valley and John himself.

"Fuck this, it's too crowded. Let's go," John got up with his claustrophobic paranoia and went to another compartment taking most of the other guys with him. However, I stayed behind unwilling to give up a definite seat.

Holding a Eurorail Pass in my hand, I nervously waited for the conductor. This little, unofficial piece of paper with handwritten dates, that signified a beginning and an end, left me unconvinced. In doubts of its validity, I hoped for no problems, but trembled anxiously as he swayed down the aisle towards me. After a quick glanced at it, he moved to the next piece of paper.

The unknown tension released, "What a great way to travel. It is just like shopping with a credit card; no fuss, no money exchange, no guilt over the loss of money, just the travel and the fun." My words went without acknowledgment.

Somehow, John and the rest of the crew got off at the wrong station, leaving me stuck with a whole bunch of women and Tim, the artist. I thought out loud, "Fuck, I'm stuck." Then I realized that everyone was looking at me and listening to my condescending grunt. I smiled, hoping that a token smile was a good enough apology.

I contemplated trying to find John's hostel, but the thought of being alone in the refugee city of white trash scared the shit out of me. So I turned to Tim, "Dude, what are you planning on doing here?"

"I don't know, I guess follow the crowd. I was planning on following a little more male dominated group, but…" His face saw the same trouble with hanging out with ten females in a city made for sexual decadence.

"Well, it looks like we're fucked or heading off on our own." He agreed that both of us lacked any semblance of balls. We ended up following the women to a hostel, going to bars with them, going to the museums with them, and even going to the Red Light district with them.

There were some positives. We ended staying in the much nicer part of town and I still got stoned the whole time. However, Amsterdam didn't offer the same scene of disgust that John would find and that I was searching for.

I hit the hot spots; Van Gogh, the Reich museum, the BullDog, and the Red Light district, but it was tame. Tim and I also made the mistake of buying hash without a true know how of the techniques of smoking it. We wound up smoking out of a bent Coke can with huge ball-point pen holes. Finally, mastery of our contraption was had when my mind began to tingle and Tim started talking about how weird it would be to be able to kill people with your ears, all from a simple Coke can.

My venture into the Red Light district was at least interesting, if not fulfilling. The place was for the dead. Whores, junkies, and hustlers filled the streets and shops with the stench matching the ugliness. Etched in my memories forever, an oriental woman with beautiful, shiny, moonlight hair; a lean, elegant body; and a sad, unconcerned face rubbed her numb clit in a window. Noticing my lingering stare, she got up and did a little dance. I smiled back at her effort, but she didn't even notice or at least didn't respond.

Falling asleep Saturday night, I considered my first trip a bust.

On Sunday, I ran into John on his way out of the Reichmuseum. "What happened to you?"

"What do you mean, what happened to you?" my red wrinkles circled his eyes and nose in disgust. "I got stuck with all of these…knuckleheads. It pretty much has been boring. I smoked some dope and looked at the Red Light district. But besides that, I haven't done a thing worthwhile."

"You're right, this place does suck. I can't wait to get out of here. You are so lucky you were with this docile group." He looked at them nervously then moved me away from them, so no one else could hear.

He continued in a hush, "well, Friday we got our shit hole bunk bedded dorm room, then hit the city. We didn't even get stoned, but instead went right to the heart of the Red Light district. We're leaving now, so I've gotta keep it short." His manner trailed away in a quick anxious whisper.

"Four of us, Jim, Todd, Frank, and myself, went into this sex show place. It's about five bucks plus a one drink limit. We get in there and it's in between shows. Finally, we blow about ten bucks each on beer and the show starts. There were maybe ten people in the whole place. It starts fairly conventional; a little dancing, a little stripping. Next thing I know, this short black guy comes out on stage and starts fuckin' one of the dancers. He forces his huge limp penis in and out of her. She makes him stop, then gives him head, licking at it like a lollipop, a sour one." The saliva formed on the corners of his lips.

"Then a fat, naked, black woman comes to our table. Everyone is egging her on, especially us. She steals Jim's glasses and wipes her cunt with them. She wouldn't give them back until he kissed her." He shuddered before glancing behind him.

"It figures. It would be Jim," I chuckled as I felt my penis catch some blood.

"The whole time she had a banana in her other hand." John looked around once again to see who was close enough to hear. An old woman, who looked like she knew no English, caught his eyes. He continued, "she peeled it, hoisted one of her legs onto our table, then shoved it up her. She then shut up Frank's encouragements by making him eat it. Amazing, he ate a banana out of a fat black chick," his eyes became slits, as if witnessing a horrible accident.

"No way. That is amazing. Hey, when he runs for President, I know I'll be getting that Porsche that I've always wanted."

"That's not all. On stage the whole time were women playing ping pong. They were lying down and pushing and catching a ping pong with their…" he couldn't use the word again, but nodded at my pelvic area. "Man, it was gross. We left after that. This place is decadence, utter decadence. Never will I come back here. I was shocked at the way women would present themselves and we would encourage it and pay for it. The world is sick. I am so disheartened."

Frank came over and I just laughed. "John we've got to go." He looked at me, "shut up, I'm not even going to talk to you."

They left and I kind of wished I had been there. I wanted to smell the place, to watch the faces, to experience. I felt left out.

I could only listen to his story and position into my own experience with selling sex. It wasn't much, but when I was a junior in high school, a buddy and myself beat these two guys in their mid-twenties at tennis. The bet was to be beer, but we went downtown to get hookers, instead. Caught off guard and far too proud to show my fear or any reluctance, I anxiously followed.

One of them gave us twenty dollars apiece, "If you find one you like, feel free." He was an owner of a chain of dry cleaners, but we all knew him to be mob.

To get us enticed, we went to a peep show. We fucked around in the movie booths, but we put our tokens in the wrong slot and got two men butt fucking. Then, we took turns watching women in private booths. Alone, I stepped into the booth and put in my token. The wooden door slowly opened to reveal this girl playing with herself. I was so embarrassed, not for her act, but because she was younger than me.

I asked her name, as I looked at the cum stains on the floors next to my untied shoelaces. She replied by telling me that my other friend had been rude. "Yeah he's an ass." That was as cool as I could sound, the only sentence that would come. The door finally closed on her while she begged me to put more money in and whispered wetly, "You're nice."

We took off with the twenty dollars still burning in my pocket. After talking to some women on the street, the mob guy started to yell at the men dressed in drag. I kept my hand in my pocket on the twenty dollar bill. We were drunk.

Push was coming to shove and I was beginning to show the only reluctance in the gang. Nobody met my standards which were getting higher and higher as the moment ascended closer to reality. I didn't want to do it, but I was too stubborn to say anything.

Just when we saw the women who qualified, someone said something stupid to a guy walking by our car. The man was a pimp who began coming after us. We took off only to have him follow us in his car. Luckily, we lost him on the crazy triangular streets of Pittsburgh and made it back to the safe vacant suburbs. The sanctity of the twenty dollars remained in my pocket, never to be given back to my mobster friend.

I positioned those same feelings into John's brothel nightmare.

SEVEN
Enjoyable

Sex in the city,
Crack before the moan.
Hideous laughter exasperates the black,
Blood rushes to the rhythmic pleasures of the self.
Glass erupts,
Mind lapses,
Cries cover the footsteps over strewn sparkles throughout.
Hands struggle to the empty beat of remaining within,
Sirens flee,
Oblivion steers.
Discovery of a lonely aching door,
Visions of ego—created and destroyed.
I roll off and fall asleep,
Sex in the city.

Yet another boring day in class, I slipped back into my past to get some quick relief from the boredom. Looking very suspicious my hand and arm attempted to cover the paper as to prevent the other students from looking at my inner thoughts. My words were choppy and the poem only had a vague assemblance to a daydream of sex in a room in Queens with kids fooling around outside an open window and their shouts of the danger and violence of their lives of being the have-nots, but I liked them anyway. Until class ended, I pondered the words, "Rhythmic pleasures of the self." I had become slightly bitter towards sex during the last few, lonely weeks and from the shock of last night.

Lunch finally came. I avoided contact with any peers and hurried off to eat. Lunch had become a ritual experience every Monday, Tuesday, and Thursday when all of the students lined up outside of a cafeteria which was actually an addition to a fairly nice restaurant. The restaurant started thinking big and added on a banquet hall, but not too many takers came for lunchtime parties. Luckily, our university had to address the issue of upset parents over their hungry children coming back home. The university forced all of the students to take the three meal a week program and rented out the banquet hall to set up a cafeteria.

The meals were consistently weak, but were vital to my existence. From the outside, as you waited in line, the place looked fairly good, kind of like a metallic Sizzler's. The mood left as soon as the fat women started slopping the food onto our plates. Their toothless scowls barked at us, daring us to eat the bland mix of shit for food.

The food was the same processed meat, potatoes, fruit, lettuce, bread, and water every single day. The meat had already made me sick once, potatoes were potatoes, the fruit had a one per student limit, just fucking lettuce with this yellow vinegary dressing to give it a zing represented the salad, and bread and water was for prisoners. It sucked.

I stood, all alone and the very first one in line with thirty minutes to go before anyone else would dare to show up. I was usually early, but not this early. Generally, I needed to be in the front of the line, because the bread had a limited supply and I had to make them into sandwiches for dinner.

My process was to take the potatoes and make two to four sandwiches with Tuesday being the four sandwich day, because I had to stock up due to Wednesday's lack of lunch. I would wrap them in a napkin secured by rubber bands which I always had waiting on my wrist. I would keep it in my locker until I went home where they sat on my radiator to keep warm and hopefully unspoiled. If my mom only knew.

Today however, I was especially early and didn't give a shit about eating or preparing tonight's dinner. I needed to be alone and to talk to someone and John was about it for me here. I hadn't seen him all day, because he didn't have class before lunch and instead went to a gym he had joined. He was like me and hated to wait in line so he arrived early, usually earlier than me.

He finally came after twenty minutes of solitude, "Hey, what's going on?"

"Nothing," I stalled, wondering how I should break my dreadful fate. "Kristie called last night," my eyes averted from his and stared transfixed to a bulletin board back drop.

"Oh, man, that's cool," he started enthusiastically, but noticed the look on my face which forced him to shut up.

"Well, she started out with 'Don, just promise me that you won't come home.' I knew I was in trouble. But what? Well, John, she's pregnant." That's all I wanted to say for the moment. I just needed to say it out loud to fully understand the ramifications of those three words and to realize its reality. Luckily, other students began to arrive.

"Oh, man. That sucks. What are you thinking?" John mumbled repeatedly, wondering what his own answer would be.

We ate in silence. I was munching on a banana, not even laughing at the fact that Frank was sitting next to me doing the same. I left early and went for a walk by myself.

I had so many thoughts and ideas, but they had made me crazy with rage. "I could marry her and raise a child somehow. It wouldn't be that crazy or hard to do, but that's something I don't really want to do. She could get an abortion, but with what money?" I felt barely alive.

I pondered some more until it dawned on me, that there wasn't anything I could do or decide. It was her choice and my role was to offer support. I wasn't even close to feeling the heaviest weight of an unwanted pregnancy that she was, and I couldn't even stand it now. The guilt drenched me.

After returning to school, John met me head on, "Let's hang out tonight in the valley." John shyly suggested. The valley had a strong couple of weeks, but lately, the excitement fizzled with our gaining contentment.

He had already sympathetically bought the wine.

Down in the valley's harshness, I started out repeating the responsibilities, but the inability to act to him, "It is like breaking a toy, and your parents make you sit there and look at it all day without touching it." The cold air felt great shrinking my pores.

"Don, do you really love her?"

"Love, what a word. John, I'm not sure. We do allright together, but the rest of my life? I don't know. I couldn't say no, though. Too much of a guilt ridden pussy is what I am. I don't have the balls enough to do what's right for me. I always think of others first."

Silence brought back the coolness of my boiling face.

"The sad part about it all is that I know when it happened, I think. Usually we were careful, especially after she was late once. She even went and got the test before, but it wound up negative. Sometimes rubbers, sometimes coitus interruptus.

"New Year's eve, she came to Pittsburgh. We went to a friend of mine's house. Everyone was fucked up, too fucked up, so the party kind of fell asleep. Nothin' better to do when you are drunk, but to eat, sleep, or fuck. We opted for the latter down in his basement. We threw off our clothes, I was too drunk. She was telling me to cum in her. It confused my swirling head. I didn't know what I did or if I really did cum in her. The night, and especially that moment, escapes me. The next thing I know we are sitting naked in a bathroom and his parents are knocking on the door.

"It's just because I don't remember much, except her saying cum in me. I figure that had to be the night and the timing is about right. It's been two months."

The wine was gone. I was talking freely, more than I wanted.

"The first time she got the pregnancy test, we got up real early and walked over to the health center. My roommate, Stinky, gave me his St. Christopher medal for luck. It was a long wait, but she came out so happy and dancing. She was flinging her long, blonde hair all over the place and she was just beaming, as I watched from a wooden bench in the waiting area. Last night she told me that there was no dancing and I wasn't waiting for her on the bench. She said she just went home and cried.

"Man, that gets me." I needed to do something. "Let's go." We went to the one and only Pasha for a night cap and for a brief, crowded reprieve from my mental torture.

EIGHT

Sure

Learning of Kristie's pregnancy made the remorse of running off to celebrate Carnival dig deep into my psyche, but the trip was already scheduled. My confusion and pain over our proposed gallivanting through Europe extorted my mind to drain its will into endless bottles of wine. Nonetheless, I continued forward, entangled by those inebriated thoughts, that tortured every step of preparation, of Kristie, at home, crying over her stormy future and me, dancing in today's sun. Her thoughts were on life, death, and her prospects while I considered the fun and sun of Spain versus the adventure and hardships of Norway and the Arctic Circle. Sitting around, I could only laugh at the pros and cons of our naked asses on a fiord versus our balls flapping in the cool Mediterranean wind on top of Gibraltar.

Emotionally unsteady, I discussed our options to John. "John, what do you think? It will be warmer and cheaper in Spain. I think I'd rather go there."

"Yeah, we should." The reluctancy and disappointment made his voice go low and slow with the surrendering of our self-inflicted dare to travel to the Arctic Circle and Narvik, Norway. Narvik appealed to me as a way of escaping our everyday trappings of Brussels, school, Kristie, and our classmates, but was far too silly and bullheaded. Reason set with Barcelona the decision.

The goal was to show up our lame friends with the most unique nude photos. Narvik and fiords were sure winners, but the money and warmth were the deciding factors. The nude craze had developed out of a typical whimsical dare by John. To conquer Europe and the bohemian pressure of being American, taking a nude photo in the most famous spot was the requisite of a successful Carnival vacation, a ten day break from school, and a requirement of initiation into the desired lifestyles club.

While Kristie decided our futures, I laughed ironically in the absurd race to Gibraltar to beat our rivals, who were going to the Pyramids in Egypt. The universal story of the ease of men and the hardships of women was beginning to unravel in front of my daily planner.

Home packing my backpack the night before our departure, I couldn't help but to wonder why Pam and Linda had invited themselves along with us and how they had obviously teased our torso's brains until we relented.

"Don, Don, Kristie on the phone. Kristie on the phone," Albert's call ran up the stairs. Even though he hated to penetrate our sacred silence, the old man would bubble over with excitement whenever Kristie called. His feet tripped up the stairs in his continuous shouts. He knew I missed her because of my refusal to discuss her and he sensed something big was going on between us because it was her third phone call this week.

I picked up the phone and listened to a couple of sniffles before saying hello. Without a pause, she reported to me of the telling of her parents, the morning sickness, her destructive sadness, and her complete loneliness.

"Kristie…I will do anything for you. We can make it through this together. If you want to have it, we will. If you don't, we won't. I have weighed both avenues in my head and I know which is better for me, but I cannot think for you."

"Just don't leave me."

"I won't." I sounded pathetic.

"Have fun in Spain and don't think of me. I will be fine."

"See you." She started to cry and hung up gently to punctuate her last words.

NINE
Give Me A Beat

Pam and Linda, best friends, met us at the station. They had our itinerary, trains, hotels, and famous sights carefully scheduled to fill every waking hour.

Linda was allright and kind of sarcastic, but neither of us could stand Pam, particularly John whose distaste of her grew in each moment of forced conversation. He would mumble whenever she was not listening, "you fat-assed, brillo-padded head." His descriptions of others were always cruel, but accurate. Besides her looks, that were very reminiscent of a hungry rat, her whiny attitude was the final nail in John's coffin. However, the real origin of his resentment flew out of the embarrassing fact that he had dated her once sophomore year. John fessed up, "She had a great ass back then." I laughed. "I swear."

Linda, kinda cool but uptight, had pasty Irish skin with a brown Farrah Fawcett haircut and green eyes. Also, a nonexistent ass, that still could wiggle her jeans, gave her the appearance of being bulimic or anorexic.

Together, we lunged towards Paris to capture the night train to Barcelona.

Paris was a disappointment, we had most of the day to waste with Pam and Linda leading the way. "Let's go get crepes." In the Latin quarter Pam forced us to watch her fill out her hips to her crepes' song.

Before John or I could see anything that we wanted, Linda announced, "We've got to go." That was it, crepes and a another train station. Paris, what a thrill.

As we waited for our train in the South Station, John broke our second wine bottle on the floor in the bench filled waiting area. We had spread our bags in a circle to mark our area from the many screaming families and crazed loners, but the wine had made us abandon our position to a small corner of the room. The spreading wine, that seeped throughout a quarter of the waiting area and Linda's bags, signified another bad start and meant that the two of us would have to share the only bottle.

Enraged and downcast, John and I needed this wine, but not for the usual reasons. Although we were rookies, we knew that the most important aspect of traveling was that sleeping sitting up was much easier drunk and without, at least, a bottle each tonight, sleep would be violent. Luckily, Pam and Linda had reserved a couchette that spared John and I from having to listen to their idiocies for an entire evening.

Pam softly spoke to us with a stern manner, "Don't forget where we've got to transfer. We'll come and make sure you don't forget," their backs entered the couchette train while we continued down the long lines of cars looking for an unreserved second class compartment.

"Finally, John, you are free of that huge butt. I can't believe you went out with her." My face crawled upward like I had just eaten a sour grape.

"I swear, she wasn't that bad," he admittedly laughed.

"It's huge."

Walking all the way to the front, we were hit with our first taste of the French. "Blah, Blah, Blah, you Americans," the common people yelled unrecognizable obscenities at us. Scared and intimidated, we found a nice compartment, that had a family and two open seats, in the farthest car.

As the dreams of a nice, friendly couchette lingered and the smiles of a wholesome family relieved, the endless streams of drunk men scowled at us when they walked past our safe haven. "Fuck you," John would smile on edge, feeling much braver than me.

Pretty much, John and I just sat there on our best behavior not daring to say a word to scare this lovely family unit. Against our wills, the family got off only a few hours into the trip. In fear, we cracked open our last bottle of wine. At the same stop, a young, tame looking French guy, whom I offered some wine, joined us. He was all smiles and overly friendly to my gesture, "I love America. I want to go there someday and buy a penthouse."

"Yeah, don't we all," John's eyebrows signaled the fun that was going to be had.

"My name is Guyon. I am from Papillon. I have big house with horses." He repeated the only English words he knew over and over again.

We spoke quickly hoping he couldn't follow, "Is this the only English he knows?"

"Or is he retarded?" John held his ribs trying not to laugh while seeing this guy's goofy, happy smile that made us ponder his chromosome composition. Feeling sorry, I gave him some of the last bite of our bread.

After the wine was gone his English expanded, "Come and stay with me. My family take good care of you. Big house, lots of horses."

"John what do you think? We can't ditch Linda yet. It would be great to get rid of Big Ass though."

"Yeah, your right. We can't. Hey Guyon, can we bring two of our friends?"

"Yes," he was definitely retarded or didn't understand the question.

John and I took off to find the two comfortable women getting ready for bed in their marvelous couchette. We ran through the story to only find doubtful looks on their faces. "Come and talk to him yourself," John pleaded.

Only Linda came. "I am too tired," moaned Pam.

Guyon gave her the same English and she bought it. It sounded great, nice house in the country with horses, actually coming in contact with the real French culture and not forgetting a free bed and food.

As we talked, Linda moved closer and closer to me until she obviously rubbed up against me and touched me more than required. The emotions of my loneliness offered no resistance. Seeing this, John gave me looks of parental warnings and childish laughters in between his fucking around with Guyon, the retarded Frenchman.

It got late, sleep was calling. I tossed around the idea of messing around with Linda with my hormones while my head rested on her lap, faking sleep. She rubbed deeply into my scalp.

When it came down to it, I was a sucker for those egotistical moments of self-pleasure and conquest that sex offers. Kissing and feeling had no bearings on my feelings for another, but fulfilled my needs. My aching stomach reminded me of Kristie and of my lack of feelings for Linda, but I persisted to pretend to sleep and enjoyed the rub. Upon opening my eyes in a dare, I found her tongue ready to thrust into my mouth.

She stuck her tongue too far and too aggressively, making me want to stop immediately. Shutting my lips, I forced the French part of the kissing to cease. Embarrassed for her, I glanced over to find John gladly asleep next to Guyon.

"I better walk you back to your couchette." The moment was gone, but the seed was planted. I was hungry for someone and an easy target. Walking back to our compartment, I promised to myself and to Kristie to put out the fire and live up to unspoken promises of faith.

"We are here, We are here." In mass confusion we jumped out of sleep and assembled our luggage. We ran off, wondering if the two women had remembered to wake up and to get off at Papillon.

"I don't see them. Maybe we are in for a little luck."

"About getting lucky, Don?"

Blood flushed my face, distorting the real embarrassment of my lack of a conscience and abstinence. My confused head circled the area, searching for them, only to be disappointed in the sight of their huge backpacks that wobbled towards us. Pam was reading her *Let's Go Europe* when they met us. "Oh Papillon was were Salvador Dali lived. There is a museum here and everything." Linda then smiled a little too friendly and a little too early at me. I didn't bother to return the favor.

Guyon paced among us, reassuring us of his "big house with horses." He seemed very tense and I began to think the reassurance was somehow more for him. "What's next, Bill," John begun to call him.

"I call my mom, she will pick us up."

I bought a *USA Today*, the only thing in English, to pass the time. "Hey John, Scientists discovered broad wrinkles in the fabric of space. They are actually looking at them towards the beginning of time. Think about that. Man, way too much to try and comprehend. Looking at fabrics of space from the beginning of time. Too much. This is what it says, 'scientists detected faint temperature fluctuations in microwave radiation echoing from the supposed instant of creation. Though the temperatures fluctuate by no more than hundred thousandth of a degree, they signal primeval variations in the universe's topography a mere 300,000 years after its explosion.' They actually say that the variations in topography were large enough to create the gravity needed to attract more and more matter. Too much, man. Maybe people should use their amazing minds on more useful, tangible things, instead of this abstract bullshit."

John's whitening lips told me to shut up. His concentration was busy watching Guyon and trying to figure out why he was pacing back and forth. The carefree and happy retard, that we had come to know and love the night before, was long gone.

The mom came and things went downhill quick. They fought in French about something for the whole ride home. The twenty minute ride quickly turned the scene into a heavy rural area. In silence we pulled in their home which was a run down shack without a yard, let alone the damn horses. The two bedded wooden frame told us that we were a major imposition which the mother wasn't trying very hard to conceal.

Inside, we sat down in a heavy wooden kitchen to eat breakfast, and then took a nap. Guyon woke us abruptly about an hour into sleep to provide the details of a woman that he must find. Of course, his mom wouldn't give him the car, so we hitchhiked to the local high school. It was my first hitchhiking experience and it was actually easy.

We got to some town, not Papillon, and walked around looking for this woman. We went to her school and to her house. She was nowhere and he was pissed. The picture of Guyon and his mom came into focus. Apparently, Guyon had deserted from the army to come home and find his girlfriend who was fifteen. He was basically a fuck up with no money and his mom was tired of his act. His mother, who was the town's only doctor, had married some African who had run away to leave her to take care of her little town and three kids. We were the icing on the cake.

After the afternoon fiasco, we went back to the house. Guyon was really wearing on us after all of his bullshit promises and plans. Idiot kept coming to mind, so John and I decided to go for a walk to check out the area around his house and to blow off some steam.

They lived in God's Country. Earthy browns and forest greens produced a sharp picture of what an old movie would have looked like in color. The rolling hills at the foot of the Pryennes produced wine and housed sheep. The whole area was quaint, so quaint that John had to take a shit.

"Do you want to head back?" I looked down the dirt road that had taken us.

"No, I can't make it. Hey, shitting in the Pryennes, what a grand scheme. Who could say they actually shit on one of the Pryennes mountains, the home of Salvador Dali?"

He contemplated the mess. He farted to test the consistency. Hard was what he had hoped for while running and/or sticky was the worst. "Cover me." The fart gave the signal of solidness, he hoped.

As he went behind a brick wall and a shrub, I readied my camera. To good too pass up, "Dude, you're not planning on taking a picture?" Too late, his shit was immortalized.

"Come on, we had to document your shit in the Pryennes." He always bought that stuff, a story to tell your grandchildren approach.

We went back for dinner which was a treat. She did us up well with tons of spaghetti and bread that coated our stomachs for the bottles of wine and champagne that we would finished off. I was fucked up when I got up from the table.

After dinner, Guyon's brother pulled out a massive Marley joint. John was ready after missing out in Amsterdam. Running around the place, John shouted, "Wow, that was the biggest hit ever. That is the greatest joint ever. Wow. Wow." Guyon's sister snarled at him while sitting on the radiator smoking a cigarette. "Wow, Killer joint. That's Amazing. Wow," he ran up to her, taunting her face.

Acid house rock, which I truly hated, filled the free-for-all house. John continued yelling "Wow," Linda and Pam were their usual wallflowers, and I watched the sister smoke her life away on the radiator while hating acid house rock.

"I hate acid house rock," John kept saying to her. He sat next to her and laughed with his high. She didn't care or understand.

Now, Guyon was in a new fight with his mother. She would not give him money to go to a nightclub, only a ride to it. "Hey, do you guys have American Express?" Pam, of course, responded with a positive.

We jumped in the car with the mom shouting orders. Finally, it clicked in, "He was going to use her American Express. It didn't matter to me, because I wasn't going to give this asshole shit, but I spoke up anyway. To her ear, "Pam, you know he wants to use your American Express to finance the night, right?"

She flipped out and joined the chorus of yelling. John knew what to do. "Fuck this, too loud," John got out and I followed.

Nothing else to do, but to go to bed while Guyon sulked between fits of rage. "Billy, when you come to visit us in America, we'll have fun then. In that Penthouse. Oh yeah, penthouse." John was still stoned trying to soothe.

With John lying on the floor, I shared the bed with the other two. Linda stroked up against me while I balanced on the edge of the pulled out couch. I stroked back. The stroking increased.

"Come on, quit it you guys. I'm in this bed too." Pam's whine saved me and sent me into horrible dreams of Kristie.

In the morning I awoke to hear John, "Bill, oh yeah, just call and let me know when you're coming. Lots of room." My head thumped. "You'll get that penthouse yet. You've got six hundred francs, right. Almost there, Willie." John handed over his fictitious address.

"He's retarded, definitely retarded," I mumbled while dressing in the kitchen. I looked up to find Mrs. Guyon watching with a smile as I showed my shame.

Off to the train station. "Never again are we following some fuck around again, John. I'm still looking for those fucking horses."

TEN

The Horse Without A Rider

The train ride to Barcelona from Papillon was short and easy. John and I avoided the women by standing in the hall watching the shore bounce roughly off of the heavy rocks.

"Finally, I feel free from the heaviness of the Belgium grey."

I agreed. "It's got to be about sixty. Nice to feel a little air on my skin other than just the cold on my face. I'm glad we went with Spain."

"Me too, all we've got to do is get rid of these two. What's going on anyway with you two?"

"John, I don't know, man. She started rubbing my penis, I wanted to tell myself that I was too mentally drunk and too morally weak to offer up any defense, but that's just a rationalization to make myself feel better. I can't do this anymore. I'm so sick of myself and I'm driving myself crazy worrying about it."

John's look of wonderment, that was mixed with a little disgust, got lost in the translation to his mouth, so he just let me run with it. "What are you thinking?" He looked back out into the waves.

"Nothing, I guess. That's my problem, I'm morally bankrupt and it's by my own devices," I drifted away. The day offered such pain and guilt for which I could not find anywhere to hide. At least night would come where I could forget and take my ill feelings out on others. The day, however, exposed all.

Her long hair getting caught in her tears rattled through my mental images. Our words echoed. The guilt was heavy, but lightened with the thought of the oppression of responsibility. "I'm not up for it. I don't like any of my choices. I wish it would go away. Fuck," I rubbed my hand through my hair and stared out at the ocean with John. "Where to go when you can't go anywhere you want to. It seems too easy for me, though, you know. I can walk away from this pregnancy and go to Spain and play with another woman's tits. It's just not fair. I don't have the pain, only the guilt of not having the pain, but that's plastic pain. Never again."

The opinions tried to make myself feel better, but the pit wouldn't go away. The shock was gone, but reality remained, hitting me with its heavy hand and leaving depression as its bruise. The despair dug further beyond the situation with Kristie and into my existence. In one beautiful sunny morning off of the Eastern Iberian coast, I realized that my flowers had already blossomed. Life had begun its upward struggle of growing old, the process of deciding the least painful route of responsibilities. These were the same thoughts that looked my father in the face every morning and plagued him for all of these years. The steady watering and feeding of youth had sadly ceased and provided no more excuses.

"What's in Barcelona anyway?" John regrouped.

"Of course, Barcelona is where Picasso's stuff is, also, Goudi."

"Who's Goudi?"

We returned to our shared compartment. Quoting from *Let's Go Europe*, Pam read, "Goudi is one of the original and most influential architects of the Twentieth century and his buildings and houses are strewn throughout Barcelona."

"Good to know, Good to know. Where are we going to stay anyway?" Linda showed us the circled names in their travel bible.

Barcelona was beautiful; the shore, the people, the buildings. The scene was light brown sprinkled with the bluest of all blue for a back drop. The subway cars, a good sign of the character of any city except D.C., were a spotless and glossy white with little lights indicating the next stop.

Our hotel rooms, for ten bucks each, looked onto a quiet courtyard. We hit the streets running. It was carnival time and the streets were packed. As the main boulevard whirled around us, we began to feel like rock stars. Like American women in Italy, the natives loved American men and made us feel like the studs we had always wanted to be. "Hello, what is your name?" followed by shy giggles of the uncertain language rang in the night air.

"John run up ahead. You've got to check this out. I can see over the whole crowd. Not one person is blocking my path. I can see the tops of everyone's head." The photo of a blonde head jetting among the brown was suppose to capture something, but I knew the picture never would. To capture the true moment was impossible, moments move and pictures stand. I still tried.

"We'll meet you guys right back here in awhile," John told the other two without turning back. "Right outside of that, the flea market-type tent." Once again, he had ditched Pam and Linda with a few strokes of the mouth.

The blonde bigness of John and myself turned heads throughout the smashing crowds while Pam and Linda slowly evaporated into the masses. "Since I was little, I always wanted to be stared at instead of doing the staring. We are Jon Bon Jovi," his chest flew out and his shoulders flung back.

Hungry, we hit McDonald's too afraid to try to get food without any knowledge of Spanish. Splitting a hamburger and an order of fries just wet our appetite, but that was all we could afford. Sitting next to a group of teenage women, our appetites watched them eat and pick between flirting giggles. Responding, John gave them sad eyes and pointed to me. He rubbed my stomach, asking nicely with his raised eyebrows and shaking head. The bravest one understood and offered a cherry pie to me. Soon, we had filled our bellies with all of their half-eaten stuff from salads to Big Macs.

Next, we walked around to do some shopping. Carnival was the most energetic time in Europe. The whole continent was on vacation, spring was springing, and everyone was busting at the seems of being inside too much. Our spirits fed on the environment. Scared sightseers turning into adventuresome travelers, the thrill stuck to us. Cooped up in the midwest without even an ocean to stare at and to dream of foreign lands through, we were ready to live a little.

With my spirits rebounding, I felt compelled to thrust myself back into the thoughts of Kristie again. The lightened mood crumbled into the black guilt within moments. Adventures meant leaving the steady things behind with the mundane living of life. To bribe those feelings, I bought jewelry for her. Doing the same, John carefully choose a little silver ring and I followed, "She loves silver rings. That's her thing."

I would never send mine, but saved it forever as a symbol to something that I had long forgotten.

With our new gifts and a good, red wine buzz, John decided that it was time to call his girlfriend. Perhaps, it was the wine induced thrill of the moment, but something inside both of us panicked in delight and in the prospects of an overseas phone call. We ran around desperate for a phone. After a couple of hotels turned us down, our rapid eyes shot out, searching for phone booths. Sparkles broke the blackness, as we searched for the red highlighting mark that signified a phone booth. Anxiety collapsed our senses with the thought, "Where are we?" Cobblestones forced us left at a bar. "There, There, John I found it. Over here. Over here."

The door jammed, but John's agitation released the mounting pressure. He picked up the phone, "Collect call from John…513-523-8990…Hello, wait…it worked," he breathed heavy and impatiently.

I finished the wine while John waited to talk to Cindy, his girlfriend, for the first time since his departure. He called a pay phone collect in her dorm, a trick one of the students fell upon. Someone was finding Cindy.

After tracing my footsteps, I walked back to the hotel and then back again to the phone to find John finishing up and relieved. During the last few weeks, he had slowly become an anxious trigger finger, twitching and sweating, but shaking with the fear of pulling. He finally let go, "That was great, forty-five minutes for nothing. That's almost one hundred bucks for free. Easier than easy, I can't believed it worked." Jealousy discovered me.

We arrived back at our hotel to the tense feelings of the forgotten women. The cats laid ready to pounce, as we noisily came into their room. "Where were you guys? We waited almost an hour at that damn flea market."

"Sorry, it was my fault. I forgot I was supposed to call my girlfriend." He didn't care. He was on air.

"Well, that place was scary. Don't ever leave us alone again."

"Well it's over. Don, do you want to sleep in here? Those two can have the other room." Linda smiled at Pam and then towards me to wait for the affirmative.

I didn't even look up, as I weighed the moment and said, "Naw, that wouldn't be too good of an idea." Her inquiry shuddered down my spine then back up into some reasonable part of my brain.

Instead of sex, I opted for sharing a room and a bed with John. He entered the room behind me, "If you would have left me, I would of been forced to sleep in the same bed as the butt. Do you know what that would have done to me? I would have pummeled you. You know, pummeled you?" He unpacked his neatly folded clothes.

Before going to bed, we hung out with the two women and finished another bottle of the wine. I was really the only one who wanted to drink anymore, but tried to rally the troops, "I've got a game. Just freely associate. If you miss, you drink. I'll start. Spain."

The order was me, Linda, Pam, John.

"Barcelona, Goudi, ugly."

"Stupid, smart, school, depressing."

"Life, death, funeral, black. Life, just kidding."

"I will go with sky, um stars, movies, silent."

"Again night and just kidding; it will be baby, mother, family, home."

"Wrecker." John howled at my slip as Linda blushed piecing together my predicament quite quickly. Through John's and my mumbling she had to already know, but she didn't seem to care.

Reluctantly, the game continued on for awhile until I darkly ended it. Being faced with the term "child," I put all of us out of misery and straight into bed with "killer."

Back in the room with the lights out, John began to speak, "I love when you get out that dark humor. It's morbid and poignant, but somehow still funny."

"Yeah, it's great."

I awoke in complete darkness with the sound of John tripping on something.

He stood at the foot of the bed watching his subconscious fly backwards. His eyes darted, "Wow, I just had the most fucked up dream. There I was sitting in my room at home watching T.V., flicking through all of the stations. First channel ESPN, the Pirates were playing the Reds. The Reds had two on and two out with Heaton pitching. I couldn't watch, so I flicked to MTV. Tesla, or some other bubble gum heavy metal band, was on for the one hundredth time that day. I started randomly checking out the other channels. First "She's Having a Baby" was on. You know with Kevin Bacon."

"Well, we know were that one came from."

"Then it was Eddie Murphy and Nick Nolte in, you know, *48 Hours*. Then *Batman* was on. *Batman* hasn't even come out yet. There Michael Keaton was with his fake muscular chest in a Batman costume. I think I like the natural look better than his fake chest. He looked like a baseball umpire." He went back to sleep not remembering ever being awake or his nightmare account of a bad night of T.V.

During the train ride south out of Barcelona, the four of us faced the facts and decided to split into pairs. John and I eyed the nudity on the Rock of Gibraltar with new vigor while they dreamed of Portugal. Their spirits seemed to lift up with ours and they were, at least, relieved that they no longer would have to put up with our bullshit.

On our way to Seville, John and I stopped in an unnamed town with some famous mosque that everyone said was a must see. We did not really know what we were doing or where we were going, but we had a couple hours to kill before a night train would take us to Seville.

The city was dark, cold, and rainy, bringing back the sinking feel of school. The train had departed from the shore hours before and took us away from the warmth of early spring. As we began the walk to our desired destination too proud to ask directions, John finally accomplished his most dreaded, but expected moment, his ankle turned.

To know or to see John, one understands his fear of injury. His problems were two-fold, an unbelievable ability to attract personal injury and severely weakened feet, ankles, and legs which were really a result of the first problem. Upon watching John walk, faces stared first with disgust of a pompous-like rocking motion. However, the faces turned quickly with sympathy at seeing the pin like joint of his ankles and delicately placed steps.

During high school, football injury after basketball injury left seriously damaged feet that required surgery. The surgery was not as successful as hoped and had removed all of the feelings in his foot and his ankles leaving them unable to regain the proper muscles and tendons.

Without much feeling or control, he found himself consistently in the hospital with broken or severely sprained ankles, a severe hindrance that left him permanently angry at the sorrow he saw in every unknown face that crossed his path in the streets.

He had waited impatiently for his first accident and had warned me over and over again of the upcoming tragedy. When it arrived, I helplessly watched him lie hopelessly on the ground writhing, crying, screaming, and cursing a river full of obscenities. I watched those same sympathetic Spanish faces, that spurred his uncontrollable anger, stare during the busy lunch hour at his mangled and pathetic body. They stopped only for a second, then continued to walk, just like any other person who lived in a town of more than one hundred people would do.

"What should I do? Are you all right? Do you need anything?" I felt useless and wanted to cry with him.

"Fuck," was the only response.

Finally, a bewildered woman stopped and offered assistance in the form of directions to a hospital, we thought. Ignorance found its first casualty, as I wished I had not been cool and taken Spanish, instead of French, in high school. "I don't need a hospital. Just need to rest for a while," he coaxed a forced calm into his intonation for the helpful lady, as tears of pain crept down his face.

"Fuck it. Let's just go. Don, all I need to do is get on a train and rest. Get me to the station." He refused my help and braced himself upward.

"We can hang out here for awhile. It's got to be two miles back to the train station. We might do more damage than good."

"Yea, you're right. Fuck it. No, I know my ankles. I need to rest peacefully. This fuckin' street won't do it. Fuck it all." We waited a minute until his will was rejuvenated. I carried all of our gear. His patience and calm wavered as the struggles of hopping on one foot grew increasingly difficult.

I tried to ease the pain, "John, if you died tomorrow what would be the one moment in life that you would want to take back with you."

"What?"

"Not one moment, maybe a feeling. How can I explain it? I guess I'll tell you mine which will give you the idea.

"There's actually two. The first one is well, it's a little embarrassing, but it's the first thing that I thought of. Okay, it's a warm spring day, actually the Kentucky Derby was just run. So it's about six o'clock and I am outside with my parents. Dad is barbecuing away on our green painted charcoal grill. We hadn't graduated yet to the gas kind.

"My mom is standing next to our back stairs with a glass of water for the coals and a fork for my dad to check the chicken with. I am actually sitting on the stairs with my shirt off for one of the first times of the year, a little sweaty, and I am bouncing a basketball on the stairs where my feet are resting. I had just gotten back from playing tennis and it's my eighth grade year. I'm doing nothing, but staring at the cement hardness of our backyard and the junk pile on both sides of our van that barely fit into the garage.

"It was a beautifully sunny day and my face was tightening up from the sun hitting my virgin white skin that had been fully cleansed through a lot of sweat. What a great feeling, just that tightness and redness does it for me.

"So anyway, my dad is kidding around with my mom. These playful moods didn't hit often, but when they did my dad was a teenager discovering for the first time that he could tease girls sexually. Then all of a sudden, he pulls her top down exposing her breasts. 'Charlie, thanks for showing the whole neighborhood my breasts,' my mom muttered feeling flattered.

"He just got this goofy grin, like mine, where the ends of my lips disappear with the upward swoop into my cheeks, a little like the Joker. His cigarette stained teeth poked out around the black gaps that made him looked like he was missing teeth. He had a full set, but they struggled to cover the entire area they were suppose to.

"For that one brief moment, I realized my dad was a regular person, like me. He was entitled to have a personality with its goods and its bads. He could have his own little quirks. He could have sex with my mother. I never looked at him the same way after that day. He became a regular person, no longer on the pedestal of father."

"Hey, how's that ankle?"

"All right"

"The other one is less of a story and more of just a random feeling, that comes back again once and awhile. It can not be pinpointed by a little anecdotal tale, just by senses.

"It's a smell and a feeling that is in my nose that exemplifies a zeitgeist of my sixth grade era. The last time I felt that I was on top of the world. Yep, sixth grade." I shook my head smiling.

"I was on the traveling baseball team, called the Mighty Mites. I had a girlfriend and the pick of the one that I wanted. I was friends with all and I was basically the big toe of the grade school. I really hadn't come to realize yet that a painful side of life existed. No responsibilities brought me down. Tomorrow was too far away and I didn't remember yesterday.

"Anyway I can see myself walking over this hill that held an old folks home and was the way I walked to my best friend's, Eric Williams', house. I have shorts on and my Mighty Mite baseball hat on. I could smell the freedom and the adventure. I could taste them in my nose, I could feel them in my nose, I could see them through my nose."

My voiced went quiet and low. "Every once in awhile it comes back and hits me with a brief glorious moment of revelry that tells me everything will be going my way. I could be walking along, smelling it, feeling it, and just start smiling to myself and taking long, deep, and yearnful breaths through my nose to get the full effect."

"What have you got?"

"You know what it's going to be. It's that hectic moment with all of your bags heading to the train station, not knowing where I'm going or how I'm gettin' back. Yeah, that's the feeling I'd take with me. It's it. I'm living it right now as we walk along.

"It's that anxious moment like the feeling of taking off a woman's pants for the first time. Every time I am rushing for that train and wondering where I am going and not knowing what I will be doing, that's it. Yeah, that's definitely it."

"I have had so much fun here. I wish it would last forever."

"Like Dylan says, forever young."

"No, that other song. I want to be forever young. Do you really want to live forever, forever young." John sung skimming over the words to the memorable song of the forgettable group.

Making the train station, we had Seville in mind. With the swelling going down and the sun out, we were ready to conquer Seville. We had dipped in our feet to test how cold the water was, now we were ready to dive head first into Europe. We could handle anything and we were ready to grab as much as we could.

The train was our vehicle and the excitement of the many already lived novels echoed in the rattle of the tracks. Tomorrow was a new city, a new adventure. The sights of Seville, the land that any true romantic could not resist, lived through the words in us both. Seville…the land that brought out the best and worst moments in so many lonely and painful lives.

ELEVEN

Marx

"Fucking yes. Fuck Norway. It is so warm. Zing, zing, look my shirt is off. Look at this place. It's the best." John's ankle was better and he was flying high. We entered the Place des Amerique, a semicircle of red, blue and white tiles that clashed with canals on the edge of a park. The place was very Spanish with lots of white and brownish reds.

Seville was beautiful and we knew we were going to stay a couple of days. Americana was abundant and many Americans crawled by with their sweatshirts, baseball caps, and sneakers. "How come nobody here wears Nike's? Aren't they European. Nike sounds French or Italian."

"I don't know, I thought they were made in Korea or some other American blue collar, wage stealing, copycat, motherfucking country."

"Yeahhh, those bastards. Woowhoo, Seville," John did a little jig.

"Pam and Linda are long gone, the sun, the warmth, the beauty. I'm with you, woowhoo, Seville."

We did nothing, but enjoy the end of the day, laying on park benches and walking beneath the tropical trees. I read my *Fodor's: Europe on a Budget,* "*Fodor's* is getting us nowhere. Nothing to see, nothing to do. The maps suck in this thing. I miss Pam's *Let's Go* highlighted every which way. You know, I've got to call Kristie tonight. Tonight is my night."

First off, we needed to find dinner and somewhere to sleep before night's trappings. The backpacks were getting heavy and the approaching night was bringing a chill. Wondering through unknown streets eventually produced a cheap looking pension and a shitty, little cafeteria which were perfect.

Costing five dollars, the pension was on the outskirts of downtown and close enough to walk to. We didn't even bother to check out our room before making our way back to the cafeteria to finally eat something.

The food sucked and was reminiscent of a closed, rotten fruit stand, but everything was extremely cheap. They also had tiny bottles of wine that only cost about thirty cents each. While shoveling in the food, I remembered, "I'm supposed to call her at ten o'clock, what time have we got?"

"Two more hours there, big guy," John gulped in between bites.

We hadn't eaten anything other than bread since the fiasco with Guyon. Hot food tasted so good, even if the pasta was soggy and stale. When you're really hungry nothing beats steaming food. We were quietly rejoicing in the warmth and being washed away by tepid wine when a group full of obviously English people sat at our table.

To watch and to listen to them made apparent that they were art students on a Spain field trip. They fooled around, ate, and drew together until we became hypnotized to the production of their hands and pencils. Our staring became a bit too much and too noticeable, "Hi, I'm Brian." Brian was the only one more interested in his food and surroundings than his sketch pad. He smiled through his bearded face which was really just pubic hair that was not enough to truly be considered a beard.

John jumped right in, "Hey wants going on? I'm John. You guys must be from England." His chair slid closer to a slight woman who was a part of the crowd.

"Yeah, art students from London. We are down here traveling through Spain, trying to draw the landscape. This is Sarah," his hand lead to a lean, dark, pasty woman.

"Don," I didn't want to look up until my spaghetti was completely finished, but gave a nod their way.

"Can I see," John leaned over Sarah's bony shoulder.

I finished to look at Brian's only sketch. It was a straight forward sketch of the people of the cafeteria and the scenery behind them. He had a remarkable ability to create personalities on paper.

Sarah showed off her surrealist renditions of Seville and laughed at the drawing that she was currently working on, a caricature of me.

"Where are you guys from in America?"

That was a weighted question, because you never knew of the ignorance level of the geographical make-up of the United States of America. John started at a low ignorance level and went high, "Cleveland, it's in Ohio, the midwest, you know, the middle of the country."

"Pittsburgh, Pennsylvania."

"Oh, yeah, Philadelphia," Sarah continued to stare at me for awhile before drawing for awhile. I looked at me through her translation. Of course, I saw my huge Superman chin and long narrow hollow sockets covered by wire framed bottle caps. With my long face, I was a cartoonist dream, the human, walking, talking, caricature. I looked at the big head taking up three-fourths of the page and cursed myself and my misfortune.

"All right," I ripped some vengeful paper from Brian's pad and borrowed a pencil in order to start on her not so wonderful appearance. I drew miserably as the wine and nerves controlled my hands and distorted her face. A crowd began to stand around and watch.

"Hey, maybe we could make some money tonight." The thought of money brought my eyes to my watch, "Fuck, I've got to call Kristie." I searched the cafeteria for the phone and put down my pencil to make the collect call that I had promised Kristie. We had worked out an arrangement where I would call her at a designated pay phone at a designated time which was in five minutes.

I came back to the table unsure if I was going to cry, "John, it's not working. Let's go find another phone." John wasn't listening because the owner of the cafeteria was yelling at him. She had asked him to draw her and he felt compelled to concentrate on her large rolling body.

"Where do you have to go?" Brian gave me some attention

"Brian, I've got to call my girlfriend, it's kind of an emergency."

"Where are you going to call her from?"

"I guess a pay phone. The plan is to call collect from one pay phone to another pay phone. Then nobody pays. Well, that's at least the plan. But it doesn't seem to be working, the phone or the method."

"Well, let's go find you a phone."

John, escaping the verbal lashing of the fat cafeteria owner, was already being forced into the street. After a couple of attempts from several phone booths, my head was fighting the drunkenness and the frustration and it couldn't remain calm enough to think of another way to call her or to just give up. Outside of my hysteria, the night had become cold and rainy. Leading the others, I wandered the streets in our second phone panic, but this one belonged solely to me.

"I don't know Don. It might be the phone. It might be the operators. Who knows? It could be anything. What can you do?"

"But I've gotten an operator and I've heard the ringing. Some-one even answered once, but not Kristie. I've got to get a hold of her, it's very important. We've got to talk. I need to tell her some things plus I promised her." The determination of not breaking another oath bubbled to the surface and out of my eyes.

"Why don't you try to use my phone in my hotel room," Brain reluctantly decided to extend the offer. I accepted, even though he was really just wanting to shut me up at this point.

His key fiddled with the door. It opened and he let me go in and shut the door leaving me alone. The receiver was in my hands, "Collect call from Don, yes collect; 513-523-8054." The safety of his hotel room and the isolation brought comfort while I waited for the ring. It rang directly and someone picked up, but not Kristie. I tried again, but this time her actual room. "Collect call from Don, collect. Yes, collect; 513-529-2535." My ego finally conceded to the fact that she wasn't at our prearranged destination and that she would be at home in bed and should pay for the call. I just didn't want her mad at me for not getting a hold of her earlier. She had enough to be mad at me already and I didn't want to give her more.

She picked up, confirming her failure to go to the predetermined location. "What do you mean? You didn't go. I've been running around all night trying to get a hold of you…worried fucking sick. Too cold and too rainy? Too sick?" The disappointment in her and in my blurted words slumped all faith. She didn't need me or truly care. My ego was hurt, I was drunk, and the weight of the world seemed way too heavy once again. With a slam trying to smash the plastic phone and a "fuck you," I hung up and tried to throw the phone through the wall to release some of my anger. The cord jerked the phone at its furthest point and slowly began its descent to the ground. I felt silly picking it up and placing it in its proper position.

I sat down on Brian's bed. First thing first, I couldn't dick Brian like this. I knew it was not a collect call. I knew it had rung her directly. I knew that I had never heard an operator, but I pretended for a moment and contemplated about the amount of money and the ease of escaping with my wallet still full and my scruples intact. I could lie to him though. He wouldn't get the bill for a couple of days and I'd be long gone. It was another bill that I couldn't afford, but I didn't find the lie in me.

I went down and got the phone bill from the fuckers at the front desk, "Thanks a lot ass wipe." Luckily, the desk clerk, not knowing the meaning of ass wipe, nodded appreciatively. The bill was about hundred bucks. What do you know, I had about one hundred and forty in my pocket. I stared deeply at the foreignness of the old soft bills. Spanish bills were much softer and colorful than America's. Brian was sitting at the hotel bar leaving a wide escape route. I could just run and not even tell John, just take off. Train station, first train to anywhere, then home. Belgium seemed safe and warm, just like a home.

I counted to ten and dreamed of the true home that kept escaping me. A white picket fence, a dog running through the damn plants that I planted yesterday, kids playing basketball in the driveway, I was scared to go on.

I caved, knowing what had to be done. I walked over to Brian and counted out to the exact Peso the amount I owed for the phone call. He watched the bills hit his hand, "What happened?"

"Something fucked up, and the call wasn't even collect. I don't know, man. Just take it." The money was gone forever. The jaws of drunken reality took a hard bite into my arm and took all of my money. How I was going to survive from bleeding to death, "John let's go."

I abruptly ruined his fun at the hotel bar with the English art students and especially his sudden interest in Sarah. "John let's just get the fuck out of here." Pain and anger began to run through my veins again. The analysis of the last couple of minutes clenched my jaw, pumped my blood, and scattered my mind. I took off into the night, looking for any helpless object to destroy with or without him. Nothing was found, nothing.

My head was swelling. John caught up to me, "Don, what happened? Wait up." I moved quicker, becoming irritated at his voice. I hit a street sign, then a telephone pole. My hand felt broken.

"Don wait up."

"You can't catch me. You can't catch me. Look what I can do." The road was cobblestone and John had to take his time and be especially careful in his drunkenness. I hopped and ran backwards on the cobblestone singing, "You can't catch me. Look what I can do and you can't." John was the target to destroy. The anger bubbled outside of me and exploded into John's red and frustrated face.

"Yeah, Yeah, whatever. Just tell me what happened. Did you talk to her?" He remained calm and ignoring.

"Yeah, I fucking talked to her. It was too rainy and cold for her to be at the phone booth. So I panicked and called her room. She was there. Fuuuuuuck."

A pause was maintained by my screaming "fuck" for a few moments. John contemplated the advantages of being quiet or continuing to try to reason with me. He wasn't the least bit pissed about my show of anger, arrogance, and malicious prodding at his most vulnerable trait.

"John, I don't want to talk about it. Maybe tomorrow. Let's get back to our fucking room."

The room really did romantically suck. It was outside with a roof above, providing shelter. Dark, Damp, and smelly, the place, a perfect place for a zit on the butt of the world to sleep, maintained my hostility. I felt deserved, "Fuck."

My mood was dark with the lights first footsteps upon my clenched face. My head pounded with its effort to recoup what was lost in last night's alcohol binge and emotional failure. "I'm hungry, John. Too bad, I'm not going to eat until we return to Belgium. Nothing better than spending a hundred bucks for a phone call to a lover who isn't concerned enough about the life we are about to kill or to wait in cold and rainy weather for a call from me. Where is the shower in this place?" The air shot out of my snot filled nose.

"You are the darkest swill of a piece of shit I've ever known," John laughed without me.

The hotel was very interesting in the light. Upon entering, a hallway led to a roofless courtyard, which was filled with a variety of tools and plants, and housed a red brick structure. The two levels of rooms squared around the courtyard with a mixture of the owner's residence and the rooms for rent. The white, painted walls provided a perfect combination with the red brick floors and red tile roof. Rustic and beautifully simplistic, where form follows function, the place had no heater or hot water in hopes of attracting the poor traveler during the summer heat.

Unfortunately for us, it was February. The beds were cold and the shower had no hot water. Placing our bodies under a cold spicket in a moldy closet in the outside air wasn't pleasing after a cold night of sleep.

"I told Brian we would meet him at the top of the church at noon, up in the bell tower." John hung his head waiting for my next explosion.

"What church?" my blood boiled again.

"I don't know, some famous church. We walked past it yesterday."

During the walk to meet Brian, I explained to him about what had happened last night. I didn't even apologize for being such a dick, because he knew I was sorry. It was time to move on and to get through the week without any money. "John, I would like to warn you. I've only got forty bucks left." He shrugged, slightly flushed.

We arrived outside of the iron gates of the church that we thought was the famous one which Brian had talked of so highly. It was already twelve-thirty, but John wanted to try to find him anyway. Today, keeping his word had new meaning to him. We walked up to the entrance and read a sign with prices, "That's almost four bucks each. Just to get into a church. Say if I want to go in and pray. This is bullshit." A woman handed John a flower. She rambled on about something. She began to yell and point. She held her hand out. John, confused and irritated, suddenly realized that she wanted money and yelled frantically back at her, pushing the flower into her face.

She yelled back. John just dropped the flower and walked away, "What kind of fucking place is this?"

"Sorry, Brian." John searched the towers with the famous bells, hoping Brian would telegraphically receive his apologies.

The sun finally took hold, lifting the cold. A bench provided us with the perfect angle to sit and splash our faces in it.

The pit in my stomach of the humility, inflected from the night before, began to wear off with a renewed interest in the town. We worked up some energy and walked around to find anything that looked famous.

"Everything here costs money. I've never seen anything like it. It must be expensive to learn anything here."

"That's true anywhere. The rich keep the poor down by making learning too expensive. That's why poor are more happy than the rich. You know, ignorance. The rich have got to worry about the harm they are causing because they know the harm in everyday living," John was turning eloquent.

Holding our thoughts inside of how we fit into his picture, John and I stared eye to eye. We walked around the outside of another church wondering what to do, if everything was going to cost money. Finally, a bright idea hit John. Our plan was to try blending in with a tour of American students in the hopes that they would include us in the entry fee. After spotting the perfect situation, we stood silent and intent while the teacher walked around counting how many tickets were needed. I felt a little uneasy and extremely cool about the free deceit without even a blink of the teacher's eye at us.

As soon as we entered, we went on our own tour, sidestepping the teacher's agenda. When they left, we followed quickly behind and got a free tour of an art gallery. Again, we were accounted for and paid for without any effort. We began to mingle and talk with the class. I met a cute, little preppie who considered herself part of the avant garde due to her nose ring, but she still had on a plaid sports coat and nice jeans. She made no sense.

I actually was trying to finagle a dinner out of her, but she couldn't take a hint or didn't want to take the hint. "We haven't eaten for a good day and half now. I can't wait to get back to Belgium, so we can eat again." Maybe, the approach was a little too strong.

When they loaded up to go somewhere else that didn't suit our fancy, we took off.

"Hey, what's up," John scarred the shit out of me with his shout. He ran up to me with this woman talking to her as if she was a lost lover, "what are you doing here? No way..." and the other dumb things one says in these type of meetings.

The amazon woman was named Mollie and was someone who went to school with us and through further recollections, someone I knew. Joining in their conversation, I pretended not to remember her, but the picture of taking her to a Date Party a year ago was clear, almost alive. It was a grab a date where you couldn't get a date until the day of. I couldn't find one, so she was my blind date. She was much more interested in every one else at the party, so I left her. I never saw her again until this day and I hoped she didn't remember and wasn't pissed.

She was studying in Barcelona and was on some water and apple diet, weird, weird woman. Seville was the location of some lecture she was attending. She gave us directions to her hotel and a couple of handy Spanish sayings, like "where is..." and "what time is it?"

Until it was time to meet her, we bummed around unable to locate the bullfights. The engagement took us to a beautiful, Holiday Inn type hotel with a little balcony that pictured the setting sun to the backdrop of Mollie and her roommate eating apples and drinking water. She was some sort of anorexic health freak. Bored and not offered any apples, we left after the sun finished.

With nothing to do or nowhere to escape the past, we left Seville. It was only Wednesday and we had no money to spend, had not posed naked on Gibraltar, and had nothing to show for where we have been. "Toledo!" John shouted to the waning moon.

TWELVE
The Heavy Hand

As the train entered Toledo and we awoke from another vicious night of sleep, the sun had gone for good. I had always heard of Toledo, Spain, but could not remember why. We were excited anyway.

We pulled into the station only to discover that the station was not actually a part of town, but situated like an airport. In order to get into town, we had to take a bus that drove over ancient roads for a few miles until reaching any kind of life. We didn't know if we should leave Toledo all together, go into town, or just watch the trains go by. The day started out slow with watching the trains go by and wondering about taking a shit.

With the shit, that was peering out of the edge of my anus, being the decision, John and I went into the bathroom. John was perplexed, "Why would a place have urinals, but not toilets. That is completely backward. What's up with that?" John pointed to a long slit in the floor that was surrounded by tiles and a wall. "What do you think this is? Is this where we are supposed to shit? I don't see the toilet paper, but it is definitely a hole."

There was no stopping us nor my shit. My pants wrapped down just below my knees in assuming the position with my bare ass shivering against the cold cement wall. John followed. Luckily, mine was hard and fairly clean, finishing with an echoing thud. "Hey, I made it," I announced after watching my shit dangle for a moment out of my ass, then suddenly taking a plunge downward towards the blackened abyss. "Just like a dog. What are you going to do about wiping?" I quickly glanced at John's progress not wanting to put any unnecessary pressure on him.

"Oh, I don't know, but if I don't wipe, my ass will be itchy for a week. I already have the eternal itchy ass, even with proper wiping."

"Fuck. We could use my *Fodor*'s." I ripped a section out, "Hell, I will never go to Poland." The opening to the Poland section sounded charming before letting the heavy paper rip into my tender asshole.

After taking some of the appendix for my assurance or insurance wipe, I handed it over. "Ha, I'm going to use Yugoslavia. Those fucking Yugos suck anyway," his voiced echoed in the tiny building as I waited outside for him to finish.

We ate a little bread before deciding to board the bus. Toledo was a very old and brown city. Everything was made of mud, even the sky. At the top of a hill, the strategic military position for any intelligent city, we walked around looking at the free map provided by the train station. A castle here, a castle there, but nothing was new or exciting. Everywhere was the same in Europe. The place seems to be stuck in its past without a concern for its future, same as it is everywhere else. However, North America has the advantage because it has been exploited during a much shorter period and not quite as hard as Europe.

We both took time out to write postcards and to mail them with the Toledo postmark. "Cindy will dig this one," it was a picture of an old man pulling his lip over his nose.

I took my time and tried to be careful about the contents in the one I sent Kristie.

'Kristie, what's up? I am still in Spain, enjoying Toledo. As you can tell, we have changed our plans once again. Still the end goal is the Louvre and posing naked, but neither have been accomplished yet. I will be calling you when I get back. Take it easy. I miss you.'

After long and careful thinking, I produced the same old bullshit of saying nothing, but wanting to. I couldn't really bring up the pregnancy or the ditched phone call in a post card, oh well.

John blissfully lead me to a post office to mail the shiny pieces of cardboard. His relationship was taking form to me without him wanting to talk much about it. It seemed very free, but yet had a nice touch of urgency and dependency. Always ready to fall over an unmanageable edge, they managed to keep their balance, yet still lived with the rush of fear. I was jealous, wishing Kristie and I had developed a little, relational coordination. At least, we had some excitement.

Walking around, Toledo had very little to offer. However, John was feeling too good to let the place go to waste, "Don, I will be so disappointed if we don't pose nude. You know, sometimes you can't let life happen, but you gotta make it happen." We stared across a brown river towards the muddy, rambling ramparts that fortified the city. John carefully cased the area knowing that the upcoming tower was our best bet for posing.

We climbed down and over, then back up. The resolve to accomplish nudity hesitated with the picture of a policemen throwing me into prison forever. The top of the stone, square spire glimmered above, only a few steps away. Fear was nipping at my heels, "Go ahead, I'll take it with your camera. You go first." The lens displayed John already with his shirt thrown down on the ground while he worked on his belt.

For the picture, he gathered up his most serious and stoic face. Looking off to his right and upward, the pose bound his expression and dreams for the sky. The grey sky highlighted his dirty hair which matched the eroding cement of the opposing castle across the river. His chest stuck out and stomach sucked inward creating an illusion of a very small penis. A perfect compliment to his pasty skin, his shoes and red striped tube socks kept his fragile feet safe.

Fuck, it was my turn now. I swiftly got the pants off, but was too scared to take any more off. I looked around for the signs of any approaching company. Boom, my pants were on quickly, as I thought I heard voices rounding the bend, almost at the top. The picture was taken.

"Down in history. We have the proof. I bet those fools never even went to Egypt. I can't believe you kept your coat on. What a wussy girl."

My knees were still knocking and a shiver struck my bones from the fear and the cold. I ignored his taunts and began the descent.

We walked around for a little while until we came across a small road with an alley way leading back to nowhere. Somehow, the sun peaked out of the clouds and shined across a bench and a little statue. A baguette, cheese, and a thirty-two ounce bottle of Coke still remained in our backpacks.

Right then, I experienced one of those moments that will

represent the zeitgeist of an era in my life. The essence of our age and our time were crashing down, imbedding our brains in the solacing sunshine with a sense of freedom that will be hard to repeat or imitate. The moment would become emulated in the religion of our lives that was being discovered and formed.

"Don, nobody has any idea where we are right now…nobody. If the worst thing happened and I had to be reached, they couldn't do it."

"Yeah, the other way to. If something would happen to us, it would be over. We have no money and we can't communicate to anybody," I finished off the watered down European version of Coke.

Immensely intense, the moment remained in silence, completely free and pure. The thoughts of no money and nobody sung slowly to the romantic pleasures of lacking and desiring. The tranquillity sat still, staring up at the brief glimpse of a cloudy sun which warmed our heads.

Unable to maintain the momentum, we decided to head back to the station and make our way north to Madrid.

I was getting used to the endless boredom of train rides. Wine became the necessity for sleep and made my thoughts uncaring of the next hours. Through the dark reflection of the drunken nighttime, I looked at my hair, my face, and my eyes. The faded view flattered and proved the lingering existence of a tired, but comfortable boy in the dirty fringes of jeans and flannel shirt. My head bounced against the glass hoping not to be disturbed by more upsetting dreams. The people around us were invisible and I no longer cared.

We pulled into Madrid with the sun's reappearance. The town was big, confusing, and intimidating. "People are strange when you're a stranger, faces look lonely when you're alone," John sang my sentiments. We had no idea where to stay or what to do. The walk out of the station confronted our biggest decision on the trip so far, right or left.

"All I know is the area by the train station is the easiest place to find a room, the most expensive, and the worst area."

"Left it is," John turned around.

We walked forever, going into a few pensions that were horrible. Our backpacks were growing unwieldy with the dirt on our packed clothes and with the forced patience running away.

"Let's just sit down for a second. My foot is fucking killing me," he collapsed. Without a word, we concurrently counted to ten and collected a personal agenda to find a place to lay our heads and bags.

After a mile of left, we took two more lefts circling back to the station hoping the next road would be more fruitful. Madrid's scenery was unnoticed in our exhaustion. "If we don't find a place by the time we make it back to the station, we are on the next train to anywhere," his calm forced outward through his teeth. I didn't bother to look at his face to see the level of piss frothing up in his eyes, I just knew.

We finally settled on a place that was ugly, sterile, and fairly expensive, ten bucks. One bed and a group shower down the hall with the promise of hot water sounded too good to be true.

I put my stuff down and sat in the chair which was one of those old fashioned new wave metal squares with a fake, red cushion, the kind found in a doctor's office during the fifties. An hour later, I awoke in the same position, noticing that the night had reappeared and that John was under the blankets on the bed.

Nighttime, the time for extremes, swung me low and tried to bring John down with me. He awoke to my counting of money. "I've got four bucks left and I'm in Madrid, Spain. I need to get to Paris and then to Brussels on four bucks. I want to get to America on four bucks…four dollars. Four dollars and I need to pay for an abortion to kill a person's only chance at living. Four dollars and I'm in Madrid while my girlfriend is in bum fuck Ohio, pregnant, and not wanting to walk to my awaiting phone call. That phone call alone could have paid for most of it," the wallpaper caught my attention.

I continued, "The thing that gets me is that I'm not religious at all. I think that Christianity is the cause for so much of the pain and hunger both mentally and physically in the world. Sometimes, I think about some fuck writing a book, burying it in his backyard, finding it a year later, and then ruining the world with it. Now that's a classical piece of literature, so devastating as to change the world and raise a fervor of guilt and passion for generation after generation…a piece of literature, just like the bible.

"Doesn't make sense. I don't buy it. Say if we would have done the same thing with the Hobbit or with Dianetics. Would so many people have died for that book as the Bible?

"I'm not religious and that's why I have a problem with abortion. The baby has one chance. It's millions and millions to one, but boom you have created it. It could have been a different egg and a different sperm. It's like winning the lottery and having the money taken away.

"Now religiously speaking, we have souls and are part of a

grand scheme that is master minded by some benevolent old man, bullshit. Anyway, do all of those eggs and sperm have souls. When they die do they go to heaven and hell. Why not? Do birds and rats and ants go to heaven? Or for that matter, do trees go to heaven? Sure, they have no brain, but is a soul contingent on a brain. I think theoretically no, but they don't have the capacity to make up an image of a soul to comfort them from the fear of no longer existing.

"Anyway, what does it matter if you terminate a life, religiously thinking? I know everyone is born into sin. But I can't image a god saying, 'no, you died at birth before a baptism. You must go to hell.' So why would he say that to an aborted child? It seems like the easy way to the eternal bliss of heaven. No pain, no tests, no nothing, just eternal bliss. God is fake, heaven is fake."

"Wow, great stuff," he rubbed his eyes, combed his hair with his fingers, and yawned. "Don, you can rationalize anything to fit the mold you want. That's the nature of religion. That's the nature of man and of you. Nobody wants to question or to improve. I had to go to a Catholic high school. It's a wonder I'm still sane, normal, and questioning."

"If you didn't have an abortion, what would you do? Marry Kristie?" He pulled down the covers.

"I don't know, marriage is another sacrament I want to question and dissolve." My fingers rubbed hard against a granite chin.

"Well, the real question is could you support it or give it the needed attention? Or would you want to?"

"Could I? Yes. I don't need to finish school to push around paper in a fake job to make a lot of money to give my child Air Jordan's when he is two. But do I want to watch a child, live with Kristie, and begin the mundane rigmarole of adult life? No."

He laughed, "dark and funny, that's you, trapped in the dichotomy of need and want. Let's go somewhere, anywhere."

We walked around a plaza and discovered a Wendy's. "Nothing beats Wendy's, by far the best fast-food place. The hamburgers, everything, are of much higher quality. Should we go?" his lips slurped together and apart. He opened the door without waiting for my response.

The jingle of change in my pocket spoke, "Just a single." We busted through the second set of doors and looked the place over, "just like home." The burning oil soaked my senses.

At the counter, "A single please. This isn't anything like home." I showed the person behind the counter one finger and responded

"Si" to whatever his question was. He left to pack the tasty treat into waxed paper.

There it was in its shiny wrapper, a single with everything on it. The ketchup, the mustard, the fresh onions, tomatoes, and lettuce; all of it rested on a soft bun sandwiching the square of sizzling meat. A single keeping warm in the wrapper stared right at me.

Paying homage, John spoke a short little prayer of gratitude before the eating began, "My hunger is made worse by my being spoiled as a child. Not the spoiled we think of as tons of food, but spoiled with the opportunity to eat a variety of foods at a variety of times during a day. Now, I am only being allowed to eat once a day, and the food is bread and cheese. To have a hot Wendy's Single is the greatest self-pleasure I have known since discovering masturbation. So accept our small offering of words and know that we are fully appreciative." We stared at the picture of the owner, Dave Thomas, and bowed our heads to him out of respect.

"We split it even," as I slowly removed the paper. My world crashed, "what the fuck is this? Where is the lettuce? Where is the tomato? Where is the god damn real onion?" I opened the face to discover a little ketchup and mustard mushed in with fake onions and fake pickles covering a overly greasy, round burger in a bun that should have been given out in the morning of the day before. "This is a McDonald's hamburger for forty-nine cents. We just spent almost two bucks, half of my wealth, on a McDonald's hamburger that doesn't even have a two-cent slice of cheese on it." My head crashed to the imitation antique advertisement filled table, repeating, "Just like home, goddamn it."

"Man what a bummer. This sucks. At least the ketchup was free. Where is Dave Thomas? Does he know that they make burgers like this in Europe." It was all gone and tasted marvelous.

We walked around wishing for the money for alcohol. On the way, I stopped to talk to a crazed woman who was speaking to lobsters in the window of a restaurant for fun. She responded with a flurry of obscenities, I thought.

"Great, Don, now we are going to get killed by this weird woman." She followed us through the streets and her voice became more threatening the faster we walked. John finally screamed "Shut up, you fucking bitch," right into her face, but she did not flinch. Times were lean, but we made it back to our sterile pension to sleep.

Gazing in the tin mirror, "Man, I look like shit." John came over to join me in staring at ourselves and each other. The little bit of sun that we had collected in Seville was long gone, faded forever. My hair was every which way, like Yawho Serious. I hadn't had a haircut since I left the United States and my frazzled appearance showed it. The hair on my neck was now regular hair's length and the top looked like a dirty tossed salad.

John was weathering the week much better and in general, much more hygienic. He was in better shape and his hair was cut close, plus he hadn't gone through puberty quite right and had only peach fuzz for facial hair. My beard was taking form.

"Fuck it all, fuck it all," he said to his chest.

The next day we started early and went to the Prado. With this, our money was gone. We had no food, no water, no money, and two days and the Louvre to go.

We wandered through the many austere galleries and halls. "So many fucking Rembrandt's. The man painted himself over and over again because he had nothing better to do. Now, they are worth millions and for no good reason. Sure they are good, but nothing original or amazingly realistic," his scornful face yelped.

"Let's go find the Goyas. I dig Goya. They are so dark and dreary. He hit the world over its head with his paint brush," I was bullshitting. He was the only painter I remembered from my painting class. A screaming, dark face shrieking during an execution killing with the name Goya under the picture was all I really remembered.

"Don, I look at art as being good P.R. jobs with a little talent. A picture is what anyone sees in it. If you are told to see something and expect to see something, you will see it. Thus when a masterpiece is named, everyone sees it as one and vice versa. The artist's job is to get critics to say 'masterpiece' in their reviews and the rest of us will follow. Does something please the eye? Does something evoke one of the other senses? Does something hit an emotion or memory? What really is good art? That should be up to the viewer not critics, historians, nor art dealers.

"Everyone wants to save their status…from the critic, to the historian, to the art dealer. If any of them are not believed, they suffer financially. So once they choose a masterpiece, it is up to them to do a good P.R. job to create the illusion or their careers will diminish. A vicious cycle is created and the common viewer can not over step their preconceived minds. That holds for art, racism, sexism, etc. That is how the brain works. But hey, if you like it, fuck everyone else. I liked Goya's man screaming too, so fuck the Rembrandt's which cost so much money. Let's go."

We left and headed to the station. Next stop was finally Paris.

"You know, Paris has become our Wally World," John was settling into the train ride watching the black countryside become formless. "We are subjecting ourselves to all of the hardships as in the movie. I feel that we have even seen the biggest ball of string, the whole thing. All just to end up looking at more paintings before Wally World closes for renovations.

"You know what else has been bothering me. All of Europe is being renovated. Have you noticed that? What is that? What is going on? When will it end?" His words wrapped around his body. "Everything famous in Europe has scaffolding on it during the spring of '89? It's like construction on a highway. The question I begin to ask myself is when will this road be complete and enjoyable and easier on me. That is why construction takes place, to make things better. Sure one mile is better, but the next is worse and creates more traffic than if no construction ever went on. And it never finishes. Always there is traffic due to construction."

"My belief on that is that it is a grand scheme to keep jobs."

"I wish the government was smart enough for that."

Paris came with the train ride ending during another sun rise. Again, I stated that we had no money, no money to get to the Louvre, no money to eat, no money to get into the Louvre, nothing. John only could add, "I am so fucking hungry."

The walk from the South train station to the Louvre was a long one, a couple miles, maybe. We stopped and looked at Notre Dame on the way. Everything was becoming related to god and nothing impressed me anymore, not even the famous Notre Dame.

The signs said we were getting closer. We turned this way and that way, then boom, the thing just opens up into a huge stone plaza. The area was awing. Nothing compares to the people, to the space, and to the old grandeur of the Louvre.

"Wally World," I sat depressed on a step. "Now what?" We regrouped watching the people migrate back and forth in front of the glass pyramids. The little kids ran around all excited over something I couldn't identify. They would quickly become bored and tired, eventually being dragged through the same square by their parents four hours later.

"Looks like we've got to ask for money," I summized after recounting all of the money we didn't have.

"I don't know about this. Actually begging," John contemplated the concept, "Wow."

"We just find some Americans, who are older, and ask for the money. We just say we have run out and we don't want to miss seeing such beautiful art. Cake."

The romantic quality of begging to get into the most famous art museum was intriguing John. He didn't even hear my other suggestions. To me it was just another reminder of my troubles.

We needed just thirty francs, about five bucks, but the real concern in my opinion was if either one of us could actually beg. Raised a man, I have tried my hardest and spent too many of my waking hours trying to look like I know everything and can do anything, a sad and desperate way of a life, insecure and scared. However, begging for money smashed my purpose for living and was tough to swallow. I attempted to pass the act along, "John, just go ask this guy. Look at those khakis and sweater, definitely a rich American."

"Me, why not you," my cover being exposed.

I tried to act nonchalant and reasonable without looking defensive. "I don't know, look at me, my mom would be scared to give me a dime and you expect this guy to give me five francs. Image of a bum is the key to their raising the most money. For example, you see a white guy on the street who is shaven and quiet, he'll make a killing begging. But that black guy doesn't have a chance. Everyone figures him for a drug addict, while the white guy is just down and out of luck. The white guy makes a killing."

"I don't know."

"Just do it. For the sake of art."

"All right," he made his way over to the guy. I walked away a little bit and tried not to be too obvious, because I didn't want to be associated with the act. He talked to the guy forever and even pointed to me. They even laughed a little bit. John has a weirdness and awkwardness to his conversations, he'll say anything and will give it humor just by his presentation. He came back successful, leaving me jealous of his braveness.

The Louvre didn't live up to the high expectations, but I dug Delacroix's stuff. We were too excited about getting back to Brussels, food, running hot water, and beds to really take our time to enjoy. We left after only an hour and a half.

On the train ride back, I looked so bad that a random woman gave me an apple for no good reason, except my pitiful face. It made me feel a little bit better about not being the one who begged. The sensation was perfectly decrepit.

THIRTEEN
Stroke the Fury Conscience and Ego

Now that the Carnival fling was over, I could no longer run around and had to face my problems head on.

That first Monday back, I gave Kristie a call to arrange a meeting place and a time to make our illegal collect call. We needed some time to really talk things out and to make decisions weighing in the pros and cons. As a form of meditation, I immediately went into hiding, only revealing myself to fellow students during class. I thought about everything and what I wanted to do and what I thought I should do. Should and want were completely different things that were equally important. The thing that was going to make up my mind was need.

Once again, I went over the questions. "Do you need to have the baby? No, not physically nor morally. Abortion is legal and neither one of us have any moral problems with abortions."

"Did you need to not have the baby? No, emotionally and physically I am capable of raising a child in a way that I see fit and I am able to support a child with love and money. I don't have to finish college to support a family and I don't necessarily have to quit college to support a family. It could be done easily."

That was easy, right back where I started. From Kristie's side, I, egotistically, assumed that she was too lazy to want to raise a child, and if she had to, the task would be mine. Also, her pregnancy represented a good way to corral her insecurity and force marriage upon me. I didn't think she really wanted marriage, but I knew her mental instability and the thought had crossed her mind, regardless of its egotistical absurdity. Her thoughts were swaying and probably were day by day. She also wasn't dumb and knew I would not marry her just to raise a kid, which was not necessary in my eyes.

In the grand scheme of things, I figured it didn't really matter that much what I wanted. It was entirely her decision. She would have to give the birth or have the abortion, not me. That was a very shortsighted view, but correct in our situation. If she was going to have it, she was going to have it, regardless of the fact that I would be the one to raise it. If abortion was the choice, she would have it, regardless of my emotional and moral support.

I wished abortion was more of a partnership choice, but why should it be when we weren't really partners. I could hear my parents saying, "Oh he is still young and idealistic. Remember when you were like that." I bet a lot of kids from the sixties thought that same exact thought today.

"So what do you want to do?"

She paused to strengthen her voice and capture her emotions, "I have thought about it a lot, Don. You know how I feel about you. I think of myself raising a child right now, and I can't see it. I can't even handle growing up myself. I'm fucked up and I will never be able to get myself together with a child to worry about."

It was too easy. She had answered correctly with my exact reasons. It was too easy, though. I felt the guilt and continued, "We could have it you know. Live with one of our parents, the whole deal. If you wanted it, we could have it."

"Don, you know we can't. I am pretty sure I will have the abortion. My brother is going to take me to a clinic in Cincinnati, next weekend."

I sighed and coughed. "I am so sorry that I'm not there for you. You seem to be doing fine without me, though," the weak attempt at encouragement crackled my voice an octave higher.

She started to cry, "I miss you, but it is so much better that you aren't here. You would have told me what to do. Either way, I might have regretted it. I would of ended up hating and blaming you. You know how I am." I nodded with the phone to my ear. "Now, I can only blame myself."

"I still feel like I let you down, not being there and all. It's too easy for me. I feel so guilty."

She reassured faintly, "Don't worry about it. Just have fun

while you can. You'll probably never get another chance to do what you are doing. Neither will I. Oh by the way, I told Jack. I stopped over there and asked advice from him. He seems like the most reliable guy I know and the closest one to the situation. He told me to call you and tell you, so I did. Also, my dad is willing to pay."

"How did he take it?" My breathe drew shorter.

"Actually pretty well, even my mom. I guess we gave them enough crisis growing up that nothing will surprise or upset them."

"Tell him thanks, but no thanks on the money. I should bear some of the burden and responsibility. I figured it all out, I'm going to send you a money order or a check. I'll send it tomorrow or the next day."

"Are you sure? He doesn't mind."

"Yeah, I'm sure."

"Well, I miss you and can't wait for you to get back."

"Promise you will call me as soon as it is done. I want to know that you're O.K."

"Yep, I'll see you."

"Bye, Kristie."

I opened up the phone booth to a chilling windy spring rain. It was always early spring in Belgium. I looked across the street to my home away from home. Albert was farting around in the living room. I wondered what secrets and misfortunes he had taken with him from his past. He never went through an abortion, I bet. He was a one woman guy. Now, that he was old and she was dead, he wondered what it would have been like. That's why he felt up all of the young American women that he cooks dinner for. A small price for a good meal, I guessed. I would have let some woman rub against my chest and crotch for a meal.

Too much was on my mind to do anything, but think. The conversation played over and over again. Wow, what a surprise she was. There I was thinking how emotionally immature she was. Next thing I know, she was sounding like Dr. Ruth and my mom spewing out rational decisions and thoughts that has taken many others many years to develop.

Some lady stared at me, noticing the conversation I was having with myself. I smiled and played it off like I was singing. The air felt light again and the heavy burden of deciding was gone. I had one obligation which was really a doctor's concern, the actual abortion. My sense of freedom would return with a healthy and completed abortion.

I planned my strategies for getting two hundred dollars to her. I would try to get a check from somebody. I had the money to pay them, but I needed a way to send it. One of my rich friends would have a check that I could send.

Going up into my room to count the rest of my traveler's checks, I flipped through the bills, verifying the eight hundred dollars that was left out of the beginning thirteen hundred dollars. The bitterness of that phone call in Spain stung. "Fuck," my hand hit my desk. Six hundred dollars and it was the end of February. I had to make it through March, April, and May. "Two hundred dollars a month, that's easy. Fifty bucks a week."

At school the next day, the shit hit the fan. Some dumb ass got us all caught for using the pay phone trick. She had called late last night and had been cut off. She then decided that she would call back on her credit card number, smooth move. The phone company broke into her phone call and told her that she would have to pay for all the phone calls that were unpaid between Belgium and the States.

It sounded hilarious to an outsider, but I could no longer laugh at my dripping fate. I knew my bill would be about two hundred dollars. It was extremely bad timing, plus none of my friends had a check to give me for cash.

"I can't get a fuckin' break," I mumbled, walking the miles to the only American Express office in town. I presented my esteemed card and expected a money order in exchange for traveler's checks. I have been a bank teller and I knew it was easy process, plus everything was American Express. Once again, my miscalculations cost me money.

When everyone understood everyone else, the bill wound up being forty dollars to exchange American Express traveler's checks for an American Express money order. Some bullshit about all transactions must be done in francs, so I had to convert it twice getting whipped in the ass both times.

With the deed down, nothing could upset me, but I still took a shot at the people behind the counter. "Surprisingly, I have always heard such good things about American Express and traveling. Well, you guys suck ass." I ran off to get rid of the money order and to pay off Kristie. It sickened me to think that the money was really hush money to my conscience.

In a twisted celebration, John and I went to the valley that night to get drunk. "I fucked her and sent her my last money. When I boil it all down, that's all I see…no bloody fetus being thrown into a waste basket can. Some schmo probably goes, 'and the foul,' hitting his buddy while lobbing the fetus of my dead son into a waste basket can."

"Dark again, I see. I love it."

"All I do is lick the stamp. What would you do?"

"Go home, take care of it, work and save some money. Start all over again next year."

"Sounds good."

"Well, I've got enough credits now to graduate, if I want. I'm just going for that second major." His head jerked, pissing me off.

"Asshole, give me the wine. I want to know when you are going to cheat on Cindy?"

"Jezz, tough. I would like to say never, but I have that natural humanly weak instinct to conquer and to mate. I am not planning on it, but if I was presented with the situation…of course, you've already answered that question for yourself."

"Fuck you. It's only been twice and it was strictly physical not mental."

"So far."

We laughed at my coldness and ease at rationalizing anything away. "I only cheated twice on her before leaving for Europe…no make that three. But what really is cheating? Just because I told her that I dig her, doesn't mean we are together forever. Just because she wrote her favorite poems in a book for me to take to Europe, doesn't mean. Fuck, what does anything mean?" The momentum was gaining.

"What were the other times?"

"The first was with this woman I met at one of our parties. I remember Kristie had to watch her cousin's dog or something and I was going to meet her later on in the night to take her home. I think we agreed on between twelve and one.

"So I hung out at the party…same as usual, but I wasn't really trying to meet anyone. Those seem to be the only times that I do. I was dancing and drinking, when this good looking blonde with Kim Bassinger lips started talking to me. We got on the subject of wine and how we both liked it, good deep intelligent stuff. I actually innocently blurted out, 'I have some upstairs. Let's go crack it open.'" The silliness flushed my face. I looked down at the stream that drifted into my future.

"She gives me the green light. On the way to my room, I realized that I had just asked her up to my room which is not a lightly taken proposition. I started thinking with my dick and planned the rest of the evening…a little wine, then I went for the kiss. I still thought everything was innocent, maybe a little feel here, but nothing more than a massage to my ego. She was the most sought after woman at the party and I was feeling good.

"We are making out by the bar, and then she says, 'Don't let me be bad.' What is that? Don't let me be bad?" John and I laughed feeling a little excited. "I led her to my room and our clothes were off in moments. She kept saying, 'Don't let me be bad.'"

"I mounted her, but a rage of guilt shrank my penis. I went for the blow job then a titty fuck for the slashing pearl necklace effect. She kept saying, 'how does that feel, baby' in a psychotic trance-like voice. I also ate her out. She was talking dirty the whole time.

"Anyway, I told her that I had to meet an old buddy of mine uptown and she said, 'I did this only one other time.' I watched her put on her see through lace underwear and strap down her large breasts into a lacy contraption and then ran over to meet Kristie after washing off my face. We made love a little more exotically than usual."

"How about you?"

"Well, I had an opportunity once. She was an old girlfriend gone bad. We said we would marry each other when we were in high school, so she tried to hold me to my word last summer. She looked good and talked of our promise and the lost good times. I went out on a date with her.

"Next thing I know we are getting things on, but I stopped and took her home. She got pissed and started calling me everyday, threatening me. Finally, it all passed and Cindy knew nothing."

"That's it, not bad. I did go out with that same woman after that night. Kristie decided to break up with me a few days later, so I asked the other one out, but she was too dumb and sleazy for a quality relationship, plus Kristie changed her mind.

"The next one was with a black teller who I had gone out with the summer before. She decided to come to visit and it was our semi-formal weekend. I convinced Kristie that I had no choice and that nothing would happen. Well, I knew something would and it did." His eyes grew with the thought of having sex with a woman of a different race, just like all of the fuckers at my fraternity when I took her to the big formal. "But things changed between me and her that weekend. Wanda, her name, asked me to be the godparent of her child. I felt trapped and haven't talked to her since. She was nice and beautiful, but I didn't want to get involved with a nineteen-year-old woman who lived in Queens and had a three-year-old daughter."

"The last one was over Christmas with the woman I suspect that I will marry someday. Tracey Tandish is her name. Mean parents, huh? I got my first crush on her in first grade and ever since then we have never gone out, but have always had something going on from friendship to sex. No matter what, anyone will take a back seat to her. I never admitted it to Kristie, but if Tracey asked me to break up with someone and go out with her seriously, I would in a second. I think she would do it for me. Even though I just kissed her over Christmas, I considered that to be my biggest act of adultery towards Kristie, because in my mind I want Tracey much more and would choose her over Kristie. By not telling Kristie, I have been extremely unfaithful."

"Of course, there is metal mouth and skinny legs in Spain."

"Fuck you, it's gonna happen to you. You had better get married now, because I feel the winds starting to blow your way."

FOURTEEN

Harvest

The next month, or so, seemed to be just filler in my life. I went to visit a buddy of my in Clausbourg, France. Josh; an enigma of Jewish shortness, mounds of muscles, and red brillo pad hair; had been my best friend in high school and we had remained fairly close, even through the long distances apart and infrequent visits. How or why we became such good friends was never known, but an interest in sports and women seemed to be our common bonds.

The great thing about friends was that time and distance doesn't matter like it does in relationships with the opposite. Friends would give a fuck what the other one was doing, but they would always have fun together whenever they could. Men and women should act the same way together and stop being so uptight. I wished I would start acting like that and would stop being so uptight.

Europe at the same time for Josh and I was more of an accident than anything else. Things fell in place nicely for our already planned Spring Break together in Greece.

After the trauma of the last couple of weeks, Josh was my opportunity to get back to where I had started and to release. I had told him my sad story and he braced himself for the possibility of a stormy time.

The highlights of the trip were nude bathing in Bain de Bain, Germany in the natural hot water springs and going to a winery. He knew lots of women to hang out with, even if most of them would just be his friend. Flirting and meeting women was his world, but the actual closure meant very little. As we say back home, he was all yack and no shack.

The first night of my visit, I had to sneak into his house late at night and run out the front door in the morning, hoping nobody would look up from their breakfast. I felt like a fugitive, no not really like a fugitive, but a teenage lover, who was sneaking out of his house, trying to meet their love in the middle of the night. However, when I got outside I had to sit in the cold waiting for Josh to finish his breakfast while I got none.

The next day was a drunken fiasco where I stayed with Josh and a buddy of his in a hostel with a midnight curfew. The hostel was in the city which made it much more convenient for all.

The day had been a mess. We had gone wine tasting and drank way too much. I talked one of his fellow female students into stealing some bottles and she got caught. By the time the bus placed us back into the confines of Clausbourg, I was hung over, in trouble, and wanting bed.

We did manage to hit the town for a few before the midnight curfew forced us home. Hanging out with all of his women friends, I watched him flirt and attempt to receive some playful banter from numerous women. With the continual movement of time, he became more and more unsuccessful.

I fell in lust with one of them. She was a hairy faced Californian free love type. I actually thought she was pretty with bluer than blue eyes, blonde hair, and a nice figure. Josh didn't like her and gave me shit from the beginning. In a few weeks, he would come up to visit me letting her tag along. However, he disliked her enough to not tell me that she was interested. Knowing afterwards was good enough.

When Josh came, he could only stay for a night and it was the middle of the week. I'm not sure why he even bothered, except for bringing the hairy faced Californian.

The next weekend, Kristie's abortion ended without any complications. She called me on Sunday and let me know that she was fine, tired and sore, but fine. The actual operation was quick and easy, but the wait was long and dirty. We could only afford a clinic. Mass market abortions were not the cleanest.

With the abortion behind us, I began to loosen up and brighten up just a little, even though I still had to pay for the illegal phone calls which added up to two hundred dollars. I couldn't afford it, so I wrote my fraternity with a soliciting explanation and a promise of repayment. For once, joining a fraternity supplied their promise rewards of membership when the check arrived in a week. I was squared away with the world.

I planned one other big trip before the two weeks of Spring Break. It was to Florence with Erin, the first person I had ever met in the program. I knew it was a mistake, but she kept bugging me about it and promised a free place to stay. Florence was a good opportunity, plus she did have a place to stay for free.

Lately, she had been overly friendly; cooking me dinner and wanting to study together. Every corner I turned, I started seeing Erin. I knew she liked me, so I took advantage of the situation. Knowing full well the danger that laid ahead, I led her on.

She still had this black curly mass on top of her head that was perfectly balanced by an impressive nose. Her olive skin high-lighted her middle eastern ancestry along with the Jewish star she wore around her neck. Her frame was the tiniest I have ever seen, four foot ten inches, maybe ninety lbs., and was very reminiscent of a teenager at the beginning of development. However with Erin, she didn't have an eating disorder, but was instead addicted to physical fitness.

I admittedly liked her. Her smile was infectious with those big cheeks to accentuate it. Also, a dry sense of humor from worship-ping Woody Allen made her a challenging conversationalist.

Florence ended up being another self-inflicted disaster. First, I got drunk on the way down and fooled around with Erin. "Risky Business" had left an imprint on my brain about having sex on a real train, or whatever they did. I ended up fingering her, instead.

I woke up the next morning with a huge headache and quite embarrassed about the night before. My narcissistic and nonchalant views of sex had returned to haunt me.

Things settled down once we met her friend, who showed us the sights. Florence was an ancient city with the same picture of a Madonna over and over again. After an hour, I could no longer handle the Ufizi or another painting of a Virgin.

Again drunk, I made another fool of myself on our last night. I became fascinated by an outdoor urinal which seemed like a great idea, but was much more beneficial for men then women. I made her look at it and listen to my commentary forever. Slightly scared, she laughed along.

From then on the night escaped any recollection, except return-ing to her friend's place and falling asleep while she caressed my hair. I woke up the next morning to find red wine puke around the toilet. I must have thrown up without really waking up. I cleaned up the bathroom and didn't say a word.

We left the next night only to get kicked off of the train in the middle of night in Milan. That city was a piece of shit. I fell asleep in a frozen train station with a used needle on one end of me and a man doing Michael Jackson imitations on the other.

As I pretended to sleep to avoid conversation with Erin, I watched through my half closed eyes, a group of men robbing a young oriental tourist. As he slept, they sat next to him for a minute then took his bags.

I watched wondering what to do. Initially, I was all set to yell and wake the guy up to foil the crime, but I paused. I had lived in New York for a summer, so my second instinct was to ignore. I sat and wondered about myself and human nature.

There were three of them and only one of me, plus Erin. Generally, the poor hate Americans, as displayed by every bum in every station cursing at me. On the other hand they didn't look like violent criminals, more of the con artists type. Right and wrong paralyzed any decision.

They slithered away, leaving an Oriental guy to wake up about thirty minutes later wondering. I watched his puzzled face turn into fury when he discovered his bag was not only gone, but apparently stolen. He looked my way, so I kept on pretending to sleep.

What had made me be afraid? I couldn't really explain the hopeless feeling of knowing I should do something, but watching the opportunity pass me by. "Better to burn out than it is to rust," squealed in my head for the next week. Neil Young depressed the shit out of me, but he spoke the truth.

I considered myself a failure. It was the first, but not the last time that the realization of failure would come.

"It's better to burn out than it is to rust. Hey Hey my my. Rock 'n Roll will never die."

FIFTEEN

A Terrible Ode

Spring break was supposed to be the climax of Europe for me, but turned out to be the beginning. For John, it was the end.

Our plans included finishing a test, because our school had insisted that our biggest tests be on the days before our big vacations so nobody would cut out early, and then it was off to the South of France. Josh had already come up to Belgium to travel down with us. His break started a day earlier, so he made the trip up, even though the next day we would be heading back down. Our ultimate goal was Greece with not much of a plan between, the only way to travel.

John and I were becoming increasingly skinny. To keep nourished, I had taken up the habit of going into the McDonald's and waiting for people to leave food on their trays. These lowly measures became a ritual on the weekends and Tuesday, the days that we did not get our prepaid lunches. The days which we had lunch, I had enough for both lunch and dinner.

My plight had become famous in school. The word got out about the abortion and that I had no money. Understanding classmates saved their extra food for me or just bought me some.

John joined the battle, scrounging with me out of spirit, instead of necessity. His refrigerator was always open to him at his house. His housemom made him sandwiches and even dinner sometimes, but the romanticism of being hungry traveling through Europe was appealing, so he was more than willing to deprive himself.

Being hungry all the time was giving me an edge to the world. I would get onto a bus and just yell "cunt" or "twot" just because nobody, more than likely, would know what it meant. Since wine was cheaper than water, drinking it became habitual and I became more and more obnoxious. Once a party drinker, I was now just another dick. John, on the other hand, was always intolerable with or without wine. Offensive company carried him to new heights.

A typical John scene: we were walking past a row of parked buses. The bus drivers were on a break and resting in the shade. John noticed them sleeping and began to yell as loud as he could upon passing each bus. He would watch them jump up startled and daringly just laugh while they cursed at him.

We stayed away from the bars in general, but the nights that we indulged, wound up being nights of slam dancing, yelling and other idiot atrocities. Nobody was too excited for our patronage or for our company.

The students most frequented bar, that Albert had promised so long ago, was Pasha. Some English people owned it and would employ some of our students. It wasn't far from school and was a logical, but boring, choice as our local hang out.

Walking in the front room of the bar, it looked like any other, smoky and dark with a long bar and tables on an elevated floor. At the end of this room, one had two varying choices. To the right was a well lit game room. A typical sports type bar with a pool table and dart boards to keep everyone interested and drinking without recognition of the money they were throwing down their throats and out their urinary tract.

The room to the left was a miniature disco. It looked like the designer had just walked out of seeing Saturday Night Fever and went to work. The alternating lights in the floor and even the silver ball completed the room. The sides were lined with bleacher stairs for those who just liked to watch. The entire place, from walls to the ceiling, was encased in mirrors. Walking from one end to the other of the bar was experiencing several culture shocks in moments.

The night before leaving for our adventure, John and I blew off studying and deciding to take Josh out to the famous Pasha. We sat around for awhile shooting the shit until John got edgy. I agreed with the idea of leaving, even though Josh wanted to meet any woman whom he could "get on" and this was his best chance.

John led us and we just began to walk anywhere. "Don, what is your whole grand scheme of things? What do you want to do with yourself?" his low tone struck an odd note. John loved bringing up these challenging, abstract farces for questions, especially with a guest.

I went along, "Gee John, I'm not sure. Give me a few minutes. How about you Josh?"

"Well, I think I want to go back to law school to become an International Lawyer. My dad doesn't like the idea, but I think that's what I want."

"How come?" John continued the questioning looking for something or anything of substance.

Josh took a moment to think. By his uncomfortableness, it was apparent that this was his first deep thoughts on the subject. "I don't know. I guess it's the easiest way to travel and make money. To be honest, I'm not sure if I should qualify my goals in law down to International. It might just be a whim, you know being in Europe and all." His back pedal unconvinced even himself.

"Um," with a note of a challenging dissatisfaction.

"Well, I worked in a law firm last summer and I enjoyed it. It's kind of like being a student who has to learn everything about anything to solve the complex puzzle. It's a feeling of conquering an obstacle."

"Sounds fucked-up that law has be like that, a game," I added still wondering about my answer and the effects of "L.A. Law" on my generation.

"I don't know. I guess all white collar work is fucked-up and warped." Josh felt better.

"Don, let's hear it."

"Same old shit, I've been yapping about for years. I have teaching blood in me. I like the control and power and can only handle answering to myself, plus the hours seem perfect for an afternoon nap. But besides that, I am not putting any boundaries on myself. Whatever I do, I will just be a regular, not the top nor the bottom, but the regular."

The conversation reverted inward at John, "Myself, I find that my life is a series of progressions, leading me to some unknown spot. I don't exactly know where it is going, but I know the path to choose. My next step will be law school as well," his calculated inflection wasn't right for him.

"John, I wish I saw things more in that view. I see it as my life falling in place right in front of me, telling me this is what you will do. The choices aren't there or I just don't create them. No, I think it is that I don't want to see the choices. I'm too afraid to branch out on my own, having no one to blame." I grew slightly scared.

"Fuck it, let's just go to bed." Josh began rethinking about hanging out with us for a week.

The next day the test came and went away slowly, but when it was over the adrenaline rushed throughout the school. So many plans and expectations were about to be realized.

Almost everybody decided on renting boats and cruising around the islands of Greece. John and I, along with a few other mavericks, decided to fuck it and went on our own. About sixty people were going down to Greece together. "Don't they get sick of looking at each other?" is the question the rest of us wondered.

The three of us met at a Grocery store to buy the necessities; some bread, some cheese, some salami, and booze. The tradition of drinking a bottle was going to continue even with Josh's reservations, "You know I can't drink wine like that Don." I just smiled deviantly at Josh's squirming between him conforming or casting. "I'll get two of these big beers. You know I will get a good buzz off of it." He looked confidently down at the brown bottles, "Yeah, I'll be feeling good."

"Whatever Josh," the compromise.

We took the long walk over the valley and through the city to the train station. Since it was Easter time, we stole, well not really stole, Easter Eggs from any local merchant who was offering them.

With about an hour to kill, we went to the bar across the highway from the train station. Walking into the crowded expensive bar, but cheap restaurant atmosphere, sixty drunk, rich pricks, that were heading to Greece, appeared before us. All of them had been there for quite sometime and were repulsive. Overly anxious and drunk didn't match. Like drunks at sporting events or concerts, they become at least twice as obnoxious.

I watched and talked to many of them seeing and hearing sex and lust. While John and I were still stuck on posing nude, the rest of the students had become obsessed with fucking as many of their fellow students as possible. Even the women, everyone just wanted to fuck. Good for them. It seemed a noble goal, but one that had lost its appeal to me about the same day that I had lost my sexual appetite with Linda in Spain or with Erin in Florence.

I talked them all into giving me their eggs, so I had about a dozen hard boiled eggs to eat during the two week period. "See you guys in Berlin," they walked to their train that would take them through Yugoslavia. "Thank God, we aren't going with those idiots."

"Yeah, I start getting sick thinking about being trapped on a boat with them."

"I'm sure they will have some great stories," I was picturing certain couples forming and dissolving in hours, "but none that I want."

Our time had arrived to leave. On my way out of the bar, I grabbed a salt shaker to add a little flavor to the Easter Eggs. Just outside of the door, a man came running out of the bar, "Hey, you. This is not America. You can not take that." His accented castration for me mixed his French and English together just enough that I got the gist. I believe a loose translation was "rich, snot nose punk, thinking Europe is your little playground, using all of us for you decadent lust for a contemptuous life."

I returned the little piece of glass to the counter where it came. Walking across the bar, his continuous berating remained right behind me in my ear. I tried to act proud, but the embarrassment wore on my persona sheepishly. With my hand releasing the salt shaker in the exact position where I had stolen it, a swelling of hatred rose through my body out of my reddening skin and bulging neck. "Fuck you," I mouthed to the guy who continued to lambast me to his friends. "Fuck you."

Outside, "That mother fucker. He has it all. What the fuck? Does he have to take a salt shaker? Does he know what it is like to be hungry? He doesn't. He could go home tonight and dunk his eggs into a bag of salt, that fucker. All I wanted was a little luxury which I haven't had in months," I looked at my companions. Josh still looked embarrassed for me and John wasn't even really listening. He had heard it all before.

It wasn't the salt incident that I was pissed at, it was envy in everyone. I was jealous of people who had a home with the things that they liked or wanted close at hand. I was jealous of those fuckers who could go on a cruise through Greece. I was jealous of what I easily had once and now struggled to have.

I got on my pedestal and began, "For the first time in my life, I feel the real anger of being a have not. This has been building in me for the last couple of months. The scrounging through McDonald's garbage cans…the potato sandwiches staying warm on my radiator…the crabs from not changing my underwear for weeks at a time, everything is rubbing and working against me; the joy on people's faces eating a fucking Big Mac…the smell of people shoving Thuringers in my hungry nose…the new clothes people got…the gifts people bought for themselves, for their families, and for their friends. I am so used to being on the other side of the fence. It stings me with a bitterness and flips my world completely and cynically around.

"I thought I knew what things were like for underprivileged people. Underprivileged is not what I want to say. I'm not sure of the best description, perhaps privileged people is better. I didn't realize that my rage has always had hope to quench it. Hopelessness is the fuel of the fire, something I do not know. How can I or anybody think to understand the poor? Those rich fucks singing for a hungry Ethiopia or a trapped South Africa, what do they know? Nothing, but sympathy and shame. What do I know? Nothing."

The train left the station with a twist of the cork. I said goodbye to myself.

We made our camp on the train. After a few months of traveling in Europe, we had acquired some good ideas on how to make traveling as pleasant as possible. First was making sure you were drunk. As stated so many times before, alcohol made falling asleep much easier. Second was speakers for a Walkman which would scare people away from your noisy cabin. Third was to lay your bags everywhere for the same purpose as number two. If you can scare everyone away from your cabin, sleeping across two chairs, which was much more desirable, was attainable. Trips went by much faster asleep.

We prepped ourselves well and everything worked like a charm, except one man with a bow tie around his collar, bravely entered. John ultimately heckled him into the submission of leaving.

We drunkenly reminisced, the way you were supposed to, with Josh beginning, "Don was the one who got me to lose my virginity." What else would we reminisce about, but sex.

"Yeah it was pretty funny. I had this sex pot of a girlfriend who taught me everything that I know and do not want to know. She had a friend who was even worse. This chick even had sex with my girlfriend's little brother. He was like thirteen at the time. She was seventeen.

"Anyway, I set up this blind date knowing Josh had a great shot at getting laid. His parents were gone, things were perfect. The plan was to drink a little beer, to eat dinner, then we would drink some more back at Josh's place."

"Yeah, we got some Grizzly Beer, I will never forget that beer. I even get it at school when I think I might have a chance with a girl. It doesn't work too often, though." Josh confirmed with a sour swig of his lasting beer.

I cut him off, "Anyway, we are at dinner, and these two decide they want a beer. During dinner, I was watching her hand rub his crotch under the table. I reluctantly gave them the keys. They came back awhile later with horny eyes and wet lips. Then, we quickly returned back to Josh's, worried the moment would fade. I could see the look of fear in your eyes as you knew your time was nearing.

"Everything went according to plan, Josh had sex in his twin sister's bed and I had sex in his. How did I end up in your bed, anyway?"

"I can't really remember, I think we started downstairs and you went into my room. I had no choice."

"Good old Jen."

"Yeah, I came in about two pumps. I still do."

"You know, I still hate Jen to this day. She is such a whore. When she fucked Claudia's little brother, I lost any warm feelings towards her. I still feel kind of bad about letting you lose your virginity to such a whore. It can taint you for life."

"Yeah, it puts very little emotion into having sex."

"How it should be? We are animals. Anyway, the worst part is, Josh's mom found out about the whole thing."

"How?" John giggled in delight of our ease of exchange.

"I am not sure, maybe it was my sister. Or maybe my mom just guessed."

"Yeah maybe she found cum stains, but it was funny. 'This place is not a whore house Josh.' That was awesome." I joined John's snickers, then grew seriously pensive. "I know Claudia ruined me for life sexually. She was so easy going with sex. She taught me all kinds of positions, etc., but I never really liked her. I just thought I needed to lose my virginity and I had already hit sixteen. I thought I needed to learn for the time when I really liked somebody. After Claudia, sex seemed like just a game, a good story to tell. I have no real feelings for sex. I guess it's not that bad of a concept, you know?"

"Yeah, I guess you have a point, Don. Sex isn't really an indicator of feelings. Lust is lust, love is love, but sex is different with love. It means more somehow," John was almost done with his wine. I chugged mine not wanting to be out done.

"You know Don, I think the thing that warped you the most was Chrissy." It was Josh's to turn laugh.

Her long, black hair and pointed face fondly erased the picture of Claudia in bed. "I dug her. She was so perfectly loony, but I thought she was hot."

"It took you so long until you asked her out."

"Yeah, I took her out and was so nervous. She made all of the moves on me, then came New Year's Eve. We double dated that night." I smiled at Josh feeling good about the good times we once had together.

"With Julie, another one of your famous dates, while I labored along with Julie."

"I liked Julie," those words slapped against his shoulder in a joke.

"Shut up, I know you did, bastard."

"I should go out with her. She was your mental match, just as sarcastic and you couldn't handle it."

"I could, it was the hair on her face, plus she was whacked out about sex."

"That's it for Josh, number one looks, number two sex, wait I minute, looks, religion, sex, then personality."

"Not true, looks, personality, religion, then sex. You must admit that sex is not that important to me," making his irritation of me known.

"Yeah, because you suck at it and feel so uncomfortable."

"No, I'm just afraid."

I finished up my wine just ahead of John. Josh was still nursing his first beer and fidgeting at the prospect of sex and women which both scared him and kept him up at night. That's what an overbearing mom will do for you.

"What about Chrissy, Don?" John finally became interested in something.

"Well, New Year's Eve came and we went up into my room. My parent's were at a party. I have this thing with New Year's Eve, I guess," everyone got my cynical joke. "Next thing I know, our clothes are off and she is sitting on my face. Then she slides down and goes to town. I can still remember the number one song of the year that was on the radio as we had sex. 'Don't you forget about me' topped the 1985 countdown. The thing that got me was that night was the last time we ever went out. I scared her away when I called her the next day. Ever since then…" the memories mingled with the reality.

John and Josh talked for awhile while my ego missed Chrissy. I had actually never fucked her, because my penis couldn't get hard enough to penetrate her tight vagina. Forgetting the pain of failure, my mind shifted into a dream of the blow job, that she had given me to make me feel better. My penis swelled with blood. I would give it all up to see her now, just because that moment of failure wouldn't leave. Moments just like that have plagued my entire life. I have a penis with a bad conscience.

The trip grinded towards the south. We listened to a tape of old soul music of the mid-eighties, like Cameo's "She's strange." John and I were screaming the words. The moment capped off that feeling of high school, Chrissy and Claudia. Times I wouldn't want to see again.

Out of talk and wine, we went to bed.

Sleeping on trains still sucked no matter how drunk or how much room one has. I was woken when a young couple got into our cabin. They talked at first quietly, but the whispers became impassioned by an argument. Loud whispers were worse than regular talk.

At first I tried to translate what they were saying, but between the mumbles, the fast pace, and my bad knowledge of French, I had no idea what was happening. The man made a power play and got up with a macho slam of the door. However, he came back about thirty minutes later in a sympathetic tone.

He lit up a cigarette. "You can't smoke in here. Where is the light? This is a no smoking car," John exploded into the confusing confines. He threw his luggage about the compartment, trying to get up and maintain his balance. He tripped, "Fuck, where the hell is the light? I will show you, this is no smoking. Fuck…fuck. Stop smoking."

Everyone else was confused as he finally flicked on the lights. The couple stared in shock while John pointed at the sign, "See, it is no smoking. We got in this car for a reason." His feet hopped up and down for punctuation.

"Pardon," came back politely.

Confidently jumping in, Josh went into a wild story of John's horrible allegories to smoke. His French sounded smooth and convincing. Trying to get back to sleep, John was still mumbling, "the sign says no smoking. If you want to smoke, smoke outside." I glanced at my watch. Three-thirty A.M., which meant another five hours until Nice. I laid back down listening to John continue his sedated rage. I was dreaming of the straight jacket that would hoist him away, when the sun started our day, just outside of Nice.

"What the fuck happened to you last night?" John tensed up again from the question. I knew the better route of a simple forgetful ignorance, but Josh prodded, visibly upset. "I thought you were being raped. I checked if my hands had touched you anywhere that they shouldn't of."

"I can't stand smoke. I can't sleep with smoke in my face."

I laughed and turned on the old Walkman. The scenery was warm of firm browns and healthy greens. Only with the South of France and two nights under our belts, Josh felt a new uncomfortableness with John.

We hopped off the train with Rusty's *Let's Go*, Josh's new nickname, leading us to nowhere. We took our before photo to determine later if Spring Break was successful. The tense search for a place to sleep began.

John was surprisingly feeling good. "Our face is going to be a light golden bronze, with our teeth zinging, zinging of white to match our hair." John repeated the Zing of the teeth and a Zong for the hair with body motions to match the bright riveting of our visages. His energy from the night before refocused intensely on his sunburned dreams.

"Josh, not too expensive." I was looking through a list of hostels.

"How about this one? It's only fifteen to twenty bucks."

"Josh…"

His patience of me was wearing thin as he studied his travel bible. "Come on Don, this place is only twelve bucks, we aren't going to do any better than that."

"All right."

We walked in circles for about an hour until we finally arrived at the desired location, five minutes from the train station where we had begun.

We got a triple room with a shower and one huge bed and one little bed. The perusal of the hotel/hostel enlightened us to fact that it had nothing to offer, but a little room where continental breakfast was provided every morning.

"Which way to the beach?" We followed the pointing fingers until at first we could smell the tightening of the lining of our noses with the salt hovering in the distance. The exhilaration built as we crossed a park lined with palm trees. The horizon was only blue. We crossed a highway to discover the beach. "This is a nude beach right?" I showed our age.

The boardwalk presented itself, then the beach. The beach was a disappointment, but nobody would let any emotion show, except complete bliss. The beach, made of little pebbles and rocks, was contained by chilly, blue water. The Spring Break crowd was non-existent.

I hated the beach. There was nothing to do on them, but sweat, get sand in your pants, and dive in cold and filthy water. This beach was even worse, because you couldn't even sleep or walk bare foot, due to the pointy rocks. Its only bonus was the possibility of seeing naked women.

I threw Josh's shoe in the direction of a naked lady so he could check her out. We laughed like junior high, hormonally defunct kids.

SIXTEEN

"Come On, Give Me A Break!"

Lying on the beach, I got bored and took a walk. Nice was a beautiful site, with jagged edges cutting through the skyline and its perfect clear pool of blue skies. Actually, I had come to discover that it was the weather that really made a town beautiful. I loved Florence because the weather was nice, but I hated Geneva because it was cold and cloudy. Sunny with temperatures in the mid seventies and no humidity, Nice was perfect as a post card. It was about time.

I returned to find the rest of our trio squirting "Sun In" in their hair. "Come on Don. Just put it in. We can't let those fuckers in Greece outdue our tans. We need that blonde zing," John was obsessed.

The considerations of the dirty blondness of my hair and how goofy it would look if it turned into a myriad of orange shades. "Sun In has always been against my morals, but…since you put it that way."

"Shut up pussy and put it in."

"I just hope my hair doesn't turn orange like Rusty's."

"You are so stupid. My hair is strawberry blonde." He wasn't laughing.

The afternoon went by slowly. Finally, John and Josh admitted to being tired and sunburned. On our way back to the hotel, a grocery store restocked our usual food supplies; bread, cheese, and some kind of smoked meat. Smoked meat sounded like it would last longer than any other. I also indulged in a fifty-cent bottle of red wine that was sold in an Evian-type bottle.

We fell asleep for awhile only to wake up to John's misery of over indulgence of sun. His skin was a painful shade of pink plus he moaned of sickness, "My head is all block-up. I guess it must be allergies. Luckily, I have some stuff that clears it up right away." He showed us a hand full of white horse pills.

Josh and I went for a jog while John attempted to convalesce. The top of the cliffs, that overlooked the stony beach, dared my legs, heart, and will with its upward climb. The cliffs were filled with winding paths, little areas of woods and grass, and lots of little streams that formed story high waterfalls throughout. It was exactly like being on a miniature golf course in Myrtle Beach.

I lasted the whole run, feeling refreshed and invigorated. We ran back to eat and shower. Continuing to whimper in bed, John declined our invitation to watch the sun set and to drink my wine. Josh and I set out on our own, again.

Within fifteen minutes, the sea appeared. "So Josh how do you like Europe so far?" a bench on the boardwalk provided a perfect perch. "I haven't really had the time to sit down and talk with you."

"It's been great fun. I feel like it's a vacation from school, but sometimes I feel guilty that I haven't learned or saw anything. I mean, I expected my French to be fluent and to meet French people. I haven't met a soul, besides the people at my school and the family I live with."

He pondered out loud and into the purple horizon, "But my new friends have come to mean a lot to me. We have gone through a lot together, a really bonding experience."

"Yeah like pledging a fraternity, except you have the important bonding with women."

"Yeah," he smiled anxiously, then controlled himself. "Well they have become my friends. I'm sure I will stay in touch with a lot of them. What do you think of this place so far? I know you've had some rough times."

"Personally, it has kind of sucked. I have no money, the situation with Kristie, and I feel real uncomfortable where I live. He is a nice guy, I guess, but since I don't bring back the women he wants to meet, he doesn't include me in anything. I just don't want to be there talking to him. I guess he would like some company, but I don't provide him any."

"Don, you've been drinking a lot?"

"Yes and no, Josh. I was for awhile and then I decided it was not the way to solve my problems with Kristie, but that idea didn't make it very long. Now I drink a lot when I go out drinking which isn't very often anymore. I never go out during the week. I'm sick of hanging out with those guys. I don't know about my drinking. I don't think it's anything serious, but once I start I keep going. Does that make sense?"

"Well, you now I don't like you when you are drinking too much. You get this kind of edge to you. It scares me. Like in high school, when we would go at it with all of those guys. You guys would scare me and I felt like I didn't belong. I just hope you don't end up like them, drunk, stoned, and stupid. I don't know."

I swigged my wine turning away to watch the still orange splotches roll in with a lapping blue motion. Upon finishing, we returned home after buying another bottle. I respected Josh's feelings, but I wasn't planning on making any concessions, at least not yet.

Once inside the hotel, a guy that worked there invited us to a party that he was giving. He was from Canada and did the laundry at this place. France and the job had let him drop out for awhile. We confirmed our desired attendance and promised not to be late to the nine o'clock meeting time.

On the way up the stairs Josh ran into some women that he recognized. Enthralled, "Hey, I know you guys, don't I? You guys study in Clausbourg."

The four women turned around and recognized his face like he did theirs. They were friendly and made conversation. "Are you guys going to the party?" Josh had plans forming in his head.

"Yeah," they rang out as I continued walking away.

Girls, party, and a commonalty brightened Josh's suddenly exciting future to our uncertain night. "Who were they?" I obliged him.

"They study in Clausbourg somewhere, I think I met the one with the short blonde hair before." Hormones bubbled out of his pearly white teeth.

The good news woke John up. It took a good fifteen minutes of convincing him to go to the party with us. "Come on," we ruthlessly chanted. He rolled over shook his head and rolled back over facing away from us.

"John, we've got to go. Take the skirt off, pussy." Nothing.

"John, I am going to jump on your fuckin' pussy ass feet and rip them off and put them on the window sill to dry and make you stare at them all night. Your dried blood will cake and make them stick there forever to rot and smell worse than you already do." Finally, a laugh.

"John it's a party. How can we not go?" Rusty paced anxiously. I opened the new bottle of wine and offered it around. Rusty continued, "there will be girls that I know from Clausbourg," his voice squeaked out of desperation.

John took the wine and looked blankly at Rusty, "all right, dicks. I'll go."

We met downstairs and took the long walk through a tunnel and across several highways to this guy's apartment. He, being Wayne, had assembled a pretty good crew of people; a group of Canadian women that looked like heavy metal video vixens, a whole slew of guys who mostly traveled in pairs of two or three, the four women whom we had met earlier, and us.

In order to save each precious drop of wine, we hung back from the rest and stingily shared the bottle. I was feeling the bottle before too long while the underpasses orange lights energized the illness. We walked up a whole bunch of stairs and into a tiny little apartment. Wayne had some beer and some others brought the rest. A circle of drinking and meeting formed.

After finishing the wine, I partook in the socializing. Josh was talking to the four from Clausbourg and John was on the floor in the middle of everyone. I contemplated listening to Josh's cheese out, hoping to get lucky, or listening to John's loud and weird attempts at grabbing the center of the party or the center of someone's night. I sat next to John.

I wound up next to one of the heavy metal queens who was fairly attractive with her long, straight, blonde hair, her athletic build, and angular bone structure hidden under the paintings of cosmetics. I looked around at everyone listening to her and realized she was the center of the male desire.

"I think Canada sucks," a bitchy tone complemented her roll of eyes, flick of hair, and shrug of arms on to leg routine. "Why don't they get their own identity? I mean, all we do is act like Americans. You know, we don't have a Canadian culture."

"Yea, I've never heard anyone say, 'You know, you are suppose to do it like they do in Canada,' or 'Hey I saw them doing that years ago in Canada.'" I peeped in with an obnoxiously mocking valley dude tone.

"What about hockey or Canada Dry Ginger Ale?"

"Fuck hockey," she looked pissed at John for questioning her authority and beauty.

"Fuck Wayne Greztky," was my attempt to spurn on a debate and John, but it was a no go. He moved on, looking bored.

She continued with her lambasting of Canada. Because I had agreed with her, I was the launch pad of some deep frustration probably brought upon by being ignored as a child or losing the Ms. Canada competition. She rambled on about the economies of Canada and how it was solely being supported by and supportive of America. "They might as well be taken over by America. Break them into states and vote for the president."

I grew tired and bored, "what do you mean them, aren't you them?" I walked away.

Once again Josh was making moves and John was drawing attention. I kept following John. He was talking passionately to a bunch of guys and in particular to the fattest one with a round curly top. "Don't you just want to turn on the T.V. and watch some football?" John was off and running on his favorite game, 'Name all the things that bug you about Europe.'

The guy was on the edge of his seating with excitement, "Yeah, but I want it to be the football of the seventies when football was real football."

"Like the Steelers."

"No, not the Steelers," he looked at John like he was a dumb little child who knew nothing. John laughed at him. "The Raiders."

"Yeah, John Matuzack," John egged him on nodding his head, bugging out his eyes, and shacking a fist. He stopped as he noticed the chord he had just struck with John Matuzack.

"John Matuzack, ah man, you know it. Fuzzy me." He offered out his hand palm up and thrusted his fingers upward and continued to move the fingers up and down like pistons, "Fuzzy me."

John looked hard at the fingers and cringed towards my direction. You could read the thoughts, 'Do I act like an idiot and keep him going or do I act like a dick and ignore.' He hesitated for a moment as he watched the fingers wiggle in front of him. He slowly let his hand and fingers greet the waiting wiggling fingers. He fuzzied him and laughed hysterically at the gesture and at the guy. This guy didn't know how to take it so he backed off and tried to incorporate another conversation. John just continued to look at him and let all of his anger out in the form of hideous laughter. He kept saying, "Fuzzy me." John was drunk and ready to play with this guy's head.

I kept following him with the anxiousness of a "To Be Continued" T.V. episode. He spotted his prey, the video vixen. She was bitching to someone else when John broke into the conversation, "You are the best and biggest farce I have ever met. When I make a movie I want you to be my farce." His finger jabbed at her lower shoulder, just above the breast.

She looked at him funny, unconcerned by his finger, but unsure of the meaning of farce. Was it good or bad, she did not know. Farce sounded negative to her, but being in a movie was her girlhood dream. She smiled and said, "Thanks."

"No, thank you," John said in between another hideous fit of laughter. "Thank You."

I needed more to drink, so I went into Wayne's refrigerator and acted like I belonged there. I grabbed three beers, one for each of us. Mine had a cap that needed an opener. I tried everything hoping not to draw anyone's attention in case the beer was theirs. Attempting, I ripped my shirt and my skin. I went into the bathroom and tried to knock off the cap against the porcelain toilet, but it wouldn't budge. Next, I broke the toilet paper holder, "Fuck."

I guiltily left the bathroom to find Wayne's roommate waiting for his turn in the bathroom. To rid any suspensions, I met him head on with, "Hey I think someone broke your toilet paper holder." I had forgotten about the 'who smelt it, dealt it' rule. He was kind of pissed and watched me for the rest of the night.

Finally, a neighbor came and broke up the party. She yelled at us in French as we marched single file down the stairs. Josh did the translation and filled us in about her being the landlady and kicking Wayne out. John said "Hi" to her on the way down the stairs.

We moved towards a bar somewhere in town. I was way too drunk and the night came and went with my swirling head outside of my body. Sitting in between John and I at the bar, an American, middle-aged man began telling us how free willed he lived and how much cooler he was than us, "You see it doesn't matter. I don't have a name or need a name."

One of the women piped in over my shoulder, "He just asked you your name," referring to a laughing John.

"You don't see. It doesn't matter."

John was ready, "I see. Since it doesn't matter we can call you what ever we want?"

Sarcastically, "Sure."

"I see. I see…dickhead. Everyone meet my friend Dickhead. Don, this guy's name is Dickhead."

I looked up from the beer that I didn't want and grunted, "Hey, Dickhead."

I watched the group of people that had dwindled down into the four women from Clausbourg, us, and Dickhead. A waiter empathetically approached and politely forced us to sit at a table in the corner to prevent our thunderous and uncouth behavior from scaring away the rest of the well paying patrons. Luckily, we had lost the fuzzy man and the video vixen and her friends.

Unfazed by our hatred, Dickhead continued to argue, but this time his topic was fidelity. Practically everyone was yelling at him. "It doesn't matter if I cheat on my wife, I love her."

John had enough. "You are so full of shit. The only one you cheat on with your wife is with your hand. You aren't even married. Let's stop the facade, you know and have nothing." A piece of spit flew onto Dickhead's chin.

Dickhead, stunned with the anger in John's raised voice, thought about everything and said, "It doesn't matter what you think." John went into his laughing fit again.

I phased out for awhile looking around the bar, which was just like a TGIF Friday's, pretty generic, and the four women. Three of them went to a small school in Ohio which was the home of our esteemed Vice President at the time. The other went to Illinois. They were upper middle class pieces of flesh and bones from anywhere, U.S.A.. They were like everyone else I had ever known, generic, just like the bar. I didn't bother to meet them.

On the other hand, John began talking to a short-haired blonde sitting next to him and to a long, brown hair woman with a long angular face. Josh had the other two, while Dickhead and myself were being ignored. Looking into my beer, I thought about throwing up.

"I know you, we went to grade school together," John was on a roll tonight. He began guessing everything about the blonde haired woman, hitting her life story on the head. I was too drunk to make out the particulars, but everyone else seemed astonished at his accuracies.

Then the conversation turned into a debate about John's validity. It was getting pretty heated when I spoke, "John's full of shit. He is making it up, and just guessing right. Just look at him, goddamn it," my malicious tone was unwarranted. The table gathered into an uproar about how could I say such a thing. Knowingly, I joined Dickhead in the doghouse and returned to the foam and shut up again.

"We've got to stump him." They persevered in the interrogation of him and his knowledge of the short-haired blonde mop. John confidently and correctly gave his assessment of her attitudes, beliefs, and past.

"Ask him her sexual experiences," I blurted out, "it will get him."

The two women, that Josh had been taking to me, shot me a glance. Their eyes rolled up pointing to the Ray Bans that rested upon their nicely coifed hair. "What?" my face shrugged. "I just said sex. Did I miss something?"

"Typical, male."

"What do you mean by typical male?" staring at the baby fat of a red faced, blonde hair, snooty bitch. Josh cringed, as his prospects left with my mouth opening.

"You would bring up sex." I still didn't know what was going on. "Did I miss something? Is sex that taboo?" I looked hard into their faces waiting for my vicious reply that Josh's face warned them about. I thought for a second, looking at everyone which kept their eyes upon mine.

Tons of lewd questions about her apparent problem with sex came to mind; 'Did her cousin Joey rape her?' etc., but I didn't. Instead, my head plopped down with a chuckle. I was too drunk and missed something far, far away, "I'll bet Dickhead would agree with me." I got up to alleviate myself.

Finally, the night closed to promises of our meeting tomorrow for a trip to the beach and bed.

The next morning I awoke to Josh at the foot of my bed shaking my toes. "Let's go. I want to make the beach by eleven."

I rolled over only to hear my answer in John's mouth. He mumbled, "All right."

Our free breakfast followed by a shower rejuvenated my spirits. Josh did his pushups and isometric exercises to push out his already huge muscles for the beach. "That's sad, Josh, a slave to your body."

"Come on Don, I haven't lifted in a week. I feel small." His smooth muscles rippled upward to a tiny head.

"Shut up, you're only doing it because we are going to the beach with those girls. Which one?"

"Lynn."

"Lynn, she's a real winner." John laughed with me in between the sniffles of a stuffed up nose. "John, what's your girlfriend's name?" I was offering no mercy.

"What are you talking about?"

I laughed, "What are you talking about?" I mimicking his early morning whiny denial. "Like you don't know. What's her name?"

"It's Kelly, but it was nothing."

"Nothing?"

"Yeah, come on I knew her in elementary school. I swear I know her from somewhere."

"Cut the shit, John. You were guessing right. Don't give me your shit."

He quickly grinned and looked away, "It was nothing, just having some fun."

The admission was all that I needed. "Should I write Cindy and let her know? You might as well forget it. She is already counted. She will be yours."

"Yeah, right."

"Yeah, right. Just another notch, man." I reached for my knife. "Count it. I might as well notch it now." I walked over to his bed post, looking triumphant. Josh watched from his sit up position. The blade went into the bed frame with one stroke. I met the previous cut with an exact duplicate to complete the V. "Notched!" I yanked out the V. "Notched."

Laughter broke John's tension, "You're just trying to get the heat off of your attitude last night and your little misfortunes of love. How many times have you let down poor sweet Kristie? How many?"

"Notched."

"Guaranteed, nothing will happen."

"Notched."

"Come on guys, they are waiting for us." Josh huffed in between sit-ups.

"All right let me take my allergy pill." John gulped it down. He stopped for a second to swallow, but nothing happened. Gagging a few times to get it back up, his head and eyes rolled towards the ceiling. His final gag was very loud and raspy.

I asked, "Are you all right?" Showing me a finger to let me know to wait a minute, he made a few faint sounds. The escaping noises demonstrated that he could still breathe, so I thought nothing of it, but watched curiously.

Jokingly, "Do you want me to give you the Heimlich?" He looked up at me bug eyed. He showed me his finger again, gagged again, then shook his head in confirmation. I still thought he was fucking around, but I placed my hand somewhere below the ribs and right in the middle and pressed hard and even. Relaxed, I acted like nothing was going on, still thinking that it was a joke.

A second later of frozen time, his horse sized pill flew across the room. "Man, you just saved my life," his lung gulped through his throat and out of his mouth.

"Yeah, I know. Let's go to the beach."

SEVENTEEN

Morissey and the Shiverless

"Hey guys, what's going on?" On the way to the beach, Josh zealously positioned himself next to Lynn and Jen, the two women from Clausbourg that had enamored him last night. They both had their hair slicked back and Ray Bans covering a small portion of their sun burnt faces. Don Henley's "Boy's of Summer" floated in the air. They had identical, slightly chubby faces with girlish bodies, skinny but a rim of fat throughout.

John and I were paired with the others. I walked next to John's Kelly and he walked with her best friend, Tricia. Tricia looked like the other two, but taller, skinnier, and more angular. Kelly was completely different, at least to me. She had short, blonde, bobbed hair and a face that reminded the passing world of a Madonna in a classy more innocent mood. Ripped Army shorts hung over a white bathing suit and she wore no shoes.

Kelly and I lagged behind John and Tricia. "Notched," I announced to the air.

John gamely offered out his hand, "Fuzzy me." Our little inside joke was safe.

Kelly and I talked lightly, mostly about last night. "I am a little fuzzy about things, especially once we got to that bar. The wine destroyed me."

"Yeah, you looked out of it."

"I just remember being yelled at for bringing up sex."

"I have no idea what that was about. The whole thing was bullshit anyway. I am an easy guess," she shrugged it off easier than me.

I watched her womanly figure move. A flat stomach stretched into breasts that stood facing slightly upright. Her arm's muscularity cut the air just beyond her curvy bottom. The legs were stretching out as far as possible to keep pace with my James Dean swagger. I laughed out my nose after she noticed me watching her, "Yeah, definitely bullshit. He won't admit it, but it was definitely bullshit."

The immediate attraction to her contradicted her obscurity to me last night. On the beach, I gladly positioned myself in front of John to place myself beside her. He had purposefully done the opposite.

After an hour, I couldn't take it. Lying in the sun was driving me nuts and making me hot, plus Josh was busy ignoring us and making an idiot out of himself trying to impress Lynn. He turned his back on us and whispered in a sweet voice for only her to hear.

"This is boring, anyone want to go for a walk," hoping for a yes answer from Kelly. No takers came my way. "How about a swim?" They looked at me with a crazy faces. It was March and the waters were freezing, but I wanted her attention. No takers came. "Fuck you guys, I'll go by myself," in my best Jack Nicholson.

Fighting the painfulness of the jagged beach, I skipped above the rocks. I jumped in and listened to my body scream out with a huge shiver. "Fuck. It's cold," I screamed at the god of water temperature.

I spun around towards the shore to find Kelly jumping in behind me and clumsily swimming my way. With a poke of her head out of the water, she leaned her head back to produce that greased back power-broker look. "Hey, this feels great."

"It's too fucking cold." I dove under her and swam to shore. She followed.

The day slowly past by. "I still hate sitting in the goddamn sun."

"Shut up and relax, ass," John started to glow feverishly describing the hair zinging and teeth zanging process with a new zest. "Let us be thankful for this wonderful day given to us by the rays of the sun." Then, he proceeded to talk everyone into a consensus decision to leave, in order to check out Monaco.

"I'm starved," John looked into the sea from the boardwalk on our way out.

"Yeah, I can't wait to eat tonight." John and I had committed to eat one meal a day. Luckily, this hostel gave us a free continental breakfast, but it also meant our only meal was in the morning.

I dreamed of the rolls we already had, "Why do they call it continental breakfast and why does it suck? Don't they know that it's supposed to be the most nutritious meal of the day?"

"Yeah, where is the fruit? Where is the cereal? Just bread." John looked at the rest of them.

Only Kelly paid attention, "I don't know. I hate breakfast anyway. Brunch is it for me."

"Not quite breakfast, not quite lunch and ends with a canta-loupe." The two of them glanced my way in which I offered an unknowing shrug.

We got to the beginning of a pseudo front yard of the pink palace which was home and supposedly a famous mansion at one time, but now was just fragments of itself cut into tiny pieces over the years. The place was as small as the house I grew up in and the yard was only ten feet by ten feet. I studied the place until a familiar face, standing at the door, came in focus taking a second to register. Florence flashed before me and the red shit in and around the toilet bowl. I panicked.

Then Erin's voice appeared in my head, "I just heard from my friend in Florence. You know the place we stayed. Well, she said that you puked behind her bed and in it. I guess it really smelled bad when she got back and it took days to go away." I didn't remember throwing up behind her bed, but it was definitely possible. In fact I knew it had to be the truth.

I hid behind a tree, "John come here, remember that story that Erin told me about me puking in her friend's bed. Remember I thought that I puked in her toilet. I cleaned it up the next day and opened up the window to remove any traces of smell. Well, that's her friend." She walked into our hotel. "Fuck."

John laughed, "It serves you right."

"Fuck, she's the last person I ever wanted to see again. Walk in and walk back out and let me know if the coast is clear," a cynical laugh bubbled out between my teeth shaking my tongue.

We snuck up to our rooms and prepared. I wore a pair of green khakis and a green stripped oxford. My hair swirled on top of my head with a huge blonde gob slapping in front of my face. I was trying to impress Kelly and hoped she would notice. Josh, also working on his image, wore tight jeans and a tight polo shirt to highlight his chest, one of the only male chests that could hold a credit card.

"You're still shorter than me, bastard," I jealously blurted out while waiting impatiently as he flexed and taunted in a mirror.

I looked at John who, swept up into our clean look, was shaving. He raised his eyebrows, "Don't start Feller, remember you're already notched."

"It looks like you're the one on the prowl, big guy."

"Yeah, save it dick. You are just too embarrassed to talk to her after being notched. You want to so bad, but you won't. A stubborn proud bastard, both of you," I included Josh in my accusing pointing.

Before getting on the train, we went to the local grocery store for the making of sandwiches and wine. It was already four and I was starved, but we waited to eat. I felt guilty about breaking our one meal a day promise and about the extra money leaving my pocket, but our state was critical.

The train ride was a short distance, but a long trip. It was similar to riding a subway with too many stops and too many yellow lights given to the conductor. The countryside was mountainous and rugged with little vegetation to soften. The city appeared past a mountain that the tracks wound down into the station. The mass of tourists, which we followed hoping that they were in the know, hiked up an intimidating cliff. Josh became conscience about his Let's Go tag name and left it in the room forcing us to be on our own.

We walked to the famous castle and looked at how nice it was. "Who cares about these fucks anyway? Stephanie still gets diarrhea like the rest of us." The other women grew to ignore John's lewd comments, except Tricia who seemed to be taking a shine to him.

Getting ice cream, we stopped to watch the people excited over nothing. About ten yards away and sitting along a curb under a tree across the street, John's face peaked in and out around the legs of hundreds of people passing us by. I sat with the rest, but slightly away from the next closest person. In between the moving legs, John was laughing hysterically about a picture he had just taken. He motioned to me, but I couldn't understand his crude attempt with sign language so I walked over.

"There you are, with that dumb ass, sad face sitting slightly down from the rest, as if casted away. It is perfectly symbolic. I am so glad I have that on film. It's going to win awards, major awards. Everyone eating ice cream, but poor little Donnie."

I walked back discouraged. "What do you say we get those sandwiches going?" Josh looked my way from his private conversation with his buddies, Tweedle Dumb and Tweedle Dee, both of whom I considered dumb, simply because their presence bugged the shit out of me. Today, they had matching pink shirts and nicely pressed pants with the same identical hair, faces, and sun glasses. Sickened, the shivers caught hold of my bones. He nonchalantly shook his head and frowned.

The snide look was so condescending, that I wanted to cut off his little penis. I shot back the look to help him understand my disapproval with the panhandling of his personality to pick up a cunt. We silently ate as our friendships endured an unexplainable test. I began to wonder if it was me.

Afterwards, the casinos attracted our attention. On our way we wound down through the ramparts of the castle to a huge marina, up through gardens, and across sculpture gardens. John got silly, "Take this photo." He gave the camera to Tricia and he laid down on the grass in front of a feminine floral arrangement. He pouted out his lips and hips.

"Wait," I jumped in and did a similar pose. "Come on, Josh," he reluctantly looked silly and pretended to feed John's grapes. Flash.

"Your turn." The four women got into the patch of grass and smiled.

"Lame," John looked through the lens. They changed their poses around a little bit. "Lame, but it will do."

Next we ran into a sculpture garden. I posed with my hands on a huge cast iron butt while Josh did the same with a pair of breasts. I took a picture, that never came out, of John through a series of statues with explicit holes that ran across the grass.

We finally made our way to the casino. "Ten bucks to get in. Forget it. I just wanted to look at it, anyway."

"I'm with John, forget the gambling. I can't afford it." I moved to the back of the pack.

"Not me, I've got to go," Josh chimed with the girls responding positively. "We're in Monaco, you've got to gamble."

"Well, good point, but…we'll go to the beach and get drunk," I produced the two bottles of wine from my book bag.

"I'll hang with you guys." I looked at Kelly and John looked at me. The tension of John's neglect of and my obsession for her, crashed the scene in its apparentness. My heart fluttered with suppressed emotions.

We got directions to the beach and agreed to meet there. The sun was going down just as we found it. The beach was a big horseshoe cut out of the land with little fine pebbles acting as sand. Only a few strangling couples remained enjoying the fading red shadow.

"Much better than Nice. You can actually walk barefoot on the rocks." John was picking them up and throwing them into the water.

I took my shoes off, "I've been wanting to do this since I started thinking about going to the beach. In Nice, I feel like I am lying on a basketball court, a painful one at that." I got out my handy dandy Swiss army knife, the cool kind with the magnifying glass, and opened the wine.

We passed the bottle and took more momentous pictures. I twisted my body into the sand until I was covered in pebbles past my knees. Kelly posed with me for perspective. "Don, I think we are getting better at this picture thing. Don't forget we've got to pose on those steps," John said while squinting into the glass hole.

Taking a chance or giving a test, my words said, "Yeah."

Anticipating Kelly's reactions, "We've got this thing about posing nude in famous places. We posed on a famous fort in Toledo. It was a warm up, shall we say."

John interrupted, "We shall."

"For the big one, the Parthenon is the target," I looked for disapproval or lack of understanding, but found neither. "I'm planning on going with the shoot the bird pose." I took off my oxford and rolled up the sleeves to my T-shirt. I thrusted one arm towards the sky and towards an imaginary bird. The other arm bent up towards the ear. As I looked thoughtfully posed on the precise moment to let go of the imaginary arrow in an imaginary bow, I flexed my muscles. I knew the only resemblances to strength in my thin soft frame was my biceps which were overdeveloped in my stint at pretending to be good at tennis. The ploy was another shallow attempt at impressing her and quenched the burning.

John joined in, "I'm going for the more classic flexing of the stomach while lying on stairs pose." He fell to the ground and rolled up his shirt revealing the burnt stomach. He relaxed his torso, facing towards the sky, with both arms propping up his back to reveal the lines on his stomach. He flexed then relaxed then flexed.

The wine was gone and burned my desires for more. "I can't wait for Greece."

"Those guys are going to Greece, too," Kelly spoke up.

"Good, that will make Josh happy."

"Yeah," she laughed. "He's pretty obvious about it."

"Yeah, he's like that. His number one priority is getting women to like him. He doesn't even care about the sex."

"Well, he doesn't have a chance. She told me that she isn't really interested. Plus, she's got a boyfriend."

"It doesn't matter. Rejection gets his motors working harder."

John jumped, "You aren't going to Greece with them?"

"No, I've got to get back and teach."

"What?" he sat on a wonderfully placed log of drift wood.

"I tutor English to French businessmen. I've got to be back on Tuesday."

"Good pay?"

"Better than nothing. I don't have the money to stay over here, so I've got to do something. I was only planning on a semester, but I knew I couldn't go back yet. So I'm working and not traveling as much. I couldn't go even if I wanted to." She joined him on the trunk.

John felt no mercy, "How much you got?"

"I've got about a thousand bucks."

"That's tons, Don only has three hundred dollars left."

"Yeah, but that has got to be able to pay for my plane back."

"Oh," John still saw an angle and a mission. I recognized it in his tone and concurred. To him, it was just a challenge, another quest to keep things interesting. To me, it was more in my loins.

"You've got to go. When are you going to get the chance to go to Greece again? I'll tell you, never."

I added, "He's right. Plus we are planning on doing it on nothing. Maybe two nights in a hotel at the most, one meal a day."

"Well, I could. My grandmother, who just died, left me five hundred bucks. I was kind of hoping to use it for graduate school, though."

"Graduate school, that's what the government is for. They don't give out cheap loans for Greece, do they?"

"Nice John." We high-fived. "Anyway, your grandmother would want you to go to Greece."

Kelly laughed a little nervously as she contemplated. We were eager to conquer. "You've got to do it. Carpe Diem."

"We'll see."

The others showed up. "Hey, I think Kelly's going to go to Greece."

"Maybe," she tried to shut John up.

"How was the casino?"

They sat down with us, "Fancier than shit."

"Did you guys win some big bucks so you can take us out for some drinking."

"Nope, lost it all, twenty dollars," Josh confessed.

"Nice beach, huh? Lot better than Nice." Sitting in a circle based on the driftwood and enjoying the chill, ghost stories came to topic.

John started, "There was a group of us bored one summer night. We were sitting around in one of my friend's backyards, drinking and bullshitting. Nothing really to do, so our conversations turned to the perverse. I stated that I had always had psychic powers since I was little. Actually, I think we all have psychic powers, but some discover it and others don't.

"Of course nobody believed me." John began to feel the story, as the six of us began to close around him. "I looked at one of the women, whom I really didn't know. She was quiet and someone whom one of my friends coveted to sleep with. I stared at her for quite some time while the group quieted and watched me. I looked her in the eye and said, 'You want to talk with your grandmother don't you?'" His tone went deep and his voice turned to a whisper drawing us even closer.

"She turned away. I said, 'Don't be afraid, I know. Let's talk to her.' I told everyone to get into a close circle. I had never done this before, but I had some hidden instinct guiding me. We all joined hands. I told everyone to focus all of their attention and energy on me. 'Don't look at me, but concentrate on me.' I told her to concentrate on her grandmother and to look at me. I began to call her to come forth. With the energy, I began to loose control of my body. Then suddenly with a huge rush, she came through me. She spoke through me. 'Hello, Monica,'" his voice shrieked in its pitch. Returning to normal, "The girl went hysterical and let go of the chain. She was crying with a joyful disbelieving.

"Everyone looked at me amazed. They told me of my contorting face and pumping veins. 'I've never seen anything like it.' They no longer disbelieved in my powers." Everyone was mesmerized by John, except me. I still sat away from everyone and looked off into the Mediterranean, denying the odd feeling the story had left. Shaking my head in jealousy, I wanted his storytelling powers and creative imagination. Everyone else had a look of scared belief. He finished, "I never saw that girl again."

A long paused cast its chilling effect into the air. John triumphantly and arrogantly looked at the submission on everyone's face.

He felt like he was our master. Suddenly Tricia broke in, "I had a similar experience."

She was unshy and looked straight at John throughout most of the story, only glancing at the rest of us during breaks to see if we remained entertained. "I don't know if any of you have ever played with a Ouija board or know what one is." Everyone nodded with recognition. "Well, we were fuckin' around one night at school my freshman year. It was late and nobody felt like sleeping and my roommate had a Ouija board, so we started to play.

"Next thing we know, it starts moving on its own. My friend yelled, 'write it down, write it down.' It spelled out a name. 'Evelyn McCue. Please help me. Deliver a message.' We looked at each other in disbelief. I didn't belief in ghosts or Ouija boards, but the thing was moving on its own. I swear it was.

"It began moving again. 'Tell Bill McCue from Rantoul, Illinois that I am fine and waiting." A fever rushed through me. Tricia looked slightly frightened reliving the tale. I believed those words she uttered out of confession, "I swear it." I fought to dodge her trance by glaring out to the sea again and mumbling, "bullshit."

She continued, "It stopped, we waited around all night and every night for the next week. Nothing so we called directory assistance in Rantoul. Sure enough, there was a Bill McCue. We called and he answered, but nobody had the guts or the belief to tell him what had happened. My friend who called just held the phone in embarrassment as he continued to chant, 'Hello, Hello'."

"We called back the next day, pretending to be the phone company, and asked his address to verify our records. We had decided to send him an anonymous letter. We wrote it up by simply saying. 'Your wife tried to contact you through us. She told us that she is fine and waiting. I hope you believe, because we do.' We sent it off unsigned. We watched that Ouija board for another week, not moving it, not touching it. Finally, it moved again. It simply said. 'Thank You.'"

I had to get up and walk off the chills this time. I pictured Evelyn's ugly wrinkled face gently but powerfully sending that message. It must have meant the world to her. I reached back for reality and quoted "bullshit" so only the ocean could her. I did not want to believe.

John looked at her with admiration. I expected to see a little jealousy or even a competitive admiration, but it wasn't there. He just lovingly admired what she had said. I began to believe him too.

"I have one more," John finally said. "It's really quick and I have never dared to tell anyone before. Nobody ever believes my first story anyway," he looked down shyly, playing with his shoe-laces. "But you guys seem different, I feel a kindred spirit, a bonding. I don't think our meeting was an accident," Kelly and John exchanged glances, then he looked at Tricia's calming face. "Yeah, it definitely wasn't by accident.

"Well anyway, this is how I remember it. When I was little." He looked up, "I had a so-called imaginary friend. I would sit in the closet to talk to him all day. My parents were slightly worried, but they felt it was semi-normal. After awhile I would come out of the closet and tell my parents what my friend had told me. It would be stuff that a little boy wouldn't know, like about politics or about science.

"After awhile it freaked my dad out and he asked me, 'What does he look like?' very forcefully. I was a little scared at his tone, but answered 'he has an umbrella and wears an old fashioned gangster-like hat. He has a black suit on and a black overcoat.'

"The next time I got out of the closest my dad went storming in. It was a big walk in closest and he shut the door behind him. I guess he wanted to prove to himself that nobody was in there. A half hour later he came out, made himself a drink, threw it back and wouldn't talk about what had happened. I never saw the guy again, and my dad has not spoken of it since that day."

"Wow, that is fucked up." Josh looked white while Jen and Lynn shivered in the strong wind.

"I don't have any stories. I am not really sure if I believe in spirits and the such. I guess I never will until it happens to me," my confession shot away from the rest and out to the black curls.

Their following questions bounced off of me, "You mean you don't believe their stories? What made those things happen then?" The chills left me, "I just can't believe."

We were too spooked to hang around in the dark and headed back to Nice. On the way back to the train, I asked Kelly, "Do you believe them?"

"No, but I do believe in spirits, but not the dead spooky kind. My own religion, I guess. I definitely don't believe those guys, but they were good stories." I had heard enough for the night and anxiously awaited the cooled sheets of bed.

EIGHTEEN
Lighten Down

John and I tried to rally the group behind Kelly and her debate on Greece. The immediate indifference to Kelly from Josh, Lynn, and Jen went by unnoticed. With Josh, I knew it was a little more than indifference and more of a dislike. His hostility towards the situation remained beneath his patience which I hoped she would not expose.

"All right, I will go. I've got to get the money, though." She lied to shut us up as the train found its home.

Back at the Nice train station Tricia, John, Kelly, and I walked to pay phones to allow Tricia a call home while the remaining half retired to bed. Unable to dare to pull away from Kelly's presence, I ignored my dizzy head and heavy eyes.

The first and second round of the NCAA's were being played and Tricia was consumed by Illinois' chances. She had to call home to find out the results. John flirted and teased, "With Hansen, forget it. Once March comes, his collar gets tighter, the circulation to his brain is restricted, and he starts putting in his best friend's son who is number twenty at the end of the bench holding the towels. Liberty hasn't been the same since he was on the cover of SI as the best high school junior. God, I miss the NCAA. It feels so weird not to be watching the highlights on ESPN at eleven." He circled the free-standing phone.

"Yeah, it is pretty weird not to know what is going on.

Something could happen and we would never know," my body shrugged against of row of red and orange plastic lockers becoming sick of Julie's conversation with all of her family. It was a short twang of homesickness, "Sometimes I just want to turn on T.V. and watch anything, even bowling or pro volleyball."

After Tricia finished, we ran into our host from the night before, who was also in the train station calling home. He repeated into the plastic salt-shaker top, "I've never been happier. I can always go back to school. Mom, stop worrying." He was smiling and waving very friendly at us. I smiled back with the thought of him moving out of his apartment without a toilet paper holder.

"Kelly what is it going to be? Time is running out." John knew she was annoyed, but unable to figure out his enthusiasm. His voice was calm and sincere as he spoke using his great acting abilities, but the eagerness and joy of bugging the shit out of her appeared in his glossy yellow-tinted eyes.

"I've got to find an ATM machine, a BNP machine. Have any of you seen one?"

"Wow, an ATM machine, that's something else I miss."

"You just miss the money, Don."

"Hey, I'll help you look for one," my opportunity appeared.

Julie was ready to go back and John volunteered in a gracious motion of chivalry to accompany her. For the first time, I was to be alone with Kelly and I couldn't stop shaking. "Don't choke, be cool," I chanted inward trying to recapture a common pattern of breathing. She walked slightly ahead of me with a flowery dress, waving in the nightly breeze, that was underneath my worn and too big jeans jacket. The dress and her sweater nicely complemented her infatuating snake-like curves, forcing my breathing to reestablish its rapid unsteady pace. The blonde hair was held back with a white bandanna showing me her too blue to be true eyes for the first time. I reeked of my sappiness.

"Hey that's a nice dress." She responded with gentle and knowing laughter. "Not too smooth, huh. Conversation isn't really my forte. The dress just looks good on you." I had said too much. The big moment was running on by me.

"So what is your forte then?"

"According to Josh it's drinking." She looked at me questioning, giving me the green light to continue. "He's been bummed out at me since we left together. I don't know what it is? Well, yesterday he told me that I am drinking too much again and that I'm getting a little too close to some sort of violently demented edge which he is fearful of. I don't know? I don't think I'm such a big drinker, especially compared to my friends that I grew up with or my family. My mom's side has had continual bouts with drinking. They say it is hereditary." My lips and shoulders agreed with my last sentence. She watched me talk with interest as I prodded for some sympathy and attention. "I think the biggest problem I have is that I grew up with friends who based their fun around drinking. If something was going on without an opportunity of getting drunk, we wouldn't go. I think I'm socially retarded for life. Somewhere along the line, drinking became evil to Josh. I guess he never fit in when we were drinking back in the days. What kind of ATM machine are we looking for again?"

"BNP."

"Fuck John, if you can't afford to go, don't go."

"Well, do you think I would do something out of the pressure to do it, let alone pressure from some guy I don't even know?"

"Maybe. Sometimes I need a little outside inspiration."

"Yeah, well I don't," she was getting short. "I want to go, but the money issue will decide it for me."

"Where are you from?"

"I grew up in Chicago, but now we live in Indiana."

"Where?"

"Highland Park, Illinois and Crawfordsville, Indiana."

"I've heard of Highland Park, but Crawfordsville? Sounds like a bait and tackle store."

"Not too far off, it's about an hour north of Indianapolis. Just a little college town."

"Like the rest of the Midwest."

"I thought about going to University of Ohio, but too many people were going there from high school. I wanted a new start."

"Why Ohio Wesleyan?"

"My sister went there. I did the exact same thing. Same sorority, same major, just wanted to follow in her shadow."

"Do you like it?"

"Well, it's all right as far as educations go. We do volunteer work during our Winter term. Almost everyone studies aboard. They do make an effort at being very liberal arts concentrated. The social life has grown boring, that's why I'm still here. I couldn't imagine going back and getting drunk with hundreds of the same people at some dumb ass fraternity. Which one are you in?"

"Sig Ep. Does it show?"

"You aren't the happy-go-lucky frat boy image, but I see you in one. At Ohio, you've got to, plus I noticed your T-shirt today. You probably hear that you don't look like you are in a fraternity all the time…too quiet, too pensive, too independent."

I laughed, "Independent, pensive, quiet, sounds good to me. Actually, I get that shit all the time. 'You're in a fraternity?' You know with that smug look and snotty voice. Then I ask them about everything that they think is wrong with a fraternity. They come back with fraternities exclude people, promotes misogamy and rape, harbors dumb jocks, and a variety of negative adjectives to shoot holes through me. I ask them if they see me in that same light. They usually fumble around with something, maybe a 'that has nothing to do with the concept of fraternities.'

"Then I go into my preaching about how I can sympathize with the pain and hatred of a black man and how he must feel when he knows people are looking at him and shivering with fear because he must be a crack headed, murdering and raping thief. How I see that look when I wear something with my letters on it in a woman's eyes which labels me a 'Snot-nosed, rich, dumb ass, shallow rapist.' I finish up with how it is prejudice either way.

"I watch their reaction to my absurdities, then admit that the comparisons are an exaggeration, but the principle is right on the money. I agree that fraternities have problems entrenched in their traditions and methods, but generally speaking it is not the system which is the cause, but a symptom. Fraternities ideals are high; brotherhood, community service, balanced men, etc., but more often then not, those principles are lost and the place goes awry. No fraternity has the credo of disrespecting others, especially women. The problem comes from the members and no one else. The members are the simple result of the society in which they live, which is all of us. Society promotes men to be bombastic, selfish pigs. Any situation which forces men and women to live in separate buildings promotes these problems."

She searched out my eyes searching for my intentions. I focused on the black ring around her left pupil and then looked away, knowing those words were the closest to any kind of a truth that I knew. I paused for a moment then briefly looked back into her eyes and mouth. Admiration was what I wanted to see, but I saw her heartbreaking disbelief.

We got to a BNP and she took out the moncy. I stared at the

thousands of francs in her hand. "Wow, what that could buy?" I caught myself before I could contemplate the food that it would buy me and fired on top of it, "I didn't think you had the money."

"BNP lets me take any amount out, but I've got to pay it back as soon as possible. That's why I've got to call home."

"They just let you take it out? What a bank!"

"Yeah."

"That's weird, I was a teller last summer in New York. We couldn't do that."

"Why were you a teller?"

I lied, "I wanted to get out of Pittsburgh and away from my family for the summer. I have an uncle that has a house in Connecticut and in the city. It was weird. I actually have an uncle and his gay lover who we called an uncle in New York." She looked at me with renewed interest, but I was trying too hard to impress her again.

"Long story, but they were getting a divorce and they both have a lot of money, especially my uncle's lover. So they squabbled over it the whole time. I was a tennis ball being bounced back and forth. The other uncle lived in the city, Greenwich Village, and the real one lived in Ridgefield, Connecticut. I was a man without a home or too many homes.

"It was a great experience, anyway; met lots of people, got to live in the city and in the country. Plus, it gave some job experience." My mind went back to the desolated loneliness and the smell of the grass in Connecticut compared to the crowded loneliness and the smell of sweaty people in the city.

"So anyway, these guys used me as their method to argue…dumb fucking bastards, both of them. This cost this much, that cost that much. I want this, I want that. That's all they talked about to me. Like I gave a fuck, but I had to sit and listen and wait for them to take vacations and leave me alone to my own devices."

We finally reached the hotel where she used the pay phone to get the final verdict. "Nobody was home. Good night, Don."

I watched her door open and shut. The lightness of having a reason to wake up ran through my feet. I couldn't sleep during my mad, raging tossing and turning while thinking about her. These feelings had happened too often to me, but I was invigorated. Kristie no longer existed in my infatuation.

I woke up to Josh's pre-beach routine. In between grunts, "Don, you didn't?"

"What? With John's fucking girlfriend? No."

"Get off of the notch thing already. Fuzzy me?"

Our fingers intermingled, "Oh, now that you have a new girlfriend?" I couldn't help myself.

"Come on, I think she is actually cool. She is really nice." He waited for our disagreement to his synopsis of Tricia and the flippant flailing of his arms.

I looked at Josh, "So is Kelly." He didn't bother.

Onto the beach, the seven of us went out together for the last day in Nice. The train left for Greece, via Rome, at six o'clock. First thing in the morning, Kelly had finally reached home, but their reluctancy rubbed off on her. We were losing. "Fuck your job, fuck it all, fuck fuck." John stumbled and hurt his foot during the last two fucks. He hobbled around holding onto my shoulder.

"You're lucky I'm here. Saving your life, supporting you, and where is the thanks?" I sat down on a blanket of stones.

"Thanks. Kelly you should have seen him in Spain. I tripped and thought that I had broken my ankle. I'm yelling and screaming while resting my weight on him and he is carry my bags. It must have been two miles back to the train station. Where were we?" The pride in our demise glittered his chin and cheeks.

"I forget, some monastery for the Moors or something. It was suppose to be beautiful. Well, that's at least what *Let's Go* said." I motioned towards Josh completing the joke.

"What?" Josh looked pissed as we all laughed.

"These guys don't know your nickname, do they, Rusty?" John rubbed Josh's brillo head. "Rusty!" He spoke to Kelly. "Every morning we've woken up with Josh at the foot of our bed wagging his tail saying with his cute face, 'come on. Let's go.' Faithful just like a dog…a dog named Rusty."

Rusty perked up in his frustration in his inability to come up with a quality come back, "Hey Kelly, when are you going to take off your top? This is a nude beach, isn't it?"

John said, "Yeah, we've got ours off. Nudity isn't something to be ashamed off."

After a round of "Come on"s from all three of us, she laid on her back and said, "I was just about ready to before you asked. Now it's too late."

"Yeah right." But she ignored. I added, "All I have seen in Europe is nude paintings and the such, when did it become so taboo, I mean nudity. Doesn't make sense."

"Taboo, I think that's twice you've said that in two days, Don." John huffed.

"Kelly, isn't that Ned and Degan?" Jen suddenly blurted out between her pink splotches.

Kelly looked up and her eyes jumped, "Degan? Hey Degan." She sprinted barefoot across the sandless beach, impressing all of us. Her trot took her between two opposing and surprised bodies.

Ned, the one on her right, wore a plaid bathing suit, white T-shirt, and raybans. His face was clean and tanned with a perfect mat of black curly hair like a Kennedy. He just kept laughing and patting Kelly's shoulder making me jealous.

Bob, whose last name was Degan, looked around Kelly to Ned with a smirk hiding the rest of his face. The doughy Irishman wore no shirt and ripped Champion shorts. His three day old beard matched the long rolling curls that wound down his neck and finished at the shoulders. His shoulders hung low and swung in rhythm with his hips. His feet seemed not to move.

We were all introduced after which Degan burst into a run towards the ocean, throwing out an unspoken challenge to Ned and Kelly. They obediently followed and I found myself doing the same without much choice. His magnetism immediately moved all of us in complete admiration for his every word and gesture. His strong shoulders carried his heavy physique out much further than anyone dared and he stayed in much longer than anyone dared. His body cut the water with two openings in which he dove through.

The twists of fate pushed John, Josh, and myself into the back seat, as they reminisced and retold their trials and tribulations of Europe. Kelly forgot about me and was laughing in her complete joy. Holding back anxieties, my ears gripped each and any word, trying to pick up any clues about Kelly and her love life.

Degan and Ned seemed to be a good team. Ned was definitely the straight man, who kept them honest. Everybody knew and liked him. He was the kind of person that you slapped on the back or just randomly yelled his name in a large crowd. No one could resist. He never got mad and always laughed, but every action he took was reasonable and calculated.

Degan had the perfectly opposite characteristics to fill the Yang of their circle. The man never laughed, except for a stupid smirk that remained transfixed and brought about a self-consciousness onto anyone who dared to seriously converse in his direction. Life was his joke and his lies were the tests for his class. No one was ever sure of what he was truly thinking. Sometimes he would go for hours without a word. Few people knew him, but everyone recognized him walking down the street. He intimidated with a free spiritedness or perhaps an uncaring for everything. The silence and freedom made him king of himself and pulled everyone along behind him, even if they loved him or hated him.

Together, Degan pushed and Ned pulled to keep things fun, safe, and relaxed upon a middle ground. Their fights made their understanding more complete and a respect always present. After my quick yet thorough synopsis of the two, I knew that they would never hang out after Europe.

With everyone in Europe, Europe was Europe, distinctly separated from the rest of everyone's life. Nothing compared. The boredom and uncertainty brought us close together which no one who didn't participate could break. However, the situations and feelings could never return, leaving a void without a reason to continue on with the friendship. Just like Degan and Ned, John and I would be friends for life, but never hang out together.

"Guys, Greece is calling us. We've got to go and get ready." I grabbed my things slightly pouting of the imminent loss of Kelly.

"That's where you guys are going next?" asked Ned.

"Yeah, tonight a train to Rome, stay a night then Brindisi for the ferry to Greece." John started to join me in the walk back to the hotel.

"We will be there in a couple of weeks. We are going to see all of Italy and then Greece." Ned followed us and the rest were behind him. The moment was awkwardly presented with my eyes squinting into the orange and white.

"Kelly are you coming or what?"

"What?" a pause accompanied by a lightening of her face, "I guess."

"Typical. You would. No guts no glory," mouthed over my shoulder. I remained ahead of the rest wanting to sulk and anxious to get out of town. Nobody had heard my snide and spoiled comment. A grocery store appeared and I went in determined to be alone, "I'll meet you guys back at the hotel."

I bought three, one gallon jugs of shitty red wine knowing the unlikeliness of finishing them without throwing up, but the recklessness and the thought of a forgetful night on a toilet sounded great.

I went back and finished packing with the rest of them. Downstairs, Degan and Ned were hanging out and waiting with Kelly around a white iron grill table and matching chairs. A huge weeping willow, that dripped low, provided a cold shade. Sitting down next to Kelly, I joined the waiting game. Knowingly, Degan broke my imposed silence, "Hey Head, how come you aren't going to Greece with these guys?"

After smiling at Degan for his help, I had to ask, "Head?"

She looked wrinkled and concerned over Degan's question. Her mind appeared to be unsure on an approach, "Well my last name is Moorehead. Thus the nickname, Head which of course stems from more head." Her eyes left mine to give Degan a stern, motherly look.

"Head? I don't know if I can call you Head."

John joined us, sitting down next to Ned with a slap on his back and a huge grin. "Head, that's fucking absurd."

I laughed heartily. "Yeah, how come you aren't going, Head?" exaggerating the last word obnoxiously. "You guys want some wine." With the twist of the lid, I offered the first swig to Kelly and then to Degan. The bottle was being passed.

I looked at Degan sensing that I had an obligation to him. What was it, though? Then it just came out without even thinking it, "Why don't you guys come to Greece with us?" The question was so monumental that time plunged into a spacelessness, floating with the question mark remaining fixed above our heads. Degan slowly turned his head upward and then down at Ned. He shrugged, telling Ned exactly what he wanted and asking him if it was all right. Looking back at him, Ned half-cocked his head and raised an eyebrow in consideration. A long paused ensued leaving me with the answer. I gave the bottle to Ned in celebration.

"All right, now I've got to go," Kelly announced slightly perturbed.

"Fuck, but we've only got a half an hour until the train leaves. Let's get you tickets." Kelly and I ran off to the train station to get tickets, but the line was long, so we took our chances and made our choices. She went back and packed up her stuff hoping the line would dwindle. While waiting, John made the arrangements to meet Ned and Degan in two days at ten o'clock in the morning in Rome at the train station.

She ran up to gather her belongings when I saw it coming my way. Her fat puffy face and wavy blonde hair appeared around the corner of the entrance to the yard. She noticed and recognized me right away. She pointed and quickly whispered to her friend, "He is the one that puked in my room."

I contemplated hiding first. Then I looked around for an escape route. Nothing was attractive, except a tree trunk that was too skinny. I knew that denying her due was not the right way to go. By the time I had exhausted my possibilities, we were standing face to face. She began pointing her finger, "I've been waiting to tell you that was the most disgusting thing I have ever seen." Her fat on her face squashed with rage, recalling that first glance at what was causing the horrendous odor in her apartment.

Then she gave me a snotty "I beat you" look and head tilt. I gallantly let her have the moment. The puke and its smell probably were really gross. "Yeah, I'm sorry about it. I didn't even know that I did it."

"How could you not know?" in a parental scolding manner.

"Look, I didn't mean to make an excuse. It happened, I'm sorry. I probably cost you discomfort for a day or two. For that I am sorry and only that. I didn't create the problem to make you suffer. I feel no remorse of myself, only for you."

She didn't really understand, so she took the conversation as hers which is all that she was really after anyway, "Well, I am just glad that I finally got to tell you to your face. It is off of my chest."

"Good. I've got to go. Off to Greece you know. I'll send your regards to Erin."

Kelly was packed and among our group in minutes. "Are we ready?" she threw in an anchor woman's hard and tired toothful smile.

At the train station, John and I waited with Kelly on the long line to get tickets. "Hey, Don, we'd better get on. The train is leaving in five minutes. Kelly, we'll see you on it." John walked away as I looked at the line ahead of us. It didn't look favorable.

"Hey, Don if I miss it." She handed me a piece of paper with a cryptic address. "Stop by in Clausbourg."

I smiled, "Good luck, see you on board."

The train pulled out as John and I managed to capture seats. Italian trains were renown for their overcrowding. Luckily, we were still in France and still got seats. After a few stops, the train's aisles would be filled with obnoxious assholes.

The other four members of our gang sat in a compartment a few down from ours. I was glad for the separation. Both of our compartment's were completely full, promising the separation until Rome.

I got to looking at the people as the train tensed, ready to leave. John sat next to me by the window. Across from him was an old Italian man that smiled each time I looked his way. His brown sweater under his brown suit went well with his Fodor hat. Next to him was a Japanese or another variety of Asian tourist. He seemed scared and confused still wearing a blue winter-like jacket. The other two were a couple who seemed way past their prime and hated each other for it. I was sad, because the station was gone and no Kelly.

Just at that moment, I saw her lugging her Army bag past our cabin. I hopped up to help with a little too much excitement in my actions. My arms went up, with my palms facing her body, in a motioned that told her to stay in the hallway. I went out, "Hey, I can't believe you made it." I saw it in her eyes too, but was it for me or for Greece? "Tell the Chinese guy that you have reservations for this seat. He will never know. I don't think he knows any English or French."

"I can't."

"Come on. You will end up sleeping out in the corridor. There are no seats left, plus we have got the wine." She wrinkled up her face similarly to the woman whom I victimized with my puke, but with far less fatty wrinkles. "Come on."

"All right." She went up to him and played the part beautifully. She looked confused then checked the seat number twice and talked fast and confusingly. He just shrugged his shoulders and apologized with a bow. We laughed without shame.

Immediately, we dug into the wine. Passing it around with some leftover food, I was in such a good mood that I offered everything to everybody in our cabin until it was gone. The couple, looking at us with disgust that they should have been saving for themselves, answered crisply, "Non," while the old man took our leek. "I am so sick of leeks, I couldn't eat that thing anyway," was my answer to John's scornful look and hungry growl.

"Don, let's go out to dinner tomorrow. I'll buy this one, you the next. Fuck it, we'll put it on our Visa cards."

"Deal."

Quickly changing his lightness, John stared into Kelly with a long intermission, "So Kelly what is your goal in life? That's been our big question of the week."

"To fulfill the erotic."

"Wow." John leapt with unexpected joy, "that is the best one I have heard yet. Go on. Wow, out of nowhere."

"To fulfill the erotic isn't about sex, though. It is about fulfilling what one desires, to be completely and totally selfish and self-sufficient. I don't mean that in a money grabbing way. Too many people confuse wealth accumulation with selfishness. It is the opposite. Acquiring comfort is fine, but comfort only goes so far with wealth. At a certain point, usually the beginning of existence for most people, comfort goes out the door and impressing others is the sole motive. A bigger car, more expensive car, why? Prestige. A faster more expensive car, why? Prestige. I will buy a car that I desire, not for my neighbor.

"Selfishness is doing what you want to do without concerning others. When I have that, I will have reached my goal. I am still too egotistically selfless. Altruism is the downfall of society."

"Wow, altruism is the downfall of society." John looked like he had just had sex. I was still dreaming of her lips forcing out those words.

"What makes you say it in terms of erotic," I begged for more.

"Well erotic comes from desires that are at the edge of our fantasies. Erotic implies tearing down the walls of the reality and pushing it to the ends, the erotic end."

"I am a fan of both altruism and reality, if not I would hate myself. I am entrenched daily in both. My goal is a simple happiness. Happiness with one's self, but doing something for others can make one feel good about oneself. It depends on the motives. To impress others, I agree is bad, but to impress oneself is good. For example, I would rather go home, have dinner, watch football, have sex, then sleep for twelve hours. But if I forced myself not to do what I wanted and, let's say, feed food in a soup kitchen for the simple joy of helping, then I have performed altruism in a constructive, pure way. My cause and means helped me and accidentally helped others." I surprised myself with the clarity of a thought that I had never fully developed in my own head, let alone out loud, especially with my head spinning in wine.

"Sure, but if I might be so bold, you are lying to yourself with either your watching football or your working in a soup kitchen." She said it very matter of factly, without any malice or any doubt in my character, but the slighted conversation threw me back. She was right, but I wouldn't admit it. I tried not to show the truth and it must have worked. My deceit never appeared in her blue eyes.

John joined, "Both of you guys are fucked. I believe in the

extreme conflict working to produce the always better. Capitalism, relationships, anything; extreme conflict is the way to go. Without it, we all fall into mediocre pit of massive goo. For example, Democracy, not a true democracy, but the one we have, is fucked. Our government is based on compromise, no true winner or loser in our legislation. They compromise everything down to fuckin' water. Piece of mind or spirit, whatever you said, is a breeding ground for nonconfrontational mediocrity. Fuck.

"I can buy Head's idea of fulfilling the erotic, assuming that definitions of an erotic clash between forces which produces a higher level of whatever. Erotic fits in with my extreme concept. Don, your thoughts are nice, but too shallow. Dig a little deeper next time."

I laughed as he talked himself into a ball of introspective energy with fists ready to release it. His voice rose throughout causing a panic on everyone's face.

Bed time came, "Kelly why don't we share our seats?" I saw no response so I got nervous and added, "you put your head at that end, mine will be here. Unless my feet smell too bad."

We made a perfect rectangle. I felt a closeness to her that made me want to give her a hug and a kiss good night. I was too nervous, though. Instead, I fell lightly asleep with the wine confusing my dreams and preventing REM. From my light sleep, I woke up to find my hand caressing her leg. I whispered apologies, but heard no reply. I fell back asleep comforted in the fact that I wasn't caught, but desperate in not knowing if she was feeling the same way.

NINETEEN
Sitting Next to Expectations

Rome arrived at ten o'clock in the morning. I yawned and smelled my crusty, heavy, hangover breath. "Rome, never thought I would ever be in Rome. Boy my breathe smells like the rotten goo of the road kill deer that won't even be scraped up off of the road."

"On a warm summer day at that."

"Exactly."

Kelly shook her head, "Wonder what's doin' in Rome?"

"Can't say I really ever wanted to come here. I guess we've got the coliseum and all that Catholic shit, like the Vatican and the Sistine Chapel. We need *Let's Go*. Where is Rusty? Now that he's got his new toy, he doesn't need us."

"Bastard."

At the station we met up with the others. Of course, Josh had planned our day with the others. "First a place to stay, then we go to the Vatican, then the Sistine Chapel, then cap it off with the Coliseum."

"Does any of that include bathroom breaks?" in a half-hearted effort at a joke. "Just kidding," and I gave Josh a little jab to the chest and wrestled around with him. The morning was beginning to feel a little bit better.

Finding a place to stay was as difficult as usual. If you had used *Let's Go*, you'd better make reservations, if the place took them, or get there first thing in the morning. We went to a few places and they

131

were all full or had raised their rates since landing the dubious distinction of being listed in *Let's Go.* What a job that must have been, working for *Let's Go.*

We finally found a little pension with empty beds about ten blocks away from the train station. It was empty because the place was so far away from the station and was not on the way to anything else. The rooms were just extra rooms that an elderly couple, who owned two floors of a walk-up brownstone -like building, had. They kept one floor to themselves and the other to rent for ten bucks a bed. They had seven beds left which was perfect. The three men had to share a room with some woman whom I never saw more of than her luggage, while the four women got a room to themselves.

The place was very sterile and sharp, not sharp as in good looking, but sharp as in sharp, after World War II prefab thrown together in mass, lacking all form and flow, and not much thought to the visual architecture. Its form never quite followed its function.

We threw our stuff down and started out against the day. First thing was the Vatican. The place was huge. The weekend before Easter inaugurated the shape of an overzealous excitement. The place was just massive. We walked into the main church, maintaining a boy/girl separation.

Josh spoke to me, "this place is too much. All of this ornate stuff is just too gaudy for me."

"No doubt. Just think of all of the hungry people they could have fed." I didn't need much to get me going on religion.

"Instead, they built and spent all of this stuff to celebrate their grandness. What grandness? Filthy rich, spoiled bastards. They preach suppression and abstaining, but for what? I'll tell you, so they can get their hands on more of the cookies in the jar," John summed up everyone's exact sentiments.

"The more I see the origins of Christianity, the more I wonder." I looked at the Baroque pulpit flowing from above.

"Judaism is where it's at," Josh staked proudly.

"It's all the same. Hey, get under the crucifix, Josh. This will be one to take home to the boys." The boys were our friends back home, who were mostly Catholic and prejudiced against the Jews. They mocked Josh and his religion, mercilessly. Josh never minded or never paid them any mind, considering all of them as dumb-ass, pot heads, so he willing took the picture with a chuckle.

Next was the Sistine Chapel. Another bus ride got us to its sacred gates. We saw the sign with a list of entrance fees, "Five bucks to get into this place," John cursed the sign then sighed.

"And it's even under renovation." I remembered the talk back at school about how much brighter the renovated side was then the original, but it wasn't interesting enough to sink five bucks into seeing.

"Churches really shouldn't charge, maybe donations, but to charge seems very exclusive." Tricia said walking away, "I'm not going."

"I can't afford five bucks," my budgeted mind perused my empty pockets.

"I don't want to afford five bucks." John cursed the sign again threatening to spit on it. "They do this shit in Spain to. Don, remember when we snuck into those churches with the large groups, maybe we could do it here," my nod lied. The failed phone call to Kristie the night before our Spanish coup was the pain that rung.

"Who cares? Michelangelo was just another temperamental asshole artist who only worked for the money and glory."

Kelly added, "I don't know about that, he was on his back for how many years and he didn't get paid shit."

"Well whatever, I'm not going in. I'll hang out here." John left the sign to join Tricia who had already crossed the street.

"Well, I really want to see it. I bet it looks pretty cool, too famous to pass up."

"I'll be out here too. We'll be waiting for you on those steps over there." I joined the opposition.

I followed the gang to the steps where we would meet the others later. They weren't really steps, but a gradual decline broken up by a step every fifteen feet. The brick laid path was wide enough to be a street and held park benches and trees on each side. We laid down in the middle of it all and fell asleep. Nobody spoke or woke up until the others had returned.

"How was it?" I looked up to see Josh blocking my sun.

"Amazing, too bad you guys couldn't go."

"Oh well, what's next, Rusty."

"I want Italian ice cream," the Bobbsey twins rang out in unison.

"First Ice cream, then I thought we would walk to the coliseum. There's lots of Roman ruins along the way."

"Sounds good."

We saw Roman ruins and the Coliseum. Nothing too exciting, but the fact that you could say that you saw them. I even willingly forked over the money to see the coliseum. I would at least have something to write about in a postcard to my parents.

The coliseum was funny. You got inside, looked over the edge, and that was it. Maybe you read about how they filled up the bottom with water and had fights in boats, but that was it. I guess the age of the thing makes you wonder and feel impressed, but it didn't do it for me.

Instead, I sat back and wondered why old things were so cool. Everyone lived in the past. It was a horrible cycle to get stuck wishing for yesterday or even yesteryear. I figured it was because memories can mold the reality anyway you want and make it so sweeter, but I didn't really know. Everything old was harder, cleaner, more fun, more this, more that, less that, but it all boiled down to horseshit. It was just like my dad saying kids aren't the same anymore, and he was a teacher. I think he was the one that changed. Same as it ever was. Same as it ever was.

Then it dawned on me that I and everyone around me neglected the present. We made plans to see the past. Planning tomorrow to get a feel of yesterday puzzled me forcing me to walk out, bummed and rethinking my motto for life.

As planned, we went out to dinner which wound up being a mess. The food, supposedly real Italian cuisine, sucked. It was pricy and average tasting. Dividing the bill didn't work for us, either. Everyone got pissed because some had more and some had less. I hated when you couldn't just split the bill. What was a few dollars between friends? I guessed a lot, because everyone was griping. Our big traveling entourage was finally beginning to wear thin. John, of course, made the biggest scene with everyone, including the waiter. He said the food sucked and didn't want to leave a tip. I put down some money after he left, unable to not reward the man for his work, regardless of its quality.

"Let's get some wine." Nobody even looked at me, let alone gave me an enthusiastic response. Instead, it was bed time.

TWENTY

Long Walk in A Black Gown

The trek to Greece was going to be forever. First, you had to get to a small shithole town named Brindisi. You left Rome at ten in the morning and didn't arrive in Brindisi until five in the afternoon. Next was the ferry, which took the entire night and morning. Then, a train took you to Athens and arrived pretty late at night. All in all the trip took about thirty-six hours.

I woke up early and went to a travel agent to get tickets with Head. With the trains and ferries included, the trip was more expensive then flying, but taking the ferry was hopefully going to be twice the fun. She spent almost all of the money her grandmother had saved during a long lifetime, but remained undaunted. She was ready for anything. The rest of us were set with our Eurorail passes with an additional billion lire docking fee which equaled ten bucks.

Head and I scurried back to the pension in order to pack and get food supplies. With only minutes to spare, the entire gang of seven walked along the train hoping to catch a glimpse of Degan and Ned. The last car was in sight, our doubts were quickly fading into reality.

We hopped on the last train and there they were, sitting there with dumbass grins raised above newspapers, "Doubted, didn't you? We were really testing to see if you would walk all the way to the end." Laughter ensued.

Our heads hung in respectful shame to their grins. Kelly, John, and I dunked ourselves whole into the thrill of destiny. The rest didn't really care either way, but I knew of their necessity to the scheme.

After a boring day of travel, the coming coast hinted with the dead smell of fishing. "Do we get off here?"

"The line keeps going. I don't know." Josh looked through the several pages in *Let's Go* on traveling to and from Greece.

"I'll ask…next stop it is," Tricia was wrong. Brindisi was gone and slipped farther north.

In a panic of fears, the next stop appeared hours away on the map. "Wait a minute. Are Head's tickets still valid? Will we miss the ferry? How far is the next stop? Blah, blah, blah." Their voices sprinted past comprehension.

My faced turned red with absolute anger that was besieged by a horrible temper and by the repetition of no patience at the most random of times. I kept it in and took a few deep breathes, but my neck shook. Wondering how we could do something so incredibly stupid, I walked away from the bumbling pack.

John followed, "This sucks. Man, you look pissed." He whispered, "You all right?"

"Yeah, I can't stand it. I'm going to explode. Traveling during the day has shredded my patience." The black bubble subsided in seconds with the conversation, "I'm much better now. Thanks."

"What do you think?"

"We get off at the next stop and turn around. If Head's ticket isn't good, they will kick us off at the next stop, Brindisi. Dumb asses. If we miss the ferry, that's when you see me really lose my cool," was followed by a hocker trapped in a threatening cackle.

"Well, let's think. If we miss it, fuck it. We'll blow these fools off and go to Sicily."

"Good idea," the consequences of Sicily with Head played tricks on my mind. The anger was reapproaching in acceptance.

"They've got better ruins anyway. It's probably easier to pose nude on them to." John lived our dream.

The crowd came back our way, out of our seats waiting by the door at the end of the compartment. In the distance, Tricia was overheard scheming with Head about passing her Eurorail back to Head after the conductor looked at hers. I told everybody that it didn't matter, but nobody got my point. "If not, Sicily. Fuzzy me." John spoke in an obvious code, leaving me without a choice. So I had to fuzzy him.

As it turned out, the conductor didn't even check and we had about four hours to kill before the ferry left. We loaded up on supplies in a huge grocery store. I bought lots of bread, cheese, and crackers. To wash it down, I gathered up two jugs of wine. Ned looked at me astonished, "you're going to take wine?"

I said snobbishly, "Dude, of course, we try not to travel without it, like American Express."

Degan wouldn't let my attitude slide, "Just two?" and ambled away.

I smiled and grabbed two huge jugs and told John to grab two additional small one. "For tonight, we shall drink."

Getting on the ship was a huge bureaucratic nightmare, check after guard after check. Unseasoned water travelers, we staked a huge corner on the rear of the upper unsheltered deck. Only a few weirdoes joined us, but logic escaped in the post-warmth of early evening.

Immediately, we began to frolic in our food and wine, sitting and bullshitting in a circle. "What sea is this, Adriatic, Aegean, or Mediterranean?" Everyone had their guess. Others joined in our party to create a nice mix of twenty weary kids.

A brother and sister, who must have been given a whole bunch of money and a Eurorail pass, introduced themselves to me. They were as wholesome as a Maine night and as fucked-up as the Maine people. Extremely goofy, the two sat smiling, but never laughing at anything, except each other and their joys of incest.

Another group of three women, who were reputed lesbians from Canada, also joined us. Nothing really made them reputed lesbians, but their short hair, manly manners, and our discriminating imagination. Mostly, it was John's imagination that played with the lesbian idea. Overly fascinated in talking to them, he dragged Ned along with him for laughs.

Degan, Head, and I smoked and finished off a lot of the wine. They remembered old Dead shows, his brother's acoustic guitar jams, and getting stoned. I watched and listened to understand them more. I concluded out loud, "Degan, I think you are the most laid back person I've ever met."

"No doubt," said Head.

"Untrue. Until, I can fall asleep standing up, that's when I'm laid back. I did once, but haven't since. I was talking to my sister. Next thing I know, she's nudging me. It was in high school, but not since. I have lost it."

The night got blurry real fast. I went down to the bathroom to contemplate puking or shitting. Wrapped in the cool comfort of the porcelain against my ass, I remembered that John had disappeared. I figured that he was fucking around with one of the Canadian lesbians which forced me to put my head between my legs to puke, but nothing came.

Then, John came booming in the room laughing at the mirror.

"John?" I peered through the little slit in the door.

"Don? Are you shitting?"

"Yeah, or puking. Waiting to see which one will make the door stand still. What is so fuckin' funny?"

"Nothing man, I'll tell you later." He turned away and his voice and laugh was muffled. He was talking to someone else when the door slammed. Then he was gone leaving me with my intestinal dilemma.

I went back to the deck, unsuccessful, to find Degan arguing philosophically with some bushy-haired, blonde kid, who was probably years older, but didn't shave yet. Next, I went over to Kelly who was standing by the rail watching the black ocean. She bought me a beer.

"Man I'm fucked-up. I tried to puke, but no go. This beer feels good, though."

"Yeah, I'm pretty fucked-up too. What is Degan doing now? Get him over here." She bought another beer and showed it to him as bait.

"Degan, you pussy. Shut up and let's get to work on this beer." He turned and had the devil in his eye. I actually shuddered as his eyes became pointed red and pulsated. He drank in silence and commanded me to follow.

We went to the No Duty Shop, going straight for the liquors. "It's so expensive in Europe, we might as well buy it without the tax." He bought some shitty brand of whiskey for fifteen bucks. I chipped in six bucks, but regretted going into my pocket.

"Let's find John and Ned to get some help on this," was my plea. Obliging my last will, he let me look everywhere for John and we even did our best reconnaissance imitation, running and covering each other as we spied on all of the rooms. It grew old to the delight of the passengers who were still awake. He was nowhere and probably lost overboard for good.

Ned was still on top and drank with us only to get Degan off of his back, but mostly he ignored us. After a few big gulps, I had reached my limit as my whiskey-stained puke hovered around the top of my throat. The rest of the night became a test of my ability to outwit Degan with fake chugs, as he alone continued to put dents into the submerging level, whose credit partially went wrongfully to me.

"Look Degan, no more. I have been bested. I can't drink anymore. I'm going to boot." The disappearing water rushed up against the stained iron and spun around looking good and white, but it made me feel like shit in its black colorless white. My stomach was begging. Compassionately, he smiled calmly at me, but the devil in his eyes remained. His lips kept going upward, reaching for the crevices of his nose. In his rejoicing red costume, he held the lid of the whiskey and contemplated and compared it to his fingernails for awhile. Then, looking back at me, he threw it overboard, the second grandest gesture in my life. I took a deep swig then another and spit it over the edge and yelled with vengeful pain.

I lost the grand gesture a few minutes later and started passing the bottle to anyone besides Degan to help me out. The level didn't move and Head wouldn't have anything to do with it or me.

Luckily, Degan got caught up somewhere else and never came back. I was left alone with Kelly for the first time since we bought tickets in the morning. It was my second chance with this gorgeous woman hidden in a baggy pair of ripped jeans and a whole bunch of extra large flannels which protected her from the freezing salt air.

"I was hoping to stay the night up here, but it's way too cold. I would love to stay awake all night digging the stars."

"Yeah, I'm just drunk." That's all I could say. Fortunately, I was too scared to talk and make an ass out of myself. "I'm just too drunk," conceded my defeat in some way and relieved me in another. Degan and the booze had stolen my attention and purpose away.

"Let's go find somewhere to sleep," she grabbed everyone's stuff and went below deck.

Looking for a good spot to sleep, I kept scanning for Josh who was nowhere. He probably was pissed at me for blowing him off or something, but I was completely convinced not to take a chance and leave Kelly's side.

Most of the seats were taken, but a few by the bathrooms were free. Looking, Kelly finally saw Josh, Lynn, Jen, and Tricia sleeping on a table. Ned was by himself asleep on the floor in some corner while John and Degan were dead somewhere unknown. Degan probably fell in and someone probably got pissed at John, killing him.

Head and I were safe and laid next to each other across a row of four plastic chairs, like the ones in airports. It actually wasn't that bad. Somehow the black suddenly lifted from my eyes and entered my head. It was morning and I felt horrible. I woke up scared and looked around to find Kelly sleeping peacefully, her face pressed together against her bent arm and her lips pouting out. Her lips moved slightly in and out until I got lost wondering if I would ever get the courage or the right opportunity to lay my own lips on them. The sigh went downward until I felt my penis expand from the need to pee and her lips' movements. Peeing appealed to me more than masturbation, so I got up and pissed.

On the way, I found our luggage untouched and John sleeping next to it, still no Degan. The ship circled around gradually forcing me upstairs. The rest of the group was already back on deck into the position we had claimed last night and bundled up allowing the early sun to soak their faces. The sun smiled and said nine o'clock.

I went back down, woke up Head, and carried everyone's luggage on deck. John stirred and followed incoherently and fell back to sleep. I turned to speak to Head and caught her look for a moment. The blonde hair was flying frantically emphasizing her bed head. With her head tilted back, the sun captured her eyes and turned their colors to a rich light blue, better than the deep ocean's. Holding her skin and lips tight against the wind, her trance was broken with my eager mutterings, "Hey, did you happen to find Degan?"

She took off with the energy I never had, but always needed. Nothing could stop or ever damper her thirst. She bolted ahead leading me through every imaginable corridor until we set eyes upon his decrepit body clutching onto the empty bottle of whiskey.

He laid slumped in the corner with the guys he had been arguing with the night before. The bottle reappeared in his opened eyes as he laid staring at us with his lone movement being the heavy heaving of his chest. "Wow, he's still asleep. That's nuts."

"Sleeping with his eyes open, that's freaky. Degan…Degan," I savagely shook him.

He moved startled and gained his composure after a wipe of the crusty hangover on his lips. "What's up?"

"We are all up top. We've got your stuff."

He looked around and had a hearty laugh, "Wow, what happened to me?"

"Degan," my head shook, "last I saw, you had thrown the cap

to the whiskey overboard. I tried to keep up, but you wanted more. I gladly lost your wrecking ball after that."

"Whiskey bottle? I remember buying it and then boom, blank."

"Dude, no idea, but you had something in your eyes last night that wouldn't let you stop."

We went up top, laughing in the blissful memories of not remembering.

John was awake and talking to Josh. They were doubled over laughing. "What's going on?" I interrupted.

"Nothing," they unconvincingly repeated while glancing back and forth at Head's ears and then themselves. She got the hint and left to watch the water and the Greek islands slip to and fro.

"You've got to listen to John's story. Go ahead and start over for these guys."

John blushed and caught his breathe. He started with the usual disclosures. "All right, you've got to keep it quiet. You are going to think I'm crazy, but this is what happened last night.

"Okay. You remember the crazy lesbians from Canada. Well, I was hanging out with them. I knew the one liked me. The tall one with short, black hair. You know, the one that spoke like a man. Somehow, I ended up alone with her up here. Next thing I know we are kissing. She's getting all crazy and rubbing me everywhere. Well, I started feeling guilty so I tried to dog her. That's when I saw you, Don, in the bathroom. I was all set to blow her off, but she followed me into the bathroom. So I stuck with it," his shoelaces dangled against the green astro turf.

"We went into a boiler room. You should of seen the place; two floors with black grates, grey oily machines pumping, and hot steam everywhere, a really weird place. I thought I was back in the medieval period. It was so incredibly sexual. Anyway, we start going at it with each other. She rips off my clothes and stripped herself down totally. I said, 'I won't have sex with you, but you can give me a blow job, instead.' She said that she wanted to taste all of me and started to stroke my hard on.

"I almost came, but I had to make her go down on me. She sucked me dry, swallowed and everything. Get this, she says, 'man, you taste funky, like Paprika.' No shit. So she starts rubbing her clit and giving me a crazed look. I'm ready to fuck her when Cindy suddenly hits me. I look at her and say vially, 'I want to shave you',"
John stuck out his lips and shoulders as he repeated his line in a good Mick Jagger imitation motion and face.

"I ran back to find my bag, it's no longer on deck, so I find you sleeping downstairs and get out my shaving cream. I even woke you up Don, but you were out of it. I ran back to her. I'm standing over top of her and her pussy is just dripping wet. I'm shaking up the can. Shwish, shwish, shwish." He did an accompanying shaking of his hand with a pretend can of shaving cream.

"I'm just about ready to do it, when some guy comes in. He must of worked there. He started yelling, so I walked over. I begged him to give me a minute with that all knowing smile. He agreed. So I walked back over, but something came over me. I don't know what, not really guilt towards my girlfriend, but maybe a self-respect. I told her that we had to go. She got up and dressed and as we walked out she looked at me and said, 'well I guess I know now to never suck a guy off without having him eat me first.'"

He beamed. I said, "Come on."

"All true, Don. Crazy night, huh?" his eyebrows went up.

Everyone just laughed and shook their heads and laid in the increasingly warmer sun. Greece, its little islands, and sea gulls captured our eyes. The islands had amazing thrusts of rock with beautiful beaches and trees and houses stuck in the middle of nowhere. I pictured Greek tycoons flying their helicopters there and to shore, sometimes taking their speedboats to the main island. The water was so deep, innocent, and blue.

I sat in joy with Kelly, "This would be the life, no cars, no people, no authority, no…" I could think of lots of other no's that I would want, but stopped. "Well maybe not. I would have to be rich and that's not something I'm striving towards."

"What are you striving for?"

"To be that seagull." It flew in circles hundreds of yards away.

"Sounds good."

"Well I guess the life's probably not as glamorous as Jonathan Livingston, but…"

"No nothing ever is."

"So what are you striving to be?"

"Who cares!"

"Uhm, that sounds even better."

Shore finally came and we went looking for the train to Athens. Tricia, Lynn, and Jen left during the night for Corfu, leaving Josh greatly outnumber and slightly scared. I laid back to watch the mass of people enjoying the day. Dancing to Dead tunes on his Walkman on top of an exhaust pipe, Degan's body wiggled in all of its glory.

I felt good, I felt relaxed, I felt excited. The possibilities were endless.

TWENTY-ONE
Lord, Buy Me Something Nice

Greece, fucking Greece.

The trains in Greece were ancient, full of creaky noises and worn away cushions. They puttered along stopping at every possible station. To look at the faces of our accompanying travelers revealed their long, tired, ugly, hungry, and anxious stares which opposed our own sharp, cheap, and thirsty looks. No natives were in sight, only faces like ours and those trying to sell or steal from us. Every couple of minutes some English speaking guy came and tried to convince us that his hotel was the best. Each tried a unique pitch; cheapest, most American-like, best location, most native; anything to strike the right chord.

Only a few of them were actually Americans, the rest tried to use their English or similar accents to underline the exotic natures of their hotel. Already with our minds made up, they became boring and annoying. Our decision was a man in his fifties with an French accent who was dressed in safari type khakis, red bandanna, and desert hat. His hotel's brochure, that boasted over a hundred tapes of American albums at their bar and a free beer to boot, was hard to pass up.

Josh, Head, and myself sat in one row with the others up ahead, but in sight. Josh was trying to drop little hints and complaints about our plans or lack thereof for Athens. It was getting more obvious and obnoxious.

I generally agreed with him, but didn't want to hear it. "Josh, you're only bummed because there are no women here for you to chase. No sympathy from me."

"Untrue, Don." He looked at Head and at the hair in front of him. "All right, so what? You are the same way."

"What?" I also looked at Head but then down at the tiled floor.

"I fully admit to meeting women as my biggest concern. I don't get any excitement out of sitting around drinking and listening to music, but you're no better."

"Come on, every time we went out you had to go somewhere to meet chicks and they were chicks." Kelly allowed my chauvinistic slip and nodded in agreement. "We would drive around all night trying to find where women were stationed. I enjoyed hanging out with the 'Buddies' and drinking and circle jerking."

"Bullshit, you came out with me every time." He contemplated his next accusation. At first, he looked out the darkening window which changed his mind. Then, confidence grew back into his forehead. He scratched his brillo pad, red hair and flexed his biceps, his famous pipe shot. "I understand why you are trying to convince me that you are above that," he looked right into her eyes and said, "with her in our conversation."

He had me and was right on target, but I wouldn't concede him the victory and tried to conceal it in my face. I laughed to give myself time to think, but it kept blank. "Yeah, right," the tone was sarcastic. "I try to impress only myself. The day I start trying to impress women is the beginning of my death." The lies sounded good, but I was still too embarrassed to look towards Head.

Josh and I stared each other down for a second and declared a truce. The train rattled along with Athens only about an hour away now. The crimson dawn was quickly slipping to an oppressive violet. The ocean switched sides of the train and lapped right beneath me, stretching out its arms to welcome. Keeping to myself, I contemplated how the water switched sides until Athens was announced by a fat and messy conductor. I was grateful for the view, but the geographical implications destroyed my hopes and eagerness to be intelligent.

Outside of the station Degan found the safari man who did the best sales job. "How far, sir?"

"Only about fifteen minutes that way." His manner of pointing fit his outfit.

"Lead the way, Pepé Le Pew."

Always a salesman, in forty minutes he presented our five dollar a night room. We first saw the bar which was beautiful with picnic tables and benches arranged around the nooks and crannies of the room. The long wooden bar had a big metal backing, that acted like a mirror, enlarging the room. A man told us where our rooms would be and gave us two keys for two rooms with three beds each. He explained some rules, but nobody listened. We were already making our way up the stairs before he was done. Josh, John, and I took the room upstairs while the others snaked through a long, narrow hallway on the first floor.

The rooms were no Best Westerns, but the sheets seemed fairly clean and new. Ours had a sink and a toilet fitting in a corner and the beds around it. The sink and toilet cost a buck fifty more a night, so Josh took dibs on it before anyone else could make any other suggestions.

I threw my backpack on the bed then let my body follow it. The paint on the ceiling was chipping away, unveiling several cracks in the roof. The rain, leaking through, hit my face waking me from my short dream with the realization of the fakeness that took awhile to sink in. The dark faded wallpaper zigzagged where the ceiling and walls met. The nicest place, that we had stayed in yet, spun around our slumped bodies.

Josh was washing his face and brushing his teeth. John spoke, "I can't believe it, fucking Greece. It has been amazing so far, perfect weather, perfect company. I'm amazed that something has finally worked out for us." He paused and looked at the design of the wallpaper and noticed the same bad technique of putting it up that I did. "I think this is the best place we've stayed in yet. Beats the fuck out of Holiday Inns. So, Don what's up? I feel like I haven't talked to you since Rome."

"Yeah, kinda weird. You have been hitting it off with Ned pretty well. It's like you guys grew up together."

"I don't believe in much, but I have a weird feeling about the unique fit that we all have." We both looked at Josh drying his face and hands. He wiped away the little white crusty remains of the toothpaste. "Like it was always meant to be. You and Head and Degan, I don't know what is going on with you guys. Degan is pushing you dangerously close . Plus you and Head are in love or something. What's up with that?"

I laughed at his unconscious slip to a favorite Cheers episode. "Nothing man, I just think she's cool. Still, I've got to go home to Kristie."

"Ummm," he grunted. "I haven't heard that name in awhile."

"That's why we are having so much fun. When you first get out of the cage, you got to test those unused legs and run wild."

Josh yawned, sighed, and moaned, "I'm beat."

"Yeah, me too. Let's get that free beer."

"Agreed."

Josh rolled his eyes. "All right, but bedtime is just around the corner."

I admired his desire and discipline to see a city like you were supposed to. He badly wanted to get a fresh start on tomorrow, but wondered about its possibilities. "Hey, there might be chicks down in the bar," was my only consolation to him.

"Don't start Don." He laughed at his twisted thoughts, "You know, you've got a good point."

"Tonight we ride."

We checked out the others' room, then went for the bar. Their room was an exact replica, but had windows in place of the toilet and sink.

We got our beer and sat together. I wanted to test Kelly some more that night. I don't know exactly why, but I had a sadistic side to see how far someone would go, especially women. If I couldn't go as far as to fart or say cunt, then I knew for sure they were not for me.

Actually, the word cunt really bothered me. Women could say cock, but not cunt. They could say vagina under their breath, but never cunt. Why? If someone offered me a good explanation, I would buy it. It was a word describing a part of anatomy. Sure, it was slang and derogatory, but so what. Four letters forming a syllable was four letters forming a syllable. There was no difference between cock and cunt.

"John tell these guys your story about the ferry."

He paused and blushed. He was anxious for the opportunity to tell the others about how cool he was and how cool his experiences were, but, "I don't think I should with a girl present."

Kelly picked her head from reading the carvings on the picnic tables. "First off, I am a woman and secondly you don't think I have lived your story and then some or, at least, heard better in my day?"

She was passing, so he began. Degan and Ned picked up the list of the American albums available at the bar to listen while Josh looked at his unwanted beer, bored, but interest was gained after Kelly's quick commentary.

He went through the story very animatedly. He used his hands, torso, head, and eyes to highlight every little detail. He was fun to watch. As I listened to how the little details changed, I wondered about the truth. Hey, it didn't matter, it was just a funny story. He paused in embarrassment and apologized to Kelly, every so often, annoying her with the extra attention that he threw her way.

After the story, Josh apologized for being so tired and went up to bed. By this time we had had several beers, but not too many. A perfect hum existed numbing my sense of tiredness. We began to meet the others in the bar.

I got stuck with a group of Californians. After my last experience with the guy who fuzzied in Nice, I worried about what was being raised in that state. However, that guy was nothing compared to these clowns. John began to grill all of their dumb thoughts out of them, so he and Ned could get some laughs. Most of them were annoyed, but two remained, finding him a challenge. It became absurdly comical.

The couple, who remained, was made up of a nameless man and woman. The man was generic looking; part on the side of a neat head with neat clothes. He was neat. The woman was a long, blonde haired, bubbly bimbo. They went to some architecture school in California. About ten of them were traveling together to see the architectural gems of Europe. Dreaming of being an architect since I was little, I was disheartened at the prospects for such an interesting art filled with such dickheads.

The woman readily gave her view on life, "Everything comes down to money. Everything everybody does is for money." She babbled on and on about how righteous she was. John was reeling her in making her look dumber and dumber with each reply.

She flabbergasted me, "So how much would it cost me to fuck you?" Startled by my bluntness, she played with her long, straight hair and ignored. "Seriously, how much would it cost me to fuck you?" I was aware of John and Ned laughing hysterically, but I wanted a serious answer, so I didn't acknowledge them. "You said everything is about money, so how much?"

She got very serious and contemplated. She hadn't thought about that twist, but considered it a legitimate question. "I don't know."

I blew a deep, wicked breath that vibrated my lips and made an assimilation of a mocking laugh, "A hundred, a thousand, or what?"

"The actual transaction of money cheapens that gesture automatically." She looked so proud. "It would have to be in form of a gift."

"Dinner, flowers, what?"

"I'm not cheap."

I repeated her mocking motion with my shoulders and neck. "A car?"

"Yeah, definitely for a car. It also depends on my liking of the person. The more I like them, the cheaper it gets. For you it would have to be a car."

"It almost makes me wish I had a car, so I could make you put your…" I changed my mind on saying cunt. "body where your mouth is."

"You wouldn't even be a good lay."

"A good lay?" I watched her lashes flick, each time revealing less and less in her eyes. "A good lay, that's hilarious. You are the sickest person I have ever met." My voice sharpened, "What the fuck goes through your mind? You are going to die sad and ugly. Your sad, painful death has already begun. You amaze me."

She tried to gain her poise backing away from my advancing rage. "Naive and stupid," she shook her head. Her friend came to her defense by striking up conversation with John and Ned.

I ignored their conversation, trying to avoid any more conflicts. Somehow, John got this guy to do the stupidest thing I have ever seen. John held a can of Noxema which Head had given us to help our dry, burnt skin. "I bet you can't spin this thing on its side with your finger."

He contemplated the dare without even wondering why he was about to do it. He looked at all three of us proudly. "Give it to me."

He did it. John looked at Ned trying not to laugh. The laughter squeaked out as a high-pitched fraudulent giggle. How could this guy not feel stupid? I searched every inch of his face and posture to find these thoughts, but nothing showed, except for his pride for spinning a tin can on its side.

"You can't do it with two fingers." John handed him the can trying to look as serious and challenging as possible. He did it, again. Then something rushed through his body. I was waiting for some kind of explosion. John and Ned both sensed it and their smiles left their faces. He held the can high and tightly showing John the Noxema cover. He looked at them so strangely and then paused, poising himself to speak. We waited anxiously. Then suddenly he thrust the can back down to the table, held it on its side, and announced, "I'm going for three." Holding up three fingers secured the most moronic scene I had ever witnessed in real life. I felt like Monty Python was writing the script for the night.

I doubled over with laughter and awe. I couldn't even watch the feat of spinning a tin can with three fingers. I leapt up roaring. The whole place stopped, wondered, and watched. My body shaked across the room until I found Head talking to another couple on the opposite end of the room.

I interrupted and told the story. The recognition that it wasn't meant for words came about half way through the story forcing me to stop and excuse myself for interrupting. With patience, I sat still and quiet until the couple left Head and myself alone.

"Don, do you think I swear too much?"

The question caught me off guard and I instinctively answered no. She explained to me about the disgust she had felt towards those two, especially the woman and her constant use of the word fuck. She also hated the man's views on everything. "Another conservative fuck with his eyes and mind shut to everything outside of his nice, little room. I did it again. I said fuck again. Damn it."

She seemed so affected and concerned that tears seemed eminent. A pity for her confused mind, that twisting her ideals and behaviors over something so unimportant as words, tickled my nose. Trying to fit the world into her intentions was not an easy task and was making her scared and sad. Her concerned depression was so sudden and untimely. I couldn't say much of importance. "Yeah this whole fucking place is weird."

"Hey let me know every time I say fuck, okay?"

"Okay. Let's go to bed, my mind is tired."

Degan was face down on the bar sleeping. Ned and John had already made their reprieve. We woke him up and placed him into bed. As he shuffled out through the door, the bartender began yelling at him about the tip he didn't leave. He kept mumbling apologies about wanting to listen to Rush. "I proclaim myself a Rushhead. I am sorry," were his last words as he fell into bed.

I looked away from Kelly, "Goodnight."

"Yeah, we better get some sleep." By the time she had finished saying that I was as far away from her as possible.

Scared, like a beaten child, my heart thumped and pushed everything to my loins. I didn't want to confuse myself anymore, so my eyes stayed down after I placed half of my body outside of the door. "Hey, sleep with the angels." It was a saying that one of my roommates from school always used. I liked it, so I stole it.

Her growing grin showed her top teeth and formed crinkles around her eyes. I felt so much that I barely made out her reply, "You too, Donald." I hated the name Donald.

I fell asleep and did sleep with the angels that night.

TWENTY-TWO

Slippery Straw

We woke up, once again, to Josh tugging at our feet flipping through his dog-eared pages of *Let's Go*. I felt surprisingly good, even though I couldn't remember the number of beers that I had finished. The memories of the last few being forced down my throat flipped my stomach for a few moments until I got the courage to get out of bed.

We went back to the bar and read the breakfast menu. I counted my money and had spent too much last night, but I was still close to plan. Thankfully, a cup of coffee loaded with sugar extended an additional spurt. As I counted to ten before stopping the white flow of sugar, John gazed at me like I was insane or stupid. The sugar floated on the top for a second until the white went to brown then black winding up somewhere below the surface. I put my head down close to the cup and listened to my spoon grind the sugar against the bottom. The deep aroma of old coffee stung my nose helping unblock my snots. I breathed deep and free.

Josh went and got the rest of the gang. All six of us had the continental breakfast which was only a dollar twenty-five. Our plates went down with a thud as the bartender from the night before kept a steady watch on Degan. He ignored and pulled a cigarette from the breast pocket of a plaid flannel shirt.

"What a night, huh?" We all laughed at the picture of his face down on the bar and his heaving shoulders while he slept oblivious to the harsh words of the lady wiping up the bar everywhere, but where he slept.

We filled in Josh about the dumb ass Californians. Again, it proved much funnier in person, but the three of us who actually witnessed the event uncontrollably laughed while John repeatedly performed his impression of the guy going for "Three."

Josh took control after breakfast and walked us through Athens on route to the Parthenon. Stopping at markets, I indulged and bought myself a leather hat for ten dollars and a pair of mukluk socks for two bucks. The hat reminded me of something Jim Morrison would wear. So I took off my shirt and paraded down the street doing my best James Dean swagger. I swung between Morrison and Dean singing "L.A. Woman," like Elvis, and saying "well, then there…" like Elvis.

We walked through food markets and got the cheapest food ever imaginable. We loaded up on olives, bread, meat, and cheese. Our future looked good.

Head, who was a strict vegetarian, forced us through a meat and fish market where they slaughtered the animals in front of you. An old woman snapped a chicken's neck and handed the still jerking animal over to her customer. "If you guys can walk through this and still eat meat, then eat meat. But to go through life not knowing what happens to them is not fair." Her tone was harsh and critical. Nobody dared to argue, but no one was affected enough not to eat the lunch meat we had already bought.

Josh leaned over and conceded, "She's for you." He had known all of my latest string of girlfriends, who were vegetarians, and not liked any of them. He also knew that I couldn't help but to fall head over heels for one.

As we made our way through the buying crazed crowd, I wondered what would happen if everyone all of a sudden saw us foreigners and decided they hated us enough to kill us. We were submerged in what seemed to be thousands of little olive skin heads yelling orders everywhere. We were the coffee bean that sticks out so sorely in a glass of sambucca.

Atop of the mountain which housed the Parthenon, we paused for a moment pondering the greatness and sadness that had taken place so many years before in the Ancient Greek societies. The place was much more effective than anything Rome had to offer.

I tried to sneak into the park without paying and got busted. The guard yelled at me feverishly. I showed the sad, desperate face that

I possessed and he took pity. He used sign language to tell me, "I won't let you in, but try the other gate." I thanked him with a nod and motioned to the others, who were already in, that I would find them inside.

The Parthenon was our goal for the trip and we had finally succeeded. Like any other monumental goal, achieving it was always anticlimactic. Our biggest excitement came when John reminded me of posing nude.

Ropes were everywhere making posing on it difficult. I didn't mind the ropes nearly as much as the thousands of tourists, especially the families. I pussed out which infuriated John. He sulked about for awhile, but in the back of his mind, he admitted that it was impossible.

On a wall on the edge of the cliff, my eyes followed the others with curiosity. Head took off by herself to let her ragged, cut-off jeans and a blue and yellow tie-dyed slide against and mold into the blue day. Her sandles molded on the rocks as she looked deeply at every aspect of the old marble. I threw rocks in her direction, but not close enough for her to notice. It was just a little game in my mind to pass the time.

After about an hour we had exhausted the mountain and left inquisitive about an opposing mountain that climbed up 1,000 yards away. Looking up from the city, the two mountains looked like breasts stuck high and firm above a stomach.

On the way over to this other mountain, we passed a prison stuck into the mountain. "Hey this is Socrates' prison," someone decided.

I looked around and thought this was our moment. "Hey let's pose nude here. It is perfect, better than the Parthenon, more cerebral. It's perfect."

Everyone liked the idea except Head, but Degan talked her into taking the picture. We ran up next to it, when nobody was around, and dropped our pants down to our ankles. She took two pictures, one with my camera and one with Josh's. Snap, the moment was preserved with our boyishly proud hips thrusting towards the shutter.

Upon arriving to the top of the new mountain we posed once again, this time with our shorts on, but our shirts off. With muscles flexed, the white marble of the Parthenon gleamed in the far background. We struck every ancient stance possible, as Head was a sport, taking pictures with all five of our cameras. Sitting on a rock and eating our lunch, the sun was bright and began to turn our faces red to brown.

Josh's next action had some park in store for us. It was already about four o'clock and the rest of us had seen enough of the sights, but we humored him and he humored us. Before the park, he let Degan and I go to a liquor store.

We had no idea what we were reading while we both perused an assortment of wines and liquors. Degan called me over pointing down to the bottles of Ouzo. My head nodded in agreement as he picked one up. Its label read thirty-nine percent, "Just thirty-nine percent. That won't do."

"Yeah what is that, about eighteen proof. Anyway it's only two dollars a bottle." He grabbed another.

We walked through the nice park, but it was still just a park. A secluded expanse of dirt opened its arms, so we sat down in it, forming a tight circle. I opened the first bottle and handed it to Degan, "make the first toast."

"To the lizard king and Don's hat." He grabbed my hat and took a big swig. The bottle continued around the circle of Degan, me, Josh, Ned, Head, and John.

I toasted, "To the thirst of today."

"To Ouzo."

"To Greece."

"Too easy guys, to the smiles of our days and to the desperation of our nights." Head's face winced with the gulp.

"Wow, to the legacy and impossibilities of our friendships."

Degan thought hard and laughed, "To wiping boogers."

"Good one, Good one." I paused trying to top him. "To wiping our butts more than three times and not hopping in the shower to clean effectively."

The toast continued until we switched to saying something nice about one another. Josh got the most complements that ranged from his big biceps, his curly strawberry blonde hair, to his expertise in *Let's Go*. The first bottle was done.

John stopped the game, "You know Josh you've got the body of a Greek statue. Let's make you into one." Our heads joined together in the picture of him disrobed down to just his BVD's. The creativity continued with a wreath, made out of the closest thing we had to olive leaves, and with a big rock that would act like his discuss. The cameras came out and Josh twirled around, like the model he had always wanted to be, in love with himself. His chest bulged and his arms rippled with every flash screaming towards his catwalk. The Ouzo had kicked in.

We staggered throughout Athens singing, yelling, spitting, and taking pictures. The day was surreal almost like an acid trip which dripped of heavy colors and funny faces. By the time we had returned outside of our hotel, the bottles dripped dry by Degan's and my own challenging desires, prompting me to buy two bottles of wine. We went to the bar with them, but it was the same dead scene.

Waiting for the night, the town held tight giving us reason to take it head on with the intentions of meeting either a native woman or a raving communist. After changing into warmer clothes, I went down to find everyone. Instead, I only found Head hanging out in her room. "I'm not going to go."

"How come?"

"Too tired."

"Yeah Josh is already in bed. He decided he's going to leave us for the islands tomorrow. Says he knows where a buddy of his is. Rather hang out with him than get moldy with us, I guess." By this time I was standing right next to Head. A chill went through me as I looked down into her eyes. After holding each other's stare transfixed together, our eyes moved down to each other's lips.

My stomach turned in nervousness. I knew what was coming next, but I was so scared. I wanted her so bad, too bad. My stomach continued to flip like it does every time I kiss someone for the first time, not a pick-up in a bar, but someone I have cultivated a friendship with for awhile. My knees shivered in weakness. Eyes shut, I headed slowly for her mouth hoping hers would be there accepting mine.

The door swung open and there was John. He felt the excitement in the air. "Oh sorry…we're leaving, Don." The others came in with the wine dangling down from their arms.

Ned was head-butting Degan. Nothing was fazing him, so John and I took turns trying to dent his skull. I was always a successful head-butter and cockily grabbed the back of his neck and thrust forward striking my hairline with the middle of his forehead. I fell back slightly dizzy and looked at him. He smiled and said, "Nothing."

"Come on Degan." Then crash. Ned was dancing on his bed and head-butted a hole through the window. "Fuck, let's get out of here." We followed yelling, screaming, spitting, and swigging wine.

Aimlessly, our night walked to nowhere until our wine was finished. Ned threw a bottle. Smashing glass threw itself into tiny sparkles that scattered amongst cement. John went to throw the other one, but I gave him a reprimanding glance and he properly disposed of it. Defeat and boredom conquered us, but not the night.

A disappointed devil came back into Degan's eyes that wanted to recapture our lost energy. In a suicidal scream, he crossed the street right ahead of a bus daring it to hit him. A yell in a frightful pitch crossed with him, "No," but he was gone. My heart stuck into my throat with a taste of helpless throw up.

A lifetime passed before the bus got through the intersection revealing Degan's dumb ass smile. "You fucker."

"Asshole, we thought…"

"Forget it." We made it back safely with a thud into our beds feeling bad.

As I watched the room spin above my head, I tasted the bad burps of throw up and Ouzo and remembered my brief encounter alone with Kelly. "I wonder what will be next."

TWENTY-THREE

Needle, Sunset, Junk

The next day we woke up to find Josh already gone. His note told us of a plane to Mykinos whose departure was confirmed by my watch. His leaving precipitated a tinge of sadness, but hopefully he wasn't upset about anything. I don't know what he would have been upset about, but I wasn't sure. I hadn't done anything bad, except not letting him have his way the whole time. Oh well, I was too easy on myself and let it go. He would forget, if not forgive.

The rest of us got ready to leave Athens, ourselves. We bought all of the necessary goods for another night of travel and ate a Gyro. "When in Greece, do as the Greeks do." The lamb, or whatever it was, ran through me like shit through a goose. For fifteen minutes, I sat on the toilet, dripping with sweat. Refreshed and light footed, I headed with our group for the train station after paying our bill, plus five dollars for the window. No one could figure out exactly how the owner had known and how a window could only cost five dollars, but he gave us no trouble. We gladly paid the man.

On the train we opened our first bottle of wine that had the taste of vinegar and liquid soap mixed together. Doubtful, Head asked a fellow passenger their opinion on the validity of the wine and its ability to be consumed. They nodded an affirmative, but their eagerness indicated that they really didn't understand the question.

With the threat of poisoning ourselves a major concern, Degan took a swig then laid his head back and boldly let the wine swirl around his throat. "I don't think we'll die," came with a sigh.

After giving him time to slump over dead, John rallied behind his battle cry, "It is a must, a test. We have to finish it." So we unthankfully did.

I joined Degan and Head at the back of the train where a car had wooden tables planted into the tile floors. Without a word, I sat down to begin to write a letter to the forgotten. The pause in between sentences enabled me to hear their talk of school and friends.

> Dear Kristie,
>
> What's going on back in the states? Finally I'm having some fun and enjoying myself. You always told me not to worry about those little things. Now, I find my tensions slipping away, not even coming to form in my mind.
>
> I can't wait to come home, though. I feel tired of the fight, but I will keep it up until that plane lands and I get my first paycheck. It's not easy always being hungry and not having a place to go which offers comfort.
>
> Spring Break has been amazing. Sunny everyday. We are beautifully bronzed. Josh, my friend from high school, has stayed behind in Greece and now it is just John and I heading through Italy. We our hanging out with a couple of people we met, two guys and one woman from Wesleyan. It's kinda of weird, but we have become instant friends.
>
> Next for me is the long travel up to Berlin. It will take a couple of days and most of it will be alone. Supposedly a couple of friends of mine will get on my train in Austria, but I don't know for sure.
>
> Well, I'll see you soon. I'll call you when I get back to Belgium. Take Care and Have Fun.
> Love,
> Don
>
> P.S. How was your family's move to New York? How convenient for us.

I smiled at them and got up returning to my solace in the other car. Hearing my name whispered as I left, I didn't bother trying to figure out what was being said.

We made the ferry and bought some more wine. This time our experience had properly reshaped our expectations and removed our previous mistakes, but it also removed the fun. We cased a good place to sleep and positioned our bags to secure it.

Stuck in stories of where we had been and what we had been, the drinking went along at a nice slow pace. The lackluster attitude was provoked by our eminent fracture. Ned and Degan were stopping off in Corfu before going back to Italy, John was on his way to Vienna, Head had to get back to France, and I was set on Berlin. Tonight was our last night together. Everyone was trying to make it last. The favorite story was the convincing of Head to come and how Degan had given that famous glance at Ned, confirming their entry into our plans.

After the wine was gone, I felt pretty good, slightly out of control but not ugly, violent, or sick. I worked coolly and collectively towards Kelly, so I would have the opportunity to be on the deck with her and alone. Our time together dangerously drew towards an end. Degan had run off again while John and Ned secured my single, dire intention with their usual prankster activities.

I was feeling much more confidant as we watched the water slap up against the steel sides and fall back down taking on the water color of the ship. Hurried in my intentions and in my motion to kiss her, the moment became forced. She kissed in return, but the reluctancy propelled and spilled my hopes. Sensing it, I pulled back to see the concern on her face. She also saw it in my face and tried to lighten up her look asking me perkily, "What would Kristie say right now?"

The bombshell hit, reeling me back, gasping for thoughts and explanations. A good strategy seemed hard to find, so I reacted with a shrugged and steered towards the truth. She noticed the efforts in my thoughts and the resolve in my conclusion of not to bullshit her.

"Well, she's a woman I was seeing at school when I left."

"So you guys still have something? I watched you struggle over that letter."

"Well, we do have something, but it's not love or even like, for that matter. I guess it's more of a…I don't know. I don't know that I've ever been in love; we had fun, but it ran its course."

"Well what's the something you have left?"

"It's…" I gulped hard and stared into the night sky, hoping for help from above. I laid my cards on the table knowing none would come. "She became pregnant right after I left. She had an abortion." The cool air felt great. The tension poured out of my legs as I stretched my arms apart trying to catch every refreshing bit. "I have to go home and settle everything. There are a lot of untended feelings waiting. The only thing that will resolve them is me coming home. I know she feels bitter towards me and I feel guilty. We both need to get them out on each other. At least I do, for my sanity. They may fade away, but will never die unless I face her. I need to stand naked in front of her and let her take the knife to every inch of my body. It sounds strange, but that's the something."

"Oh, It must be tough."

I let go of a long sigh and a small tear came about. "You know, I really needed to tell you. I don't know why, but you seemed to be some sort of a savior." The darkness hit and stopped the conversation. We stood quietly looking at each other for awhile. I studied every inch of her face and her long and hard suck on a Marlboro. Her face was smooth and tan with her blonde hair alternating from blowing in her eyes and flowing back with the wind. My soul jumped into hers, knowing that I would continue to fight and that she wouldn't resist. Our destiny for something finally revealed that tonight would be the beginning.

We went to bed in each other's arms. But before we fell asleep, I remembered the question I had wanted to ask, "So you saw my letter?"

She smiled, "Yeah." We gazed at each other until our eyes fell from the weight of our week together. Innocently, our bodies didn't move nor did our lips try to kiss each other. For a change the company felt nice and clean.

We woke up the next morning to Degan and Ned bidding us goodbye and John complaining about a bloody nose that had been bleeding for three hours. They left in the darkness onto the island of Corfu with only a "See Ya." Head and I went down to the front of the ship and watched the sun head up over the horizon.

Unfortunately, we stumbled upon a guy that went to my school. He told me of the many on the ship with him, sinking my anonymity to the world. I offered him a bite of my breakfast, a cucumber, but he declined with a snub, telling me of the breakfast that they offered on board. With the clouds intermittently breaking up the sunrise, the tide was turning with reality that always crashed into the dream.

We gathered John and our stuff to venture on top. I was tired, but for once, wasn't hungover. My bearings seemed out of whack, but my spirits remained fairly content. Frozen in this perfect painting, the scene of Head by my side and John at my feet brought about a guarded warmth. The only impediments were John's constant complaining about his bloody nose and the reappearance of the other kids from school.

As the trip went on, the seas got rough. John became increasingly worried about his nose and tried to rally fellow passengers to his rescue. A few offered home remedies for bloody noses and one got him ice. He intermittently shifted between being close to tears and laughing at his calamity. Because I was often a victim of bloody noses and laid little importance upon them, I tried to keep things light. Even though the bleeding was now going on five hours, the chances of death before clotting seemed an impossibility.

As the waves got more turbulent, John's panic increased with loud yelling and assorted carrying-ons. His hysteria and the rough sea added up to a series of huge blood infested pukes on the astro turf deck. These big pieces of clotted blood hit the green astro turf carpet and swarmed around like little red leech demons making the onlookers sound like a crowd watching a gory horror show. Eventually, the red worms would adhere to the surface like Velcro. Skeeved in amazing disgust, I went below with John to barf in unison. In between pukes I managed some laughter, "Boy, I'm some help."

"You need help? Look at me, I'm on my way out of life and you need help?"

We were both seasick and worried. Fortunately, Head was our saving grace, keeping us feeling secure as she watched us like a mother, laying on the deck, holding our stomachs, and laughing to keep the proper bend on the moment. John's facade appeared as if it had been beaten by an L.A. gang and left for dead on the green astro turf of a football field. On the other hand, I was just a useless bag of mush, bitching about the waves. Every once and awhile, I would get up, yell fuck, and ask Head in hysteria about what we should do, if anything.

Finally she went to the bridge, where the captain kind of understood her, and was offered a helicopter to take him to shore. Declining, she instead got the captain to find a doctor and tend to our dying friend.

A suave Italian and an old fat Greek, both doctors, were the next ones to come to our rescue. They talked among themselves about what was going on or about their golf game for all we didn't know. Finally, they acted and took John below, outside still, but in the shade. They elevated his feet and put ice on his head. Impressed, John felt relieved that someone was doing something for him. He laid quietly and slept while Head and I talked about anything.

She sat Indian style across from me with her Army shorts on again and a sweatshirt representing her college to keep warm. She put on the mukluks that I had bought the day before and huddled up behind them. I couldn't help, but smile. We decided that we had to talk about our lives from the beginning until the day we met and then continue on into what our future would be like.

I began, "I was born in a small Midwestern town. All right, I was born in Pittsburgh to a common, middle class family. My dad struggled with teaching high school math and coaching tennis while my mom stayed at home to raise her two beautiful kids, Don and Sarah.

"The rest of my growing years were uneventful. I was into sports like the rest of our township. Soccer, baseball, and tennis were my main sports. Going into high school I chose tennis, mostly because my dad was the coach and I excelled in it the most. So I stuck with it." My speech sounded like an essay reading.

"I was a spoiled tennis brat with a hot temper. I did pretty well, but it was no longer fun so I quit the competitive aspect and just did some teaching on the side.

"Socially I hung out with the cool group, but didn't let it consume me and had a variety of friends. We were big drinkers and socially it was our driving factor, more so than women, except Josh, of course. I think that's why I fall back on it so much now in social events.

"My family is interesting. Immediate family is boring, my sister just got married and she works as a temp. My dad is pissed about paying for her education at the University of North Carolina, but she's daddy's girl. She just got married last week, and here I am, no invitation, no nothing. They couldn't afford to fly me home and it was the only time she could have it. I say bullshit and will always be slightly offended by not going to my own sister's wedding.

"My dad is a pisser, a strict disciplinarian. He makes us pay for C's and below at school. He divides tuition and room and board into the total number of credits. So basically, it costs nine hundred bucks a class. My sister graduated with a two point, but will never pay anything back. Again, I'm a little bitter. Another good story about my dad is when I was caught drinking in ninth grade. He grounded me for an entire summer. But that is much too long and involved to be properly relayed.

"My dad's side of the family is boring, but my mom's is crazy. She has got step this and ex that. One aunt was married four times, one uncle married four times, another aunt married three times, and another uncle who is the gay one.

"They come from big money, but my mom got none. She was a step away, so to speak. One aunt tried to cure the world of heart disease through jello enemas and another uncle is a recording engineer who has yet to record one. It's pretty funny."

"So what's your tale?"

"I grew up in Chicago and moved away to bum fuck Indiana after my senior year. Indiana was where my mom had grown up, and they redid an entire house for themselves. I have an older sister and a younger brother. That's right, I'm the dreaded middle child.

"I followed in my sister's footsteps and went to Wesleyan and joined the same sorority. My dad sells wholesale truck tires and my mom stays at home. My dad always seems to be going, but my mom likes the freedom and quiet time. My brother is still in high school and I don't know him too well.

"I major in Biology and English and don't know what I want to do. My deep convictions are simple; women's lib, animal rights, and the Grateful Dead.

"Besides that…"

Our conversations continued in that kind of background vain for hours. We got heated on a few topics and agreed on most. Disappointed in some of my thoughts, I found myself bending some of my philosophies to meet hers. I have strong convictions, but found my convictions stronger for her than any other cause.

Humor was our common thread, but mine was based on a dark cynicism while hers was more progressively sarcastic. With my humor jabbing at myself and hers trying to take on the globe, our personalities mixed well and kept us from getting at each other's throats. During this acquaintance period, I kept reminding myself of my raison d'être, Love is Nonexistent. But now, even that seemed to be liquefied.

Throughout our gibberish, John remained calm and his bleeding slowed until the boat arrived at port in Italy. Immediately upon docking, we went to the front of the boat and were led to a waiting ambulance. Perfectly on cue, his nose began to gush. For a second, I pictured him hitting it to start the bleeding again, because the timing seemed too perfect.

We rushed through the streets feeling important and went directly to the hospital. Italy was fucked. Doctors have days off on Sundays, so no one was there to really help him. Sympathetically, a nurse looked at him and gave him a coagulant to slow the blood flow. Then she looked at us and told us that we all had to go, even with John's nose still bleeding.

That was quite a blow to John's confidence of the place. He was counting on being taken care of and there we were standing in front of the hospital with no where to go, no map to help us, and John's blood dripping everywhere.

We walked the streets looking for a hotel. I pulled out from the very back of my wallet the credit card my dad had given me for those "just in case emergencies." I figured this was as close as I could get.

After about two miles of aimless walking, we came upon a hotel. We needed someone to speak English, but nobody did, so we ventured on. John resumed his panic mode about never finding a hotel or somebody to help him. The straw broke his spirits.

The mad man yelled and screamed, "Fuck Italy, I'm going to Germany where they have arrived in the twentieth century. This place sucks." Then as the anger wore off, it turned to fear forcing tears down his cheeks. Threatening to hop on a train, he started walking away from us towards the train station. Head and I didn't know what to do. She went for the ignore while I went for the rationalizing. It became obvious that nothing would calm him.

With the tears and blood alternating splats on his T-shirt, we finally found another hotel. John had already given up and started off towards the train station, but I convinced him to wait and I bet him that he couldn't find it anyway. He succumbed and fell into a corner of a building to sob pathetically, murmuring something about dying. I still didn't see the life and death concern in the predicament, but bleeding for over twelve hours straight was a concern.

We got into the hotel and the attendant luckily spoke English. The ensuing relief made me feel like crying. The hotel was sixty bucks a night and the man behind the desk immediately offered his assistance. John laid down in the efforts of regaining some sort of composure while Head and I worked with our savior.

A doctor arrived. After his five minute evaluation, he informed

John that he had to go back to the hospital. "Thanks buddy," but he did give him another coagulant shot and gave us another one for later. He also filled us in about a NATO air base that might help.

Kelly and I left to get some dinner in order to give John some time alone. He was sick of us and was ready to kill anything. "What the fuck," I figured that I might as well live it up and eat at a restaurant. I treated Head to a nice pasta dinner, our first date. Discussing our best bets on the outcome and how we couldn't wait for it to be over, we had a fun and a relaxed dinner. "The head butting and the drinking must have really done him in," I thought out loud.

When we were gone, John called home which was a big mistake. He wound up blubbering into a phone to his girlfriend and to his mom. His incoherence and tales of death scared the shit out of both of them. When we returned he was in tears again. Giving me the phone number, he implored me to call both back and explain the deal and what we were going to do. My light mood was very unconvincing and left them just as frightened.

Finally, everyone fell asleep. I woke about every hour and checked on John. Head didn't sleep at all waiting for something big to happen. Finally he asked for the other shot. I looked at Head, "where is the needle?" She handed it to me. "Do I go for a vein or just the butt?"

"The butt."

I hesitated over top of him and wondered if I could fuck this up and if I did, what would happen. Head noticed, "I'll do it, I've given tons of shots before."

"Why didn't you say so earlier?" The pressure subsided.

She took the needle, walked next to him, and stuck it in with extreme confidence. She slowly removed the needle. "Wow, that was the best needle shot I've ever had. Amazing. You should be a doctor."

John seemed better.

TWENTY-FOUR
Sipping Red Through A Funnel

In the morning, we started our day by getting the NATO base on the phone. Going around in circles, I spoke to some guy in charge of their medical facilities. Finally, the chase ended when he asked if John or I were military personnel. The "no" response was the incorrect answer.

"What do you mean? It's an emergency." John heard me and the hysteria began all over again. He tried to grab the phone from me and began to shout at the man. The terror in John's voice moved him enough or luck had found us because he agreed to send a nurse and an interpreter to meet us at the hospital. At the time, their gesture went unappreciated. Thinking that it was the least they could have done, I was dead wrong. The guy could have just hung up on my whiny voice. Instead, he made these two people do probably the last thing they wanted to do.

We got a cab to the hospital and of course on cue, John begins to bleed again. Relieved at the situation, he finally just laughed at the blood all over his body. Cakey and crusty flakes fell off in the wind all over the cab. The absurdity made him laugh some more.

The fucking cab driver took us the longest way to the hospital, the dick. I knew, but what could I do. If I yelled at him, he would have gone a longer way. So I kept my voice inside, "Fuck him."

We got there just ahead of the translator and the nurse who helped John checked in. A nurse quickly escorted him behind two sterile swinging doors. Alone in the waiting room, Head and I stood around wondering what to do. Nobody ever came back, so we left.

First off, I recounted our combined money left over. We had forty bucks to blow and I could still make it to Berlin, if neither of us ate or drank. She set aside ten dollars for herself, just in case. "What should we do for him?"

"Well, I would want food and shit to read. How 'bout you?"

"Sounds good to me Head," saying Head was beginning to sound weird.

We walked up and down the main drag. During the walk from the train to the ferry or vice versa the main street was the way one went. The situation forced the street to an utter grotesque tourist trap. Loitering salesmen constantly haggled you for something. Men followed the foreign women and crazed people ran up and yelled at everyone. The place was Dante's Inferno. Today though, the boats were scheduled to come and leave at night. It was ten o'clock in the morning and the town did a complete reversal. Kids in school, families shopping, and young people flirting made us fit right in, unnoticed. The town seemed real again, but the show was hiding, gearing up for its nightly freak show.

On the main drag, we found a bookstore with English books and newspapers, but their selection was bad and their premium was high. The only name worth looking at was Vonnegut, the perfect doomsday author for John's attitude. We bought it along with a couple of magazines and a newspaper. The rest of our money was spent on food for him; water, pretzels, and apples; a nice selection.

After checking out of the hotel, our bodies released and sat by the water for the rest of the day to ponder our strategy. "Should I stay?" I looked at her sincerely hoping for the right answer.

"Well, Don, I don't know. Let's think about it." She had on the same flowery dress as she had in Monaco. With her hair down and her sunglasses on, she now reminded me of Don Henley's, "After the Boy's of Summer have Gone," but in a good way this time. It was that "Dead Head sticker on a Cadillac," not "the hair slicked back and wayfarers on" line that was for the Bobsie twins, Jen and Lynn. The "Don't look back, you can never look back" line kept speaking to me.

Forgetting, she opened her mouth, "Well if you stay, you'll fuck-up school and sit here spending money that you don't have, doing nothing."

"Yeah, I could sell my advice to suckers like me on the way to the ferry."

"If you go, he'll be alone and scared and if anything happens, he could be lost forever in the jungle of Brindisi."

"Thus, the dilemma."

"What do you think?"

"Well, the only reason I would stay is the what if. But he's a big kid. I don't know, I think I should go."

"Well, I'm going. You can go north with me for awhile, but I'm going tonight." We checked out a map and found a night train which would take us through Bologna. In Bologna, she steered through Switzerland to France while I veered east to Venice then up through Austria to Berlin.

"John really wanted to see Venice and even Florence, if we had the time. Oh well." A variety boats came and went until visiting hours.

We got to the hospital a little early and waited outside under a tree. A fat, old policeman walked by, placing tickets on cars and throwing the receipts on the ground. Watching him carefully, Head's face slowly let itself become enraged. She blurted, "Don't you care about your city?" Her cry wailed to a shrill, but he didn't bother to look up.

She ran up next to him and followed, "Don't you care?" He mumbled something incoherent, but derogatory, then threw down another piece of paper. She continued to follow him picking up every single piece that he dropped. He was irritated and she was enraged, but they both keep their distance as each did what they thought was their job. Her convictions held firm.

She sat back down huffing and puffing with curses intermingled, "fuckin' dick."

"Oh, by the way, you just said fuck." My smile held its cuteness.

We went inside to find John. I tried asking a nurse at the front desk, "Do you know where a John Feller is?" I spoke loud and slowly as all people speak to others whom do not share their common language.

She looked up, confused at first at the sounds emanating through my black and pink hole with bones sticking out. Then something clicked and she smiled pleasantly, "Oh, the American." She pointed up the stairs and to the left, giving us the name of the Ears, Nose, and Throat department in Italian. Still uncertain, we asked as soon as we made our way up a set of stairs. Through the hallways, large factions of children followed. Snaking our way through the growing crowds, the visions of the grandeur returned of being that famous rock 'n roller.

The small children gained braveness and began coming up to us with a touch and lots of giggles. The older ones trailed behind, speaking the only English that they knew, "What is your name?"

I couldn't resist, "Sting" and Head responded, "Madonna." I don't think any of them were big English or American rock and roll fans yet, but I thought it was funny. They looked at us with momentarily blank faces, especially with Madonna. Then they giggled.

A nurse in the Ear, Nose, and Throat ward took us to John. She also welcomed us with the greeting, "Oh, the American." A couple of turns and some doors, then there he was, lying comfortably, finally relaxed. The room contained five other patients who curiously watched John and his friends. The atmosphere reminded me of an early sixties movie about some hayseed town and its hospital. Old metallic beds painted white, bare white concrete walls, and green tile, which looked like it was imported from my elementary school back home, created a sterile yet primitive feel of nowhere, 1962.

Lacking excitement or anxiousness in our visit, John spoke evenly, "Hey guys, what's going on?"

"How do you feel?"

"Better."

"Well?"

He wanted to tell us all of his internal woes, but wanted the satisfaction of having us wait and then ask. "Well?"

"Well, what did they do to you? What have they said?"

He looked at our bags and smiled. After handing them over, his eyes perused the variety of books and magazines. He took the time to look up a few words in the dictionary and paged through his groceries. Finally he began, "From what I have gathered." He glanced and smiled at an middle-aged man, who laid directly across from him, and continued, "he speaks German and has been translating the Italian into German, as best he can. Anyway, from what I can gather, I have a ruptured vessel in my nose and my healing process is fucked. They think it's because of malnutrition."

"Oh great." I wondered what was going to happen to my empty body.

"Well, the worst part is that they shoved a huge paper or cottony thing up my nose." He held his hands apart by a foot. "It is clogging up my sinus cavity to stop the bleeding."

"Well, the big question is how long are you in for?"

"Ten days to two weeks," his head hung dropping to his chest. "There's no way I'm staying here that long. No way." His will and anger were gone.

"Ten days to two weeks, wow." Open air hit the conversation. The big question was still unopened and unspoken as we all contemplated how to handle it. I couldn't stand it, "How do you feel about me staying or going?"

"Well, you should go. What the fuck are you going to do here?"

"Yeah, I know, but I worry about that what if."

"Hey, that what if will happen with or without you. What are you going to do that I can't do?"

"Clot my blood."

He told us stories of the nurses and the other patients. He was being treated like a celebrity leper. His eyes would open from a nap only to see little kids standing beside him staring. They would run away frightened. The nurses would all come over to examine him and just begin to laugh. His shot routine was becoming nationally famous. Visiting hours ended.

"See ya."

"Yea, see ya, back in Brussels, I guess. Enjoy the rest and the free food."

"Too bad, I'm never going to make it to Venice."

"I'll say hi to it for you, and hi to Berlin as well. I'm sure we will be taking it by storm."

We left John sitting nowhere and doing nothing. But all fear, that had left him, made me feel better on the quiet walk back to town.

Passing an exchange window, Head got the idea to leave a note for Degan and Ned.

Degan and Ned,
John is in the Brindisi hospital. Should be there for awhile. Visit him if able.
Don and Head.

"No way."

"Yeah you're probably right, but it's worth the effort," she said.

On the way out, we also ran into some guys whom I went to school with. They seemed genuine in their promise to visit John, but who really cared. I was getting the fuck out of Dodge.

With two bottles of wine in hand, our night train picked us up.

A sudden remorse and confusion flew over me as I listened to Kelly talk away and lead me through train after train. The search through the entire train left us seatless. Our only option was to settle on the very back of the very last car and sit on the floor by the bathroom. The train tracks reappeared out the back window and ran away from us.

With the wine gone, I gave in. Trying to be manly, noble, or true to my intentions, I tried to void myself of sex. However, the wine changed my mind. Her lips kept moving and forcing blood into my penis. I wanted her and went for it.

We started out kissing gently, feeling each other's lips, teeth, and tongues. With my penis being fully erect and yelling with pain to release everything, I passionately and violently thrust my tongue throughout her entire face and neck. I laid her down and grinded my hardness onto her groin area. Our blue jeans rubbed together making me raw and hungry.

In the moment of passion, I accidentally thrust open the back door. The terror in our eyes spoke of the tracks whizzing by and looking painfully sore and close. The amount of distance in hanging over the edge to shut the door seemed easy, but not without numerously dangerous possibilities. We looked at each other and wondered if trying to shut it was worth it.

Then, a mystery man came out of nowhere, grabbed the door, shut it, and gave us each a cigarette. We said nothing and gratefully smoked them patiently before hustling back to our tangling of clothes and mouths.

We woke the next morning, laying in each other's arms, tired, sore, and hung over. As I have never been able to do, she started the morning with a smile at my disheveled appearance and my intense smell. I hadn't showered in a few days and my breathe reeked from last night's alcohol and cigarette binge. I gave her a kiss anyway. Neither of us mentioned the night before and headed straight into town; Bologna.

Bologna seemed boring; a park, maybe a few other famous pieces of architecture or art work, but mostly there was nothing to do. We once again pooled our money that we didn't have and decided to try my trick.

"It's easy, you just sit in a booth and watch people eat. Hopefully there will be an upstairs or a separate eating area where the workers can't watch you. Then, you just stare at them and look hungry, sad, tired, desolate, yet safe. You need a hard image, but a gentle look. Then when they are done, they will leave their trays there, knowing you will eat it. And if worse comes to worse, you rummage through the garbage after them."

It took an hour of endless walking and being lost until the yellow arches appeared behind a mountain full of scaffolding. We sat and I went to work. Our efforts retrieved a half eaten Big Mac, a nice piece of a fish sandwich, lots of fries, and several half filled drinks. People always get more than they want, especially with drinks. Unfortunately, the McDonald's in Bologna did not have my favorite, Chicken McNuggets.

It was nice portions, but not enough. Next, the hungry Head showed me something much better. We went to a supermarket, walked around and ate when the coast looked clear. I had a whole endive, some cookies, some paprika potato chips, a tomato, a cucumber, and an apple. We strolled on out of there and then ran when the door shut behind us. Our legs carried the rest of us back into the big park in town. Finding a park bench, we fell asleep until our separate trains had to be caught.

Head's train was the first one to come. I grabbed hold of her for one last kiss and watched the curves walk away. I looked down at her address and phone number after she got on the train wondering how long I would wait until I used it.

After that first taste, I was an addict, not able to wait to see her again. My reluctance seemed gone and my conscience forced thoughts of Kristie, but her image kept drifting away, always smearing back into Kelly's or Head's or whatever I called her. I sat in the station, smiling with content and excitement to get back to school, so I could give her a call.

TWENTY-FIVE
Sliding in Galoshes

That afternoon Venice rolled into the teared window of the train. I think it was that afternoon, but it could have been the next day. The days had blurred. My only certainty was the battle between daylight and the fuzzy, cold, rainy climate. Amazingly, today was the first rainy day, that I had seen, since leaving Belgium years ago. Tired and very alone, the too many days on the road had worn me down and out.

The train crossed over some sort of water then Venice's city appeared. Excitement eluded me with my thoughts of no money, no map, and no plans. The next train out of here didn't leave until ten P.M..

When I arrived at the station, a sense of familiarity stung the air. It was everywhere, but nothing was attainable or helped my mood. The train station was the same, the atmosphere was the same, the people looked the same, and the architecture looked the same. Boiling it down, Venice lacked. All those great people during those great years and I was trapped with nothing to do in a cold city that stunk like a backed up Hoboken sewer.

Finding lockers to put my stuff in, my hand dug into the pockets of my jeans and coat in hopes of a miraculous discovery of change. Nothing, but a sock full of the exact round-trip fare to in and out of Eastern Germany, crossed my fingertips.

Like all other train stations, this station lacked a bench for me to recoup. With no alternative, I sat outside to the stairs leading up to the station to watch the hurried world climbed aboard long, wooden, overly dressed canoes, and to figure out where every one was going. The long and slowly ascending stairs provided a perfect view of one of the canals and of the gondola business.

As I sat, I ran into a few people that I knew. They were all people who disgusted me and forced me to move along, pretending like I was on a mission to see the city in a hurry. Not wanting to look like a liar, I searched the streets and canals through the mist.

After about a mile, my feet were too tired to continue. The city seemed like just another old, dirty, European tourist trap. The image of a city, sinking to a slow, ugly death, materialized after each step. The people latched on trying to prop it up, but were failing miserably and pathetically. The city was taking everyone down into the depths of its sewer water, never to return.

I saw my life doing the same. Death was inevitable and we were all slowly dying. Dying, like the bum, like the drug addict, like the aids patient, the world was constantly dying. As soon as the sperm hits the egg, the world began its tedious, melancholy, desperate death. Like Venice, our grip clung on to what already was, wondering how we could stop the process. All of our energy was sucked into slowing the process, only to make us weaker and make death more painful and slower.

I arrived back at the train station laughing in tears, "I am nothing and I deserve what I have." The rain picked up as the day no longer tried to stop the fall of darkness. I picked up a Venice radio station and listened to the hellish repetition of acid house music. "As long as my death does not end up in a constant state of acid house, I guess I did a not bad job of living." Kristie and Kelly clobbered my mind again.

Finally, the train arrived and I hopped aboard. I was supposed to meet some friends on it, but they fortunately never showed. The reservations for this train were made months ago when I had money, so I treated myself to a couchette. Their beds were empty, but three others had people in them. They were from Germany, an older couple and their son, who looked to be in his early thirties. Their ancestry was apparent with their three short mustaches and their words being cut-off with the sounds of hockering. Their faces smashed up as I took my shoes off and laid down on the top bunk. The sweet pungent odor of my feet and hair slowly drifted down filling the cabin. They would get used to it.

I laid there the entire ride, wondering about my future until sleep overcame. Desperately, I needed a good night's sleep. The exhaustion played with my mind and oppressed my mood. As far as I could see, senior year, a job, a wife, kids and my future offered nothing. The last three-fourth's of my life would be the exact same thing day in, day out. But what could I do? I was not one to fight the system. We called out for order, for responsibility. What was I to do? The abstract thought of it was too much and too depressing.

Wondering about one's purpose and meaning usually left people short of their expectations. Expectations acquired as the child didn't match the reality of the grown-up. Things ended up being money related which determines the turning of the earth. The actual want of people was never considered. Maybe Head and her bullshit about fulfilling the erotic was a good, clean, and new outlook on things.

"What are my erotics?" First off the top of my head was rock stardom, women, sleeping late, drugs, and lots of attention. I thought deeper. My only other thought was an author/adventurer who could taste life and observe it. Making some money and making some love and sleep definitely fit into those schemes. The sleep thing was undeniably motivating me the most. I couldn't really define what I really wanted, but I knew that the definition was just as hard as having the balls to do it. I doubted if I had either the brains or the balls, but I reassuringly fell asleep, promising to try to discover what life offered besides sleep.

The morning came and I woke up from a horrible dream. Back at school, my senior year was winding down. I was at a party and I decided to borrow a buddy's car to get some food. Things got really scary and blurry finally focusing with that car crashing into the bridge part of an overpass. I was on the underpass. The car and myself were uninsured. Returning from the police station, I got drunk and shot a kid in the leg with a BB gun. Upon my second arrest I protest, "But I only pumped it three times and he was over a hundred feet away. Tell that pussy to take off his dress." That was the end for me. I was kicked out of school and all of my dad's money was gone. He had to work for the next five years to pay off all of the damages or kill me. He decided to kill me. He threw a bucket of acid on me and I melted away without a scream. The spiraling dream alerted me to the abundance of my unneeded tension.

Next, I was in Heidelburg, I thought. The Haufbrau House, in which I had a beer before buying tickets to Berlin, erased any doubts of being in Heidelburg. Now, everything was gone, except my mind which had Kelly tuned in. Oddly, I alternated between calling her Head and Kelly. Today, she was a Kelly.

Heidelburg was boring, but bright. The backdrops were gingerbread houses and the set from the *Sound of Music*. "Oh well, no Vienna for me."

Waiting for the train, the inevitable comparisons of Kristie and Kelly began. A soft moment of sanctuary filled my visions of my sore penis rubbing up against Kelly's denim. A smile brightened the industrial ugliness of the Heidelberg station. She seemed so beautiful to me, too beautiful. "I am ugly and simple, I don't deserve such a fine woman." The chin and glasses that appeared in the window of a store, that I stood in front of, made me a cross between Clark Kent and Jay Leno. My body was skinny and becoming softer. These thoughts of her were in only the simplest and purest ways; the effect on me. "She's too good, only the beautiful hurt," Prince began singing to my incoherent, jumbled brain. All of the answers appeared in his songs.

My body felt so tired, it didn't want to hurt, anymore. The joy couldn't even have been handled. Maybe, it was all a passive aggressive trap, but I conceded that my real problems stemmed from a good dose of no confidence and too much time alone. I looked up to see the workers behind the counter of the store asking me to leave with their stares. I continued on.

Kristie was so much simpler. I just had to perform in bed and say some nice things with a promise of commitment every so often. She didn't care about my shortcomings and didn't expose any. In fact, she made me look like the greatest thing. She wasn't overly good looking, she wasn't intelligent, she wasn't motivated. I could grab the reins and do my thing. It all seemed so easy, but I couldn't forget the tears nor the constant turmoil that she forced upon me. Seldom a moment of sunshine shone through our bedroom window. Reverting back to the realities of school and my room, "maybe that is it, I have no windows in my bedroom. It's a great place for sleeping and for not looking when having sex, but not enlightening enough."

"Next year, I will have a window in my room," a big step up in my life. Pessimism was so easy to fall back on, but dreams and desire needed to be worked for. Kelly required work. She was her own woman and would force me into being my own man. I would have to prove myself worthy more than to just her, but myself. I was scared. I pictured those walks, laughing almost in tears with her.

Those questions, where I racked my brain for what I thought was a correct answer. I saw her pretty smile and her eyes. "What is happening to me, trapped in a consumer, transaction world? I am no Plato, I am a man who wants it now and quick, hassle free." I definitely had too much time alone.

My brain's scattered thoughts went back and forth between the idea and ideals of trying to make ends meet with the two women. The pros and cons weighed heavier and heavier, but the picture remained. I wiped it out, trying to remember Kristie with her long hair and her own beautiful smile. It wouldn't come, just that dumb ass, tie-dyed T-shirt surrounding her lean shoulders which balanced her blonde hair. I saw that smile after drinking some Ouzo, with her face capturing every moment and every drop of the sun. She skipped along while walking. I seemed happy.

I've got the two women blues, I don't know where to turn.
One has got a knife while the other makes me burn.
I've got the two women blues.
My body is yearning, my head is aching.
A moment to escape, some time by myself.
Maybe I'm stupid, maybe I'm faking.
I guess I'll put them both on a shelf.
I've got the two women blues.

I looked at the words on my notebook and laughed. I was interrupted, "Don?"

A whole bunch of fucks from Brussels, one being Linda appeared on top of my head. The world crashed and my brain shut off. Nothing to do, but suck it up and get to Berlin.

On the long ride to Berlin, someone gave me a copy of *Rolling Stone* with Madonna on the cover and I borrowed the "Like A Prayer" tape from a buddy and dreamed. As Berlin came and the men in the machine gun poked at me, I stared at the picture of Madonna on the cover and listened to "Like a Prayer" over and over. I had too much time alone.

TWENTY-SIX
LM and IS Curves

I made Berlin safely. Fifty students from Belgium and myself met at a hostel to begin a field trip to enrich our lives in International Economics. For some unknown reason Berlin was our city of choice.

Berlin turned out to be not so bad. The west side was a complete capitalist trap with whores and drugs at every corner. I frequented many establishments and talked to the women with a concern for their purpose in life, hoping for some insight. Instead, I ended up getting a free hand job and being called a chicken, "bac, bac," for not wanting more. With a fresh cum stain in my underwear and free sandwiches every morning, things seemed all right there.

On the East side, I saw a part of life that I probably never will again. I met a local woman who spoke English and who took me to a local bar, a restaurant, and a night club. She showed me the bullet holes from World War II, graves of the Jews in a wall. In between, she spoke of the mood of her country, hope mixed with anger. Her belief that change would come and save them all fought against the depressed stench of hungry desires. She believed in the her generation and in the generosity of America which allowed me to feel proud of my country for the first time.

Leaving East Berlin, I was accompanied by a friend, Pete, and another strangler who claimed to be a Prince from Niger or something like that. He showed me four passports; one Diplomatic, one

German, one American, and one Nigerian. It sounded cool to me. Anyway, the three of us were leaving when we arrived at the gate, precisely at the prescribed hour, midnight, to return west. The prince led us through the gates of prosperity. After letting the little black prince go through to his freedom, the soldier kept saying, "Nine, Nine," to my friend and myself.

Baffled, the fright of not being allowed to go back flew into our minds. In ten minutes our Visas ran out and we had no money and little hope. I was thinking about where the U.S. Embassy would be when someone in line informed us that we had to cross where we came in through, which was at least a mile away. I was drunk and tired, but we began to sprint with terror, yelling out of our dry throats. The stoic guards pointed their machine guns at us.

Then out of nowhere our little angel, who showed us the city, came zinging around the corner. She picked us up and took us to the correct exit. We made it through to freedom. I have never been so afraid for my well-being as that. On the other side, I fell to my knees and kissed the ground and got a fifth of whiskey. My nameless friend, Pete, and I split it on the way home. He even bought it. "Thanks," I offered between heavy pants.

I never did see that prince again. I was so pissed at his face and his little shrug that emphasized our apparent demise from the other side of the wall. My dreams of him and those guards made for a horrible night.

The next morning at breakfast I recited my tale over and over as I made my sandwiches. The hostel served little pieces of bread and cold cuts for breakfast. This amazing luck let me eat like a champ.

Finally, we were allowed to leave Berlin after three days filled with lectures and three nights drowned in drinking. It had become just as mundane as regular school.

TWENTY-SEVEN
Bad IV

The train ride back to Belgium was very slow and painful. I actually felt excited about my bed and the cafeteria. Spring now had taken over life and everything approached summer. The season caught my spirit and lifted me back to good intentions. I tried to write Kristie on the train ride, but nothing came out right. Instead, I watched the seconds tick away wondering how much longer I had to go. Not even my Walkman's new batteries could save me from boredom. Finally, we got back to Brussels and I took the hour long walk back home.

Albert was waiting for me, "How was your trip?" he asked without curiosity, just politeness.

"Oh not bad. Greece, Italy, and the South of France were beautiful. We ran into a bit of luck with the weather. Berlin was very interesting. I had a good time." I couldn't think of anything else to tell him. He just kept looking at me waiting. "I'm tired. I've got to get some sleep." In front of his eyes, I slinked up the stairs. His lack of fondness for me was becoming too apparent, so I decided the best thing, that I could do, was to at least stay out of his way.

The next morning, I had to go directly into the Dean's office and explain John's situation. "Well, he got a bloody nose that wouldn't stop, so we went to the hospital." I started laughing at how funny the dreadful tale of a bloody nose sounded. The Dean watched my suspicious lightness of manner and tone. He struggled over whether

I was telling the truth or if John was off with some woman, fucking his life away in a remote island never to return, but still hoping for the college credit.

"They said he was malnourished and couldn't clot it. They said ten days to two weeks." The funniness ran away in his doubt so I began to play it straight. "I have the address and a phone number if you want to call." With a wave of his head, I was free to tell the tale to the rest of my fellow students. With John's bloody nose and my Berlin stories, I became the "Celebrity of the Day."

Ignoring my new found popularity, I went for my first jog of the year. The thought of jogging energized me, so I ran with it, so to speak. Slowing past John's house, I looked upward to his window hoping to catch a glimpse of him, but only a darkened drape appeared.

Thinking about him having the worst time of his life made me laugh. Nothing could bring me down until I got home that night and a box was waiting there for me. I recognized Kristie's address and her writing. Albert looked down at it and up at me with excitement. He loved the turmoil. His secret fantasy must have been to be on a soap opera. I disregarded his curiosity and took the box to the seclusion of my room. Canned food lined the box with Spaghetti-O's and Ramen Noodles looking the best. To balance the good and the bad, I enjoyed a cold can of Spaghetti-O's while trudging through her letter. While eating, I smelled her presence.

The opened letter was soaked in her perfume. "Oh great." With a sigh I read about her feelings for me and how much she missed me. "If she only knew," my head shook for her ignorance. In between her script, my principles began to detail the plan of our break-up. My conclusion was a nice short letter to tell her to wait for a phone call at a designated time and at a designated location giving me two weeks to prepare a strategy. Two seemed enough time to carefully weigh nothing or everything.

A couple days later, I again went jogging past John's house to look for a sign of his return. The Dean told me that he would be home anyday, but still nothing. Jogging up the cobblestone path that used to lead us into the now forgotten John's valley, I kept my head down so I wouldn't trip on one of the stones.

"Hey." My head jumped up to see sunglasses looking stupid against a newly paled face. John looked frail in his jeans and red and white horizontally striped shirt. I had always thought that horizontal lines made you look bigger, but I hoped it was the other way around for his sake.

"Wow, what's up? How are you feeling?"

"Great man, better than ever. I slept and ate for over a week. Good to be back, though. Wow, Brussels looks and smells a lot different."

"Same old shit. It will hit you when you go back to class. You look good."

"Fuck you, I'm nothing but bones. But I'm feeling good and we only have a little more than a month to go in this rat hole. It will be nice to get back. That's the one thing that is keeping me going," his voice riveted in its hushed air.

"Yeah."

"So how was Berlin?"

"Crazy, the place is nuts. Whores, drugs, you name it. East Berlin is a hole. It's backward. I almost got stuck there. Good story. I'll save it for later with a bottle."

"No more drinking man. Not for me." My right eyebrow rose. "I'm taking medicine anyway."

"All right, but don't leave me hanging. We still have a long way to go until things return back to normal. I still need you to run around with and your fresh daisy like perspective to keep my chin up."

"Shut up. So you fucked around with Head while I was on my death bed? Didn't you?"

It was a sheepish smile and a slight blush that kept me from lying. "Yeah, but not until we left you. We fucked around on the train. Another good story for that first bottle of Belgian wine."

"Yeah, so what's up with that?"

"Well, Kristie is still waiting."

He laughed, "I've heard that shit before."

"I don't know? This is a tough one. I actually like Head, but I may not even see her again. I finally have realized there really is no reason to hang on to Kristie, but the whole thing is not fair to anyone. Hey, maybe I'll get a good conscience someday and become a complete mess."

He laughed some more, "You'll see her. Ever since you notched me, you did yourself in. You've probably got her address with you."

"Fuck you." He walked past me towards his home.

The next day, my first letter arrived from Kelly.

> Dear Don,
>
>   I'm back at home and bummed. Nobody got too pissed at me not coming back. I guess that

shows you how good of a job I am doing.
How was Berlin? Seeing the wall must have been amazing. And your trip back?

She mentioned some other trivial stuff. I scanned the words looking for a sign.

It came,

> …and so I met this guy named Don and he and his friend talked me into going to Greece and drinking a lot. So, we all partied and then were left alone. John started bleeding and Don and I sat by telling stories so we wouldn't have to talk about the blood and the fear. So, now this Don and I are friends and I'm bored to be alone.
>
> When I woke up on the train I had no idea where I was. I fell asleep before we left and couldn't remember where I was going. I was scared. Even if I had been waking up in the strange bus station, there had always been the face of a friend close by to reassure me. Now a strange Italian man stared into my eyes.
>
> Love,
> Kelly

It was in a smooth and neat cursive that looked so artistic on the page. I showed it to John, "You shouldn't of made that notch, man. When you call her, tell her thanks for everything. You know she called me down there. She picked up my spirits when I needed it the most."

I read and reread it, looking hopefully for something more. "Does she really want me to call or come?" She did and knew I would make that call as soon as I couldn't stand it any longer. Strangely, I needed her with a desperation while the thoughts of her raided my every move. The warmth and familiarity of the letter kept me hanging on.

The day came to call Kristie, I nervously dialed the number from the phone booth. I still hadn't decided what route I was going to take. Somebody else picked up.

"Is somebody named Kristie there?"

"Snags, what's up?"

My college nickname really through me off, "Who is this?"

"Hadlich."

"Hadlich, what the fuck are you doing? I mean what's up?"

"Well I saw Kristie standing here. She told me she was waiting for you to call. Then I forced my way onto the phone. I don't want to take up your time, but I wanted to say hi."

"Yeah this is illegal and I have been busted before. Say hi to everyone would you?"

A pause and a muffled buzz elapsed before, "Hi, Don."

"Hey what's up?"

"What's going on?"

"Well, I just wanted to call to hear your voice." My heart sunk. I blew it and I didn't have the strength to go back. Over the phone was all wrong and created a void where I had nothing else to say.

"Thanks. It sounded like Spring Break was fun."

"Yeah, best time yet. How was your Spring Break?"

"All right, just worked."

"Thanks for the food."

"I even put Spaghetti-O's in there for you."

"I liked the perfume in the letter."

The tension eased a little. She laughed, "I had no idea of the proper amount, so I just drenched it."

We shared a little more laughter. Silence came back.

I couldn't stand it. "Hey I better get going before the cops come and arrest me and take all of my money, which is none."

"All right, take care and let me know when you your flight gets back into New York. I'll pick you up. You know, we live there now."

"Thanks. Oh yeah, could you bring me a bologna sandwich to the airport? I'm dying for some bologna and mayo."

"Bologna and Mayo? All right, will do. Take Care."

"You too." We both waited for the sound of the other end to click signaling the end. It was like getting the last word in. I finally put down the receiver and kicked myself.

I stood in the phone booth, "I'm a fucking retard." Stuck in a gasp, I pulled out a crumbled piece of paper from my pocket. Kelly wasn't home, but I left a message with the lady who owned her apartment, telling her the time I would arrive in Clausbourg, which was tomorrow.

The train ride to Clausbourg was only a couple of hours until its arrival. When I got to the station, Head was nowhere to be found.

I waited on the platform for a moment, then walked around the main terminal by the board with all the departures and arrivals. I went back to the platform. "Fuck," being the pessimist I figured she didn't get the message. I weighed my options.

I asked someone how to get to my treasured address in my best French. At least I was finally making an effort to speak it, "Ou est La Rue de Oretgno," showing him how it was spelled on the crumpled piece of paper.

The directions came back in Franglais. With a hearty "Merci," I was on my way. Without any problem I found the street, but of course it was a main avenue. It was like walking down Sixth Avenue in New York. The first address was 1090 and it needed to be 8010. "I hope these numbers go up and quick," but they didn't. After a half-hour the number sat on top of my head.

"Fuck, there would be a hole bunch of different fucking buzzers." I didn't care if I was speaking to myself and looking like an ass. The buzzers made no sense, had no scheme, nor a familiar name. I looked outside and up the long brown stretch of the apartment building walkup. "How do people move in with all those stairs? It's too tall to be a walkup."

I thought for a moment. Making an educated guess, I rang one of the buzzers. The door opened its gates to let me go up. With the apartment number in hand the climb lasted eight flights until the number six appeared. The bell brought a woman who searched me with a funny look on her face. She was fairly young and European with her scraggly brown hair falling down on her shoulders and partially hiding a weathered face. Her brown eyes ran up and down my body as I did the same. She was definitely European, thin as a bean.

"Bonjour, Est…Kelly, I mean, *Qu'est c'est* Kelly, ici?" my flustered mind wouldn't work. I had tons of French knowledge, but choked in the clutch. Recognition in her eyes afforded me the opportunity to relax.

"Hello, I am sorry, but you just missed her. She went to meet a friend at the train station."

"Oh, I am her friend."

She laughed and told me that I could leave my stuff. I said, "Thanks, but no thanks. *Ce n'est pas probleme*." Back to the train station, I went.

I got there again and tried to figure out where she would be. Looking up at the hanger like green building, I was tapped on my shoulder, "Hi, what's going on?"

It was the tall blonde with the hairy face from California who Josh had brought for me to hook up with, "Hey, how is it going?" Her name mashed out in a blob, just like my memory of it.

"Did you come here to meet Josh? I think he went to Geneva or something like that for the weekend."

"Oh no, I…" Head came running up next to me.

"Where have you been?"

"Me?"

"I'm sorry, I was a little late."

"Yeah, I walked to your place and back again."

"Oh well, it's great to see you," her smile proceeded her bright eyes that ran back and forth between me and the Californian.

"Yeah, you too."

The blonde felt dumb and coughed. I ignored her because her name still wouldn't come to me. Finally, she announced, "Have fun. I'll see you around."

"Oh yeah, it was good seeing you again." Her leaving wasn't even acknowledged with a look, but the temptation to check her out one last time made me fidget.

"Who was she?"

"I can't remember her name. She came up with Josh to Brussels to visit," stopping short of informing Kelly of her sole purpose which was to sleep with me.

"How's John?"

"Fine, he just got back the other day. He seemed recharged. Looks good, but he lost tons of weight." We looked over each other and I bent down and gave her a kiss on the forehead when she looked away. She blushed.

"I've got a present," I pulled out two bottles of wine from my book bag. "Best in Europe is the Belgium Resiling. Much better than the Alsace shit coming out of here."

"Hey, Clausbourg has got the premium beer, Kronenburg, that couldn't be touched by anything Northern."

"Is Degan coming?"

"Yeah, in about an hour."

My laughed got caught, "I knew he would be for some reason. Let's hit a grocery store and wait out here. I don't think I can make that trek back to your apartment yet."

Degan and Ned were a great surprise and I couldn't wait to see them again. When they arrived, the bottles were uncorked and passed around.

Ned started, "Where the fuck is John?"

"He just got back and is still resting up. He would have loved to come, but he was worried about what else you would do to him, Ned."

"You know, we stopped by the hospital."

"No fucking way," the picture of the note, that she left in Brindisi, and the astronomical odds hung mystically between us.

"Can you believe that, and you had no faith," Kelly admonished.

"None…That's amazing."

We finished up the bottles and went back to drop off our stuff. It was getting late already so we bought two more bottles before the liquor stores closed.

In Head's little room, the wine was emptied in whispers, as to not upset her landlord / roommate. Landlord / roommate was a very precarious position to get into. After that we headed into town to whoop it up and to keep our eyes open for Josh, just in case he was in town. At the bar I recognized some of his classmates, but they had no idea who I was. It was nice. We drank Kronenburgs, Clausbourg's highly touted beer, until our bellies were full and then snuck back into Head's place.

Getting caught meant serious trouble. We quietly ate a can of corn niblets that I still had left over from dinner. They taste so good cold that all of its juice was consumed.

I laid down with Kelly on her bed while the other two slept on the floor. We teasingly fondled each other's genitals, but my blood still raced uncontrollably passionate.

The next morning was inaugurated in each other's arms. She checked out her apartment and was gone for quite some time. The three of us looked at each other and smiled, knowing she was busted. And she was, but she still sweet talked her way out of it.

She stormed back quietly into the room, "I shouldn't have to put up with that shit. I pay good money to live here. Oh well, we can't do it again tonight. We'll have to break into my school and sleep there."

She showed us the town in the light. Clausbourg was fairly hip, because of the presence of the European Parliament. Lots of parks and statues were all background for its big cathedral. We checked it all out, posing at statues and taking goofy pictures. We even got yelled at by an elderly man for not appreciating the significance of a certain piece of art.

The statue was the head of a man, eight feet high, poking out of a square pool of water and surrounded by columns. We posed behind it with our heads poking up the exact same way. That's when the man berated us about our limited appreciation for the French man or some other kind of marketing shit drilled into everyone's conscience in order to sell the piece and to justify the tons of taxpayer's money that was spent on it. Head berated back. She spoke fluent French and was very impressive in doing so. French, a very sensual language to watch someone speak, was such a beautiful language as it rolled and made one use their lips and tongues.

Continuing on, the four of us decided to head out to Head's best friend's house for dinner. We only had a faint idea of how to get there. A bus here, a bus there, then we had to walk about so far. Kelly really didn't know.

We got to what she thought was the stop, actually it was the last stop. The bus driver told us that he thought that it wasn't too far. Getting out, our aimless procedure followed what we hoped the bus driver had directed. Of course, it was wrong and we turned around. Ned and Degan played kick rock, finally having some fun and getting a break from the weariness of traveling together for such a long time on so little. Shorts weather had arrived in Northern Europe and they were digging it.

A dirt road eventually led us to the place.

I was very anxious to meet Tonya, one of only two true friends that Kelly had in Europe. Kelly had the suspicion that she was truly a lesbian and hadn't come out of closet. They even talked about it where she divulged that she had wanted to kiss this woman a couple of years ago, but it never came to fruition. Lesbians were very intriguing to me at the time and I was aching to meet her.

Every boy's fantasy was to be in between two women, a strange phenomena called Dad's Penthousetition. Dad's Penthousetition struck little kids, who came across Penthouses at an early age, and forced men into lusting after lesbians yet hating homosexual men. I was stricken, but recovered from hating homosexual men. The hating became benign and wound up being in all of my coolness, "I just don't understand them."

Tonya's story was simple; she was in love with one of the Ecuadorian guitar players that hung outside of the famous Clausbourg cathedral. He wanted to come to America and marry her. Yeah, right.

She had prepared us a little repast of salad and chili. She was another vegetarian. It was good to consume something more than bread and cheese for a change. Even though she didn't want to go out with us for the night, she began drinking, so we followed in her insistence. Beers from some where in France were our choice tonight and drunkenness came easily.

With something to prove, Tonya bashed America from the onset. I was feeling surly, so I poked back, "You know, I'm becoming to despise American bashing. It just seems like the hip thing to do for young Americans here and for the young Europeans. It is only out of jealousy and an unfounded jealousy at that."

Yes, I had hit a nerve, "Americans have all of the power and they broker it so they can keep accumulating more power and wealth. Ignorant, fat cats is the best way to describe Americans."

"You are an American?"

She was on a roll, "Yeah, I am an ignorant, fat cat." I bit the ole lip. "Me, Me, Me, and More, More, More. They hold countries hostages economically and force the deaths of millions in order to maintain their standing at the top of the heap, capitalism of politics. It is gross."

I was drunk, but not too drunk, "Yeah, but it is so easy to criticize every decision that anyone makes. There are always at least two sides and not every one is going to be happy with what side gets what. We spend the most money in aid. At least we try. You may think that their only reason to give aid is to keep countries dependent on us, but they could really be trying to do what is right. Is just sitting back the right thing to do? What would you say if we were completely isolated?"

Kelly threw that "you better stop now before I kick your ass" look my way. I didn't even really believe or care in what I was saying, but I wanted an argument. Even though I knew better to continuing an unwinnable argument, I forged forward killing the buzz. Eventually, I ignored her as she kept rambling to nowhere throwing in a "Yeah" every once in awhile to encourage her to shut up.

Ned and Degan were obviously jamming to Michelle Shocked, a nice swirling country blues mix of the joys and pains of being young. "I know Texas always seems so big, but you know you are in the largest state in the union when you anchored down in Anchorage," they sang.

Beer gone, Tonya pissed, and the rest of us drunk; it was time to leave. "Off to the big city," was Degan's parting shot.

The bus didn't arrive for an hour forcing us to make the choice between peeing on the road or in our pants. I had never watched a woman piss before without a toilet until Kelly sat down just like a catcher and let it rip. "Off to the big city," it was.

We got back to town and had nothing to do. "Let's go to a bar."

"No, I only have fifteen francs to last me until Monday."

We looked at Kelly for a destination, a purpose for our efforts. Our journey lead us to a Sunoco. "A Sunoco in Europe, that sounds like a beatnik poem." However, it was the only place open after 6 that still sold liquor.

"Kelly, they have our wine here." I announced over the aisle. Our wine was 4.2 francs and was in a water bottle with a plastic top. The flavor came only in burgundy red and the size was two liters, perfect.

We all got a bottle and headed to the nearest canal which crisscrossed Clausbourg. Creating laughter about anything, the wine smoothly filled our minds with thoughts to giggle about. Suddenly Degan looked at Ned. They had an amazing inane sense about each other's thoughts. "Yeah?" Degan asked. Something bad was about to happen to me. Ned hesitated, then quickly got up and jumped into the canal with Degan a step behind. I looked at Kelly with a sigh, "You know I have to." I was a little smarter and stripped of my clothes first.

"Be my guest, but I'm not going."

I raced in, pretended to have fun, and swam briefly, then rushed back to the safety of shore. Ned's head disappeared into the Texas tea of night's water in a swoop of Degan's power. Ned's hand came up full of black sludge that he soon discovered to be all over his body. This sent them into to hysterics as they both ran out laughing.

For all we knew, the crusty cake that stuck to our bodies was shit. Ned was pulling lumps of solid waste from his hair, "Are the canals used for sewage, Head?"

"I don't know, but the water doesn't flow too much. It just kind of sits there and stagnates. Plus I've seen scores of rats swimming along."

"That's a bummer." I shivered in disgust, grabbing the ground.

Upon finishing the wine, our feet began to take us to our new home, Kelly's school. We did not dare sleep at her apartment again, but we stopped by to get blankets and luggage.

Kelly broke into the school without any problems and led us up to the main lounge area. The building was dark and very small. Inside, there were only a few tiny classrooms which offered very little comfort. Kelly and I took the couch in the lounge, while the other two hung their clothes and settled in on the floor.

They seemed asleep, so I woke Kelly up with a kiss.

"Ummm, I've been waiting for that all day."

The passion carried us away, until her clothes were completely off. Not wanting to be caught in a very embarrassing situation, we scurried off to the Dean's office to continue. After various efforts of struggling to fulfill her inner burning, she wound up naked, satisfied, and asleep, while I was fully awake and fully clothed, staring out a window.

I stared at her naked body.

Her bronzed arm, cutting across her creamy stomach with her firm breasts, comfortably balanced upward while her nipples with cottage cheese bumps protruded. Her pointed chin, her sharply cut face, and her blonde bobbed hair finished the landscape.

I ran back down her body, measuring each subtle curve closely. I bumped over her light brown pubic hair until I slithered down the firmness of her leg.

She was beautiful, so beautiful that I was sure I would not get the distaste of disgust for her that I felt for every other woman I had known.

A horrible rumbling started in my stomach and catapulted me to a trembling that engulfed my whole existence. That very moment spoke, telling me that she was not the one. I knew at that very second that no one could ever fully know or fully understand me. Reaching the top of that mountain, my scream reached every corner of my brain, "I can never truly discover love. Love does not exist. Love does not exist," came out in a silent chant.

Life was a series of hopeful encounters fading into lonely realizations. Now, I had the world figured out and was much wiser than the rest of mankind. My body and mind switch into a perfect synch that reached the pinnacle of existence, a comfortable realization of a sad fate.

Saddened, I watched the night drift away. I covered Kelly up with both of our blankets. Huddled under my coats, I fell asleep losing my guard, forgetting everything that I had learned, and ignoring and denying the truth.

The next morning, Ned left to see some relative, who lived close by, leaving Degan, Head, and myself. We walked through town, kicking around and looking for a good time. None was to be had. We contemplated getting stoned, but I was worried about drug testing at my summer job. Instead, we sat in the main square and watched the swindlers swindle, the musicians play, and everyone else do their thing.

We ran into Josh's twin sister. The gesture of his best friend and his sister coming to town while he was off chasing skirt somewhere else baffled me until the redemption of carelessness came. Oh well, neither of us had told him that we were coming.

I finally decided to leave, "Look, I've got a huge paper due tomorrow. I've got tons of work left to do." I was lying. It was almost done. I really just needed to edit it, but I was still nervous about it. The paper sucked and I would rather spend my night staring at it, knowing that it sucked, instead of ignoring it. My customized conscience worked miracles.

"Come on, why don't you stay tonight?" It was Kelly's turn to do the annoying.

"We could get fucked-up again tonight, no stopping us. What do you say?" Degan had that look today, but it was less evil and more caged. His skull was hiding in a pen while we waited for the explosion that would never come. Instead, he just grinned.

"All right." We walked back to her place, but the paper lingered in my mind. I took comfort in knowing that a six o'clock train could still be taken.

"I'm still going to go. I'm too much of a pansy ass."

"Don, how much time do you still have to spend on the paper?" Kelly looked out her window nonchalantly, not even waiting for answer. "What time is your class? You are going to spend that whole time on the paper? Go back in the morning, finish it, turn it in, then go to bed."

"You're enjoying this aren't you? It's my whole grade for this class. My paper sucks. It's on some dumb ass trade thing with the European Community. How can anyone in their right mind put any sort of effort into that?"

They walked me to the train station with me leading the way walking the whole route on any crack in the sidewalk that would break my mother's back. Degan balanced on the edge of the curb and Head tried to push either of us off. Sometimes, it was the simple things. Running, jumping, yelling, laughing, drinking, spitting, barefoot on grass; that was the life to be had. That was the feeling I took leaving Clausbourg. The hatred of the night before was forgotten. Spring was in my heart and soul. Life was exciting and new and I was already plotting my next rendezvous with Kelly.

TWENTY-EIGHT
Toothpicks Dipped In...

Something new, life became fun. More importantly, though, was my realization that school was a joke. With that monkey off of my back, I could now play.

Another key was recognizing that there was nothing I could do to myself to make up for Kristie's abortion. Starving myself to death just wasn't the way to apologize to anyone. Making myself have a rotten time wasn't the way to make her feel better. Nothing was going to massage my ill feelings so I just let them go. "Goodbye."

John and I started playing basketball all over the playgrounds of Brussels. We would play with the little kids who would want to kick the ball, instead of shooting it. However, the NBA was becoming much more popular in Europe and everyone knew who Magic Johnson was, so they tried.

Also, I even began to jog every night.

With Head easing my mind, John's role began to change. We wasted away the weekdays together only to go our separate directions during the weekend. Before, the opposite predominated. Also, our wasted time replaced our displacement of anger.

The next weekend after my first visit to Kelly, I went to Paris by myself. It was the first time I had really seen the city. With map in hand, I did all the tourist things that I was supposed to; the Eiffel Tower, Musee d'Orsay, Sacre Coeur, the whole bit. I was exhausted when completed, but I felt like I had to get a feel for the city. The only thing I bagged was Jim Morisson's grave. It was the real reason that I went, but it required so much more work than I wanted.

John's girlfriend had come for a visit and I couldn't see Head for two weeks. So I hopped on the train and walked around Paris, ridding another weekend.

Eventually, the time came for me to call Head and tell her that I was coming. She told me to come to her apartment this time, "No mix up." On Friday, I tried to sneak out without anyone knowing where I was going, in order to avoid any schmoe tagging along. But I didn't make it.

Pete, the nameless friend who was stuck with me in Berlin, trapped me. I felt kind of obligated to him because of the terror in Berlin, the bottle that he had bought, and the offer he made to buy the rest of the time remaining on my Eurorail. The extra time on the Eurorail, which was two full weeks after my last final, developed out of my money situation and the strong desire to get back into the states. Selling it was a necessity for money. So he came, but I was pissed at the prospects of having to entertain him. "Don, do you think I can get laid down there?"

"Better chances there than here. Everyone here already knows the kind of dick that you are." The sadness in his ex-girlfriend's eyes, when he told her it was over, replayed while he proceeded to fuck everyone and anyone that he could right in front of her ego. She went all the way to Belgium with him and then saw her self-esteem get crushed by his two fingers. She was too good and cool to keep down, and wound up having fun, but everyone thought he was the biggest ass for the way he handled things. Of course, only after he had used them all for sex.

We bought two bottles of wine and a fifth of whiskey and the three of us sat around trying to drink it all. "Kelly, Pete wants to get laid, what do you think his chances are?"

"Pretty good, enough dumb bimbos here that won't realize the kind of ass that you are."

"Wow," he faked a drink of whiskey. "News travels fast."

"The way you're drinking, you must be serious about getting laid. You can't be too drunk to fuck and can't be to sober too have the balls…huh, wussy boy?" My comments produced a hearty chuckle from all.

"Yeah, Yeah."

We went out to a bar to meet Josh and I was a complete mess. The bar kept hiding the clues to what was going on. Josh and I had spoken earlier, promising each other to help Pete find somewhere to stay and possibly some pussy. He had ninety women in his program and he thought most of them were trying to experience the zest of life and might try Pete, thus supplying a bed without our efforts.

As I walked in, he saw how fucked-up I was. I said hi to everyone, told everyone Kelly's name, and just stood there. Josh didn't even bother to get up from his corner position. Pete took care of himself, getting a beer for appearance's sake. He offered, but I shook my head horizontally, feeling the whiskey and wine sloshing back and forth.

I looked over at Head who was as equally numb, "Let's get some air." She grasped at words, but nothing was produced. We walked outside and found a corner in the alley way and made out. We violently grabbed and rubbed each other. "Let's go home."

I went in and made Josh give up his corner spot in between two women by insisting that he came over to talk to me. "Dude, sorry, but I'm too fucked up. I've got to get home, before I puke."

Josh was pissed, but had expected it. It wasn't the first time that Kelly made him feel slighted. "I'll call you tomorrow. Should I take Pete with me?"

"No something will happen to him."

"See ya. Don't worry about him, he's on his own."

The air straightened out my head a little bit. Kelly unconscientiously staggered towards home, walking in front of me. She had on a loose light blue denim shirt with a T-shirt underneath. Since it was cold, she had also put on a sweatshirt on top. Her compass was off and insisted in going the wrong way. "Kelly, isn't it this way?"

"No, no, a couple more blocks."

"Are you sure?" I looked up at the street sign that read her street name. She kept on going. Too tired to play, "Come on let's go this way."

"No, it's this way."

"Just humor me, we can walk that way, but let's go down this street a little bit." She turned to discover her apartment. She didn't remember her confusion moments before and inconspicuously led me straight into her bed.

In the morning, we woke up naked and lying spoon style. I was on the outside. I hardened, signaling us to begin fooling around. Things suddenly picked up and I was on top of her. Nerves struck

my functional body, reminding me about my upcoming perfor-
mance, my unworthiness, and my last sexual disaster with Kristie.
While attempting to place my penis inside, I became partially limp.
My frustration and further attempts completed its deflation.

I rolled off, embarrassed, to watch the ceiling, "I'm sorry. I
don't think I can yet."

"Don't worry about it. Let's go get some breakfast."

On our way out we saw Pete walking down the street. We
redirected him towards breakfast and got the supposed scoop on
what he did last night. "I was pretty fucked-up and nothing was
going my way. My rap must have been horrible, especially with me
slurring and falling and leaning and twisting every which way.

"The end of the night came and your friend, Josh, had already
left." The thought didn't make me feel the least bit of responsibility
or sympathy. "I was talking to the last couple of women left and
trying to stay with them. It was useless, so I asked them where a
chcap hotel was. One of told me she would go in on it with me,
because she didn't want to travel all the way back to her place. My
luck was changing.

"I split a fifty dollar room somewhere. It was all right. Anyway
no sex, but I did cum by virtue of someone else's hand."

"Good for you." Breakfast started and ended in silence. His
story, insensitive and cocky, had grown old. I could give a shit if he
was fucking every woman that looked his way. Apparently, he
wasn't since he made such a point about telling us. That's usually
how it was: nobody ever walks the talk or talks about the walk. It was
either/or. You were walking or you were talking. You were shacking or you were yacking.

He felt the chill in our air, "I'm going back."

A joyful sighed released, "Oh no. Are you sure? You don't want
to hang out?"

"Yeah, I'm tired and I spent all my money last night. When's the
next train?" I told him and he was off. What a relief, but I worried
that he wouldn't buy the rest of my Eurorail Pass.

The day was ours so she showed the lesser known places around
the city. We walked holding hands and laughing. The bright sun
permitted us to wear T-shirts. After a coffee house and an attempt
at a crossword puzzle, the day wound up with us laying down to tan
ourselves along the same canal that I had jumped in weeks before.
I still couldn't shake the sex thing off of my mind. I was glad we
didn't have sex, but I was worried about the long term, emotional

strains that my sex drive was experiencing. Also, the crabs, that I had attained in Spain, were forgotten to be told and continued to be suppressed by my subconscious. At this stage, I doubted she would believe my story of lack of hygiene.

Each time I went to see her, I would pour vinegar on my pubic hairs for a week and comb out the little buggers. It was painful and would sometimes rip my skin apart, but I was worried about my credibility if I gave them to her, plus they itched like mad. I don't know if the vinegar worked, but I remembered being a kid when a lice epidemic went through the school which forced me to shower with vinegar. I kind of remember that it killed the lice, but not the eggs. It made sense, since the lice kept coming back once a month.

She took me to dinner then we met Josh out with his friends. He was still a little bitter about yesterday and paid most of his attention to the latest crush in his life. Head and I got bored and went home fairly sober. The pressure of her bed and the opportunity of sex rushed back to my thoughts. Drunkenness would have made it easier.

We undressed apart. My body sagged in the middle and sunk on the ends. Noticing, a physical fitness plan was laid out in my head for the summer. I followed her under the sheets. Our mouths met and her feelings for me were finally showing. Up until this weekend she was holding back. Was it the pregnant girlfriend, a lack of trust in me, or was she not sure that she really liked me? I didn't care, because she was finally opening up. Content caressed our hugs. Even though my loins were excited, my hands and intentions stayed in check. She feel asleep on my chest, our heaving breathes in synch.

The morning came and we settled for a lazy day. Lying around in the depths of short talk and long touches until the afternoon sun produced guilt, she read a poem.

Pondering
How much you see
Without my knowledge?
Could you have known
about me?
Do you know
I conceal?
Should I dread
Your wisdom?
Collapse the walls

Divulging nakedness.
I can't conceal
I won't deceive
Knowingly, you read it.
Defenseless
I built myself.
Sheltered
Embrace us both.

I kept the piece of paper and read it and read it again looking for the clues of her heart. She was wrong, I couldn't read it. Blinded by my own obsession and self-doubt, I reveled in her written confession. The last stanza was really meant for me. Now, I was sheltered, embracing our dual fates.

TWENTY-NINE
Pretending

The quickly deteriorating time in Europe, that still remained, inflamed me. Even though I had missed out on a lot and hadn't seen it all, I needed some time alone and a set routine. The toll of my weary fight settled into my indolent actions.

John and I made our usual after school trips to our playground. We had found a series of four hoops that shot out from one stem. They alternated in sizes from regulation to five feet. Dirt and grass covered the area under the hoops with big mud patches under each. Because of the ridge created from the erosion under each basket, I could dunk on the regulation size. All the kids would watch and be wowed. I was not a bad athlete, but I could never make my six foot two inch frame stuff a ball in the basket. On the edge of being able to dunk, I needed a little help that the lip provided. A soccer ball was easy, but when the transition to a basketball was made, I miserably failed attempt after attempt. These hoops made me look good.

Today we were there again to show off. We were regulars and had a steady bunch of regular kids whom we taught little moves to and then beat-up on in games. Fun was had by all, but those little fuckers always wanted to use their feet.

Today, we were taking the back way up through the valley and into the back of the park, "How was the visit from Cindy? I know she stayed up in your room."

"Yeah, we went for it on the last night. It had to be done. While

I ate breakfast, she snuck out the front door. We were luckier than shit."

"Yeah, could you image getting caught? The look on that poor, old woman's face. You would've destroyed her along with her wonderful and pure, Catholic soul."

"It would have killed her. Then the old man, Giuseppe, would go out back and sharpen up his ax, hunt me down, and kill me like the evil soaked pig that I am."

"That would have been hilarious, a fitting ending to your life. I hope mine is on the toilet with the squirts."

"No way, it will be just like mine. When you go to Kristie's house for the first time, you know, he will be grinding up that ax. He's probably doing right now as we speak."

"He's down in the basement, mumbling to himself, with a yell every once and awhile. 'Don, that mother fuckin' bastard, if it's the last thing I do.' He keeps on sharpening that ax in his yellow pitted t-shirt waiting patiently for my return and demise."

"Speaking of Kristie, how did things go with Head this weekend?"

"Fuck you, dick. Things went well."

"Did you yet?"

"Did I yet? What the fuck kind of question is that? Did I yet?" I laughed, "No…the consequences and pain are still lingering in my penis. I can't muster up the courage, even though the opportunity has presented itself a couple of times. Did I yet?"

We walked around the pond and past the little overpriced cafes. The hoops and kids appeared just beyond. Seeing us, they stood around waiting, "Look at them, all pathetic."

"Yeah, but they can kick our ass any day in soccer." I tried to juggle the ball with my feet. It was in the air for a few moments until I had to use my left foot. The ball squirted ahead. I caught up to it and kept running until the orange ball slammed through the orange metal and the nylon webbing. The kids cheered then we proceeded to kick their preteen asses in basketball. Such a small and easy feat made us feel so big and cool. I wished I was little and getting my ass kicked.

The sun was going down as we made our way back to John's in a quiet and grey descent. The plan was to steal some food from John's family and then hit the fireworks that were in the honor of some sort of liberation of Belgium from something. Why we kept celebrating, when I remained so trapped, was beyond me.

John checked out the house yelling for an answer. Nothing came, signaling the commencement of our regale. We snaked suspiciously into the kitchen. The white cooling coffin offered us many choices; salami, pepperoni, left over chicken, bread, cheese, spaghetti. A little bit of each was taken.

With our stomachs full, we laid down on a patch of grass at the bottom of John's valley. July Fourth excitement was in the air, but a naiveté to patriotism existed. Belgium really had little identity. Wrapping around my sweatshirt and blowing my ever lengthening hair, the cool air sighed into my ears. Other students passed, but we turned down the offers to join. Tonight would be sober and relaxing.

"So how are things really going with you two?"

The red lights dripped down the grey, covering, only to be erased by yellow lights and a boom. The flashes danced upon John's ruddy visage with his eyes dancing against the midnight fire. I laid back on my two elbows and crossed my feet. It wasn't like the Fourth of July at all.

"Pretty good, I guess." John watch the last month jump across my face to the rhythm of the light above. "John, I really like her. Man…I just have a lot of fun hanging out with her. I'm not sure what it is. Well, I don't trust it or me. Let's just say that I haven't completely bought off on the idea of me and her," I lied to him.

It wasn't that I hadn't bought off, it was that I wasn't given the opportunity to buy off. Out of control, the worry that this might be that mystical thing called true love grabbed my coattails and still remained along for the ride. In fact, I had no doubts about my feelings and was diving head first, hoping the pool was full and it was the deep end.

"I had a dream about her. You're not going to like it."

I saw the graveness, "This isn't any of your shit is it?" He looked at me waiting for the explanation. "I mean, I never really did buy into those ghost stories." He waited, "It's your acting, man. Sometimes I think you think stuff up and try to test your acting and improv ability. I don't believe in ghosts." He was annoyed, "I don't mean to bum you out, but it's like reading the Bible. I just can't believe it."

"You really don't believe in ghosts, huh? Well, I guess it's just got to happen to you someday, then you'll believe. You don't even believe in spirits or psyche."

"No," silence. The fireworks worked onward. I waited and hoped for the finale. Sometimes, I needed to think before I spoke.

"I know you don't believe, but I've got to tell you this one."

"Go ahead."

He sat up and positioned himself for the camera. "Well, I had a dream the other night. Someone was trying to kill me. You came and stopped them. You were having a huge struggle, the biggest struggle of your life. Boom, then I woke up."

"Of course, I was there saving your life. How many times now." Unimpressed, I continued to hope for the end of the fireworks.

"Yeah, that's the point. You have saved my life twice. I am a big believer in three's and this will be it, the third." I thought about it for a moment. "The first time was with the pill, right after we met Kelly. The second was the bloody nose in Brindisi with Kelly. And in my dream, Don, it was Kelly. I saw her face during the struggle with you. She looked so calmly and lovingly at you, but her body was trying to rip and pull you into nothing. I woke up and couldn't get back to sleep, everything was starting to make sense.

"During the dream, I had a very distinct feeling, that she wasn't interested in me, but really you. She was trying to get to you through me."

"No way. She has been there every time I've saved you."

"No, you have defeated her each time. But the third time is the charm. Man, I've got a bad feeling about it. She is evil and she is fighting good, you," he pointed into my chest. "She is making you soft through love and then will destroy you."

I laughed, but he was unconvinced, "Come on John."

"I've got this feeling and I'm never wrong. Don't let her come up here and see you. It will be the third time. Don, I know you have a hard time believing, but I know. I have the powers. Don't let her ruin you. She will destroy you. I knew it since the first time I saw her. That's why we had such a connection that night, because we knew each other. I am afraid. You are the opponents and I am the playing field," his frothing pleads turned desperate. The finale rang out along the valley. The echo resonated up my spine, producing chills that ran bumps up and down my arm.

"She's coming this weekend," I contemplated with blades of grass twirling in my hand.

"She's coming to finish you off," his head shook to tell me I told you so.

I slept uneasily that night. In the morning I got a letter confirming her visit:

> Dear Don,
>   Blah, Blah, Blah…
> Love,
> Kelly

I looked for any evil clues or misplaced 666's, but found nothing. The thoughts hid in the back of my mind, restraining the excitement of showing her my life in Brussels.

On the day of her arrival, the school was jumping. It was the last weekend before finals and the school held a huge gala. Everyone was hanging out in the Cov, the student lounge, drinking, reminiscing, and lying. I opted out and found John before leaving to meet Kelly. He was wound up and ready for a good time.

At crunch time, I felt a little left out, but I did not have the twenty-five dollars for the party. "I kind a wish I could go, man. Have fun, would you? I'll stop by tomorrow in the morning, all right?"

"Sounds good. Are you nervous? I know I am."

"Fuck you. See you tomorrow."

"Let's hope."

I grabbed some wine and headed to the station. She was waiting with a red sweater covering the top of a dressy, flowery, long skirt. She smiled as I spoke, "I've got a great place for us to go."

Our trail headed straight for John's valley with a long oratory about the history of John and his valley. With the conclusion of the growing wilder story, we perched upon the bridge where we once offered our corks to the gods. I failed to mention that part because I knew her crusade against garbage and other worldly injustices. I was changing.

She opened up the bottle which she had brought and told me of her school and her work. "Fuck, who cares about that shit. Let's toast to not caring about that shit." She was changing right along with me.

We finished up the bottles and it was time to make a decision about our night. "Well, everyone here is at the reception. It probably won't be over until late."

"What do you want to do?"

"Well, I've been giving this some thought. I think we should return back to my place before the guy I live with gets back. I know his routine. I think we can get away with it." I laughed nervously as I pictured Albert walking into my room and seeing a naked woman.

"Are you sure? We would be fucked, if you get caught."

"Yeah, it would be funny, but I've only got a week left. What can anyone do?"

"All right, how much time do you think we have?" her voiced grabbed onto my breathy nervousness.

"Enough." We got some more wine and headed towards the park with my basketball hoops. The wine was making me dizzy and confessional, "I've got to tell you something." My tone was too ominous, "Well, it's weird, but I've got to get it off of my chest.

"John had this crazy dream with you trying to kill him and I was trying to save him. He has this crazy feeling that you are evil and I am good and his body is the playing field. He also believes in three's and the third battle is coming up. The third is his unlucky charm," I took a long breath. The breathy nervousness reappeared.

She laughed and looked at me like I was fucked, "What are you fucked?"

"You know, I said the same thing to him, but he is convinced. I just wanted to say something just because it has been on my mind or at least he keeps trying to put it into my mind."

She laughed and farted. The joy of her flagellation shored up my nerves. Finishing the wine, we headed for home.

At home I showed her the Old World style of living with Albert. After seeing all of the rooms, I realized that there was a door almost directly across from the top of the stairs, but was partially hidden by an indentation. We both looked at it, "I don't know what room that is? Wow, I've never even noticed it." I was ready to walk on by.

"Let's go," I nervously obeyed and led the way up the wooden stairs that laid beyond the door. The freshly turned on light smelled rusty, like burning plastic. At first, some regular boxes and other miscellaneous stored things jumped out at the edges. The back wall came into focus where a concrete ledge jetted out of the wall and formed the foundation for an altar. The old pictures, candles, and perfectly laid out clothes sent chills throughout. I wanted to just leave, but the curiosity got the best of us.

"Wow, that must be his wife." I held up the old picture and a manly, yet handsome, woman in her early twenties. Long, braided, brown hair swung from the back of her head and covered the lacy grey dress. On a bench were clothes which matched the ones in the picture. It was yellow of age, but the frills and lace were kept in good condition.

Next to the dress was an old army uniform, grey with black trim.

Colonel Clink on Hogan Hero's appeared to put it on in front of my eyes. "He was in a German prison camp in World War II, you know."

Next to the picture was a series of medals and accommodations then a box of pictures. The stale air began to smell of a burial betrayal. I had to leave. The sanctuary into his past was broken.

We headed straight for my room jumping into bed with my ass kissing the cold concrete. She laid down next to me and began to kiss. I caressed her and took off her clothes. She followed.

She pulled down the sheets and got on top of me. Her nipples were hard and pointing upward to the ceiling. I touched them, letting her grab my hard penis and lead it into her. The wet warmth wrapped around me and began to move in circles and up and down. I saw the concentration in her face. "Don, just be careful."

Those words rang into my head. I had heard them before and failed, miserably. However, it was much too late for my weak will. The pleasure sung on my mountain top as I pulled out, came, and went to sleep.

Later in the night, I awoke to Albert's heavy steps. He was drunk and tired, but safely home. He appeared to me, fifty years younger with the uniform forcing his back straight, standing at the top of the stairs and wondering about something that I couldn't decipher. He could have been just resting. Finally, he made his way into the bathroom and I heard the toilet flush after the door eased closed.

The night's sleep was long and confused. Thoughts of Kristie, Kelly, and sex tickled. I was doing it again. Had I not learned? Sex to me was like a drug. Knowing the harm, I still loved and needed the feeling. In a desperate choice of my feelings, I lived my life for the thought of being accepted, liked, and relieved.

The sun eased through my light cotton curtain, exposing my watch which said eight-thirty. Sleep would not come back. Albert shuffled into the bathroom and down into the kitchen. His steps circled the downstairs. We had to wait for church which wasn't until ten.

Kelly finally woke up to my whispers and touches. This time I made my way on top of her. A few moments later, Albert walked up the stairs. His footsteps stopped and I imagined him outside my door wondering if he should open the door, knock, or just keep going.

Our lovemaking stopped in anxious wonderment about what he was going to do. The steps started again and were fading away. In a sighed, I rolled off, "he couldn't have known."

Finally, his car started, enabling us to rush around in an attempt to shower and to get dressed as quickly as possible. Within twenty minutes, we were out the door and walked to my school, then down to John's. From there, the three of us walked through the valley then up into town. The sky was blue in the highlights of seasonal change.

During a bread lunch, John filled us in on the night before. "It was weird. Jenny, you know Jenny? Jenny is the nicest, straightest person here. She is just a smart, nice, asexual mound of cuteness. It was the weirdest thing. We are dancing together and she is holding me real close looking at me with those eyes. Kind of like fuck me eyes, but in her case, kiss me eyes. She's rubbing, the whole bit.

"Anyway by the end of the night her friends are asking me about her and about my girlfriend. I was so confused. Finally, I just went up to Jenny and told her, 'Look, you are the nicest, most beautiful thing, but I'm in love with my girlfriend.' She cried and left. What the fuck is going on here? I say about hundred words to the girl in four months and then she falls in love with me over a couple of dances. Maybe, she just wanted some."

"Jenny? No way John. What would she want with you?" He gave me that knowing sarcastic look that made me laugh, "John, I've seen you coming out of a shower. My question remains."

"Well, did you want her?" Kelly asked.

"Yeah, I had to use all of my might to say no."

"That's even worse than cheating on your girlfriend. The sin of the mind was committed. Even if you didn't go through with it, you wanted to. The actual act is insignificant. In fact, you cheated on her and yourself."

"Huh? Have you two been conferring?"

"On her because you wanted to and on yourself because you didn't."

"Make me feel better. Don, you told her about my dream, didn't you?"

"Of course, you knew I would."

"You really think I'm evil?"

"No...I don't know? I just believe in the psychic and coincidence. Everything has a meaning. You seem so nice though, but that dream was so vivid."

"Maybe, you are a little jealous about the time I steal away from Don? Maybe in that sense I am evil."

"Let's drop it."

"Good idea."

We went to the park and played basketball with some kids. Kelly watched, disregarding John's mumbles under his breathe. It momentarily broke our trust.

Disappointedly, John went home and we went our own way. Kelly met Albert and they spoke together in French. He kept looking at me with concern over Kristie and my relation to this new woman. He was still very cordial and warm. Perhaps, I was paranoid. The T.V. blinked in front of us.

For dinner, we ate breads and spreads, because Albert went out to leave us to his devices. We cleaned everything up, like new, and hit the town. It was already nine o'clock when we wandered up in front of John's house. Kelly picked a handful of purple and white flowers along the way which were probably weeds, but still was in a nice arrangement. After several knocks, John's housemom peeped her head out of the gingerbread window, "John is not home. I am sorry."

We felt horrible for waking her and left the flowers on her door step. It was a nice touch of pardon. With nothing to do and not much money, the city and the bars offered something more than nothing. In order to sneak into my room, we had to stay out past midnight.

Finally, we allowed ourselves to go home. Staring at his window, I opened the door with a gentle touch. The presence of a light did not shine against his tiled sill. Nothing stirred, so she hurried in behind me. Each step, my eyes jetted to the top of the stairs and my ears turned each corner until they reached the front of his door. Our nerves forced a jog at the top of the stairs. My door opened, smothering us in safety. We went to the bathroom together and fell asleep too scared to make love.

The morning was a replay of the day before. We ran out of the house after he made his visit to pray to his maker. We went to the school because I had to study for a few hours. Kelly left me alone to meet everyone and to fuck around in order to pass the day away. My concentration was on her and how she moved about the people and needed nothing to find a good time.

Her body clung to a sweatshirt and blue jeans with sandals to protect her feet. Her pulled back hair revealed her forehead which wrinkled every time she laughed or smiled which she did a lot.

Not giving a shit, I managed to get my notes down to a couple of study pages. A big, blonde woman, whom I was studying next to, told me that she had gone to the rival high school of Kelly back in Chicago. The scoop came out of Big Bird's mouth, "She was well…a whore. She used to come to parties with people in my high school. Her and her friends were considered, well huh, whores."

"Gee thanks. Now I can be a little more aggressive with her in bed." That was not what I wanted to hear, but hey, I had wanted to be a slut back in those days.

"Don," Kelly was behind me.

"Kelly this is Margie…Margie, Kelly. She went to your rival high school."

"Hey, Margie. How you doing? Let's get out of here. You've got almost twenty-four hours until your test. What are you going to do, study straight through until tomorrow? Do I have to go through this with you again?"

"All right."

On our way out, "Margie, I don't remember her. I bet she liked me back then. We all were a little bit too much."

"She said you were a whore."

"Just looking out for my own interests."

Head had to go, so we walked to my place to get her stuff then all the way back to the train station. Along the way, we stopped at a Pizza Hut, her treat. It was a nice and quiet meal, because it was late Sunday afternoon and those crazy Catholics were still hanging around the church or their families.

We got to the station. "Kelly, I've got an idea. Why don't you just leave tomorrow? You could help me study tonight and then leave after we hang out tomorrow after my test." The words just blurted out without much thought behind them. I was desperate for her presence.

"Where will I sleep?"

"Good point…wait I've got it. I will ask Albert if it's okay. I'll tell him that you missed the last train and need somewhere to sleep. I'll sleep on the couch. He won't like it, but what can he do." The pit in my stomach caved in from nervousness.

It worked. I gave Albert the sob story. Answering, he placed a blanket on the couch. After explaining the exciting complexities of International Economics, we collapsed into sleep after sex. The thrill of economics and its various curves and reactions turned her on too much, so we stayed up an hour longer making love.

I slept a few hours with her then snuck down on the couch to be woken by Albert. That morning, all three of us ate together before Kelly and I went off to school like the young couple madly in love. Albert, watching our images disappear over the horizon, worried about what was going on.

I took the test and John and Head went off to play together.

After completion, I finished to find them in the midst of an ice cream fight. The soft serve was smeared on their entire faces, except for their nonstop smiles. "Boy, did I miss out. The test went really well. Oh, fuck it," my hand wiped Kelly's shirt to capture a chocolate treat.

Off to the park once more where we laid in the grass and wondered about the complexities of life. As usual John began, "This country is fucked, all of Europe is fucked and smashed by all of the years governed by the church."

"This is a good one for you Kelly. It'll really get your blood pumping. In Luxembourg, our neighboring country, they pay the women to stay home and be with their children. Four hundred bucks a month, all because the Pope says so. He believes women should be at home tending to the children and to the home. Men need to be out their hunting the food," I interjected proudly with my tidbit of knowledge. Balancing a blade of grass on my nose, I blew upward in the hopes of knocking it off and catching it in my mouth. The effort was fruitless.

"Catholics and Republicans are the two biggest swear words in my mind. I do agree with someone staying home with the kid, but it shouldn't be qualified with a sex."

"I wouldn't mind staying home with the kids or splitting it into periods." I tried for some brownie points with her.

John just said with a poke in my sides, "Fuck the Pope."

"Yeah, fuck the Pope. What a sick display of wealth is the Vatican. All of that Baroque shit and the money spent on it could have really done something. Religion sucks and fuck the pope, mottoes for our age." A small piece of his flesh sank between the knuckle of my thumb and middle finger, the infamous scorpion bite.

"Fuck, quit that. That hurts."

"Most do suck, except some forms of Buddhism. That's the religion for me, a pick-your-own religion." Kelly touched my arm suggesting that we stop and begin our Buddhist enlightenment.

John got up and added, "No religion, that's where it is at. Nothing can be sacred." The basketball went into his hands and he faked throwing it at me. Shooting and missing, his soar, skinny ankles took him to the balls location.

"I disagree, the only sacred things are the things we keep inside of us for no one to see. The things that we do and no one else sees, they are sacred. Art is ruined when gazed upon, words are destroyed when spoken, the world is ruined when lived in. Snow is much more beautiful without the prints." I liked what I was saying.

John missed a few more shots before leaving the park for good. We walked Kelly to the station for her train with a kiss and a promise of a phone call.

Finals went by, Brussels went by, my fellows students went by. I had little remorse except for the pounds I had lost and for the loss of urgency to return. John was really ready to get out of here, so we booked the first flight out after our finals that we could. The confirmations arrived, letting us know we would leave Friday morning. I called Kristie to tell her of our plans. The waiting bologna and a ham and cheese for John signaled that our demise was still open, but evident.

"Follow the wave where it takes you, Don. Head's done you some good. She's makin' you take life much less seriously now. Remember you've got to be able to laugh."

"At yourself, that's the key. I think the darkness has left and my situations don't seem as constricting," talking to myself again.

Our last night out on Thursday would be a big one; drinking a bottle each in the valley on the bridge, dressing up like EuroDicks, and being obnoxious at Pasha. A symbolic, yet sad, good-bye to the fucked-up four months. The freedom of youth was slipping away and we were almost done fighting the power.

Thursday morning, it hit me. "GO TO KELLY," so I did. I finished my last final and apologized to John, promising my speedy return. I left with an unsure, "Keep those bottles cold." The station was only fifteen minutes away by bus. On the bus, I looked in dismay at my outfit. A shower had eluded me for the last couple days, my sweatpants and T-shirt had dripped yellow with sweat, and my favorite Giants hat had flatten down my muddy hair. I ran to the phone and let her know I was coming. The spontaneity felt great, I was in Clausbourg by one.

We hugged and kissed for awhile, then I apologized for my basement gym like smell. The overwhelming excitement of finishing finals had finally struck. Grades didn't matter. Actually nothing mattered, but being there and I was. The moment hit my endless smile.

We drank beer and made out along one of the canals. With my finger slipping up into and out of her dress, we contemplated making love by the river, but somebody would walk by each time we worked up our nerve. I missed my intended train to finish off a twelve pack with her. Finally, I won the struggle to leave. Just barely, I made a train that would get me in Brussels by nine. John would be pissed, but new love was my excuse.

Before hopping on, the reality of possibly never seeing her again sent me sprawling and looking for an agenda, a promise, anything to hold onto, besides the pictures. "I wonder if I will see you again?"

She smiled and kissed me with meaning, "Who knows? Just think of me every once and awhile."

On my way into the train, I looked back. How could I not?

I thought of her the entire trip back. The beer swam into every nook. I even contemplated masturbation. The beer and love was making me crazed. I finally fell asleep until Belgium was announced from above.

Immediately running to John's, I knocked at his door to find him waiting. I just smiled and commanded him, "Let's Go!"

THIRTY
Pickin' Apples

The runway, the exit, the baggage claim, the customs line; John laughed at me. The agony had climaxed with an acceptance of the inevitable. The weekend was going to be with Kristie while I wanted Kelly.

I followed John through customs and the now long, light brown hair came into focus. The nervous smile caught my sinful face. We hugged. First things first, John ate his ham and cheese while I indulged in my bologna. Not too much could beat the mayo / bologna combination. Not a crumb remained. The last picture was taken, survivors shaking hands in conquest.

John was transported to his new terminal and we exchanged phone numbers and smiles. "Good luck and see ya 'round," and a wink was what I was left with making me really feel alone. I don't think he has winked since.

"I'm so glad to see you. You are skinnier than shit."

"Me too. So how's it going? What's in store for the summer?"

"Working at Bloomy's? It sucks, but the pay and hours are good. I have seniority since I worked over Christmas and Spring Break."

"How's New York? Big difference from California? Sounds good. It looks like I'll be in Connecticut being a teller in Brooklyn again. That picture still seems wrong to me."

"Good, we'll be able to hang out. I like California better, but I'm making some friends here. I think my parents hate it though."

"Yeah, hey I know what I really need…it's chew. I've been dying for a little BeechNut." She took me to rent movies and to find chew. It tasted great, plus it meant that she wouldn't kiss me until I brushed my teeth.

Meeting her parents went smoothly. I actually wasn't nervous at all. He was a fairly nice guy and kind of a wimp. His wife and kids pushed him around and his voice told of his waiting for a quick death. The only present scars of his disappointment were the ring of hair around his ears and the belly above his belt.

Her mom was not interested in anything that didn't revolve around her. However she did look me over with sex in her mind. I wasn't sure if her thoughts of me were with her daughter or with her. Her skinny short frame slinked past me to reveal a firm butt and a closely shaven neck. Short hair was becoming much more appealing.

I fell asleep after fifteen minutes of some movie. I awoke the next day very early trapped in my listening to a family's moving around and its preparation for the same day as all of their other days. Nobody talked, just moved.

After everyone was gone, I explored. The house was the typical Long Island box; two small bedrooms, plus a master bedroom, a light and airy kitchen mostly in yellow and white, a large brown living room, with a small blue dining room. It could have been anywhere. A small dog that was no doubt a pure bred that somebody spent too much money and time on followed me around.

I didn't bother waking Kristie and sat down to look out on the small green patch surrounded by grey wire. People growing up in suburbs of New York were mutants. Too many people, not enough land, too much money, and not enough things to do with it.

She awoke and led me into the living room taking off all of her clothes and mine. She laid me down and mounted me, "You don't have to worry anymore, I'm on the pill and mom is paying."

I laid still as she went to work, finally making me cum. Her face seemed to smash into my reality making me pissed at my situation and for not saying no. My struggling to get her off mistakenly portrayed a man encapsulated in fits of pleasure. Cuming in her after the last time which produced a child was expectedly awkward, guilt ridden, and tense. I had definitely gotten her pregnant. She let out a little yelp, "I still have a scar or something in there, you cum hurt."

"Sorry."

I left that night, back to Pittsburgh until my summer job started.

I felt no remorse about not referring to a new love in my life or for having sex with her. She would start to feel my distance, but we did make plans for my Connecticut arrival.

Home in Pittsburgh, I laughed until I cried about the shit I had pulled over the last months. "Don't I care? Don't I have my own personality? What the fuck am I doing? If this is fulfilling the erotic, my erotic sucks." Actually, I was just grabbing at anything I could call mine, but the strength to push it all away was nearing. Kelly would be back soon.

In fact the next day, she called. "Don, guess what? I thought I was pregnant. I even was thinking of names."

"What? What happened?"

"I got one of those Home Pregnancy Tests and it was positive, I thought. Those things suck. Thank God it was wrong."

My mom was standing next to me on the phone. "Yeah."

"Your parents there?"

"Yeah."

"Well, I've got to go anyway, I just wanted to hear from you. I will be stopping in New York on my way back. I want to visit you. I will write with the details."

"I can't wait. See you then."

Another one, great. Was it my virility or what?

I promised myself and to a god, that I didn't believe in, that I would use condoms and thanked that Lord for his sparing of me. The partly cloudy sky called out and I obliged.

I rested until it was time to hit New York. Well, it wasn't New York, but a suburb in Connecticut. It was a great opportunity to be completely by myself and to regroup. Unlike last summer when I did the same thing, I felt like I needed some time alone and was fairly excited about it.

My uncle sent me the keys to his townhouse and I jumped onto a plane with a sparse collection of clothes. Of course, Kristie picked me up and stayed the next two nights with me. I cooked her dinner and we talked about general things. I filled her ears with stories of Europe. "I thought you hated it there?" her betrayal showed through.

She left early and fairly upset. I wouldn't touch her, or it was more like I couldn't touch her. We both knew our time together was short. The tension grew along with our arguments. Her laziness and her lack of intelligence pushed me to the annoying edge. Her emotions bothered me, leaving me to ignore them instead of appeasing. She left promising to call soon.

That night Kelly flew into Boston and drove down with her sister who was actually staying a few miles down I-95 from me. I had a couple of drinks to calm my nerves. The anxiety and anticipation was too high and the drinks made me feel cooler, calmer. After meeting her sister, we were alone.

She looked great with her hips wanting me to touch. We had a drink and went immediately to the bedroom. The sex was glorious for awhile then turned sleazy and disappointing. Actually, she wouldn't stop. My penis was sore and scabbed. I couldn't take anymore, but she insisted making me relinquish my title, "Master of my own Castle." Periodically, I obliged her obsession. The visit lasted for three days and four nights of barely leaving the bed.

Kristie called soon after and asked to come up. It was my last weekend before work started and I wanted the company, bad idea. Lying with her, angry and feeling alone, Kristie's breath heaved across the room. I watched her fetal position jerk upward in rhythm. The phone rang and it was Kelly. The words didn't connect, as I contemplated the significance of lying in bed with Kristie and talking to Kelly. "So what are you doing?" My lies began to build.

I got off the phone and Kristie rolled over, "Who was that?"

Nobody seemed to notice the shock in my voice or face, as I wrestled with my growing awareness of a conscience. "A friend from Europe." I went to bed, anxious for Kristie to leave so that it could never happen again.

Work started and I got to see Wanda, my fling from last summer. She was no longer interested in me or my money and made things easier on me. She looked good, but kept far away unless help was needed. The ways of the world became clearer and uglier.

My days became boring routines of constant motion. The recipe of an long and anal life:

> Wake up to two bowls of cereal at six A.M.
> Walk to catch the 7:07 train which arrived in Grand
>   Central Station at 7:47.
> Subway, # four or # five, to Boro Hall, arriving
>   approximately at 8:25.
> Read paper and prepare for work.
> Work.
> Lunch, three sandwiches (bologna or tuna fish) at
>   the Brooklyn Promenade.
> Work.

> Leave work, approximately at four-thirty, hoping
>   to catch the 5:05.
> Arrive at my front door by six.
> Change clothes.
> Jog three-four miles.
> Shoot baskets.
> At seven-thirty, prepare dinner (chicken, pizza,
>   spaghetti, accompanied by a salad) and lunch
>   for tomorrow.
>
> Options:
> 1) Drive in convertible to the beach.
> 2) Read and listen to K-Rock.
> 3) Watch T.V.
> 4) Grocery shop.
> Write at nine until nine forty-five, if mood struck.
> Prepare for bed and lay out tomorrow's clothes.
> Sleep.

I would see their hurried old faces, swimming upstream for some crazy goal that only ended up being death. I would look at their same face every night and wondered what I was doing with them. Collecting three hundred dollars a week and spending a lot of time to myself was the answer.

The first summer was a challenge due to the radically different climate of the inner city and its perils, but now I was immune and not even amused. My calls to Kelly and John seemed to be my only treat. Europe really had been fun.

Kristie and I fell out of contact quickly. The phone calls went from once a week to once a month to I'll talk to you at school.

My uncle was gone for the entire summer except for two weeks. The freedom grew boldly in my mind. "I think I'm going to come and see you."

"How?"

"Drive."

"You're fucking stupid."

"Yeah, I won't then."

"Too scared?"

"I guess. I'll decide in the morning."

"I'll be waiting anxiously."

The whole night I looked at maps, tried to calculate the time and the risks involved, and worried. I fell asleep with the car filled, the oil checked, and my bags backed. I awoke nervous wondering about the consequences of being caught stealing my uncle's car and driving seven hundred miles to Indiana and back. He would be pissed, but I wouldn't die.

I called in sick at work, confirmed with Kelly and headed for the road. It was eight A.M.

I cut through the New York handle and crossed the Hudson. Slowly I made my way against the constant metal onrush. With the top down Route 80 turned into the twisting green of the Jersey and Pennsylvania border. The car kept up with the yellow morning glow.

Northern Pennsylvania whizzed by in five hours, almost three hundred miles on the dot. In intervals, I wrote, chewed tobacco, and pissed in a Gatorade bottle to keep awake. My results were a shitty non-coherent mumble of meaningless jumble for words, urine stained shorts, and a headache from the chew. An example:

Searching the road I already passed,
I fear my soul died a ways back.
What can be done?
Contemplating hell I'll never see,
I thought my heart pure without blood.
Can I really know?
The others, wanting the controls,
block my path, pass me by.
I pay no mind
continuing to where I want and need to be.
The mind struggling in decisions,
blazes its path,
finding its cool comfort.
I follow no one,
knowing not where I am or will be.
The haunting road eludes in the fog
of the unknown and
of the incomprehensible.
I continue on that never completed journey
not feeling my past,
not seeing my future.
Exit Fourteen B of the Beaten Path.

Hitting Ohio seemed like a relief, but upon further review the road stretched endlessly onto a mountain which never came. The forestry of Pennsylvania gave way to an overpopulated brown with white picket fence broken about. The summer day foamed and formed into drops which forced up the car top. I poked at my red skin and watched the circle of white disperse and disappear back into red. The explanations of the redness of my skin at work would be funny.

Her house was getting close. I made the correct turn off with the lights still out. The sun was just about ready to leave when I turned into her driveway. I love Indiana just because it is at the end of the time zone and remains light the latest into the day.

Her house was tall and deep. The brown painted wood allowed a porch to begin in the front and sweep back most of its length along the right hand sided driveway. A large tree covered the front, next to the porch. Dogs madly barked and jumped about looking at this stranger. In a logical disarray, flowers littered underneath the tree and formed a red, white, and yellow boundary which marked the separation of house and driveway.

No one seemed home, but I still approached the house with hope. The house was the perfect dream of every young girl or naive couple, big and old. America worked and produced every day at the hopes of acquiring Kelly's house.

At first I laughed when no one answered my knock or the dogs' barks. The irony of driving twelve hours and finding no one home was too much. Dark and bitter escaped from my hollow lips, "Fuck."

"Fuck it," so I walked down the street to find a phone to call to see if I was in the wrong town or if I was the star of a *Twilight Zone* episode. Again, no answer. "Fuck it," I walked back to the number listed on my piece of paper. It seemed right. The towering green gave an assemblance of an approaching thunder storm overhead. The air was light and moving, feeling nice against my legs as I sat down on the porch to pout.

The shadows captured the entire surface. The blue sunset above had not yet begun its phasing into purple. A car pulled into the driveway, "I knew you would get here when I was gone." A tight old almost see through T-shirt wrapped around the curves. A pair of cut-off jeans poked through the bottom showing a dancing bear patch. She ran up and gave me a hug as I watch her parents crotch out of the old wood paneled Mercury station wagon. She gave me a kiss. I felt good and her energy lifted me up further.

Her dad walked over and offered his hand. The round face matched his round glasses looking very much the WASP with his ruddy colored cheeks, chinos, and polo-type shirt. He covered his bald top with a left to right swoosh of his strawberry blonde hair. Now that was real strawberry blonde as opposed to the ruby colored of Josh's hair. Josh could be her dad? In a few years, short, big stomached with skinny, once athletic, legs.

Her mom was less than friendly and I could immediately see that she was the biggest force in Kelly's personality and looks. She introduced herself very properly and walked inside. Her curly brown hair was the only material difference between the two. The big cheeks and pointy chin collapsed around a pouty mouth which must have drove her husband crazy in those courting years. Fiery blues eyes were also present under smoke tinted glasses. Ordering all of us around, she told her husband to get me something to drink. He laughed suddenly realizing the control she had gained over the years which became so obvious in front of strangers. He liked it, less to worry about.

We went inside and I was led to my room and then given a tour. I carried and nursed a cold Coors throughout. "You let them drink Coors?"

"Yeah, I explained to them the support of the Contras and the support to the Right-to-Life movement, but neither was impressed. My dad bought it by mistake, and wouldn't return it. Practicality has to fit into the life of any sane and righteous person. At least they recycle."

I checked out my room, it was her little brother's who was off to Washington to do an internship with NASA or something. He had spaceship pictures and models everywhere. His music collection was mostly rap and more particularly Erik B. and Rakim. An odd mixture. No athletic trophies adorned the walls or tops of dressers, but his room was overly masculine with blue wallpaper with civil war soldiers spaced evenly up and down in red stripes. "Very patriotic. I like it."

Kelly led the way, "My mother grew up in this very town, but my dad had to move to Chicago for awhile. That was when I was in high school. Right after I graduated, they came back. He knew the whole time that Chicago was temporary and this always would be home. Anyway, he bought this house when we were in Chicago and gutted it and built it the way he wanted to. He and my mother did almost all of the refurbishing."

"Pretty impressive."

The house had four bedrooms lined up in a L, starting with the parents bedroom at the top of the stairs beginning the bottom spot of the L. Her older sister's room was the corner of the L, then Kelly's, then her little brother's. Kelly's room and her brother's room had a secret entrance through the closet which made the evening look very prosperous.

The innards of the house matched the picture perfect American look of the outside. Everything was orderly, simple, and basic. The colors were either blue, brown, white, or pink. Furniture was plenty and cluttered which gave the home its homey feel. Downstairs consisted of a huge living room which ran along with most of the porch, an incredibly large kitchen with table included, and a modest dining room and formal living/reading room.

The backyard was half blacktop and half garden with only a small strip of grass which contained a table to eat on and a few chairs. The garage ended the black top about one hundred feet away. The garden wrapped off of the garaged and wound along the left side of the back yard. "This is great."

We drank beers on their porch while my leg shook from too much mind stimulating substances and not enough food. They ran down into my lungs and filled my body coolly and slowly. We decided to go for a walk.

We kissed allowing the excitement and many lonely nights to run into our loins and make the blood pump. She lived in a college town filled with parks and lawns. "Let's find someplace a little more secluded," she huffed. We walked over a hill and down into a small knoll lined with trees. Black roots webbed the brown mud. We took our clothes off and let go of it all.

I chased her back to her house with a stick poking and prodding all of her limbs. I needed to rid my mind the guilt of having just had sex with their daughter upon my return to her parent's house. The little game of teasing did the trick and we were back to the porch, beer, and Rickie Lee Jones. I was never a fan of hers, but the night seemed too right.

Time for bed and I was exhausted. The driving, the beer, and the sex came down hard and wobbled my mind and body. I crawled into bed after a goodnight kiss. Just at the point of my thoughts turning into dreams, Kelly walked into the room and laid on top of me with a big smile.

What could I do? However the bed was too squeaky, so we

moved to the floor. She danced on top of me in the moonlight of her brother's window. I watched her shadow wiggle up, down and around among the space ships upon his wall.

I felt my cum run back down my penis. She was warm and constricting with her muscles trying to keep the pressure within. I was happy and relieved that she was on the pill; no more worries, no more condoms.

I woke to breakfast and to her dad drinking coffee at the breakfast table. The sun was shining and sneaking through the white curtains upon the yellow tablecloth. I joined him and read the sports, the Pirates finally beat the Cardinals. They never wanted to beat the Cardinals. Of course, the Mets had won again, and I hoped my gift of a Mets hat to Kelly would not jinx the Pirates' chances this year.

"So Don, how is New York?"

I used the standard lines, "Great learning experience. Completely different culture is the urban one. It's fun and eye-opening. I have lived such a shelter care-free life. I have some appreciation for it now. Wouldn't want it any other way."

"I grew up in Brooklyn."

"No way, that's where I work, downtown on Court Street."

"I grew up in Greenpoint."

"That's Russian or Polish or something like that isn't it?" "Most people are usually one or the other." He studied my face, especially my lips. From me blowing on my coffee or the way I talked, he watched. I looked briefly into his eyes and thought about having sex with his daughter. Was it really that tough for a parent to think of their children having sex? I don't think he felt that way or at least ignored the situation.

Her two dogs came running over to me from outside. Kelly's mom had let them in, on her return from her morning jog. Eggs were placed on my table and I looked up at Kelly and smiled letting her into my thoughts.

"I am not going to eat them, but I know they will be eaten in this house, so I make my parents buy the organic eggs, where the chickens are not in a little pen, producing eggs for some asshole's wallet."

Kelly's dad looked up from the paper and raised his eye brows, "She's tough."

Kelly sat down next to me and touched my knee, "So what do you want to do?"

"What are my choices?"

She went through a whole list and nothing sounded too crazy. I couldn't even remember what we did when night came around. I was in a perfect state of content bliss, until…

"Don, you know I went and saw my friend Kent after seeing you." My mind wandered trying to keep my heart from dropping revealing my fears. It did. "Oh no, Kent and I are just friends. I can't see anything more than that with him. But anyways, he asked me how you were and how my trip to New York was."

"All I could say was okay. Something was bothering me. It was sleazy…just sex."

Was this a test? How do I respond to this one? I stalled with a "Hum…well it bothered me a little bit too. I'm not too big on putting much value or importance on sex, but I couldn't get enough of you that weekend. I feel that sex is a simple pleasure and a human instinct and I try to leave it at that, but something was different that weekend. I can't explain it and it was kind of sleazy. In relationships, they seem to go in cycles. First, the meeting, the testing, the ground breaking and the rules setting. Then, the sex period comes and can carry a relationship for quite a while. Then comes the discovery. Discover the good and the bad features, the habits, anything and everything is found. Then boom. Contentment."

I went out on a limb, "The evil word contentment, that's where relationships grow sour. In the sex stage, the relationship is either right or wrong, but sex can carry it through, but when contentment is reached, then it can grow bad, kind of like being out of practice. Anyway, I thought and still believe, that we were getting the sexual phase out of the way to move onto discovery."

I don't know if I really believed that, but I wanted to. Sex had been the downfall of all of my relationships, because that was all we had. But this time I was hoping for and planning on more. She mulled it over seemingly satisfied.

Next thing I knew the day and night was gone. Once again, we capped off the night on her brother's floor. More comfortable, she fell asleep on my chest. I listened to the night's chirps and cars finding their way home. The whistle through her nose and the feeling of belonging started to inch into my heart. I wondered if the next time I had to bring her up again to anybody else if I would use the word girlfriend. Things looked doomed.

Early the next morning I had to say goodbye. Kelly woke me up with a kiss and I packed in silence as she went through her tapes and picked out some Dead mix and read a pamphlet on Animal Rights.

I watched her every move hoping my car, or my uncle's car, would start and not blow up on the way. I heard the phone conversation, "Hey Uncle Mel, I'm stuck out here in fuck knows where in Pennsylvania…The car is on fire and I'm not sure what to do about it." I reminded myself to check the oil when I got gas.

Gone, I had sun the whole way and jammed to the stereo whose passenger side speaker had blown out, "He'll never notice." I missed her already, but knew it was just the leaving that was sending my heart and mind into the dumps. I got to the Tappan Zee bridge and waited in traffic as the Dead concert in Giant Stadium started on the radio. They played to the wideness and majestic beauty of the Hudson. How did they know?

The driveway appeared and I finally felt relax. The car had performed well and the only clue to my weekend theft was the fourteen hundred miles, but I knew he wouldn't notice or if he did wouldn't believe it, due to absurdness.

I fell right to sleep and couldn't believe that I had last worked only three days ago. I was refreshed.

THIRTY-ONE
Licky, Licky, Lie
Somethin' in the Sky

After that long trip, the summer turned greener and sunnier. I picked up a Kerouac book at Kelly's request and went through the metamorphosis of deciding my life's goal. I was to become a writer. Since those weeks alone and reading *On the Road* and *Dharma Bums*, that calling came to mind in a matter of why not.

To initiate myself, I sat down every night and wrote for an hour to see if I had any talent or if I even enjoyed it. Of course, I did enjoy it and didn't care about my talent. Listening to my thoughts and conjuring up new ones on a glistening lined paper stimulated my senses. Slowly, but anxiously, all kind of shit from short stories to poems spewed from my head and flung against the wall trying to stick. My writing aspirations were in a locked closest not wanting the expectations or the wondering from anyone which would ruin its purity and harmlessness. I even hid it from Kelly.

The summer remained only half gone, so the urge reappeared to plan another trip to Indiana. Also, seeing John who lived not too far away in Ohio was inevitable. This time I finagled my boss into a day off and headed out to Kelly's after the promise to John that I would be at his place soon after.

Once again the British racing green streak of a convertible headed through the towering grey of the east through the beautiful, changing green slopes which finally reached the endless mall of the Midwest and finally to the arms of Kelly all in between a night of black, making sleep desirable. Twice I had to pull over and sleep on the side of the road, each time waking up after exactly thirty minutes of rest.

The sun had been up quite awhile when I arrived. She ran out the door and her hair was freshly cut with her neck clean, shaven, and tan. Her eyes rang out kissing me with all of my impatience smacking her back. She looked sharp and wholesome and felt so smooth. The warm skin wrapped underneath me cooking my desires like a microwave, from the inside out. The muscles in my stomach shivered up and down until the ends of hairs on my toes quivered.

She greeted me with a flippant, "Hey." Sitting down exhausted at her kitchen table, her dad gave me a cup of coffee while I took my glasses off and rubbed my eyes so hard I felt an eyeball squish in my fingers. After breakfast I rested on her front porch swing until she expended all talk of the books that she had read over the last couple of weeks and of the travesties of being a woman in working America. Without listening to her, I dreamed of the day she could and would read a book of mine.

We went for a walk and shopped for a present for her brother's birthday. This time he was home, back from D.C., but I hadn't seen him yet. His personality and looks danced in the bare form of imagination. She drove my Volkswagen with the top down allowing me to watch her groove along to the road and the music. "Yeah, I just heard about this new group, The Indigo Girls. Sounds good, huh?"

"Yeah, I think I've seen them on MTV. They aren't Christian rock, are they?"

"God, I hope not," she continued to dizzily bounce.

"Me too," was my reply as I really thought about the contradictions of her comment.

Her short blond hair went as far back as it could in the wind which wasn't very far. Her face had become very tan and her lips were dry and pouty. Catching me in a stupid gaze the lips returned a quick smile in between watching the road and checking her rear view mirror. "It's good to see you again so soon. I missed you."

"Me too. I couldn't wait any longer to see you. I had to come." That was all that needed to be said, all that I needed to hear.

After an unmentionable dinner we headed towards John's. The Italian dressing of the salad continually returned the zesty flavor to my mouth. With each burp, I blew out towards the window hoping Kelly wouldn't notice it.

To John's, we drove along the rolling back roads of Ohio. The black pavement cut around farms and formed boxes that gridded the state. The black air was surprisingly cool for the last week in July, but felt great reminiscent of the first cool day of sweater wearing or the first warm day of shorts wearing. "Was it half full or half empty?" came to mind.

Not a word was spoken as the music pounded out "ShakeDown Street" through the gray and black striped cloth seats. We sang and danced along with our seats and with our smiling eyes. Something in the air flashed kinetically between us. I screamed as loud as I could with every inch of bliss and laughed. Kelly joined in. This love had become maddening and I seriously started to consider if this was the happiest time of my life.

The car seemed frozen to time, but rocketing forward. The cool air smacked our Indian red faces shut. Fading after each moisturizing lick of a tongue, the tightness in my lips faded back from the white. Our hands reached out and held on tight only temporarily letting go to switch gears. The magic ended when John's house appeared and "Fire on the Mountain" ended.

Actually it wasn't John's house, it was his girlfriend's mother's house. He was living with his girlfriend and her mom for the summer. If you ask me bad news, but he seemed content working for the Water Works of the town and coming home to people interested in him and his future. I thought it was strange and never really got my bearings of the surroundings or the understanding of the developing relationships of a man, a woman, and her mother under one roof.

He greeted us with beers and hugs. Cindy, his girlfriend, was much more reserved and simply said hi and turned away to return into the kitchen. The motion obviously tried to hide her face which read of her reluctance of accepting us. Her lacking of an individual connection with us turned her mind a little green. The surprise was the contradiction to her mom always saying that love meant sharing and experiencing everything together. We posed a threat to the thesis of her relationship with John.

John and I wandered out on the porch to do our guy bonding thing, while Kelly was stuck inside to make herself fit into their tight circle, "So Don, what's going on?"

"With what?" I sounded a little defensive and tried to make up for it with a smile.

"With you and Head?"

"I gave her my Letterman's jacket. I guess it's going pretty well."

He wouldn't let my glib remark change the subject, "You seem like a changed man. I don't see that fury in your eyes. Love can do that."

"Fuck love, John. You know better than that, there is no such thing as love. Just another word."

"Yeah, keep telling yourself that. You know it's entered your mind a lot lately. Don't try throwing that macho shit my way."

"Macho, that was suppose to be intellectual shit." We laughed and I got some more beers. Entering the holy kitchen, I smiled knowingly at Kelly with a close of the refrigerator. They were talking about stained glass windows or something like that.

Returning to John, "How is it livin' here? Weird?"

"I'll tell you if you ever live with a woman, there is a point when you become feminized. You stop thinkin' about sports and you begin to talk about clothes, furniture, and jewelry. It's not bad though, both seem to give into each other's interests, but it is an inevitable phase."

"Yeah, I guess if you are so close and dependent like you and Cindy. I know with Head, independence is a major criteria. I'm still torn on wanting my own life, but wanting it with somebody to share it with. Selfishness."

"Dude read a little Ayn Rand, you'll feel better."

"I've heard it will just fuck me up."

"Not you. That's like a criteria for me choosing friends. If they think Ayn Rand is fucked then I know they are closed minded bastards."

"Hypocritical, huh?" I touched my leg exposing a white spot which quickly returned to red.

"A little, but we all have are prejudices," he stared hard at my face in a increasingly louder voice.

"Yeah, it's good to see you," a little nervously.

"I miss you Don, I need someone to push me. Sometimes without a push the adventure goes away and things get stale." Finally, he looked away.

"Yeah, I'm still discovering how to be adventurous. I do notice that you are much more relaxed. The fire is gone."

"That pains me to hear," staring at me again. "I really like Head, she is very special. You know what image never leaves me? The image of her just handing over her HaufBrau House T-shirt just because I thought it was cool. It was such a nice gesture."

"Yeah and when she left the flowers for your house mom."

"It brought tears to her eyes."

A car raced down the street and U-turned passing us again. Cindy's front yard was long and open, appearing to be a continuation of the road in the dark. "You don't still have that feeling of her being evil and trying to kill you, do you?"

"No, but I must be honest with you. I'm worried about you and her. Too much love and passion. Best of friends with too much passion is good, but not for you and not for her. Something must give. I see you fifty, still athletic and cool, but alone, very alone. Your destiny is to run around meeting and leaving permanent scars on the part of the world which crosses your path. You know, roaming into and out of souls."

"Fuck, I'm too tired and lazy. My intentions aren't noble enough, but thanks, you bastard. I don't want to be fifty and I don't want to be cool. I'm a hermit. I like to sit around and think. I like the quiet mundaneness of it all."

"It's not a choice, its something that will happen."

On that note I got Head and chatted with the whole group before suggesting bed. I smiled uncomfortably when the mother went upstairs to make our bed. Cindy followed her and I asked John, "Where are we sleeping?"

"You mean, is it together?"

"Yeah," my mouth shot downward looking like Bob Dylan singing "Tangled up in Blue."

"Well, Cindy and I do, so you will too. Her mom is really cool about that kind of stuff. Raised in the sixties and suffering through a divorce will open you eyes to the youth and the reality and the desires that come with it."

"Sounds good," I smiled nervously again at Head.

We crawled into bed with the coolness of the fresh blankets and pillows that wrapped around my body and released the tensions and the weariness of a sleepless forty-eight hours. The bed creaked and the floor moved when I rolled over and kissed and hugged Kelly. She smiled and I sheepishly rolled back over knowing that this wouldn't work. She laughed at my pout so I crawled into the nook of her shoulder and fell sound asleep.

I awoke with the room screaming with the day's new light. Angrily, I searched for curtains and contemplated falling back to sleep, but it wouldn't come. Kelly woke with my restlessness and instantly flashed an eager perky stretch. With a roll on top of me she gently slid my penis into her. She grimaced with every slow and careful movement. The agony of attempting to eliminate all noise and pleasure brought a quick and painful point of climax. In an aching roll of my eyes, thoughts teased me with the most obscure baseball players. Mario Mendoza and his infamous Mendoza line were the best I could do. My eyes opened, fixated on the stairs which bore the figure of Cindy's mom. She, embarrassed, ducked down, picked up something, and headed back down the stairs, trying to hide her shocked expression.

I looked up in my own shock at Kelly only to see myself, but the trauma and shame weren't enough and were far too late. My explosion forced her body to engulf everything I had. Pissed, she denied the sensation and rolled over, "Fuck."

I shrugged, "Oh well, what did they expect?"

"Not to actually see us having sex." I nodded feeling ashamed for cuming without remorse after being caught.

Breakfast was ready after the four of us showered. I forced my eyes into the mother's face. She acted normal, but her thoughts still came across and they were accepting. She read to me, "Young love, how beautiful and how jealous I am."

We left after a round of hugs and promises of next visits. Now, Kelly and I were off to visit my best friend and roommate at school, Jack. He was another two hours east, New York was nowhere to be seen.

We rolled up to his driveway and he was waiting with his jetblack hair styled and parted perfectly with only a few strands searching for the rim of his wire framed glasses.

Jack looks exactly like me, tall, skinny, and a bony face and body. His distinguishing feature was his blue eyes contrasting the hair. Chicks dug him for that and his general smoothness and sincerity. I constantly berated him with little winking jokes about his eyes and how the babes dug him until he got pissed.

He lived on the outskirts of an air force base; flat lands occupied by flat houses, one floor and a couple of rooms. Driving by, it was dot after dot. "This is middle America…the beauty of it all."

My scalp was still tingling from the rush of the wind, when I gave Jack a quick manly hug. He and my friends from high school are the only ones I hug. A special bond exists with them while the others end up just being acquaintances that run in and out the doors.

I felt really proud of Kelly and let them talk while I watched Jack for his reactions. His approval meant a lot, not so much of the woman, but of me. Trying to hang in his shadow, he filled the big brother and best friend role for me and I often found myself doing things to impress him.

Unfortunately, Jack was only cordial and not taken back by her like I was. Showing us the hot spots of Dayton, Jack wound up taking us to some park somewhere. A long rolly park, its offering to society was a castle-like tower that was famous for something and that dared me to climb it. Even with my fear of heights, I conquered the jetting rocks and peered down from the fifteen feet that I had just climbed to enjoy the fear which trembled my heart and rolled my stomach. I wondered if it was me or was Kelly really as cool as I thought and watched her beaming face from the perch. I watched them laugh below, 'She's cool. He's cool.'

I frantically and clumsily fumbled down clinging to each protruding stone. Jumping the last four feet down and hopping into the car, I followed Jack's directions into the sun looking for a cool place to eat and have some beer.

The night had a bad edge, so we headed home with some beers and watched T.V. on his pulled out sofa bed. I awoke to Jack's shake and the saw the sun already up. Time to go back after a needed tomato juice and a western omelet at Denny's.

In the car again, Kelly put on some music and I gave her a kiss during a red light. Even though the reunion with Jack wasn't as good as hoped, I could laugh in my pride of her all the way back.

This time her parents loosened up towards me and took me out to dinner to have famous bologna sandwiches. They were huge four inch hunks of fried meat placed in a bun with tons of ketchup. Weary of the traveling I was able to tune out the night and everyone's conversation. Amongst attempts to concentrate on the conversation, everything still escaped forcing the wrong words at the right times. Suddenly the lights and people faded into the moonlight shadows on the floor of Kelly's brothers room. He was staying at a friend's house for my convenience or for our sexual convenience.

I looked down into Kelly's tightened face as I paused regaining my composure. Looking hard at her, my life flashed before me; the old girlfriends, the loves lost, my mother, my sister, my gaining age, and the look of John's girlfriend's mother. Like her, I accepted by moving up and down in Kelly, releasing until I fell limp onto her heaving breasts. Her nipples poked my stomach as I clinched her head like a walnut in a nutcracker.

With the morning, I had to leave again, but not after restraining her attempts to force me to prolong the visit. Quickly, the green trees left my soul and turned into the grey of the shit that belongs to the city and its forsaken suburbs.

THIRTY-TWO
Nobody Really Knows

The longer the summer lasted and the hotter and muggier it got, the more I wanted to leave and head back to the cool shade of Kelly. The phone calls became more frequent and longer. The letters and books were sent without fail week after week. It was a crash course and all of the crazy studying of finals.

I had a horrible dream during the middle of the week. Freezing from the overuse of the air conditioner, the night terrified me and appeared foreign in the moonless haze. Eleven o'clock was early enough, so I called Kelly.

"Hi," she sensed the urgency.

"What's going on? Is everything all right?"

Her rusty voice soothed, "Yeah, yeah. Sorry about calling so late, but I needed to call."

She was relieved and her voice relaxed, but the questions still existed, "So what's up?"

I needed to answer, but hesitated for a quick contemplation of what I really wanted to say. "Kelly, I've enjoyed the last couple of months immensely. Well, I just woke up from a terrible dream which now escapes me, but the feeling lingered of the need to call you. Usually, I would have denied it and laid in bed worrying about something that I couldn't discover. Instead, I submitted to the night and my need and called you." I knew I had said nothing, but my confidence and resolve took ground.

"I, well, you know, how I feel about love and commitments that are locked unfairly with the four letters...but I wanted to tell you that I do love you, but for all the right reasons. I care for you, I want the best for you, and I enjoy talking to you, touching you, and seeing you. I don't care about what happens to us and I don't need you to be able to carry on with my life. I just think you are a special person and I like hanging out with you." A deep breath refilled a pair of exhausted lungs.

"I know that if you were gone forever, tomorrow, I would look back fondly and yearn for the old days. But I don't want you to go away without telling you about my feelings for you." I paused and qualified, "I don't want to scare you or me either, so let's leave it at that. It's like my parents, I never tell them that I care for them or love them, which is wrong. I don't want to make that mistake with you."

"Thanks, I feel the same. I don't know about what will happen and I don't want the pressure of promises. But I can't get enough of your mind or your body. The conditional love is mutual."

"Thanks...Good night."

"Good night. Don?"

"Yeah?"

"Sleep with the angels."

"Will do. You too."

The phone rang a couple of days later, "Don, I'm sending you an essay on some of my beliefs. I've been working hard composing it. Let me know what you think."

It came the next day:

I remember I was three, because I played with Kathy, when I used to tell people that I wanted to be a lawyer. Adults would try to warn me that men usually became lawyers and I would look nice in a nurse's dress. I tried to retort with, "My daddy says it doesn't matter as long as I'm the smartest." Ignoring, they would walk away. My preschooler mind translated that into a win. With them walking away, I didn't hear their words to the person by their side that being smart was for boys, and boys only.

Slowly, I learned to become feminized and to fit into society. I kept my shirt on, so to speak. My mother taught me to cook and to wear dresses past my knees. My bedroom only saw pink and I played house with all of my dollies. I knew that I someday, somehow would grow out of it.

I reached adolescence and found that I was no longer competing with boys, but for boys. Painting my face and staring at myself, I no longer understood self-satisfaction. Men began to decide my worth at how well I could change my looks to fit their needs. My personal beauty was gone.

I read in the magazines how to falsify my beauty to fool men. The pressures left me self-conscious of my weight and trying to hide my body. I spent my days meeting my girlfriends in the bathroom to verify our good look and outfits. I watched older women with boyfriends and longed to be them. I figured it was the only way to be happy. The day never came and I went to college still lacking so called happiness.

The pages continued which summarized into the following results on women due to society:

Private beings, untrusting of each other.

Psyches based on shame.

Accepting not questioning.

Without sexuality.

Weaker physically and mentally.

Self-denying.

She proved it with signs of such travesties that are in our everyday life:

Prostitution.

Pornography.

Anti-masturbation for women.

Rape.

Anti-lesbian attitudes.

Work force barriers.

The term "girls."

Signs that read "Men at Work."

She summed up her thoughts with:

While I dream of individuality, my children sleep in their beds. Will my son know the intimacy of parenthood as my daughter will? Will they equally risk poverty and success? I demand of them to share equal respect of themselves, of their entire sex, and of their entire population. I know my daughter, at age three, will smolder the fires of discrimination as I once did. I dream that her daughter will no longer face those fires that have been flooded by compassion and mutuality of generations of effort. I can see my toes dangling in those same flood waters.

I immediately began to write my reply and critique which she would never see. The pen guided the way, my mind followed.

'Well Kelly, you have so many good points, but you try to take it places that you can't go. Like me never knowing what it is like to be a woman, you will never understand men.

Men and women are too broad, but must be used in the generic sense. Those terms and that generic sense is what is wrong with the relationship between men and women. Since they are used and I am a product of the second half, I will take the liberty of using the terms, but not without the previous stated reservations.

I, like you, grew up being told what to do. "Don't cry, you little baby," my dad would yell at me. "Stop acting like a girl." I did and my feelings have been inside ever since. The conditioning was so strong and effective that I don't even take my feelings seriously. I don't even admit to having any.

"You wussy girl, take the skirt off," my friends poked and prodded until I tried to run the fastest, lift the most weights, drink the most beer, fuck the most women, beat up anybody, and know the most. Yes, being a man makes you want to be the best, but it forces you to be in constant competition with your fellow man. We are mavericks without friends, without feelings, and sophomorically proud of it.

In respect to my teachings about women, they are weak objects there for our control. A good woman will stand by you, cook for you, and be ignored by you. Any women with similar independence are our friends, but cannot be our partners. They are whores, who will take you for everything you are worth. All of this has been reinforced by each and every man I ever came across.

We joke about masturbation, but never admit to having to use it. We lie about women and tell outrageous tales of what we convinced them to do; sex without their consent or understanding. The worse kind of these men are glorified in our movies and in our books leaving us to continually applaud them, never questioning their actions.

I started drinking in sixth grade to be cool. I started lifting to be cool. I started dating to be cool. I never thought of what was cool, the rules were already laid out. I followed blindly.

Like women, men are alone too. However, the major difference is we are taught to strive and achieve while woman are taught to restrain and watch.

The problem does not lie on men and women, but on the society that perpetuates itself. When a man sees a woman he sees just that, their vagina and their breasts which makes them different from him. He looks back to all of the woman he has known and what women are supposed to be like and he sees them through that tainted mirror of his teachings. In reality he should see nothing, but an empty skeleton for which he knows nothing.

To change I have no clue of a realistic solution. Cultures evolve through force of revolution with resolution. My only wish and my only advice to any revolt is to make it positive. Without the positive, the revolution is just as evil as the powers in control.

So my advice to woman and man is to revolt from within, bettering yourself and helping others. If the change is based on hatred of the others, it will not be true and will fail. See people as people, not as sexes.'

I folded up my handwritten cursive and tucked it away. Instead, I wrote her and told her how much I liked her writing. My thoughts were very poignant and accurate in many senses, but I couldn't bear or wouldn't dare to argue with her. I could hear her say upon reading my scripture, "You don't understand, you're not a woman." She is wrong, that is like saying you don't understand the poor or the homeless. She still tries to help their causes and pretends to have the solutions. I don't try to understand or to have solutions, I just know what shouldn't be and it is our fault, all of ours. Too many want to close their eyes or just yell at the problems.

Finally the summer ended and I headed for home. On the way to the bus, on the way to the airport, and on the way home I reread *Dharma Bums* wondering if I should take up Buddhism. "No," I mouthed without sound, "just another evil label." Instead I took up these words as my own philosophy: happy. Just in my swim shorts, barefooted, wild-haired, in the red fire dark, singing, swigging wine, spitting, jumping, running—that's the way to live. "Thanks, Jack Kerouac."

As soon as I was settled back at home. I made plans to leave to visit Kelly. The phone and the letters weren't good enough anymore with my light and growing fires. I wanted her to feel my new heat.

THIRTY-THREE
Song to Speak

Back home and away from the fakeness of the Big Apple, the realistic pictures returned shimmering in the heat. I had my parent's car which was to be my graduation present after I bought it from them. The silver Mercury adjusted to its new driver and revved with excitement as I charted a new course to Kelly's from the southeast instead of the northeast. The streets to her house were now very familiar and inviting to me, no longer permitting the feel of a stranger.

Like the first day of vacation, she greeted me with those same wild eyes and anxious expectations. The flickering light shimmering between her lashes drove me nuts and always stayed with me. Knowing my joys, she had just gotten a fresh hair cut. This time our time together had actual plans, a night tenting, a night with John, two nights in Pittsburgh, ending with a night of nothing at her place.

Arriving into friendly confines of her light kitchen, I finally met her brother who wasn't as wormy as I thought. He had her sharp chin and her blonde hair, but was less meaty and stood four inches taller than the closest in her family. He ignored my curiosity leaving to go somewhere else but there, a noble place to go.

I helped her and her dad assemble the tent and gather some cooking gear. A purchase of beer and shrimp cast us off on the ten miles from her house to a campsite on a series of lakes. The park was nice, but more residential camping then rustic. Most tents were parties, not vacationers trying to experience life the way it used to be.

I aided the set up with her in charge. My tenting experience collected dust over a time long ago during childhood. Scouring amongst over-picked brush, we eventually collected enough wood for the night leaving us ample time to walk the area heading towards the lake before the light left the barked bases of the woods.

We talked to several along the way asking directions. They were so friendly and taken aback by our intense love. "Are you guys married?" and, "Why are you so happy?" The blushing felt good in the remembrances of our youthful vigor.

Just before dark we started our fire. The fire was my task and it worked out surprisingly well. A couple pounds of shrimp danced among the bubbles from the thrusting blue turning to yellow. Smelling its glory, I ate until no more could be forced down out of respect of my once hungry and weak body. Matching my intake, Kelly happily ate the simplicity. I have never really understood how a vegetarian could eat fish, but not livestock. Their argument always took the road that the fish aren't pinned up and slaughtered, grown only to die. Untrue, in some instances they are produced just for consumption and they are mindlessly slaughtered, ending tragically and unnaturally. But I didn't bother to ask her.

The shrimp, the beer, the fire, and a cassette of Derek and the Dominos, it was as if we were being filmed for a Milwaukee's Best commercial. The beer loosened up our conversation.

"Don, what do you really want to do?"

"With tomorrow or with the rest of my life?"

"I know what we are doing tomorrow," she said it sharply to highlight her unacceptance of my sarcasm. In a predetermined fit of wants, "I know what I want to be doing tomorrow." Her eyebrows went up and down catching me off guard.

"I'm going to be a professor or something like that. Work for awhile to get experience, before I decide that is not what I want to do. Then go back to school and work on being a professor. I like to teach, of course tennis lessons are my only experience. That's just one aspect of life though, the earning of one's wages. I want to have kids. I think it will be the biggest challenge and learning experience. It's something I don't want to miss out on. How about you?" I prepared myself for her obvious beginnings of a planned conversation.

"I don't know, yet. Peace Corps perhaps and then see where it takes me. But I do want to have kids, but I don't want to be married."

"Yeah, why marriage? Who thought it up?"

"The churches to keep them in power and to keep the rest as subordinates."

"Yeah, I definitely don't need a church to bind me to a person." Déjà vu struck. Her words fit into every unfilled crevice of me.

"Don, you and me," she paused thinking with her face, scaring me. My heart sank seeing the serious contemplation going on. Finally, "I figure we will go out for the year and then I don't think we will be able to sustain. I don't know about you, but there are too many things I want to accomplish. You travel much quicker alone."

I was relieved, because I could worry about that when the day came, but for now she was thinking of a year commitment. It felt nice, "That's what I figured too. I'm lazy and don't care nearly as much about traveling light. But you, you need to go and discover. I am just content today. I'm happier than a pig in mud."

We retired to make love in the tent and to fulfill her rising eyebrows. The smallness of the two person tent engulfed us, smothering us without anywhere else to go, but into each other. We settled down to sleep and I requested her to sleep on my chest making me big and powerful like a father and his small child. The nylon fuzz of a night told us that the days were getting shorter.

I awoke to the rain pounding with rhythm above. Bouncing off of the top and cavorting down the sides, the rain remained steady. Our tent was put up well and didn't leak. Everything else was placed away into the car, safe.

Kelly wrestled in her sleep not knowing the rain was her opponent. Finally she lost and awoke. Capturing the rain, her mouth smiled and crawled on top of me. With the dancing rain and her gyrating body working in synch, I lost myself in the moment. The world disappeared except for the sensitive urging and yearning tip of my penis. My eyes remained shut long after I lost control and let the frozen piece of art die.

"Don, I'm going to get off of the pill."

"Yeah, it's probably the best thing to do. Condoms suck, but at least they are safe."

"Yeah, condoms do suck…we'll see."

Dreams came back into the view. "We've got to go. Don? Donald?"

"It seems so perfect, I don't want to ruin it."

"Come on, my parent's will worry and be pissed at the thoughts of what we are doing."

"No," but I put my shoes and shorts on. The outside of the sleeping bag chilled my nakedness with the moving front. We headed back to her house to the constant questions of what were we doing. Kelly ignored and I stood waiting and wondering in quiet the rest of the day.

I called John, "Not again. You've got to come down."

"I don't have a car. I could ask my dad for his, but it's new and I know he wouldn't want me to take it."

"I'm sorry that I have to do this, but…I must call you on this trip. I drove three times to Indiana and you haven't come here once. Two of those trips were from my stolen uncle's car which I put thousands of miles on. You have no choice. I will be expecting a call back with the good news and an ETA."

"All right."

He called back with the ETA of six. No plans just dinner, beer, and some music. We accomplished all, with Kelly's dad supplying the barbecue and the Bud. Neil Young and her back yard did the rest. We listened to "Old Man" over and over again at John's request.

"This song is so beautiful and makes me want to call my dad and say 'Hey.' He used to make me listen to this all the time when I was little. He didn't have a good relationship with his father and was determined to be close to me. He has done the world for me. Just last year he wrote me a poem about being a father. I cried over and over."

"I wish I was a little closer to my family. All I have is my immediate family and we are all so determined to be independent from each other."

"Don, you are just stubborn. You could be as close as you want."

John agreed and I knew it to be true, but I also knew that I had no choice. I couldn't let myself get close to them. "You know what is funny, my mom thinks that Kelly is the one, because I have mentioned her to them. It's a first. I think my mom sees me as a shy guy with all of the women in love with me, but me being too shy to actually have dates. Just like she was with my dad."

"It's true, you asshole."

"The second part is right." I announced, "Time for a game, you must tell the story of your first memory."

"Since it's your game you start."

"O.K.. I think I tried to block out most of my childhood for some reason. But the first memory is still very vivid of a three-and-a-half-year-old child. It was early summer and we were moving for our first and only time. I had lived on a circle on the outskirts of Pittsburgh. It was a very young neighborhood and I was surrounded by kids of all ages. I loved it and would play all day. Then one day, my mom told me that we were going to a nicer bigger house. I was scared and didn't want to go. It was actually our last day and everything was packed up when I finally realized she wasn't kidding me.

"I wouldn't leave the street. I wouldn't come in and stop playing. My mom kept calling, 'Donald, Donald, time to come in.' I started to cry, but stopped, facing the inevitable. I walked away without saying goodbye and with my heavy heart weighing down every step. I climbed into our V.W. Bus and left never to return. I have been a loner ever since."

"Good, my turn," John was anxious to take stage. "Mine is younger, in my two's. My father worked in Pittsburgh, but we still lived in Cleveland. I'm not really sure why we didn't move, but it all worked out. Anyway, my mom watched me, but she had something to do that day. I knew something was going on when my dad woke me up. He smiled and shook me gently, 'Hey kid, you ready to hit the road.'

"I had no idea what he meant by hitting the road, but I was so excited, I almost pissed in my bed. He took my hand and led to me to the car. I was so proud and felt so important. My dad meant everything to me.

"We were making the two hour drive, when halfway through he asked me if I had to go to the bathroom. I did, but wouldn't admit to it because I didn't want to slow him down. After awhile he turned to me, 'there is something I have to tell you.' He looked at me for a long time, ignoring the road which I noticed he usually watched. 'I'm going to raise you so you don't do what I have done, so you are a better man and a better person.'

"That's it. That is all I remember. Nobody ever told me the story and I never asked my dad if it really happened. But I can still see his happy face when he woke me before the sun was up. And I can still see the seriousness of his commitment to me driving to his office.

"I have been trying to live up to that ever since."

"That was nice. All right here I go. Mine was also with my dad. He had gotten one of those puzzle things, like a rubic's cube, when those things were cool. It wasn't a rubic's cube though, it was a series of blue octagons with a number on each of the eight faces. The idea was to strategically place the octagons on pegs so that each and every face was lying in juxtaposition with its equal number.

"I remembered the frustration I felt at not being able to do it and my dad joking with me about how I couldn't do it. The anger boiled in me and I was so mad at my dad. Everyday he was telling me that I couldn't do it.

"I finally got so mad that I made the resolution that I wouldn't stop until I had solved it. Over a course of days I worked and worked on it. Finally, the triumph came. I knew I had done it before I had placed the last two on their appropriate pegs. I grabbed a hold of my patience and reveled in the moment of placing the last two on.

"I didn't tell anyone for awhile and I drew the solution down on gray and brown graph paper. After I enjoyed it long enough, I knew it was time to show all. I walked over to my dad and placed it in front of his eyes. And without a word, I turned it upside down. The blue pieces fell quickly making little pats onto the brown carpet below.

"I picked up the pieces and handed it to him with a smile. I never shared that solution with anyone, but I still have it today. I must have been four or maybe even five.

"I have a few earlier memories, but nothing of distinction or relevance."

John looked at me, "You couldn't of done it. Your anger would have blocked you."

"You wouldn't have either," I said bitterly.

"You know I have only heard of his reputed temper. I still haven't seen it," Kelly stated.

"I hope you won't."

"It's your effect on him, he is a changed and relaxed man. You have truly made him happy." I looked away from the group to watch my feet for awhile. There we were, the perfectionist loner, the creative emotionalist, and the driven self lover; the yin, the yang, and its circle which contained us all.

Off again to Pittsburgh.

Once we began to hit the rolling hills of West Virginia I got excited. Not so much for her to meet my family or friends, but for her to see my pride, Pittsburgh. Something about the place and the people makes you always stay loyal and call it home. I talked endlessly to her about the city and the way of life which is seen there and how it should be like that everywhere. Luckily, she was driving and didn't have to pay full attention to my swelling babble.

We had two nights in the 'Burgh; one for my parents and one for my friends. My parents did us up right, as usual, by taking us to a great seafood restaurant in the middle of the residential part of the city proper. We drove through a tunnel which presented the city as a birthday present ripped open without a care for saving the wrapping. The bridge let us ride to the worn hills and see the worn city that was fighting back from an industrial disease.

We took two cars so Kelly and I could walk around the city afterwards. After driving around amongst the stained neon night, the silver Mercury decided to climb the hill which over looks the town. Mount Washington, famous for its inclines and expensive restaurants with a view, came easily as the Mercury used all four cylinders. We walked hand in hand over the stone wall that separated the quick slope from the walkways strewn with the monoculars that cost a quarter for thirty seconds of viewing pleasure.

The lights were dim in the almost rainy mugginess of August. "Are they on for the cleaning people or are they contributing to the downfall of the earth by trying to keep the city pretty with little speckles of light everywhere."

"The downfall."

We cavorted over the rocks daring a fall with each step. On Mt. Washington one had to take an incline down the hill. We approached the little slanted box of a chalet on railroad tracks. Entering we took a seat that was in the front of the square compartment, but the position forced us to strain our necks to view the city. However, I chose the seat to avoid watching the cable which slowly let us down and slowly let us worry about our fate when it broke. I hoped for a spring at the bottom which would cushion our fall or perhaps an air bag.

She was enthralled and kissed me and rubbed up and down on the crotch of my pants. I hardened and teased her nipples. I couldn't believe we had the luck of being alone. Before things got out of hand we slowed down and made it into the station at the bottom. We waited for the ride back up. This time we moved to the back of the square to allow the windows to show her the steepness that the tracks were laid upon and how the car was only held by a cable. "How do they test something like this? How do they maintain something like this?"

Another couple got aboard with us. The woman was young and tried to hide it with layers of blue and red make-up. She was petite and looked like she was huddled in a blanket while wearing her boyfriend's letterman jacket. He was big and broad, but a young face poked through the few stubbles of hair on his chin. Proud of his stubble, proud of his lettermen's jacket, he placed his arm around his mate to prove his pride of his young girlfriend. The letterman's jacket told me he was from a rival high school from the east side of the city. I was from the south.

I felt the day that I went to the store to try on my letterman's jacket. Trying to act so nonchalant, it wasn't easy for a ninth grader, who was the first of his friends to earn one, from busting out in a arrogant joy.

I smiled at Kelly and kissed her even though those two sat there staring at us from across the square. He was acting tough and she squeezed her body as close to his as she could. The August mugginess must have been burning up her sweat soaked skin in that coat. I laughed with Kelly. Suddenly a strong voice came from the little body, "So are you guys married or what? You're laughter is uh…infectious."

I watched Kelly with that same ninth grade bursting pride. She answered, "No, we aren't married, just having fun. We have a lot of fun together."

"Are you guys from around here?"

My turn, "No, actually I am from St. Clair, but she's from Indiana. We are in college."

"You guys met at college?" She stared at us with curiosity while her man still remained ridged, staring tough at us who posed some unknown threat. My eyes were fixed on his shrinking and whitening lips.

The car began to move up, "No," Kelly paused and blushed. Thinking of how she always had wanted to stay this and how romantic it sounded. She remembered dreaming of this very moment as a child and the movies filled with what she was about to say in it. She felt like a star in a surrealistic dream. The flushed cheeks returned to normal before it came out, "Actually, it was in the South of France."

We went home and kissed goodnight in front of my sister's room. I walked up the stairs and laid in my room in my fresh sheets of the bed that will always be my bed that stared upward to the moon lit posters of my unfulfilled childhood dreams.

The next day I showed her my community. We walked around the high school and the tennis courts where I worked. I introduced her around making it home in time for dinner. My mom was nervous about Kelly's vegetarianism and gave her a great big salad. "I hope this will be good enough for you," with the gentle placement of the plate.

The phone rang and it was Josh. "Nothing's going on tonight."

"Good, so what do you want to do?"

"Let's double date, a little dessert and then some beer in a park."

"Only, if it's Grizzly."

"Yeah, I don't think my new girlfriend will go for that one yet." I waited while he let the vision of his first sexual experience enter and leave his brain. "I'll drive."

"Good." I showed Kelly around my house to kill some time starting in the basement whose purpose was to allow my mother to save everything for just in case. A maze of rows went through and collected random articles of clothes, sporting equipment, sewing equipment, a pingpong table, and everything else ever in this world.

The first floor of my house started in the kitchen which looked out onto the backyard. It was orange on one wall and the rest was fake brick with matching fake wooden supports in the roof. A round table stuck crowded in the middle of its area making movement tough.

The kitchen lead to the only other room on the first floor. It was a long living room and dining room combination. The entire length of the wall was split with large and light wood panels and a light colored wall paper to match. The living room had a book case along the far wall that was split in two by a fireplace underneath a large mirror. The furniture ran along the other walls with a couch on the nearest and with two easy chairs stuck under the front widows of the house. The living room and dining room were split by a couch on the living room side and a side table on the dining room side. The dinning room opened up after the bookcases and ended with a picture window filled with a plethora of plants.

To the stairs we walked past the front door which lead to a porch. A foyer greeted our guests with a piano that was never really used. Upstairs were a series of four bedrooms; one for my parents, one for my sister, one for a T.V. and an exercise bike, and the last one for a computer and guests.

My room was on the third floor and the largest of everyone else's. It was my palace. With my paper route money I filled it with a T.V., a stereo, Atari, and a weight set. It was mostly blue and red, very patriotic and boyish. The scattered posters, pennants, and trophies in every visible spot spoke with inner confessions. I liked the confusion and clutter.

Josh arrived and we headed out for a dessert and then to some park to drink beers, just like he had promised. He had a new girlfriend whom he really liked. She was smart and pretty, but she had too many strikes against her. Ten pounds overweight, two years younger, and a non-Jew would lead to their demise a few months later. But tonight, he was in love and running around like a kid as Kelly and I drank the beers and swung on the swing sets. I looked forward to spending some time with him, but he paid us no attention while swimming in his emotions. He still didn't like Kelly, but was trying his best which was to ignore.

We came home and I was drunk. "Spend the night with me," the plea whispered under the flash of the television set.

"We can't?"

"Yes, we can. We'll go upstairs, I will say goodnight. You will shut the door to my sister's room and then follow me up the stairs. My parent's work and leave at seven. They will never know."

"I won't," but I knew her real answer. She followed me up the stairs and we made love in the bed I grew up in. I had so many dreams of making love to a woman that I truly loved in that bed. Now I was really doing it. I was a child again, the days were endless, and there was always something new to play.

We woke up and I looked for any signs that my parents knew. I couldn't find what I could identify or capture so we left in a whirl and headed back to her place in Indiana. The summer's end thrust me to the anxieties and the remembrance of school and how excited I was to get back. It had been a long time.

I spoke my thoughts to an open mind that encouraged my instincts, "Well, let's go then. It's not too much out of the way. You can drop me off tomorrow at home."

"All right."

We made it right before dark just in enough time to hear her mom yell at her over the phone, but it was too late. Jack was already there and setting up his room next to mine. We lived on the top floor of an annex to our fraternity. The floor featured six rooms cut out of two and was known as the Penthouse. Four of us lived up there with our own rooms—a great setup for any college kid.

This year I was to live with Jack and two juniors. Not many seniors wanted to live in the house anymore, but it was far cheaper. I could put up with the noise and chaos for another year.

I walked into my new room which was ripped to shreds. Last year's occupant went nuts knowing that he would not have to face this mess in the fall. I brushed the shit to the side and found a left over mattress. With a flop of dust our bed was made. The dust and junk smelled with age forming the image of a crack houses.

A lot of people were beginning to arrive in their noisy mini-vans and complaining parents. Back to the way it used to be, we listened to a friend play a guitar as the sun sank while drinking beers on the porch until it was time to go to bed. Carefully making our way in the lightless room to the strategically placed mattress, I grabbed her from behind to scare the shit out of her. The bed caught our fall and let us make love even though Jack could hear us through the plaster board walls. We felt good.

The next day came with a yawn and stretch. Leaving school and her was easy this time, I knew I'd be back. "Why are you always leaving me?" she shrugged and gave me a hug.

"My parent's wanted me to tell you that they were sorry that they didn't get to take you to dinner. I think they felt obligated since yours did."

"I think our parents are both new at the game of older kids with mates of the opposite sex."

"I guess, I'll see you soon, huh?"

"As soon as I can."

I left feeling empty. Why couldn't I always be with her? My feelings were out of control and my mind let it go down the road of my demise. "Definitely, as soon as I can."

THIRTY-FOUR
The Man Touching His Nose
in Elusiveness

Back to school, it felt exciting. A few days before classes our time was filled with a lot of drinking, fixing up rooms, and reattaching old friends. Paranoid, everyone seemed to be staring at me waiting for an even weirder version. The words leaked out of the back of their heads saying "Belgium Fuck" into my back.

They all asked about Europe and I replied shortly and snobbily not trying to make them relate to something that they had no idea of. I was a bohemian, I was poor, I was hated, I fell in love, I used my brain; none of which belong in the fraternities around America, especially not in Ohio. I felt sophisticated, intelligent, and sensitive. No longer the prisoner of my outward appearance, I struggled with the inner.

As I walked through the halls of our first party I knew that nothing changes, nothing ever does. Same stories, same plans, same names, I longed for my freedom. Ignorance forced stupidity, stopping me from the realization that it wasn't freedom that I was lacking, it was a vehicle to develop. I, like most seniors, had outgrown the environment.

After the first party I went to a bar to get drunker than drunk. Drinking still brought about my good times. Unfortunately, the night ended early, tired, fucked-up, and the feelings of extreme depression caught me from the shins.

The next morning offered no relief. I called Kelly for guidance.

"I can't explain it, I felt horrible this morning, just plain old depressed."

"Yeah, I'm not looking forward to going back at all. Maybe to see a few friends, but that's it."

"I think it's my drinking."

"Could be, I've lately been thinking that I don't like myself drunk. So why do it is the question I keep asking."

"Let's try to stop." It was decided. I embarrassingly told Jack of my revelation during the night. I hoped he would be more understanding, having an alcoholic for a brother, but he wasn't. He kept asking me why. I couldn't really answer.

I searched the night with a glass of water and a lot of empty explaining. During moments of drunken comradery, thoughts of my retarding formative years instilled the need of alcohol for success in any social setting. Who could drink the most? Who threw up the most? Who blacked out the most? Who did the dumbest things? Why wasn't I joining in?

Classes started in a countdown of days until I could see Kelly. I needed a car and talked my parents into giving the Mercury to me earlier than they had planned. Like that dog I promised to take care, I convinced them of my need and of my newfound responsibility. My dad caved into the pressures of my mother. I felt little if any remorse in my lies.

As soon as I had it, I ran to Kelly who was just starting school herself. In the darkened anxiety of Friday night, I found the sprawled out sorority house. My school had no sorority houses and I had heard horror stories of the rules and etiquette which I refused to live by. All nightmares were accepted while reaching the door to a squirrelly girl asking whom I was there to see. "Kelly Moorehead," my voice sunk a few octaves as I threw out my chest trying to impress any of her friends that might be present.

"Caller in the lobby for Head," chimed above. Her run beat down the forbidden staircase, looking as good as ever, to kiss me hard.

After a few introductions and a lot of head nodding and smiling we went to Degan's. Without a word, the shots of whiskey were waiting. I blushed and shuffled my feet camouflaging my turmoil of pride, but the strength grew enough to tell him "No thanks" and to adjust my baseball cap.

With a "That's cool," I felt much better. The protocol pushed us through campus to several parties to allow me to meet the world. We slept at her friends, but it was awkward. A fifteen dollar hotel up the road was decided upon for tomorrow. Everyone was amazed at our fondness and our unspoken language, or at least amazed at Kelly being in love.

The next weekend she came to visit me. We went to our fraternity party, "How can we not. I live here." It was much more free. Men have no house moms or rules about bedrooms leaving it to be a free-for-all, the kind Ted Nugent sang of. In portraits of the moments of mingling, the memories of nights long gone brought laughs at the sweaty crowds. My friends were beginning to ignore me, knowing that I was in love and not interested in their merry games. The label stuck on my back became "pussy whipped."

The series of meetings went on week after week, alternating between schools. At hers we would spend one night in a hotel and the other anywhere else. Out of desperation, our sexual desires were drained in phone booths, in the sitting room of her sorority house, and among the black cover of vegetation. More romantically we would swim in the school's fountain and walk through the famous abandoned stone curries of Ohio. All of it captured.

At my place we would lie in bed all day and play with each other's genitals showing each other where the most sensitive places were and watching my penis get hard and soft over and over again.

The weeks were spent alone, but on the telephone. The drinking pact was quickly thrown out of the window after a month. It was a lesson learned, but failed. Our intentions were off the mark and let us down.

I became isolated from the fraternity and all of my friends. Ignoring all of my old girlfriends, bridges were blown in the vindication of my blazing path. Dangerously dependent, she was my best friend whom I only shared things with. She was heading down the same path.

She took me to my first Dead concert. In the effort of driving all day to get to Wisconsin, the concert was almost entirely over when the faithful and patient Mercury was parked in a large grass field. After parking it, we walked through the smoky haze of color with spinning people trying to sell anything to those willing to pay. I smoked a little dope to calm my nerves, but wussed out on the 'shrooms. "I will, but I still have to drive and I'm uncertain of the effects." She let it stay at that.

We went with a friend of hers and a sort of boyfriend. I felt their awkwardness constantly making me uneasy at each turn of the night, but fun was still managed. Along the wasteful distance between Wisconsin and Ohio, we stopped in a park to rest. Caught up I played with her vagina under her huge sundress while the world went about with their playing unknowingly in the short grass that surrounded park benches and a lake. In a shivering cringe, culmination was coming.

The summer was long gone and winter was itching to take over. We were going strong until…those fatal words. I made the trip for her big date party that her roommate was in charge of, making both of them seem on edge. The night before we treated ourselves to a nice hotel room.

"Don," she whispered in the scared dark of a foreign travelers hotel. "I think I might be pregnant. I'm a little bit late."

It was the last thing I was expecting. We tried condoms, but neither of us could handle the loss of spontaneity. She had gotten off of the pill because of ill effects. In a whim I cried for a second, but knew it wouldn't help.

"So what do you think?" she was impatient.

"I can't go through it again. My mind won't let me. I'm an adamant believer in pro-choice, but my choice would be to have it. It seems like a bad excuse to blame it on the timing." I thought about apologizing, but changed my mind. I knew it wouldn't do any good and it wasn't my fault alone.

Her voice grew sharper and louder. I knew I had fucked up, "Well that doesn't matter. It is my body and my life."

"I'm sorry. Yeah, I agree completely. I would never think about telling you what to do. It's so easy for me to sit on the side and preach. But when it comes down to it, I don't have to stop my life for it. I can always just walk away…I wanted to be honest about my feelings though. I'm afraid that is where I went wrong with Kristie."

She was only slightly soothed, but sleep and the party took it off of our minds. Our usual fun lasted until we got back to the prompting fifteen dollars a night shit hole. She began to violently weep. I was scared. She was the strongest person I knew and was now shaking like a child in front of me. Instinctively, I held her as tight as I could.

She cried forever going in cycles, "Don, I'm scared for us. We have gone too far."

I thought quickly, "No we haven't. What do you mean?"

"It just is too far."

"I don't care about tomorrow. Tomorrow is yours, but today is yours, too. Today is ours. I can't imagine being with anyone else. You have brought so many beautiful things to my life. You have taught me so much."

Even though I thought I said what anyone would want to hear, she expectedly cried harder. "No, No, No, don't say that. Don't say that," her fists striking the pillow.

I waited for an explanation, "That's it, we have gone too far. I care so much about you, that's why I am so worried and why this hurts the farther we go."

"How can you say that? We enjoy being together more than any two people on this world. I never will ask for a commitment. I would be disappointed if you gave it to me." I lied like a bastard. I wanted to marry her. I wanted to have children with her. I wanted to see her get grey hairs. I was fucked in the head and almost begging to her.

She finally stopped crying, "I know. You are the most special person I have ever met." She hoped to calm my fears.

"So are you." She got on top of me and made love to me like she was reading the last page of a good book; sad, excited, and bitter. She rolled and threw her body, trying to make me part of her. I grew limp at the thought of a child and withdrew, retrieving to rub her back until she fell hard asleep.

In the morning she took me to visit Degan. She took us out to a huge breakfast. Last night was forgotten and she was making up to me with the spoils of food.

I left early worried about the truth.

THIRTY-FIVE
Rubber Sheets

The week was slipping by without a phone call from her. I knew she was going to get the pregnancy test over with as soon as possible. The waiting was anxious, but I continued to do it with surprising patience. After last weekend, I wanted to give her some space, some time. I wanted to be cool.

Thursday came with a strange feeling in the morning breezes. The sky was without a cloud and the warm weather was holding out for another day. Something struck during a Finance class and I couldn't shake it. My body ached and my mind felt heavy with the knowledge of what I needed.

In my biggest sweater wrapping against the late fall breezes, I slid into my big Timberlands. My route was east past my old freshman dorm. The grass remained green in the few uncovered spots, but the trees were swirling with the potpourri colors of Autumn. The air bit my face and tightened my pores.

I kept going until the long steep slope ended with a slowly moving creek showing me home. Glancing over my shoulder, school was no longer in sight. The edge of the stream appeared muddy and almost extended the entire width in some parts. It had been a long hot summer and the water was waiting for winter's replenishment.

I walked a half mile down stream and found my spot. The log still laid across to the other edge, but barely any water touched it, losing its significance. Without much struggle I climbed to its topside and inched my way to the middle. The water barely flowed.

Laying down, the sky moved by and I reached up. My mind connected with Kelly's. Slowly the sobbing was constructed in my knowing and admitting the inevitable. I wept until the dark began to threaten. With what little strength was left, I crawled back up the hill, past my youth, and into the only place that was of comfort, bed.

Without receiving a phone call, the feelings of remorse and shame ran away and turned into anger. She knew I knew, but why did she wait? The neon red flashed 1:04 A.M. when I called.

A voice was startled upon answering, but in fact Kelly was around. I waited. "Hello," the voice was husky from too much talking and smoking.

"Hi, it's me."

"Oh, hi. I was just going to call."

"Save it. What's going on?"

"I'm pregnant."

"I know, what are we going to do?"

"We?"

"Yes, we. It is both of our responsibility."

"Look Don, I've been thinking a lot." The classic words confirmed, but I hung on hoping for something better than the terrible fate I deserved and was about to receive. "I don't want to ever see you again."

"What? What do you mean?"

"Don, it has gone on long enough, and now it all makes sense to me. I really don't want to see you again." She was cold, her voice monotone. I started to cry, but stopped. No more crying was needed.

"Well, let's not worry about that now. What are we going to do?"

"I am going to get an abortion and you are going to pay for half of it. I have already begun making the arrangements. Well, actually my mom has."

"Your mom? When did you find out about this?"

"Early afternoon, hold on one minute."

I waited infuriated over the fact that she didn't deem it necessary to give me a call. My head was spinning and I felt faint. The phone melted into my hand as I laid down on my bed covered by hockey team logos. "Don, it's my sister, I've got to go."

"Got to go? Don't we have a conversation to finish?"

"Don, I will call tomorrow. It is late and both of us are too emotional. Good-bye." The dial tone didn't focus in so I waited in disbelief. Finally I placed the phone down purposefully and gently wondering what I had missed.

I woke Jack up through our tiny walls, "Hey could you come in here." I couldn't move. He walked in a little weary and a little bleary. "She's pregnant and doesn't want to see me again."

Jack thought for awhile and offered some phrases of condolences. "Don, I want to be honest with you. I know it hurts, but…it is for the best. She is right. Her timing sucks, but…"

"Jack, that's the last thing that I want to hear. She has come to mean so much. I get her pregnant and she dumps me. What the fuck?"

"Well, there are two things you can do. Go to her or forget her." He watched me for quite awhile worried. I was in the fetal holding my stomach. I knew those were my choices, but I also knew that I couldn't do either. I was paralyzed and wanted my life to end. I was so tired and weak, I couldn't carry on. I didn't try to see her. I didn't try to forget her. I laid in bed for a day, sick to my mind.

She phoned and repeated her desire not to see me and for me to send money. She was cold and so was I. I drove over to John's apartment to break the news.

"Wow, wow, that sucks. So how you doing?"

"Not to good."

"It must be impossible for you to bear. What are you going to do?"

"What can I do, argue?"

He thought for awhile and shrugged, "I don't know."

"Just always wear rubbers." My darkness that I was so excited to get rid of returned. "Who would of ever have thought? In nine months I could get two women pregnant, witness two abortions, and have two enemies for life. What a year? If my parents only knew."

"You're tough."

I sent Kelly the money that she wanted with a note. I wrote it over and over again. I wrote my feelings on one, but why bother as I angrily crumpled it up. Too nonchalant was the next. I crumbled that up. It took me four hours to write this little note and I went for the middle of the road.

I got a return letter in a few days. After being turned down on phone calls to her for a week, I was very anxious to read her feelings. My jaw dropped.

THIRTY-SIX

"Come On, I Can't."

The letter went as follows:

I received your sixty dollar check today and the short note you enclosed with it. I hope that this is not an indication of what you are really concerned about.

I remember all the things you told me about how Kristie dealt with all of her experiences and now I bite my tongue for anything I said against her. Don—it was not her who was confused or irrational, but you.

If your reaction to this is any indication of how you acted, then I am shocked. Obviously, so many things I thought you believed were only what I wanted you to believe.

Not once have you discussed the fact that we created and ended a life. I am not dwelling on that fact, simply because I spent days with tears in my eyes as I came to grips with it . I don't know if you have faced it.

I don't think you are any better than any other guy who wants to get fucked. Realize, Donald, that I just went through the most difficult experience of my life and no amount of money which you send will make up for my pain and fear. I am now picking up pieces and moving on, while you write nonchalant notes telling me to work hard. Do you realize how much I have to do to compensate for missing a week of class and how much I've worked to make enough money to pay my parents back?

I'm angry and I'm bitter. Because I feel like I'm doing it all for you. Because the whole time I felt like it was something you had intentionally put inside me, not even withdrawing like I thought you knew to. Because now you tell me everyone is giving you sympathy, blaming me for breaking up, while everyone I know is confused as to why I disappeared for a week.

I tried to talk with our Dean about your reaction and he laughed when I told him it was your second abortion. "Any guy who has had two abortions doesn't care anyway." I leaned back and shut up—acquiescence.

Don't expect another relationship to withstand an unwanted pregnancy. Please don't make this happen to anyone else.

Reading this today still rips right into my soul. After reading it for the first time I cried until the night developed with one fist clenching my pillow in rage and the other caressing the letter. My heart was dejected, my mind was on fire, and my legs wouldn't work. I listened to my roommates scurry back and forth to class and to the library. Jack knew and did my work in the kitchen for me.

Finally with the completion of darkness, I threw down the letter with my hopes and dreams; with my love and friendship. I heard John's prediction on the porch step only a few months ago. "Alone." I knew I would always be alone no matter what happened or where I went. It was now something I wanted.

My rage took over and with new and undaunted resolve I packed my bags for the library to sit down to write the letter of my life. Eyes focused on the scrolling pen and its ink filled ball which composed with the beauty of anger. The truth was mine, I wouldn't let her or anyone ruin me. The war had begun.

Kelly,

I'm sorry for you, but I can not bear the weight on my shoulders for they are not strong enough to carry the tin cross which you have decided to believe in and cast my way.

Let me begin from the beginning. In the hotel room, I spoke of abortion and my feelings. I told you that I couldn't handle another one because I didn't believe in the convenience of it. I didn't want another lost life on my mind. I'm not religious and I think that conception is a being's only chance at life. Does any of this ring a bell?

Now think hard, I believe your words were, "It doesn't matter, because it is my decision. I do not want to have a child and I won't." Maybe those words didn't mean anything to you, but they meant the world to me.

Just a few days later, I called you because I knew the inevitable would be confirmed. You nonchalantly broke the news to me that you had received the positive test results that morning and that we were through. You continued to tell me you had to go and talk to your sister. Too busy, I guess. In one last attempt, I asked you if I was more important only to hear your answer of no.

I cried for me, for you, and for the life that would be ended. I couldn't get out of bed for days. Finally I called after waiting days for your promised return phone call. The consequences weighed so heavily on you that you could only talk of the money that I owed you, leaving me with the only choice of giving up on getting through to you.

Yes, my letter was nonchalant. Why should it not? You treated me like a smelly sick cousin that you were forced to talk to at a family reunion. I feel my response was correct.

To the real heart of the matter. Don't begin to preach to me. I didn't rape you, our sex was mutual. My soul has been ripped in two by you and I have been cheated by what I thought was our intimacy, friendship, and now by your reaction.

> Hate me, if it makes you feel better. Do what
> you want with the thought of me, but don't bring it
> my way. You were looking for an escape of the
> responsibility and I am your bloodied scapegoat.

I left it unsigned and still smoking from my pain. I picked up my backpack and my feet. "Never again," mumbled through the cool night air while my tongue was still tasting of stamp paste.

I called her in two days and she didn't mention the letter. She told me when the abortion would take place and that she needed more money. Promises of money and promises of a phone call afterward left me feeling ashamed and desperately alone. In the spirit of one last attempt, I asked to take her to the clinic, but she said "No, definitely no."

Speaking in terms of well being finalities, she called with the news of her healthy completion. "Sorry," came to my lips for what had happened but I was cut off with a short, "my mom is standing next to me."

"Don't bother with the attempted lies," breaking our silently spoken truce. The words spoke of our tragic good-byes in the grandest of bitter rages.

A letter came in a few days continuing our written war.

> I have written many letters to you explaining
> all what I've been through, but they all sound
> preachy. I have also decided that if you really cared
> you would ask. I'm not sure if the impact of this has
> really hit you, maybe you are getting used to it.
> Hopefully, you won't let it happen again.
>
> I will enclose an itemization so that you can be
> aware of the costs which were involved. We had
> spoken of your share as two hundred dollars, but as
> you can see now that bills have been totaled the
> costs run much more than that. Your half would be
> three hundred and fifty-eight dollars. I have your
> check for one hundred and forty dollars in my
> account, along with three hundred dollars of my
> own to send my parents. I would like to pay them
> in one lump sum—so I will wait to hear from you.
>
> I hope that in the future you will share respon-
> sibility for the protection, not only the results of
> your actions. Kristie and I both had asked you to

wear a condom and had given them to you. A woman should not have to insist.

I will expect a check in the mail.

$45	office exam and urinalysis
10	pregnancy test
35	follow-up office
300	procedure
25	consultation
150	ultrasound
150	hotels
$715	TOTAL

The fury returned while I shared the series of letters to Jack for confirmation and support. He took my side without a true choice. I composed my final chapter to dispose of my bottled hatred and to pay off my debt.

> Again, I must remind you of some things. You were on the pill and went off because it didn't make you feel right. Then we tried condoms and we decided that we didn't like them—WE.
>
> I always pulled out before cuming, but some can leak out. I will take the blame for not wearing a condom, but I would like you to know that you are not innocent. We both consented to unprotected sex.
>
> You have tricked me; I thought you to be strong and of your own will. But I guess I was mistaken about your liberation, since you had to comply with my raping desires to impregnate you. Get real, Kelly. So, like you, I hope that you do not do this to anyone else either.

I signed it with love in the bloody ink of painful longings. She was my best friend and now she was suddenly gone. I had lost all of my commonalties with my old friends, only Jack remained with me undaunted. The thoughts and memories of her remained cutting me through the many darkened days and protected me in the unsure night. I had picked the rose letting it die away from the only place it can grow, the vine.

THIRTY-SEVEN
J.G. is Gratefully Dead

So that was it; I was madly in love just a few days ago or at least it seemed. Now…the blue skies and high tide were gone forever, leaving me a mumbling and bumbling piece of shit. My thunder stolen, my direction disappeared, and my will evaporated in a single stroke.

My life laid before me looking very unappetizing, "Nothing to do, but to follow the wave I guess." Every so often, I would read her letters and rediscover my pain. The words bite into me and took out large hunks of flesh each time. I started to enjoy it, to need it, and to thrive on it. Inflection of her pain nourished each new morning. For months I would be sitting in class and I would drift off, finding myself talking aloud, "That bitch, how could she do that? Never again, never again."

I broke out of my shell every once in awhile to prove my manliness to anybody who dared to listen. Drinking heavily, meeting questionable women, and doing stupid things to impress, I had fallen back to where I was. The frustration of taking two steps forward to take two steps back loomed above providing the dark and dreary.

On such an escapade, John took me out for a night on the town in hopes of recapturing something. We started the night by drinking the shit wine that my dad makes in his basement. It can be very horrible, but potent. We made it uptown to some bars feeling fine.

However, soon after I found myself alone and wondering why.

I sat back and enjoyed the music while sucking on a Rolling Rock. It was cold outside, but very hot in the bar confusing my pores. Too afraid to leave a winter coat unattended, the coolness of the beer soaked into my relieved lungs that were gasping in the heat.

John finally came back, "Sorry, but Linda is here." I pictured her naked ivory skin shimmering in the darkness of Spain turning my feeble stomach. "I'm going to take her home with me," he boldly announced.

"What? Why? What the fuck are you doing? Have fun." He gave me a guilty look, but his mind was made up. His girlfriend was gone for the weekend and he was feeling good about having the chance to be with someone else. The closure of the deal brought him gleefully to a new low in shame.

Going home, I found myself in the midst of a party. After a quick scan of the scene a stupid ass sophomore asked me if I wanted some 'shrooms. Remembering being a pussy with Kelly at the Dead, I knew this was a great opportunity to redeem myself and to spite her.

They were long, skinny and chewy, tasting like the sticks of the Pixie Stick candy fame. One last cold beer washed them down commencing my solo journey.

At first I was a little nervous and waited for some weird stuff to happen. It never did so I started to mingle and to dance feeling the groove. A beautiful full bodied woman with long blonde hair came up and began dancing with me. Her long body seemed to be the best looking there, but her face was beginning to distort through a prism leaving the colors dancing above my head. Meshing music grooved along with the lights and with the grooves of the each record that snaked through my body helping me to ignore the woman dancing in front of me.

Forgetting her inspired her to begin conversation by telling me how she liked wine. I offhandedly remarked that I had some upstairs. "I'd love some," she seemed too eager to tell her that I didn't mean it that way. "What the hell," she looked good and the horrifying déjà vu left me to follow.

As we sat drinking I worried about John's demise. It wasn't like him, plus he hated Linda or was it just me that hated Linda and what she represented. As I answered the big blonde beauty's questions, I watched my feet. They moved so gracefully, slowly and impressively with the mechanics of the human body.

The windows began to scream while one of the Lost Boys flew by yelling. Holding on as tightly as possible, I noticed she was now sitting next to me in my room. She leaned forward for a kiss which was nice and slow in a drip which told me to lead her to the bedroom. Captured by the spirit, a candle held the lightness on our faces while it danced between us on the floor where we sat Indian style sipping the cork filled wine of my father's.

We began to kiss again, and this time more excitedly. I felt a warmth on my chest. Things seemed to be coming back to life in a growing heat of intensity. I looked down to discover my shirt was on fire from the candle. The big hole growing by the second engulfed in a blue cotton blend.

What to do? 'If I take my shirt off, my hair will catch on fire. If I pat it out, my body might catch.' I opted for a burnt body, saving the hair. It worked and was out in a smelly burnt plastic polyester heap of white, black, and yellow. I laughed for quite awhile, while she remained scared staring at the gaping whole in my T-shirt chest.

"I'm okay, don't worry." She came next to me and kissed me with sympathy. Taking my hand she lead me to the bed by taking most of her clothes off only leaving lacy underwear and top. Her nipples and pubic hair peaked through the holes. Almost bare, I could tell that her breasts were huge and her big ass was firm—an amazingly appealing body. My penis grew with its image. We began to go at it. "Haven't we met before?" my eyes searched the familiarity.

Then I thought about her nipples and pubic hair. Who cares? I continued to think about big tits and little asses. Who cares? I thought about cuming into someone I didn't know. Who cares?

She interrupted, "What's the matter?"

"I'm going to take you home."

"Why? I want you and you want me." She looked at the bulge in my pants.

"She isn't for real," I thought. "No, I'm going to walk you home now." She wrinkled her forehead and eyebrows asking me why. She kept staring at my hard-on.

"Look, I think I would rather come home alone and masturbate." Well it worked and she was disgusted. She didn't even want me to walk her home allowing me to stay awake enjoying the last bit of the 'shrooms and wondering what Kelly was doing. "Who cares?"

I walked inside to out over and over, a sensation I never knew existed.

The next morning began with John's taps. "I did it."

"You're fucked. With Linda? You're fucked."

"Yeah, it's horrible. The worst part was the dog. He came running into the room in the morning. He immediately stopped, confused and sniffing. Then he ran out. He knew it wasn't Cindy's womanly smell, but another. He had better not tell."

"You're fucked."

"Yeah, but she really got into it. A real screamer and very aggressive, it was nice. Plus I got it out of my system while it was safe."

"You're fucked. Hey I 'shroomed last night."

"No way, I've always wanted to, but never found the opportunity."

"Weird, but cool. It was one long journey."

"Dude, 'shrooms. I don't know. Maybe it's you that's fucked."

Friends forever.

A few months later…Kelly and I had kept in contact, but very sporadically. Lately, she had been calling a lot getting me a little confused about her intentions. However, I remained emotionally far away even with my friends telling me that she was coming back and that we were the best couple ever. The exact words that I wanted to hear.

She began to bug me about visiting her. Finally, I agreed to the trip in a reunion with Ned, Degan, Head, John, and myself pretense. Only Rusty would not be partaking. The memories made the opportunity taste good.

John and I packed up on a warming March day that let me wear only a sweatshirt and a baseball cap, capturing a lightness that felt good and refreshing. My body shook with anticipation. What were her intentions? Why did she keep bugging me? Was it my imagination? Fuck it all. We arrived late.

As a buffer we met at Degan's fraternity house. The walk down the hall with booze in hand produced Degan waiting, drunk. He poured us shots. I threw mine back and looked behind me. Bam. There she was in full glory; my heart sank. I was in love all over again and wanted to hold her and tell her everything that had happened to me over the last couple of months. In feeble clutches, my head spilled its working guts onto the wooden bar.

The greeting came with her usual "hey" and a nice, polite hug. Permitting my eyes to wander, she displayed some extra weight and a little pale face, but she still was stunning. An African-type cap of soft browns and greens with corners on the top adorned her head. She smiled. I looked at her jeans and her loose T-shirt, "What's up? You look good as always. How is everything?"

"Great!" she forced it out as if I was the customer and she the empathetic customer service rep.

I started to cry, but bit my lip. By the homemade bar, Degan and John were watching me close, waiting for and discouraging any instability. My confidence gone, our stares met. The hatred in her eyes told me that truth; she no longer loved me. To my dismay, her feelings had angrily and despondently turned into hate.

I drank the night away talking very little to her, but we watched each other. We spoke like always in a sheer wall of quiet that told everything that she wanted to say. I, too, replied only with eyes. Her call was one of revenge making me the bearer and her the martyr. I could only agree.

Finally, the night drifted far away from my control. I was drunk, John was drunk, Degan was drunk, and Ned had left us. We went to a party where she cornered me with words, "So Don, I must ask you the big question: Any new girlfriends?"

She let her guard down, disappointing me. "No," I shot her a sad glance which suddenly and darkly twisted, "After you, there can be no other. After what you did, I can handle no others." She walked away to leave an overly attended scene of Degan puking on some guy's shoulder. In a sprint, I left having to puke myself.

I don't know how or when or where, but I ended up in someone's room somewhere with John. I was on the floor with the phone in my hands, my pants down to my ankles, and a vomit filled bucket by my side. Looking around, I saw his crusty lips yawning above me on a brown check couch. The results of the night were a mystery to John as well. The best I could figure out was I called Kelly filled with a despairing panic then masturbated. I hoped she wasn't home and puked some more at the thought of our conversation if she was.

I woke and walked around finding Degan to wake him up before our lunch meeting with Kelly. Afterwards she wanted to take us up to see her room which was now out of the sorority house and in a dorm. It was just one small room with a desk and a bed decorated with African garb.

The African garb had come from her trip to South Africa for a month. She flaunted it towards my general lazy direction, while highlighting the pictures of another man on her wall. I was still a little sick from the night before, so I excused myself to bathroom. Sitting on the toilet, things cleared up with a few burps and hockers. Always thought provoking, the toilet provided the time to conclude that she wanted to prove to me and herself that she was over me and had moved past me. She had done a pretty good job.

She didn't need to tell me; I knew that she was the victor. Back in the room I sat facing away from the others with my eyes glued to the door which I hoped I would soon be exiting. The anger was beginning to build. Degan once again saved us all, "What do you guys want to do?"

"I don't know? Leave," John laughed towards my profile.

"I know, let's get the fuck out of here and go to I.U. The change of scenery would be nice."

Kelly looked happy in saying, "I can't go. I have to work tonight."

I responded happily, "Perfect, than we won't get in your way and will get out of here." The escape featured my good friend and my dying idol running by my side propping me up each time I tripped. Just what I needed.

In route to Indiana, John slept in the back while Degan sat next to me in the faithful silver streak. "So Don how are things with you and Kelly?"

"What do you think?"

"Not too good, lots of tension, man."

"Degan, I…don't know what you know about everything that has gone on, but it was sad, a horrible way to end up…for both of us. Neither of us deserve what we are getting, neither of us deserve to be doing what we are doing, but I miss her and I miss myself…terribly and sickly."

"If you miss yourself, it wasn't really you."

"Yep, I guess I was fooling myself." I knew it, he knew it, and Kelly knew. I was not what I wanted to be and tried to be it anyway, a vicious cycle that constantly destroys what was built. I recreated myself out of a house of cards and then discovered myself uglier and more broken than when I started. Not a noble person and no longer caring to pretend to be one I, regretfully, spent too much time yelling at myself, striving to achieve both—recreation and resurrection. Doomed to be a subordinate actor with the leading role in mind and never happy nor satisfied, I failed the basic test of life—be who you are and enjoy it. Seeing it before me, "Degan, you know, you are the god our generation needs." He laughed with his evil eyes and grinned in acceptance.

On the way home, John and I began to talk in order to finish. "Well Don, it looks like it is over."

"Yep, not too easy to take for me. I guess I was still holding on, hoping."

"No longer, that's good."

"I guess. I feel that the best time of my life is behind me. I had a chance to grab the golden ring, but it was greased by the gods, those fuckers. However, I am no longer ignorant of myself, the painful death of a soul."

John laughed. "Always the pessimist enjoying the dark."

"Yep."

"I'm going to miss her."

"No you won't, neither will I. Just ourselves."

"What?"

"Never mind."

"Well, it's time to close the book. I believe you just wrote that last page."

He finally hit the nail on the head and sunk it into the wood. I looked over and started to laugh. The three letters were floating between us, e.t.c.

"Who cares?"